Praise for the novels of RITA Award finalist
Lynn Erickson. . .

SEARCHING FOR SARAH

"Intricate suspense and deft characterizations make *Searching for Sarah* a top-notch thriller. Don't miss out."
—*Romantic Times*

"Ms. Erickson teases the reader like a cat is teased with a piece of string. The reader follows the string through all the twists and turns of this well-plotted story all the way to the surprise ending."
—*Rendezvous*

THE ELEVENTH HOUR

"A fabulous romantic suspense . . . The lead characters are charming as individuals and form a wondrous relationship. Counterpoint to the sizzling romance is a brilliant who-done-it."
—*Painted Rock Reviews*

"Layers of depth . . . what a ride!"
—*Rendezvous*

"A thrilling read . . . exciting . . . compelling relationships . . . a winner."
—*Romantic Times*

NIGHT WHISPERS

"Erickson skillfully navigates the fraught task of portraying the mind of a stalker with multiple personalities. . . . The narrative is shadowy and suspenseful, leaving the reader with a creepy, unsettled feeling of expectation."
—*Publishers Weekly*

ASPEN

"A deliciously juicy romp through the winter playground of the wealthy and powerful . . . A complex and truly interesting heroine . . . Suspenseful and tumultuous . . . a sharply plotted page-turner."
—*Publishers Weekly*

ON
THIN ICE

LYNN ERICKSON

JOVE BOOKS, NEW YORK

ON THIN ICE

A Jove Book / published by arrangement with
the author

PRINTING HISTORY
Jove edition / December 2000

The Penguin Putnam Inc. World Wide Web site address is
http://www.penguinputnam.com

ISBN: 0-515-12971-2

A JOVE BOOK®
Jove Books are published by The Berkley Publishing Group,
a division of Penguin Putnam Inc.,
375 Hudson Street, New York, New York 10014.
JOVE and the "J" design
are trademarks belonging to Penguin Putnam Inc.

PRINTED IN THE UNITED STATES OF AMERICA

10 9 8 7 6 5 4 3 2 1

ONE

The light outside the Boulder County Justice Center was pewter-colored, and snow pattered against the windows. A nasty Friday afternoon. *Perfect,* Ellie Kramer thought. She saw her moment and she seized it like the opportunist she'd learned to be.

"I'll be glad to give you a lift home," District Attorney Ben Torres said. "It's practically on my way."

"Oh, no, no, that's okay." Ellie took off her reading glasses and looked up at him. "I have some depositions to finish."

"You're sure? Everyone else is gone."

"Positive. I'll walk or catch a bus."

"If there is one in this storm."

"I'll be fine. Really."

Behind Torres, Ellie could see through one of the narrow windows into the courtyard. The snow was already piling up. The weatherman had gotten it right for once, and the entire staff of the DA's office was delighted. Powder skiing in November. And on a Friday. But no one was more delighted than Ellie. It was only four in the afternoon, and her coworkers were all leaving. Not just the staff in the DA's office but almost everyone in the sprawling building. The courtrooms were empty, the café closed, only a skeleton crew remained in the sheriff's department up on the second floor. They'd all hit the roads before the inevitable traffic gridlock.

"I'll let Nate know you're still here." Torres picked up his briefcase and glanced out the window. "Helluva storm."

"Sure is." She nodded agreeably.

Nate. She'd forgotten about the security guard. *Damn.* A nice guy, but no slouch. He might wonder what she was doing in Records when everyone else had gone home. *Screw it,* she thought. She'd waited years for this opportunity, and she wasn't about to let it slip through her grasp.

"Good night," the DA said.

"Night," Ellie replied, nerves thrumming.

She busied herself at the computer until she was sure Ben Torres was really gone. The entire building was quiet, strangely quiet. The silence was unsettling in the normally bustling halls, but it could work to her advantage. At least she'd hear Nate's footfalls if he were nearby.

Ellie crossed the corridor outside the DA's office and used the security keypad next to the door that would take her down the steps to Records. She heard the lock release then she pushed open the door. Quietly. Down the stairs, clutching her briefcase to her chest. The hallway stretched before her, lined with doors.

Records.

When she shoved open the door, she was instantly assailed by the smell of old paper and damp concrete. Familiar and curiously comforting. A lowly clerk spent many long hours in the basement among the dusty files.

She reached for the light switch, hesitated, then flipped it on. She was only doing her job, she'd say if Nate found her. Sure, stick to her story. Bluff it out.

She made her way down one of the many aisles. She knew precisely where she was going, had noted the file box containing the records she sought so many times she'd lost count. Yes. Here it was. Untouched for well over a decade.

Case number 6973: The people of Colorado *v* John Crandall.

She set her briefcase down and drew in a breath, letting it whistle out slowly, then dragged the box down. This was it. *Finally.*

The concrete floor was ice cold when she hitched up her skirt and sat. She pulled the heavy box closer and removed the lid. Her hands were trembling with excitement.

She was reaching for a file folder, the first one—may as well start at the beginning—when an unfamiliar noise made her freeze. A . . . tapping. Mice? But no. Above her was a small, iron-grilled garden-level window, and snow pecked at the glass. The storm. Of course, she thought, and settled the folder in her lap. A police file. It was crammed full, and several black-and-white photos stuck out. She pulled them free and straightened them, and then she grew still, staring at the first one.

"Oh, God," she whispered. In her hand was a picture of Stephanie Morris in a hospital bed. The girl's eyes were closed; she was unconscious. Mottled markings of ruptured capillaries marred her eyelids; her neck was bruised.

Ellie sucked in air. The police must have taken this at the hospital that long-ago night.

The Morris girl looked so young, almost as if she were asleep. But, no, not quite.

More photographs. Stephanie again. The Morris house, the basement wine cellar from many angles. A dark, cluttered room with a single shelf of wine bottles.

How old had the girl been? Sixteen. Four years older than Ellie had been. Stephanie would be almost thirty now. But she wasn't celebrating her birthdays.

Ellie's mind begged her not to waste time on the photos, yet she continued to stare at them. Couldn't stop herself. Stephanie was a pretty, young girl with long blond hair. Had she suffered terribly? Was she still suffering, shut away in her coma?

She'd been raped and then strangled. Had the rapist meant to kill her? Had he merely been careless? Or had he planned all along to keep her alive?

Ellie considered the question. Maybe he had wanted his victim alive to tell again and again how horribly she had suffered. But Stephanie Morris was hardly a witness; he'd made a mistake, choked the girl a little too long.

His MO had either changed or been perfected after the Morris attack. His next victim, ten years ago, had died. And the girl after that, seven years ago, had also died. Both raped. Both strangled to death. Then he'd messed up. Left one not only alive but without brain damage. Ellie had read the police report from Pueblo on the victim who had survived. He'd been interrupted. Oh, he'd meant to kill the girl, all right.

A hollow metallic *clang* jolted Ellie and she paused, remembering where she was, what she was doing. It must be Nate, or a janitor, checking a door. That was all. It was okay. Okay. *Breathe.* She had her story, and she was a first-rate liar.

She studied the gruesome police photos of Stephanie

Morris for a long time and then tucked them into the back of the file. Staring up at her were the notes taken by the first two cops on the scene. She lifted a typed page, saw a signature. Right. Patrolman Michael Callas. And another set of typed notes signed by Patrolman Finn Rasmussen. The rookie cops. The goddamn rookie cops. The heroes.

She gritted her teeth and scanned the files, the initial crime scene reports filed by Callas and Rasmussen. They'd done an exemplary job, she had to admit, and sudden tears blurred her vision. Good police work, okay, but they had been so wrong, so quick to arrest an innocent man. Was this the law? Was this justice? Damn it, how could they have been so *wrong?*

She spent too long reading the reports, her mind working furiously. She was unaware of the cold in the basement, of her left leg having gone to sleep and the sky turning from gun-metal gray to black. The storm swirled around the building, rattling the bare cottonwood trees, and snow piled up in the corners and on the benches in the courtyard. None of that mattered; her world had narrowed down to the moment, to the file in her hands. All these years she'd waited, planned, lied, and cheated to get to this point.

The door to the steps opening and closing snapped her back to reality with a stab of panic.

Nate?

What if he saw her, mentioned it to Ben Torres? She had no reason to be here in Records tonight. Nate didn't know that, but Torres did. For a full minute she held her breath and listened, her nerves stretched taut. Nothing. Not a sound now.

Stiffly, her leg buckling, she rose and stuffed the thick file into her briefcase. She had to study it. She could smuggle it back into the storage box on Monday, take another home. Nothing was going to stop her now.

She went back up the steps, waiting at the heavy metal door, listening, then made her way across the hall and back into the DA's office. Sweat beaded her upper lip and under her arms. If Nate saw her now she was okay. Really. The overworked law student. And no one had ever checked her briefcase. At least not leaving the building. But on Monday, she'd have to come through security, the contents of her purse and briefcase scrutinized on the X-ray belt. No big deal. What sort of clerk would she be without files? It was okay.

She was buckling her briefcase, trying to calm herself, when the outer door to the office opened.

"Someone in here?" came a voice.

Who? Not Torres. Please. "It's ah . . . me, Eleanor Kramer," she said cheerfully. Then she saw him, Nate coming through the swinging half door that separated the waiting area from the receptionist's desk and the official offices beyond.

"Oh, Ellie, good Lord," he said, "I almost forgot Torres said you'd be working late. Lucky I didn't shoot you." He laughed.

"Yes, lucky," she said.

"Leaving soon?"

"Right now."

"Well, I'll walk you out, then."

"Sure," she said, "thanks. I'll just get the rest of the lights."

Somehow she made it outside, the blizzard buffeting her. She hugged her briefcase against her long black wool coat and hunched her shoulders, half running down the pathway toward Canyon Boulevard. She'd walk home, run home, anything to put distance between herself and the Justice Center. The storm didn't daunt her. She was unaware of anything except having executed her plan without a hitch.

The storm continued all evening and all night, and once the wind abated, the snow really began to pile up. Boulder, and the entire Front Range of the Rocky Mountains, was paralyzed. But the highway crews fired up the big orange snowplows, and by eight the next morning, the main arteries joining Denver and Boulder and the interstates were passable.

Celeste Steadman, Ellie's roommate for the past six years at CU, shook her awake. "We're going skiing. A-Basin and Copper Mountain are opening this morning. Come on, Jennifer and Bonnie are already getting their stuff together."

"Skiing?" Ellie sat up and rubbed her eyes.

"Yes. You know, that winter sport with the two long boards and the big boots."

"I don't have skis, Celeste, and you know it."

"There're ten pairs in the crawl space and Jenn's extra boots fit you. Now get up. And don't start in about the lift ticket. It's my treat. I don't want to argue." Celeste lowered her voice. "You know Jenn and Bonnie drive me up a wall when you aren't around."

God, it was so tempting for Ellie to take her friend up on the offer. The first real winter weekend in the mountains. Skiing, friends, fun, *men.*

She looked at Celeste and chewed her lower lip.

"Say yes, come on."

It would be so easy to give in. Hating to be a charity case, Ellie knew she'd somehow make it up to her closest friend. She always did, whether it was insisting on doing all the house chores or typing Celeste's papers. Ellie had

kept their finances straight since their freshman year at
CU. Now they were in law school together and shared
the house on Marine Street with two other law students,
Jennifer Cohen and Bonnie Brooks, and even though Ellie was taking a year off, clerking at the DA's office,
earning a real paycheck, she still lacked the money for
extras. For one, the rental house and utilities were too
expensive, but mostly she was paying off loans despite
the scholarship money she'd received over the years.

Celeste, on the other hand, was always flush. Her father, one of Silicon Valley's geniuses, sent monthly
checks whether or not Celeste needed them. For her
birthday, it had been the new Range Rover. This coming
Christmas the family was cruising the Amazon River on
a private yacht.

Ellie sighed and looked at her tall skinny friend, at her
long thin face and the huge sable-colored eyes, the bangs
and dyed dark-red hair that was blunt cut to her shoulders. Celeste was into the Gothic look this year. Last year
had been ash-blond hair and the wholesome cowgirl look,
including a lady Stetson; this year she was into black.
"Just finding myself," she always said.

"I really can't. Not this weekend." Ellie looked apologetic.

"It's the money."

"No, it isn't. Honest."

"I can't believe you're going to stick me with Jenn
chasing everything in pants all weekend and Bonnie
whining. Oh, *please.*"

But Ellie couldn't give in. Inadvertently she glanced
at her briefcase sitting on the makeshift desk beneath the
gabled dormer. With the three girls gone, she'd have all
today and Sunday to pore over the files. Uninterrupted
time. She couldn't afford to squander it.

How very easy it would be to tell Celeste the truth. To unburden herself of this heavy weight she'd carried since she was a little girl. But that would expose her secret and leave her sickeningly unprotected.

How could you tell someone, even your best friend, that when you were only twelve, your father had been arrested for the rape of a sixteen-year-old girl? How could you say, "Hey, I'm not really Ellie Kramer, I'm Ellie Crandall. You remember, *John* Crandall? The contractor who was convicted of the rape of Stephanie Morris? Well, he was my dad. He was my dad and I loved him and I still do."

How could Ellie confess that?

Sunday dawned crystal clear and bitter cold, so cold in the attic room that the inch of water in a glass by Ellie's bed was almost frozen. Teeth chattering, she threw her parka on over her pajamas and padded down to the front hall, where she found the thermostat sitting on fifty-five degrees.

The pipes. "Oh, no," she yelped, and she rushed to the kitchen, turning on the tap, praying. That's all she needed, a humongous plumbing bill.

It was an older rental place, a clapboard house in a residential neighborhood four blocks from the CU campus. It was painted yellow, lemon yellow, with white trim and a small white porch whose paint was peeling. The front and back yards were postage stamp–sized, too small to really enjoy in the summer. But they had two lilac bushes in the front, and pungent-smelling juniper bushes grew along the sides of the place. Bonnie always said it stank like the neighbor's cats used the bushes for a litter box, but it was really the junipers she smelled.

Ellie had taken the attic room, long since converted to

a good-sized bedroom by former student renters. She'd
painted it a light salmon color two years ago and even
refinished the pine floor herself. Last Christmas, Celeste
had given her a real wool Navajo rug to dress up the
place. The six-by-eight-foot rug was Ellie's most prized
possession. The oyster-colored down comforter on the
rickety brass bed was one of her best finds at the Boulder
thrift shop.

"It's twenty-five dollars," the thrift shop volunteer had
said.

"But I only have eight."

In the end Ellie had gotten the comforter for eight dollars because, for once, she'd been telling the absolute
truth.

The heat in the house finally got up to a cool sixty-
two degrees. In the attic, though the laws of physics said
heat was supposed to rise, it seemed only to do so in the
hot summer months. In the winter it rarely reached sixty.
She had the best selection of used sweaters in Boulder.
Today she put on jeans and a heavy forest-green pullover
and bundled up in the living room near the front window,
no one to disturb her, the smuggled files spread out on
the coffee table, a big mug of hot chocolate on the end
table beside Jenn's lava lamp—the most hideous thing
Ellie had ever seen.

She had read through all the files yesterday. Twice.
Today she'd study them, really study them and take
notes. It was amazing, even to Ellie's novice eyes, the
excellent quality of the police work. As much as she suspected the two uniforms first on the crime scene at the
Morris residence, she had to give the rookies an A for
effort.

The first thing Ellie had learned in law school was that
a crime scene was usually compromised in dozens of

ways by the police themselves. To begin with, there was
never an ideal crime scene. Then, whatever the first cops
on the scene—usually patrol officers because they were
nearby—had forgotten to write down would be the first
thing a defense attorney was going to ask on the witness
stand. Another given was that the least competent person
on the police force was the first to arrive.

But, according to everything Ellie had read, none of
the above applied to the Stephanie Morris crime scene.

The actual notes taken by Michael Callas and Finn
Rasmussen were included in the file. They both seemed
to have adhered to every rule policemen were trained to
follow. Neither cop touched anything unnecessary in that
house. Every step they took, everything they saw, was
carefully noted in writing. The position of the Morrises'
car in the brick-paved drive. The time of their own entry.

The cops had set up the perimeter, isolated the witnesses, noted the clothing the parents had worn, even
what was on the TV. Michael Callas was the one who
had found Stephanie in the wine cellar.

He had then left the hysterical Mrs. Morris in the living
room with his partner, Finn, with instructions to call an
ambulance, and had accompanied Mr. Morris down to
the wine cellar for an identification.

And it was in Callas's notes what had transpired when
the distraught father had seen his daughter.

The father had been understandably upset. He had held
his daughter while they waited for the ambulance. Mr.
Morris had noted, with evident distress, the blue and
green bandana around his child's neck.

Ellie read aloud from the cop's notes. " 'Mr. Morris
touched the bandana at this point and said, "Oh, dear
God, it looks like John's. He's been working on our

kitchen. Dear God in heaven, it's John Crandall's bandana."

" 'I noted the time at that point to be 11:43 P.M. The ambulance crew arrived approximately two minutes later and the victim was given oxygen and transported to Boulder Community Hospital. She was accompanied by her mother, Mr. Morris following in his own car.

" 'At approximately midnight, Officer Rasmussen and I secured the house for the crime lab personnel.' "

Ellie let the typed report drift from her hand. Neither Callas nor Rasmussen could have known it at the time, but the case had been practically solved.

There was just one problem. Ellie knew her father was innocent.

And that meant someone had set him up.

She read the case file again and again until her head ached and she had to take off her glasses and rub her temples. The evidence, the crime scene, had been too perfect; it had been the swiftest arrest and easiest conviction in the hundred-year history of the Boulder PD. June and Earl Morris, upstanding and wealthy Boulder newcomers, had been down the street at a New Year's Eve party—plenty of alibis—and Stephanie had been home, behind locked doors, the security alarm armed all evening. Shortly after nine-thirty P.M., June had phoned her daughter—just checking. After all, they'd only lived there a short time.

There had been no forced entry at the Morris residence, and that led everyone to the conclusion Stephanie had disarmed the alarm and opened the door to her assailant. The girl had not even started school there yet, as the family had moved to Boulder at the beginning of the holiday break. She knew no one except the pleasant man who'd been doing the kitchen remodel, John Crandall.

And it *had* been his bandana tied around her neck.

Ellie sat on the couch, took off her glasses, and pressed her index fingers into her temples again. Who else would the girl have trusted? A neighbor she'd met? But the whole neighborhood had been at the party, and everyone had been checked out by the cops. So who would Stephanie have trusted instinctively and without question? Someone in uniform. Someone posing as a cop. Or, perhaps, a real cop.

She put her glasses back on and reread several files, hoping against all hope she'd see something new, something everyone had missed in the rush to justice. What was she missing? What had they all missed?

Her mind kept returning to Callas and Rasmussen, to the role the rookie cops had played that long-ago night. It was fact that both their careers had been fast-tracked. Heck, they'd even received department commendations for the excellent work they'd done. But that certainly wasn't sufficient motive to have set up her father. Ridiculous.

Ellie finally dropped her glasses on top of the files and stood stretching. Then she went to the kitchen and fixed a sandwich. Her head was still pounding with the same questions she'd had for so many years. Who had set her father up? She kept coming back to the cops, the heroes, but nothing made any sense. She knew the police captain at the time had been trying to get his career back on track after a botched murder investigation. Could the two rookies have set up John Crandall to make their boss look good? But that scenario was as unreasonable as any she'd come up with.

What was she missing? *What?*

At four that afternoon, she gathered the files and her notes and stuffed them back in her briefcase. Her roommates were going to be home soon unless, of course, they'd met some interesting men, and then Ellie figured she wouldn't see any of them till quite late.

She took her briefcase to the attic and thought about the weekend she'd missed. So many good times missed. A lifetime of them. And then she thought about her mother, recently laid off from her accounting job at the Leadville molybdenum mine. No one's life had been more troubled than Janice's.

Janice would be home. Sunday was her day off at the mini-mart where she'd finally found work in the depressed Colorado mountain town. She phoned her mother.

"So tell me the latest about the district attorney's office," Janice said, and Ellie could hear her mother putting the teakettle on the stove in the background. "Are they working you to death?"

"Almost," Ellie said.

"Well, you'll be home for Thanksgiving?"

"I don't know. There's this huge trial coming up, and the DA has me working on some of the pretrial motions."

"Oh, honey . . . darn. I'd hoped . . ."

"It's okay. I can get there for a day or so one of these weekends. I'll catch the bus."

"That would be great."

"Mom," she said, then she hesitated.

"What?"

"Well, I . . . I got my hands on the police files, you know, on the Morris case."

There was silence. Then, "Oh, Lord. Oh, Ellie, honey, I wish you hadn't. I mean, after all this time. What good is it going to do?"

Ellie sighed. "Justice, Mom. I've spent the last six years learning the law, thinking about Dad. It's about all

I *do* think about. What if I could prove his innocence?"

"Is this why you chose to go to school in Boulder? Is this what it's really come down to? I always thought . . . I wanted to believe you just went home. Oh, Ellie."

"Mom, look," she said carefully, "I don't know if I picked CU and a major in law because of Dad. I think in part I did."

"And the clerking job at the DA's?" Janice went on. "You're taking this year off law school to dig into the past? I don't know why I didn't see it before. I was just too proud of you, too happy for all you've accomplished. . . . There's a word for it. Denial. I was in denial. Oh, Ellie, don't take this any further. No good can come of it. Go on with your life. If someone finds out you're Ellie Crandall you'll be ruined. And don't think you won't be. Believe me, I remember what it was like before we moved and changed our names."

"You mean before we both got to be such good liars?"

"That's unfair. We did what we had to. We did what your father *wanted* us to do. How do you think he'd feel if he knew you were digging it all up again?"

"I don't know," Ellie cut in. "Proud, I hope. Vindicated. Something. I just know I can't bury my head in the sand my whole life. Mom, there's a monster out there. If I can do something, if I can—"

"What you'll *do* is ruin your life. If you want to end up like me, living from hand to mouth, living in a hovel, then keep this up."

Ellie could hear the catch in her mother's voice. "Listen," she began, "we'll talk about it when I get home. I'll try for Thanksgiving. I really will. Okay?"

"All right, all right. Oh, darn, the kettle, it's whistling away."

"I'll let you go."

"You won't do anything more, I mean until we talk?"

"No, I won't, Mom."

"You mean that."

"Of course," she lied. "Well, I'll see you soon. I'll call first. Okay?"

"Okay. And, Ellie, I love you, honey. You're all I have, you know."

"I know, Mom," she said, "and I love you, too." At least that was the truth.

When she was off the phone and catching up on laundry, she couldn't help analyzing her mother's words. Was she going to ruin her life in this quest for the truth? The odds were certainly against her, and if anyone found out who she really was she'd be shunned—if not tarred and feathered and driven out of town.

There was an awful lot of truth in the things her mother had said. After all, her father spent the best years of his life in prison. Hadn't they all suffered enough?

TWO

Ellie pulled in front of Departures at Denver International Airport and put the Range Rover in park.

"See?" Celeste said, beaming, her new lipstick a dark splash of color against her white skin. "You drove great."

"I hate driving. And I hate driving this expensive monstrosity of yours."

"Oh, you do fine. And what could happen, a fender bender? I think my father owns the insurance company." Celeste checked herself in the visor mirror. "God, an entire week with *la famille,* disgusting."

"Ditto," Bonnie said from the backseat as she gathered up her purse and carry-on bag. "But at least *you* aren't spending Thanksgiving in Bumfuck, Iowa."

Ellie rolled her eyes. Bonnie Brooks—she still couldn't believe her roommate's parents had stuck her with that name—lived in an adorable, upscale town north of Davenport, Iowa, on the Mississippi River. *They should visit Leadville,* Ellie thought, though she'd be too embarrassed to ever invite them.

"Well, gotta go," Celeste said, "plane leaves at nine.

I'll call you and let you know what time I get in. It's
like a week or something." She shrugged. "But if it's
snowing or the roads are icy, I'll catch a cab. Not to
worry, Kramer."

Bonnie, whose flight didn't leave for hours, opened her
door. "I get back a week from Monday, but I'll take the
airport shuttle up to Boulder. God, Ellie, I wish we
weren't all deserting you like this. It's only Friday."

"I'm fine. And besides"—Ellie turned and smiled—
"Torres is heaping work on me. The Zimmerman trial."
She wasn't *really* on it yet, but . . .

"I'm so damn jealous," Celeste said. "This is the trial
of the decade, and you're working on it."

"I'd rather be finishing my last year at law school, if
truth be known."

Celeste shook her head. "You will, Kramer, you will.
Next year, right?"

"You bet," Ellie said, "now get out of here. Bring me
some turkey and stuffing, you guys. God, don't forget
the stuffing. And cranberry."

"I hate cranberry," Bonnie said, whining, and Ellie's
two roommates disappeared into the mass of humanity
crowding DIA's huge peaked terminal.

The traffic exiting DIA on Pena Boulevard was heavy,
and Ellie drove cautiously. She wouldn't have driven at
all, especially in someone else's car, if Celeste hadn't
insisted. The last time Celeste had parked her new Range
Rover at DIA, the car phone and CD player had been
stolen despite its state-of-the-art alarm and the lot's ten-
foot wire fences.

"Never again," Celeste had vowed.

So Ellie had given in and driven them, but now she
was faced with the twenty-six-mile drive to Boulder
alone. And there were ice patches still on the Boulder

Turnpike. God, how she hated to drive. Still, the sand-colored Range Rover *was* nice, and she couldn't help noticing that people turned to stare at the affluent young lady as they sped by on the left. *Someday*, Ellie mused, she'd have a car of her own like this. But red. Why not?

For now life consisted of struggling to make ends meet. She bought all her clothes at secondhand shops. High-end shops, though, because Boulder *was* Boulder. She rarely ate out. Too expensive. And she hardly ever partied. Friday nights were usually card nights, anyway, with her roommates. They played canasta and bridge a lot. But Ellie's favorite game was hearts. She was good at it. Poker-faced. And she almost always won.

She turned west onto I-70 then north on I-25, where the traffic was murder until she exited onto the Boulder Turnpike. Even Jennifer had already left for a week-long family get-together in Cheyenne, Wyoming. It was going to be terribly lonely at the Marine Street house, but Ellie guessed she'd be too busy to notice, between studying the Morris case files and doing a workup for the DA on the upcoming Zimmerman trial. She'd also researched and written a pretrial motion for the inclusion of some evidence in her spare time—what little there was. She planned on sticking it under Torres's nose and then, if she had to, she'd beg to work on testimony with the cops. Beg. Plead. Whatever it took to get on the inside track of this trial.

Boulder lay ahead now, spreading from the flat tall-grass plains to the foot of the Rockies. It was a frigid day, but clear, the snow that still covered the land so white in the brilliant morning sun that without sunglasses she'd be snow-blind. The Flatirons, the slablike mountains that jutted up at a dizzying angle to pierce the sky, seemed to be holding up the Rocky Mountains crowding behind them. No photo of the University of Colorado or the quaint Pearl Street Mall would be complete without the rock sentinels. They were *the* icon of Boulder. She'd grown up right beneath them, and her family would still be there, on land that had soared in value, if—

Forget it, Kramer.

Ellie turned onto Arapahoe Road and crossed town through the CU campus, a familiar route. She passed Fleming—the building that housed the law school—and felt a sinking sensation. *Next year,* she told herself optimistically, next year she'd have enough money put aside to finish up her degree. Then she'd take the Colorado bar exam and be on her way. She'd do criminal defense work. She'd always known that; it was the only way to keep her finger on the pulse of justice.

Celeste planned on practicing in the private sector. "If I practice at all," she'd say.

Bonnie wanted to become an estate lawyer. Jenn just wanted money. "I like the idea of working on contingency, you know? You sue some insurance or drug company, and it's a third to the lawyer. God, I wish I'd been in on the cigarette deal or silicone implants. Yeah, I can see me screwing a few rich plastic surgeons."

"You are sick," Ellie always said. "It's no wonder everyone hates lawyers."

Jenn would grin ferociously.

Ellie parked the Range Rover in front of the house then ran the keys up to Celeste's room on the second floor. She hurried to her attic room and dressed for work— basic, conservative gray today, with a muted pink rayon shell beneath the gray blazer. She checked her watch. Darn. She'd be an hour and a half late. She'd told Torres already—asked him—but there was so much work to be done before the Zimmerman trial, and then there were the police files in her briefcase, endless files.

She raced down the two flights of creaking wooden steps, the second to the last one actually cracking. Last year, and four lovers ago, Jenn's boyfriend had sworn he would fix the darn step, but then Jenn had met someone else, and the step . . .

The doorknob. It was a big old round brass job with a raised pattern on it and it seemed to give two inches in all directions when twisted. One of the many men who'd come and gone from the house had sworn to fix that, too. Oh, well. They really didn't need a secure lock. Not in this old place; not in a house full of students who had nothing of value to steal.

She hurried along the street then down to the walking path that followed Boulder Creek and wound up a long incline to the Justice Center. There was no ice on the pavement. In Boulder, the jogging and biking and walking paths were plowed before the roads were.

Ellie had a love-hate relationship with the town. It had been called Disneyland, Colorado. It had been dubbed Eden and Utopia. It had been called bleeding-heart liberal in a predominantly rural, Republican state. Residents joked it was the People's Republic of Boulder. Some found it a mecca. Some found it full of yuppie snobs and too many students. The University of Colorado students and staff accounted for a third of the population, which was approaching a hundred thousand.

Boulder was a healthy place to live. Along with Aspen, Boulder had been one of the first cities in America to ban indoor smoking, raising eyebrows across the country, sending shock waves through the tobacco industry. It wasn't that nobody smoked or drank in Boulder—especially up on the Hill, where a lot of students lived. It was just that the residents were into active, outdoor lifestyles.

You had to swallow your preferred poison in private.

There were aspects of the city that Ellie cherished. She loved hiking to the top of Flagstaff Mountain. There, she could look down at her birthplace, at the neat grids of streets in the tidy, tree-lined neighborhoods, or to the turn-of-the century facades of the shops lining the Pearl Street Mall in the heart of downtown. The CU campus looked huge from the aerie, its red flagstone buildings spreading down the Hill.

She rushed along the winding bike path and through the big parking lot across the road from the Justice Center. In the morning sun, snow plopped onto cars from the tall cottonwood trees and the pines despite the freezing temperature.

There was so much about this town that she loved: its political progressiveness, that magic feeling that here all things were possible, almost as if it were still a boom-town. The people on the whole were well-educated and intelligent. Someday she'd be in practice here. She couldn't imagine living anywhere else.

Yet this same town had caused the humiliation and the misery that destroyed her family.

She had to set the record straight.

She entered the Justice Center out of breath, hugging the heavy briefcase to her chest. Then it was through security, chatting and smiling to the two officers manning the X-ray belt and metal detector.

"Morning, morning," she said, hurrying through, wondering if they ever questioned why a clerk would carry around so darn many files.

The DA's office was halfway down the corridor leading away from the courtrooms toward the courtyard, and Ellie pushed open the door, greeted the two women at the front desk, then went on back to her cubbyhole.

"Hi, Ellie," one of the female assistant DAs said from her office.

"Hi, Joan. Say, is the boss in right now?"

"He's in Courtroom C, I believe, sitting in on the juveniles. Anything I can help with?"

"No, no, no problem. I'm just going to run down to Records. You know, the Zimmerman trial."

Joan nodded. Everyone had been working on the case in one capacity or another.

First draping her coat hastily on a peg, Ellie made straight for Records with a pile of files on her father's case. She'd bring others back, neatly hidden beneath the real files she was working on. Ben Torres was in court. Good. A perfect time to make a switch.

In Records, she took a breath and pulled down the box numbered Case 6973 and quickly made the exchange, snatching up some new files. Then she carefully put the box back and hurried to the next aisle over, where she was supposed to be in the first place. The door to Records opened, someone came in, but whoever it was never saw her. She dragged down a file box, felt the dampness under her arms. *God.* How long could she keep this up?

The Zimmerman trial was as high profile as it got in Boulder, a sickening case. Four years ago last July, Steve Zimmerman, a local restaurant owner, divorced and paying hefty child support for a six-month-old daughter, had allegedly hired a hitman to murder his ex-wife. The hitman had done the job on the ex and then simply left the infant in her crib, where she'd died two days later of dehydration. The motive for the two murders was so outrageous, so cruel, it was nearly impossible to believe: Steve Zimmerman hadn't wanted to pay child support. The whole case tormented Ellie—that poor innocent baby, left to suffer and die alone. The cops never would have broken the case if the hitman hadn't been told last year he had only months to live, and he'd found God and confessed to the murders. He'd died eight months ago, but the DA and cops had three taped sessions with him, three very convincing videotapes. Nevertheless, Ben Torres had crossed all his *t*'s and dotted all his *i*'s on this one and a grand jury had indicted Zimmerman. Murder one. Torres was going for the death penalty, too, in spite of Zimmerman not actually having committed the murder himself. Sometimes complicity was enough. Everyone thought Zimmerman would go down hard. Murder one at the very least.

Torres had assigned Ellie to prepare several briefs on points of law he was positive Zimmerman's defense would bring up before the judge. She was nearly finished with them, having pored over previous cases in Colorado in which judges had handed down precedent-setting decisions. Boring, tedious work that was typically given to the clerks.

But she'd stumbled across something in the Boulder PD arrest files: names of former business associates of Zimmerman whom the police had interviewed. On her own, she'd contacted one of the men, and she'd learned that Zimmerman had spoken to him four years ago about where a person could hire a hitman. The man hadn't told the cops, and he didn't want to testify unless he was forced to. Still . . . She was almost ready to polish up the report and place it on Ben Torres's desk. He'd have to let her in on the case. He simply *had* to. She'd finish the report over the weekend. Then on Monday, or Tuesday, before the holiday, she'd present her work to the DA.

That night she walked back along Boulder Creek and through the downtown street mall to her favorite second-hand shop. Other such shops were nearer the campus, but this was the one that the wealthy folks used, and Ellie had put together quite a wardrobe from here. The ladies who worked at the shop knew her and often set things aside for her. Tonight was no exception. For less than ten dollars, she went home with a pair of jeans and a double-breasted black wool blazer that would look great in court.

She stopped at a local grocery and then trudged up the Hill to Marine Street, her arms protesting. She liked the walk, though, past the 1930s neighborhoods of brick and wood homes with their mature trees and picture-perfect yards. In a week, after Thanksgiving, everyone would string up Christmas lights. Then the town truly became a fairyland.

She knew Boulder so well. She'd been born right at Boulder Community Hospital, the same hospital to which Stephanie Morris had been rushed in an ambulance that awful night. Tonight Ellie would read the medical report. She dreaded it.

Ben Torres set the alarm for six-fifteen and was asleep within minutes. On Saturday morning, when the alarm buzzed, he rolled over, punched the bar, and then patted the hump of Marie's shoulder beneath the down comforter.

"Rise and shine. I'd like to get on the road by seven."

"Um," his wife groaned.

"Come on, honey, we've had this ski weekend planned for a month. I'll make coffee."

"Um," she uttered again, but she made no move to get up.

Everything about the DA's life looked perfect from the outside. Marie, his wife of eighteen years, was still beautiful and trim. At forty-three, Ben was a slim graceful

man of medium height, his roots running all the way back
to a Spanish Land Grant family in New Mexico. He had
thick, fine brown hair, pale skin, patrician features, and
dark eyes. He knew, as he'd always known, that women
found him handsome, sensitive to their needs. Marie certainly had. But for all the flawless façade, his marriage
had gone flat.

Ben and Marie had met at the University of Colorado
law school. They'd dated and both had been recruited by
the district attorney's office. Marie had been proud of her
husband's fast rise to the position of DA, but she'd
quickly lost her own enthusiasm for practicing law.

He'd encouraged her to stop working, and he'd often
thought that had been a mistake. If she were still a practicing lawyer, maybe they wouldn't have grown so far
apart.

Marie still worked hard, though. She was head of in-
numerable good causes, a fund-raiser known personally
by the governor of Colorado. Busy, busy Marie. So busy
that her husband was far down the list of her priorities.
At first Ben had accompanied her to the endless dinners
and social events, but he'd given that up some years ago,
because Marie didn't really want or need him at her side.

Their marriage had turned into a comfortable, emo-
tionless coexistence that Ben often thought was worse
than any fractious relationship could be.

The worst part of the whole thing was the empty house
at night and the notes in the fridge next to the plates of
tasteless, foil-wrapped foods.

"Marie, come on, honey, rise and shine," he tried
again.

In the end they cancelled the trip; not only was Marie
too tired from a late-night gala, but she'd promised to

help prepare the volunteer list for the library's annual Christmas bazaar.

"I was going to do it last Wednesday," she said, "but I'd forgotten to write the children's day at the hospital on my calendar, and—"

"What about me? What about *us?*" Ben tied the knot on his robe in jerky motions.

"I said I was sorry, Ben. My God, sometimes you can be so selfish."

He was in no mood to fight. Not at six-twenty in the morning. "I'll make coffee," he said, "we'll ski some other weekend. I guess it doesn't matter."

"We have all winter."

While his wife set up a volunteer telephone list in the living room that Saturday with two of her lady friends, Ben drove over to the Justice Center and worked on his opening statement for the Zimmerman trial. He remained there till two then phoned Marie to see if he could pick up anything at the store before coming home. Then he turned off his computer and took his parka off the peg on the back of his door. He shrugged it on and glanced through the door toward Ellie Kramer's partitioned work space, and he paused. As he always did when she was in his presence or, to tell the truth, if he even thought about her. Which he did. Frequently.

She was, hands down, the best law clerk he'd ever taken on. She worked so hard it was difficult to imagine she had a social life at all. And he took advantage of her diligence, he admitted to himself, piling tedious work on her because she so readily accepted it and always with a bright, infectious smile. Someday she'd reap her reward. Here or in the private sector, Ellie was going to be a success. Everyone paid his or her dues. But it sometimes seemed Ellie was paying a higher price.

He stared at her desk as he dug his driving gloves out of his pockets. He knew he'd given her the much-coveted clerk position not just on her good grades and recommendations from professors. When she'd first walked into his office last summer, and said she was taking a full year off law school, he'd been instantly struck by that presence and grace, as if sunlight had suddenly filled his office.

Okay. So there'd been several qualified applicants, and maybe he'd given the pretty girl with the short, tousled curls and wide-set dark eyes the job based on something other than her record. But he consoled himself with the fact that she'd proven to be an excellent choice.

He sometimes found himself gazing out his open door at her, and he sometimes fantasized about what it would be like if he and Marie were divorced, and Ellie was out of school, in practice, and he really wasn't *that* much older. . . .

He turned off the lights in the office and headed toward the long, echoing corridor that would lead him out to his private parking space. "Milk, bread, and why not pick up a steak?" Marie had said; he needed to stop at the store, he remembered.

Ellie. In the three months that she'd been clerking, he'd not only been thoroughly impressed with her work, but he'd seen an intensity in her, an edge, that he hadn't yet deciphered. He knew, too, that against office policy, she took files home from Records. He'd been meaning to speak to her about that. Not chew her out. What sort of an ass would he be to call her on the carpet for doing the work of two assistant DAs?

No, no, he would put it in words that she'd understand, businesslike, even friendly. He'd do it soon, too, before somebody else noticed and got the wrong impression.

Sure, he liked Ellie, a whole lot, but rules were rules.

Monday, he thought. He'd speak to her in private on Monday.

"Milk, bread, and . . . a steak, right," Ben said, and he backed out of his space, his mind on Marie and the ruined ski weekend.

By Sunday evening, Ellie was deep into the bloodless medical terminology that made up Stephanie Morris's report: Crushed thyroid and cricoid cartilage. Cause of comatose state was occlusion of blood vessels supplying blood to the brain. Erythematous marks posterior to sternocleidomastoid muscles. Bruising consistent with position of knots found on bandana used as ligature. Vaginal penetration, tearing of the vaginal walls, presence of semen likely. Petechial hemorrhages on eyelids and bridge of nose. Bruises on arms and wrists consistent with forceful restraint. A concussion caused by a blunt object.

All those words, long scientific words, but what they amounted to was a sixteen-year-old girl beaten and raped and strangled nearly to death and left unconscious on the cold cellar floor.

The Morrises had been newcomers to Boulder. They'd purchased a two-million-dollar home in the fashionable Hill section, and the entire investigating team had known they were supposed to do a thorough job, leave no stone unturned. They went through the motions, even though Ellie's father had been hauled down to the police department only twelve hours after the discovery of Stephanie's body.

Ellie had been kept insulated from the ordeal. No one had let her watch the news or see a newspaper, much less attend the trial. She'd heard things, of course, and at junior high that spring semester her peers had been brutal to her. By the end of April, Janice Crandall had taken Ellie out of school and sent her to live with her grandparents in western Nebraska on the family farm. She had stayed there till after the trial, till after her father had been imprisoned in Canon City. Then they'd legally changed their last name and moved to Leadville.

Ellie recalled with acute clarity the judge's words when he'd granted the name change: "I guess I'd change my name, too."

Nonetheless, Ellie had heard her mother on the phone to John's defense attorney, to the police chief, the DA, the local newspaper, to anyone who'd listen, desperate, insisting that John had been set up. She'd even cried that it had to have been the cops, that they were covering something up.

Ellie had never forgotten her mother's words. At the time, they'd not had much meaning to her but, later, when she and her mother had been struggling to make ends meet in Leadville, their Boulder property long since sold, the proceeds gone to defense attorneys for John, Ellie had started to mull over the words. *Her father had been set up.*

She'd asked her mother what that meant, but as the years trudged along and John's predicament grew hopeless, Janice refused to talk about it.

"We can't live in the past, Ellie," she'd always said.

Well, Ellie was thinking about the future, about justice, and, yes, revenge. There were no lengths she wouldn't go to achieve her ends. All she had to do was picture her father in that prison cell, alone, afraid, *innocent.*

On Monday morning she replaced the medical reports and took several files on interviews the BPD had conducted with the home security outfit and the Morris neighbors, though Ellie was sure she wasn't going to learn much, as the Morris family and three square blocks' worth of neighbors had all been alibied.

She was on her way up from Records when she bumped into Torres. Her knees turned to rubber.

"Busy, busy," he said, blowing on coffee in a foam cup. "Those motions for the Zimmerman case?"

Ellie rolled her eyes. "What else? But I think they're about ready for your keen perusal."

"Good, good. I just hope, well, that you aren't spending all your free time, at night, you know, working on this."

"Don't be silly," she said evasively, "I do have a life."

How easy it was to evade the truth. She'd been doing it since their move to Leadville and the name change, making up a past, embellishing it if she felt like it. Even Celeste, her best friend on earth, had no idea Ellie had been born and raised in Boulder. In their freshman year at CU, their first few weeks together, Ellie had faked everything, taking wrong turns while walking to the mall, pretending she'd never climbed the hills or been to the top of Flagstaff Mountain. Everything. Oh, yeah, she was an accomplished liar. And she hated it. Sometimes she wondered if she wasn't digging a hole too deep to climb out of.

That night at home she typed up her final report on Zimmerman's business associate and then shut off the PC and turned to the John Crandall files. She was beginning to form a clear picture of the events surrounding the rape of Stephanie, the time line. Still exhausted from their move to Boulder, the Morrises had returned from the party shortly before eleven. The doors were locked, the security alarm armed. Whoever had assaulted Stephanie had to have had knowledge in that area. Either that, or the girl had let the rapist in.

Then the Morrises had searched for their daughter, been unable to find her, panicked, and called nine-one-one. The uniforms, Callas and Rasmussen, had arrived at eleven-twenty, and Stephanie had been discovered in a dark corner of the wine cellar at eleven-thirty-five.

Callas had found her. Suspicious. He could easily have grabbed John Crandall's bandana from the toolbox in the butler's pantry and placed it around the girl's neck. Thus incriminating Ellie's father.

Stephanie had been raped and nearly strangled to death, and the medical report stated that both had occurred in the wine cellar. The rapist had left no physical evidence whatsoever, except for his semen. The complete lack of evidence meant the man was very smart, very knowledgeable about police procedures. His semen had been sent for testing at the time, but DNA testing was new back then, and nothing had been found to tie the semen to any human male on record. The rapist had also been a nonsecretor, that is, he was in the forty percent of the male population that did not secrete certain proteins in his semen; those substances revealed blood type and certain genetic markers. Unfortunately, John Crandall was also a nonsecretor.

No physical evidence: no fluids but the semen in and around the unconscious girl, no tissue or hair, no fingerprints, no footprints.

And poor Stephanie couldn't even testify, because her brain had been starved of oxygen for too long and she'd suffered irreversible brain damage. For thirteen years she'd been in what doctors called a persistent vegetative state.

There had been fibers found all over her, but they'd all been from inside the house—only to be expected.

Except for the fibers from the flannel shirt John Crandall had worn earlier that day while working on the new kitchen cabinets.

The defense had argued reasonably that of course the flannel shirt had shed all over the kitchen, but the argument had held little weight.

Ellie made a bowl of Thai noodles for dinner and paced the kitchen, eating. Callas and Rasmussen. It kept coming back to those two cops. Solving the murder, John's arrest—all too goddamn easy.

Finn Rasmussen no longer worked for the Boulder PD. But Michael Callas did.

He was the lead detective on the Zimmerman case.

"These look great, Ellie," Ben Torres said after he'd done a review on the briefs she'd prepared. "Really, really well thought out. You're going to make a fine attorney, young lady."

"Thank you," Ellie said.

She stood in front of his cluttered desk and took a breath. "There's something else I'm hoping you'll look at."

He glanced at the file folder she was clutching.

"I did a little snooping on my own on something, well, *someone* connected to the case. I think you'll find my report interesting."

"Really," he said.

"If you have a few minutes to look it over, I'd like to know what you think."

He took the folder from her.

"If you could do it this afternoon?" She beseeched him with her eyes. Oh, she knew exactly how he felt about her, exactly why he'd given her the clerk position. "Please," she added.

He found her later at her desk and sat on its corner, smiling down at her. He folded his arms.

"You read it," she stated.

"Not only have I read it, but the whole staff has. Let's just say it's another big nail in Steve Zimmerman's coffin. What I want to know is how in hell you convinced this guy to talk when the cops got zilch out of him?"

Ellie thought about her reply. She chewed her lip and then looked up at the DA. "If I tell you, will you let me do the pretrial prep of the cop's testimony?"

It was Ben's turn to think.

"I can handle it," she said quickly. "You know I can. And it's only pretrial, Mr. Torres."

He regarded her solemnly then he held her report up. "How'd you get this information?"

Ellie lowered her eyes modestly. "I talked to him, that's all. I think he wanted to unburden himself."

"Hm."

"Are you going to let me work with the cops?"

Torres frowned. "I don't doubt your ability, Ellie. It's the lead cop on the case, a man named Michael Callas, Detective Michael Callas. Over at police headquarters they call him Robocop. He's good, Ellie, but he can be a nasty s.o.b."

"I can handle him." She thought she was going to leap out of her skin. Half her life to get to this moment in time. She gave Torres her best poor-little-girl look. "Please, *Ben*," she whispered.

It seemed an eternity before he answered. "Don't let him browbeat you."

"I won't," she breathed. "I'll handle him."

Then she smiled brilliantly. *Callas*. At last.

THREE

"Hey, Callas, phone," Rick Augostino called across the room. "Line one."

Michael Callas looked up from the tape he was transcribing, annoyed. "You take it, Rick."

"Nope, she asked for you by name, Detective Michael Callas."

"Shit," he muttered, angrily stabbing line one on his phone. "Yeah, Callas."

"Michael Callas?" A woman's voice.

"That's right."

"My name is Eleanor Kramer," she said, a little breathlessly. Or was he imagining that? "I'm clerking for Ben Torres, and he's put me on the Zimmerman case. I'd like to get together with you and go over your testimony."

A clerk liaising with the detective division? Torres must have really lost it.

"Um, Detective Callas . . . ?"

"Sorry, just thinking. Sometime Monday morning?"

"Well"—a slight hesitation—"I was hoping for today, actually."

"Today?" He looked at his watch. "It's two-fifteen already, and the office is emptying out. Can't it wait?"

"The trial begins next Thursday. . . ."

"I'm well aware of that, miss."

"So I'd really like to get started. I wanted to work at home over the long weekend."

"You mean *now?* You want to get together right *now?*"

"If you're not too busy," she said meekly.

"Christ." But an idea flickered in his brain. An unquenchable flicker that was disagreeable and welcome at the same time.

"I can be over there in half an hour."

"I suppose. . . ."

"It won't take long," she said, eagerly, grabbing the opening. "And then I thought maybe we could get together again on Friday, that is, if you're not taking a long weekend."

He *was* taking a long weekend. His family expected him. Tonight, in fact.

"Friday," he said, mulling it over.

"Well, anyway, I'd really like to get started today. I can be right there, like I said."

"Um, I guess so. Nothing else going on that can't wait."

"Oh, that's wonderful. I really appreciate it. And the DA really appreciates it, too. You know how committed the whole office is to winning this case, Detective Callas."

"Yeah, yeah. Listen, you know where to find me?"

"The Public Service Building, sure."

"Upstairs, detective division."

"Yes, I know," she said, and he wondered if he imagined the tinge of smug satisfaction in her response.

The first thing Michael did after he hung up was to lean back in his chair, hands behind his head, legs stretched out. He thought he must be nuts for saying he'd see this clerk, this hot-to-trot young lady, all fervent belief in justice and taut ambition. But then he pulled his lips into a crooked, rueful smile. Hell, he knew why he'd done it.

The next thing he did was to pick up the phone and call his mother in Colorado Springs.

"You're going to be disappointed," he said, "but I can't make Thanksgiving. Something's come up."

"Oh no, Michael. I was so looking forward to seeing you," she said. Her voice sincere.

"I know, but this case that's going to trial, I have a meeting today, and then tomorrow I have to work on my testimony and another meeting on Friday."

"You can't make it even for tomorrow, just the one day? The turkey's defrosting, and—"

"I'm really sorry, but I can't. You know my job." He tried to sound contrite, but he wasn't sure he succeeded.

His mother sighed. "I am very disappointed."

"I'll come down soon, real soon, I promise." Did his mother recognize his lies? "Say hi to the cousins, you know."

"Okay, Michael, take care. Happy Thanksgiving."

"Yeah, same to you."

He sat there holding on to the phone after she'd hung up. Hunched over, elbows on his desk, as if he were still talking to her. Finally he put the phone back on the cradle and let out a breath.

There was always pain when he talked to his mother or his father. Twenty years' worth of pain. They were divorced now, and he wasn't sure whether that made it better or worse. Their pain—had it been double when they were together? Was it diluted now? Could it ever be diluted?

He was relieved as hell to have an excuse to miss the family get-together. Even though they all, uncles, aunts, cousins, were fine—cheerful, normal—a gloominess hung over every gathering. There was someone missing. He often thought his mother should set a place at the table and put a glass of wine there for the absent one. Like the Jews did for the Prophet Elijah at their Passover seders. Not there in body but there in spirit.

Paul. His older brother, Paul. No gathering was complete without him. His memory, his premature death, the tragedy, the agony. Still as fresh as when it had happened, if Michael cared to dredge up the emotions.

He'd been four years younger than Paul, and light-years behind the prodigal son in every facet of life: sports, school, girls, everything. Paul had been special, brilliant, a freshman at Stanford, handsome, charming.

Dead at nineteen.

It was so much worse for those left behind. Being dead was easy. Dying was easy. Living in the shadow of perfection cut off in the prime of life was unendurable.

He'd never been able to mourn the way his parents had—still did. He supposed it was because he was not the parent, merely the brother. But he'd never been the favorite son. He knew that, guessed he'd always known it. And when Paul had been laid out in the coffin in the viewing room, Michael had seen it in his parents' eyes: If we had to lose a son, why Paul, why our most beloved?

Their anguish and the unmasked truth had scored him permanently and indelibly, and there was loneliness in his suffering. God, how he had hated that truth in their haggard faces.

But with time he'd learned to put it away, turn it off,

leave it buried. Until he came face-to-face with Paul again at family gatherings. And then there it was—the hideous truth. Which was why he'd rather work.

Michael never spoke of his past. He was careful not to drink to excess, as so many of his coworkers did. Crying in his beer simply did not appeal. It was nobody's business but his own, and he sure wasn't one of those new-age guys that went into the woods with a lot of other saps to beat drums and cry on one another's shoulders. What in hell good would that do?

He was a damn good detective, though. He'd figured out why: The best detective could have no certainty. Everyone was under suspicion; nothing was what it seemed. All evidence shifted from possibility to cause to effect to new unknowns. A detective working on a case never had peace, because peace only came with certainty. That was him to a T.

He didn't let his past contaminate the one area of his life that was a success, though. He kept things in compartments in his head: the past, the present, work.

He knew he was sarcastic and prickly. Scared the hell out of the rookies who had to deal with him. Intimidating. He liked it that way.

He got up and wandered into the room where the coffee machine was, poured himself a cup. Black. He liked the poison bitterness of unadulterated brew.

Eleanor Kramer. Clerking for the DA. Some homely little bespectacled nerdy law student. And Torres had her working with him, Michael, the prosecution's prime witness. "You gotta be kidding," he muttered.

The building was emptying out. Everyone who could was sneaking off early. Sam Koffey, the commander, Boulder's fancy name for the police chief, was already gone. Rats deserting the sinking ship on this holiday weekend. Running before a call came in, so they wouldn't get stuck with a case and have to pull duty on Thanksgiving.

One of the things about the Boulder Police Department Michael liked was its size—only seventeen detectives— and the way it was set up. Detectives weren't assigned to specialties like robbery-homicides or crimes against persons or drug crimes. You took whatever came up; you never knew what type of crime you'd be handling. No elite divisions, the kind of democratic equality for which Boulder was famous.

Michael was still working on the tape he was transcribing—pain in the neck—when he became aware of someone walking toward his desk. He looked up.

It was the unexpectedness of his reaction that stupefied him. The first sight of her was like a breath-stealing blow.

"Detective Callas?" she said.

He knew he was staring, an idiot, but he couldn't tear his gaze away. His voice was strangled in his chest.

"Yeah," he finally said. He cleared his throat and stood up a little too quickly, bumping his knee on his desk. "Yeah, I'm Callas."

She held out her hand, and he took it. It was slim and icy. She smiled apologetically. "It's cold out."

Then he noticed that her eyes switched to his gun, which hung in his shoulder holster over the back of his chair.

"Ah, let's see. I'll find us someplace to work."

He was glad to leave her there, waiting, while he found an empty room. He was shaken to his core, a unique feeling for him. By a woman.

No ordinary woman. She was medium tall. Nothing unique there. And she was pretty. But so were plenty of women. What she had was that rare quality of presence, as if an inner flame warmed her and spread outward to her skin, her smile, her eyes, to the tips of her dark, curling hair. She was one of the few women he knew he'd never regret seeing beside him at first light. And that was a dangerous notion.

He steeled himself and went back to his desk. "Do you want some coffee?"

"No, thanks." She wore a long wool overcoat, a solid black coat, and she was trying to shrug it off her shoulder while holding on to her heavy briefcase.

"Here," he said, and he helped her with her coat.

"Thanks." She smiled and he noted that her front teeth were a little crooked, an endearing imperfection.

He held her coat, standing there stupidly. He could smell its scent, the cold outdoor air, a bittersweet aroma like almond, female skin, and hair. He draped the coat over the chair beside his desk.

The room he took her to was one of their interrogation rooms, a small cube, featureless but for a table, a tape recorder, a one-way mirror, and a couple of chairs on each side of the table.

She put her briefcase on the table. It was an old, soft-sided one, scratched and bulging.

"Call me Ellie," she said as she searched in the case and pulled out a file with a rubber band around it. "Okay? Since we'll be working together."

For some unfathomable reason, he didn't offer a similar courtesy. "Ellie. All right. Miss or Mrs.?"

She flashed him another smile, and he wondered how in hell a crooked tooth could be a turn on.

"Miss. I'm a law student. CU."

"Shouldn't you be in class, Ellie?"

"I'm clerking full time. Taking this year off."

She sat, opening her file. He lowered himself into a

chair across from her. The table between them. She pulled out reading glasses and put them on, then glanced at the first page of the file. Peering over the top of the glasses, she said, "I'd like you to tell me the story the way the DA will have you tell it in court. It started four years ago, right?"

"Four years ago last July. One of Mrs. Zimmerman's friends contacted the police because she hadn't answered her phone in three days. I got the call. I took Detective Jamie Herne with me."

"Refer to her by her first name."

"Danielle."

"Okay, good. Use it, so the jury can see how personal this is to you. She was a real person, you know."

"Okay, Danielle Zimmerman. We went to her apartment; it was on Ninth Street. We had to force the door. She was dead of a bullet wound to the head, had been for a while. It was July. Hot. We called for an ambulance, secured the scene. Then we found the baby."

"Use the baby's name."

"Maryanne Zimmerman. Six months old. In her crib." His voice became a little thick. It always did at this point in the story. "She was dead also, no external injuries. The coroner told us later that she died of dehydration. The shooter did the mother, uh, Danielle, and just left the baby."

"It must have been pretty gruesome."

He said nothing.

"Go on. What did you do first? Suspects?" Her eyes were dark brown, the whites very clear. Above the rims of her glasses they held his unflinchingly.

"The husband. Steve Zimmerman. He owned Panchito's. The restaurant on the Pearl Street Mall."

"Uh-huh."

"I phoned him and set up an appointment for the next day. Meanwhile the other guys were talking to Danielle's friends and doing a door-to-door. Her parents, her sister, the regular drill. But I wanted this Steve.

"Okay, so I put him in a room a lot like this, with the tape recorder on. I was already suspicious because he'd reacted wrong when I phoned him with the news of his ex-wife's murder. He acted shocked, the whole nine yards, but he forgot to ask *how*. You know, *how* was she killed? And his daughter, little Maryanne. He was wrong. I felt it."

"Evidence?"

"None. No brass left around, no fibers, no footprints, no fingerprints, one bullet retrieved from her head. No witnesses, no neighbors seeing a strange man around, no odd phone calls. Nothing."

"How about Steve Zimmerman?"

"He was in his restaurant, the perfect host. He had two hundred alibis, people he spoke to, bought a drink for, ordered a free dessert for. All night till closing."

"This was four years ago."

"We worked on that case for six months, found nothing, and had to put it on the back burner."

"But something caused you to open it again."

"Yeah, that crazy son of a bitch Hugh Radway confessed. He had cancer, got religion, and didn't want to die with the killing on his conscience. It was the baby that got to him."

"You might not want to call him a crazy son of a bitch in court," she suggested.

"Okay," he said drily, "I'll try to remember that."

"I'm sorry if I was condescending."

"Don't worry about it."

"You had a deathbed confession, so the case was re-opened," she prompted.

"We got three separate videos of him, a written confession, and two doctors' statements asserting he was in his right mind. He said Steve Zimmerman had paid him five thousand dollars to kill his ex-wife so that he wouldn't have to pay alimony or child support anymore."

"Now, did this Hugh Radway tell you if Zimmerman specifically told him to kill the child, Maryanne?"

"No, Zimmerman didn't tell him about the baby."

"Maryanne."

"Right, Maryanne. That's why he confessed. Said it bothered him, but what could he do once he found the baby . . . Maryanne there?"

"We're going to have to consider all the questions the defense will put to you. Now, Detective Callas, I have to ask you one thing. It's not personal, but the DA's office has to know. Do you have any, um, things on your record or in your personal life that could be touchy on the stand? We don't want a Mark Fuhrman here."

He locked gazes with her, but she didn't blink. A shutter closed down over her eyes, and when it lifted he saw a flash of a bizarre, dark emotion—contempt, abhorrence?—but it was gone before he could wonder.

"Nothing," he said evenly. "I got a parking ticket once, that's it."

"No ex-wife or child that could make you a target of Zimmerman's attorney?"

"No wife, no children."

She stared at him, and he felt as if he could drown in the depths of her eyes. "Why not?" she asked.

"What?"

"Why no wife or children?"

"What the hell?" He ran a hand through his short hair.

"Is this something I'm going to get asked in court? You preparing me?"

"No," she said steadily, "I'm just curious."

"Well, *Ellie,* I'm not sure it's any of your business."

"No, it's not. Sorry." She took her glasses off and pinched her nose. Then she looked at him again. "I think we have a very good case. You make a credible witness. I understand Hugh Radway's videos are compelling. But, as you know, a court trial is a crapshoot, and no one can tell for sure what any given jury will do. So we're leaving no stones unturned." She went on. "Were you aware that we've located a new witness and are entering him onto the witness list?"

"No, I wasn't."

"I, well, actually it was me who found him. An acquaintance of Steve Zimmerman's who admitted that Steve approached him four years ago, inquiring if he knew any hitmen."

"You're kidding."

Ellie smiled knowingly.

"And *you* found this guy?"

"Well, actually, detective, you found him. Four years ago. You interviewed him but got nothing."

"Really."

"Really."

"And he just opened up to you, told you right off the bat"—Michael snapped his fingers—"that Zimmerman asked him if he knew any hitmen?"

"Let's say I was persistent."

"What'd you do, wine him and dine him?"

She looked up sharply but then her features softened.

He made a noncommittal grunt but kept his gaze on her vigorously. She had short, dark, tousled hair pushed behind her ears and high cheekbones. A long neck and slim hands. That smile was devastating. A bell tolled deep inside him.

She stood. "Well, I guess that's it for today. I really do appreciate your time. Uh, do you think we could do this again on Friday, or are you . . . ?" She cocked her head questioningly.

"I'll be here," he said gruffly.

"Oh, good. Terrific. I'm going to prepare some questions for you, things we expect the defense to ask." She was stuffing the file into her battered briefcase. She glanced up at him. "I know we're going to win this one. Ben Torres is confident, too. Everyone in the office thinks you did a great job on this."

"You consider four years late a great job? I don't."

"Well, but we have him now."

"Luck, pure luck."

She straightened. "I've always believed, Detective Callas, that we make our own luck."

He led her out of the room to his desk, where her coat lay draped over the chair. She gathered it up and turned to him. "Happy Thanksgiving," she said brightly.

"Happy Thanksgiving to you, too," he repeated.

"See you Friday, right?"

"Yeah, sure."

"Now, point me to the stairs. I'm all turned around. Oh, there they are." She gave a quick, self-deprecating smile, a wave of her hand, and she was gone.

And the room was unquestionably dimmer for her absence.

Michael spent Thanksgiving Day alone, not that he minded. He was generally fonder of his own company than that of most people. He had no patience for people's foibles and weaknesses; his irritation level was close to the surface. A woman he'd dated had once told him he was unfit for the human race. He'd agreed with her.

He wondered that day as he worked on his chimney if he'd have been an entirely different person if Paul had lived. Probably. Yeah, he'd probably be a swell guy.

He'd bought a piece of property a few miles outside of Boulder, on Canyon Boulevard, a winding, mountain-rimmed highway that eventually led into the heart of the Rockies. He was building a log cabin on the piece, had been working on it for three years now. A year ago he'd completed it to the point where he could actually move in, but it wasn't finished, not by a long shot.

He enjoyed the physical labor and had done most of it himself, except for the concrete footers, the heaviest beams, and the electricity.

He'd been working on the stone chimney for a couple of months, patiently chipping the rock, laying it, working from the floor up. He had in his head how he wanted it to look: French country style, dry-stacked, flat stone in layers with no grout showing. It took longer, but the result would be worth it.

Every facet of his cabin had been carefully and lovingly crafted, even when Michael had to teach himself the craft. The outside corners were mitered, held together by bolts, which were hidden by wooden plugs. The windows were fitted into their openings perfectly, the doors hung precisely, the floor, made of random-width knotty pine, was finished to a satiny sheen.

It was important to him to use his hands, he'd found, a kind of therapy. He was building something concrete, seeing real progress, because his paying job was so intensely cerebral. And so often without discernible progress.

It was cloudy outside, a little warmer than the bitter

clearness of the day before. The forecast was for a couple days of seasonal temperatures then another arctic cold front, what the weathermen loved to call an Alberta Clipper. It was shaping up to be one hell of a winter, and it was only November.

He fit a piece of stone into a slot, tapped it with the blunt end of his trowel into the soft grout, and stood back to see how it looked. Good. It looked good. Another couple of weeks and it'd be finished. The top would be slow, because he'd have to use a ladder, but that was okay.

His kitchen was state-of-the-art, not that he cooked much. Everything built-in, pale washed cabinets to offset the overpowering darker wood. A big central granite counter. The cabinets were practically empty; he'd never fill them, but he'd wanted to do it *right*.

He threw out the rest of the grout he'd mixed, left the pile of stone for the weekend on a tarp, and pulled a frozen turkey dinner out of the freezer.

"Happy Thanksgiving," he said. Not bitter, barely sarcastic.

A picture of Ellie Kramer came to him without warning. Ellie in his spotless new kitchen, a ruffled apron around her waist, pulling a roast turkey out of his wall-mounted oven.

Jesus. He was losing it. But she stayed there, puttering around the kitchen, smiling, and he got to adding details to the picture: a white sweater with a gold heart on a chain lying on her breast. A delicate watch and gold hoop earrings. A skirt, stockings, heels. He imagined the way her breasts pushed against the sweater, how her hips curved, the line of her throat and chin, the deep, smoldering darkness of her eyes. The crooked teeth.

"Happy Thanksgiving," he said again, and her voice came back to him, the way she'd said it yesterday, the way she'd asked him why he had no wife or children. Not even flinching when he told her it was none of her business.

No wonder Ben Torres had hired her and no wonder he was letting a lowly clerk work on the Zimmerman case. She was *good.*

That new witness she'd found . . . Michael wondered just exactly how she had gotten the man to open up. But as quickly as the question had popped into his head he dropped it. Hell, he guessed he'd rather think of Ellie in an apron.

Shortly after he ate his deluxe turkey dinner with mashed potatoes, gravy, and baby carrots, the phone rang.

His mother? He cringed inwardly.

"Yeah, Callas," he said into the receiver.

It was not Mom. "It's me, Stone."

Pete Stone was an informant, a guy in his late twenties whom Michael had busted years ago on drug possession. At the time, Stone had been a student, and Michael had gone easy on him. First, the young man hadn't been selling to kids. And second, Stone was a natural-born rat.

Stone no longer lived in Boulder. He lived in Wheat Ridge, a Denver suburb. And even though Denver wasn't Michael's beat, Stone still proved useful. For twenty dollars a pop. It was worth the money. And Stone didn't call often, only when there was news on Michael's quarry.

Michael found himself holding his breath.

"Your guy got on a plane to Mexico today. Baja." Pete Stone waited.

"Okay," Michael said, thinking. "I want to know exactly where."

"I'll try."

"No good. I need a town."

"All right, all right, I'll see what I can do."

"You find out, you get paid, otherwise . . ."

"Okay, Callas, I hear you."

Michael hung up. He'd been after his man for over a decade, following his every move, waiting for him to make that one fatal slip. Hell, Michael had countless pages of notes on the man, filling notebook after notebook. The guy was no slouch, and he was well connected, real hard to get to. The worst part of the whole deal was that sometimes, in the darkest hour of the night, Michael would awaken and hope the man would strike again, finally make that fatal error and Michael would have him. Then Michael would lie in bed, sweating, despising himself for his thought and banishing it back into the ugly corner of his soul. How could he anticipate the rape and murder of some innocent girl? What kind of a monster was he?

Still, it was the only way he'd ever see Finn Rasmussen behind bars.

Ellie phoned him on Friday after lunch, and it wasn't until he heard her voice that he realized he'd been waiting with avid anticipation to hear from her.

"How about I come over in an hour?" she asked.

"Sure. I'll be here." He thought after he said it he was trying to sound too casual, fake. But it was too late to alter the impression—she'd hung up.

The strange thing was, when he saw her, she was wearing a white sweater, just as he'd imagined. No heart locket, only the sweater, and gold studs in her ears, which were red with the cold.

"Hi," she said. "Did you have a nice Thanksgiving?"

"Ate like a pig," he lied.

"Me too."

By now he noticed that the other guys in the office were sneaking furtive peeks at her. Did they perceive her glow as he did or were they simply curious? Robocop Callas hanging out with a cute young chick. Jim Chambliss ambled by, trying to look nonchalant. Michael knew damn well he'd made a bet, and the others had sent him over to find out who she was.

"I was just on my way to get some coffee," Chambliss said. "Wondered if either of you would like some."

Michael would be damned if he'd introduce Ellie. "No, thanks," he said.

"None for me," Ellie said, "but it's the thought that counts. By the way, I'm Ellie Kramer from the DA's office. Detective Callas and I are working on the Zimmerman case."

Shit, Michael thought.

Chambliss grinned like a moron. "Jim Chambliss." They shook hands. "Real nice to meet you."

"We're trying to get some work done here," Michael growled.

"Oh, sorry," Chambliss said, but Ellie smiled sweetly and waved a hand to show it didn't matter. He had the urge to yank her hand down.

They sat in the ice cube of a room again. She pulled out her file, put on her reading glasses, and started firing questions at him that she had listed on a sheet of yellow legal paper.

"Why did you originally bring Mr. Zimmerman in for questioning?"

"Standard procedure."

"Was his lawyer present?"

"No, he was given the opportunity but declined."

"Did you know Hugh Radway had a criminal record?"

"Yes."

"Fraud, burglary, armed robbery?"

"Yes, I knew."

"Yet you still considered his confession to be credible?"

"Absolutely."

"Why?"

"He knew he was dying. He had nothing to lose."

"Did you know Hugh Radway had a sister he was very close to and that this woman was divorced and destitute?"

"No, I didn't know that."

"Her name is Thelma, and she's suddenly doing much better financially. Bought a new car and a trailer."

"And . . . ?"

"Her dying brother, Hugh, is suspected of taking money for his so-called deathbed confession and giving it to her."

"Bullshit," Michael said.

She cocked her head again. "Excuse me?"

"I said bullshit."

"Not in court, I hope."

"Where'd you get that story from?" he asked angrily.

She smiled. "It *could* be true. Radway was a slime-ball."

"Yeah, but he spoke the truth."

"It goes to his credibility."

"*Christ.* The man's dead."

"Yes, so he can't speak for himself, and the defense will bring up his record, his personality flaws, and anything else that could impugn his credibility."

He shook his head in irritation.

"I'm only playing the devil's advocate."

"I thought you were on our side."

"I am. Although I eventually want to practice criminal defense law. It's more challenging."

"God, one of those," he said.

"I might change my mind, who knows? Now, more questions?"

"Fire away." Christ, this law student was right out there swimming with the sharks.

It went on. The Inquisition. She pissed him off a few times, but she never lost her cool and he felt like a jerk. He knew there'd be plenty of tough questions when he was on the stand. She was doing her job.

She finally put her legal pad down and took her glasses off. "Enough?"

"Hell, yes."

She was rubbing her eyes, and he abruptly had an urge to put his hand on her head and feel the silky dark curls.

"It's late," he said, amazed at his own voice, the words that emerged of their own volition. "You doing anything? Want to get a bite to eat?"

Her hand dropped, her eyes fixed on him. "My goodness, I didn't really . . ."

"No big deal," he heard himself saying. "Some dinner."

She sat there for so long he thought his heart was going to leap from his chest with apprehension. The small room was utterly still. And very warm now.

She smiled. "If I go out to dinner with you do I still have to call you Detective Callas?"

He felt the heat rise up his neck. Shit. "No," he said in a surly tone.

"Okay, then, I accept."

Goddamn. He wanted to ask her why she'd said yes. He was missing something. A girl like her? And he'd been a rude bastard to her. Why would she go out with him? Didn't she have a dozen young law students hot to get in her pants? Didn't she have something better to do than go out with *him?*

They ate at the Caffe Antica Roma, right on the Pearl Street pedestrian mall. They got there early, and the place was mostly empty. He envied the ease with which she adapted to every situation. Like a chameleon, she fit in to the background. She didn't seem to be the least bit discomfited at being out with a police detective probably ten years her senior, a man she'd just met casually in the line of work.

She talked easily of minor matters, the severe weather they'd had lately along the Front Range, rush-hour traffic delays in Denver and on the interstates, the phenomenal growth of the area.

"Are you from Boulder?" he asked.

"Well, almost. I've been here for, gosh, eight years now, since I started college. I'm from Leadville."

"Leadville?" He raised a brow.

"I know, everyone thinks people from Leadville are inbred and ignorant, but it's not true."

"Apparently not." Leadville, a small town at ten thousand feet altitude, used to be a gold mining boomtown and had fallen on hard times.

"And you, where are you from?" She took a sip from her glass of red wine.

"Colorado Springs."

"Your family's there?"

"Some of my family." He wished she'd get off the subject. "Now, why aren't you home in Leadville over the holiday?"

She shrugged. "Too much work." And then she neatly turned the tables. "Why aren't you down in the Springs with your family?"

"Too much work," he said straight-faced.

"Oh, God, I hope you didn't stay here just to meet me." She sounded genuinely distressed.

"Of course not."

Their pasta dishes came, and she began to eat, a healthy appetite, he noted.

"Um, this is good," she said. "How's yours?"

"Very good." Actually, he had no idea how it tasted. He ate mechanically, too aware of her. The slim wrist as she twirled the pasta on her fork, the deft touch of a napkin to pasta sauce on her lip, her smile, the way her soul came through her eyes, palpable, mesmerizing. Dangerous.

"Why'd you pick law school?" he asked her over dessert.

"I believe in justice," she said promptly.

He grunted. *Justice.*

"And why are you a detective?"

"I believe in order," he said.

"Practically the same thing."

"Maybe."

She licked the spoon and put it down, leaned forward toward him. "Why do they call you Robocop?"

He felt the flush on his neck again. Man, she asked hard questions. "How the hell do I know?"

"Did you see that movie?"

"Yeah," he admitted.

"Well, then you know Robocop was a good guy."

"He was a goddamn robot."

"Not exactly. Remember, he kept having flashbacks of his wife?"

"Weird movie," he muttered.

"I liked it." She sat back. "He was very idealistic, kept trying to do right. Is that the way you are?"

"Yeah, sure, just like that."

"I think it's a compliment, that nickname. And I think you're embarrassed about it."

"Listen, Ellie, it's no compliment."

"I'm going to take it as one."

Boy, she knew how to put you on the spot. He got very busy looking at the bill and getting out his credit card. He wondered briefly if he could turn the receipt in for expenses.

Robocop. Damn, how embarrassing. She was right, not that he'd admit it to her. She certainly went for the jugular, not the least bit intimidated by him. God knew, he'd scared off plenty of women. Not Ellie Kramer, though. She kept coming back for more. And then he had to wonder why.

He found out, to his surprise, that she didn't have a car, so he drove her home. Marine Street, on the Hill near campus. A typical older clapboard house with a fraternity house next door. A nice Range Rover parked out front.

"I have three roommates," she told him as he pulled his pickup truck to the curb. "But they're all gone for the weekend."

Was this some kind of come-on?

"How about Monday?" she asked then, and he knew it wasn't; she was only being straightforward.

"Okay. Give me a call."

"I'm going to meet with Ben Torres that morning, and he'll probably have some suggestions."

"No doubt."

"Thanks for dinner. I really enjoyed it."

"You're welcome." Then he astonished himself once more. "Maybe we can do it again sometime."

"I'd like that."

She'd like that. She sounded as if she meant it. "Let me come around and get the door. This truck is pretty high."

"I noticed. How come you have a truck? I had you figured for, oh, I don't know, an SUV."

"Really? I look like an SUV?"

She smiled in the darkness. "You know what I mean."

"Yeah, well, I have this truck because I use it for construction. Carrying things, lumber and stuff."

"What are you constructing?"

"A cabin."

"Oh, wow, for your own use?"

"I live in it. It's not done yet, but I'm getting there."

She was studying him through the dimness. He could feel her eyes on him. Finally she said, "Well, aren't you a bundle of surprises."

"Not really. I like to work with my hands."

She was silent for so long he was beginning to get uncomfortable. But then she said, "My father liked to work with his hands, too." Her voice was low and sad, and Michael felt that he'd gotten past her façade for the first time, but he couldn't figure out how or what it meant.

"What does your father do?" he asked.

"Oh," she said quickly, "it's a long story. Some other time, okay?"

"Sure," he said, but cop that he was, he'd filed away the too-light tone of her voice. He wanted to put a hand on her arm, a simple gesture to tell her he'd like to see more of her without having to verbalize it. He didn't have the guts, though, and the moment slipped away.

"Well," she said in a more cheerful voice, "I'd better get going."

"Hold on, I'll get that door." He walked around the

truck, the air cold on his face. Pulling open her door, he reached up to help her down.

She slid over and put a foot out, feeling for the running board, her hand in his. It was, as usual, cold, but her grasp was strong. She was so damn unself-conscious; nothing got to her. And he didn't quite buy that.

She landed on the ground with a little thump, her hand still in his, and she was close, facing him, her breath pluming.

"Wow, that is high. Easier getting in than out," she said. "Thanks again. See you Monday." Then she stopped and looked up at him, her face a pale oval in the night. "You never told me if it was all right to call you Michael. Or is it Mike?"

"It's Michael," he replied.

"Well, then, thanks again, Michael."

"See you Monday." He repeated her words stupidly.

She walked up the path to the front porch. The house was entirely dark, no outside lights, but then she'd been gone all day. On the porch steps she stopped, half-turned, and waved to him. His hand rose on its own and waved back, and he waited until she was inside the house and had turned the lights on before he got in his truck.

He drove away, heading down the Hill toward Arapahoe Avenue, which led to Canyon Boulevard, barely remembering the drive.

Ellie Kramer. He frowned. Why did she seem to like him? Women generally didn't. Was she after something? What, his money? *Ha.* Why did he doubt her? Why couldn't he take her at face value? Jesus, he had a bad self-image.

But there was something about her. His cop's instincts felt it, sensed something. Not a lie, exactly, but an absence of the whole truth. There were so many things he wanted to know about her. And he had the distinct feeling she wouldn't answer if he asked. She was charmingly evasive and delightfully open at the same time. A paradox. She was passionate and composed. Another paradox. Something didn't ring true.

He drove up Canyon Boulevard, crossed the wooden bridge over the creek to his private driveway, and pulled into his two-car garage, filled mostly with tools and construction supplies.

The red light was blinking on his recorder when he got inside. He punched the play button. It was Pete Stone: "He's in a fishing camp outside a town called San Jose del Cabo. Took some of his employees on vacation. I assume I earned my keep? Later Callas."

Michael stood over the machine contemplating Rasmussen. Would his old patrol partner spot some nice Mexican girl and . . .

His brain shied away from the images. Michael wondered if he should contact the Mexican authorities, alert them. It would have to be unofficial, though, because the first and last time Michael had made unfounded accusations against Finn Rasmussen he'd been raked over the coals by his BPD superiors. He'd looked unprofessional, foolish. Vindictive. Everyone knew Michael had not gotten along with his first partner. So Michael had shut up.

But he'd kept records ever since then, filling notebooks with newspaper clippings, computer printouts, times and dates and locations. Names of victims. A plethora of information but no proof. No definitive proof.

Should he phone the Mexicans? But if he did, what could he really tell them?

Shit, he thought, staring at the phone, frowning.

He went to the fridge and got a beer and stood studying the unfinished fireplace. He badly needed to work with his hands. It wasn't just Rasmussen. Rasmussen was a constant obsession that Michael had learned to live with. It was Ellie, law clerk Eleanor Kramer.

He put down the beer and went to his bedroom to change into work clothes.

There was something about her. . . . Beneath all her apparent accessibility, Ellie had the faint redolence of a secret. And if there was one thing a cop hated, it was a secret.

FOUR

On Sunday morning, Ellie caught the eight A.M. bus out of Denver that stopped in Frisco and then went on to Leadville. Years ago, there had been little ground transportation from Denver into the high country, but that was before the huge population growth on the Front Range. Now a body could get just about anywhere in the mountains either in a shuttle van or by train or bus. The bus was inexpensive, which suited her wallet.

She sat near the back. The bus was crowded for a Sunday. Of course, the rest of the ski areas had all opened over the holiday, and between worker bees heading to jobs and eager skiers ready to hit the slopes, there were almost no free seats. She would have liked to have pulled out a notepad and jotted down her thoughts about Det. Michael Callas, but there was a lady sitting next to her and the situation was awkward.

She stared out the tinted window instead and let her thoughts roam. Detective Callas. *Michael.* She'd spent hours in his company, and yet, other than learning he was single, had no children, and was from Colorado

Springs, she knew nothing significant about him.

She was accustomed to understanding people easily and quickly; it was one of her survival tools. But Michael was difficult, both needy and impenetrable.

The bus sped by the exit to Evergreen and through Idaho Springs then climbed steeply toward Georgetown. Old boomtowns whose scars from gold and silver mining still riddled the mountainsides. Then the road rose steadily toward the Eisenhower Tunnel, which bored through the Continental Divide at eleven thousand feet. The forests here were stunted pines that climbed the vertical slopes in the narrow cut that the interstate followed. It was incredible country, where the craggy peaks reached to the blue heavens. Everything was white now, snow-covered, and would be till June.

The bus shot into the tunnel and the world went black till her eyes adjusted to the dimness. *Michael,* she thought again. What was she missing?

He'd been the cop who'd found Stephanie in the wine cellar. Even before his partner had come down the basement steps, Michael had been alone with the unconscious girl.

Ellie thought about the time frame of the rape. It had occurred, as closely as anyone could figure, prior to ten P.M. And, coincidentally, both Michael Callas and Finn Rasmussen had gone on duty at ten. That added up to opportunity.

She shook herself mentally. No motive for the rape or strangulation, no history there with either cop. And to believe that one of them had committed such a heinous crime simply to further his career was crazy.

Yet her brain refused to take a new track. Both cops had access to John Crandall's bandana hastily tossed in his toolbox in the butler's pantry. And Stephanie had opened the door to the rapist. It wouldn't be the first time a cop had used the authority of a uniform to commit a crime.

She saw clearly how it could have happened.

It's the annual New Year's Eve block party. The Morrises are new to town, but everyone—including the patrol cops—knows of the family already; they purchased the most expensive home on the Hill. Of course they're invited to the party.

Had one of the cops cruising the neighborhood seen them move in? Seen the pretty sixteen-year-old daughter? Begun to fantasize about her?

The cop knocks on the door. He's in uniform, but he's driving his own car, won't switch to a police car till he punches in to work.

Okay, Ellie thought. Stephanie, seeing a policeman at the door, disarms the alarm and lets him in. The security outfit had a record of it. So there was no break-in.

The man attacks her, carries her struggling to the wine cellar. Perhaps he has already picked up John's bandana or perhaps he picks it up and chokes the battered girl as an afterthought. But he goes too far and almost kills her. Or perhaps he meant to kill and botched the job.

Anyway, she thought as the bus popped out of the tunnel and began the harrowing descent toward Frisco, afterward, the cop drives the few miles to police headquarters and goes on duty by ten P.M. He could have accomplished the whole task in twenty minutes. Then the best part. He and his partner have the Hill patrol. He would have already known this. Counted on it. So the two rookies, who're unlucky enough to have drawn New Year's Eve duty, take the call from the hysterical parents at eleven-ten. Then comes the thrill, the big payoff. He is on the scene when the girl is discovered and not only does he investigate the crime right there on the spot, but he helps to solve it. The ultimate high.

Crazy, crazy, crazy, Ellie thought. She spent all those hours with Michael. If he were a mad rapist, a sociopathic murderer, wouldn't she have sensed something horribly evil?

Good-looking. Strong profile. A faintly Mediterranean look to him, a bronze glow to his skin, those golden eyes . . . Her hand in his as he helped her down from his truck.

"Isn't this your stop, honey?"

Ellie snapped back to the present. "Huh?"

"I was behind you in the ticket line," the lady next to her said. "I thought you were transferring to the Leadville bus in Frisco."

"Oh, wow, yes, I am. Thanks, thanks." She hurried down the narrow aisle.

The next and last leg of her trip to visit her mother took her through Summit County past the Dillon reservoir, Copper Mountain Ski Area, then up another pass back over the Serpentine Continental Divide and alongside the idle molybdenum mine, and down into Leadville. When Ellie had been a teenager here, there'd been signs welcoming tourists to the home of the celebrated Molly Brown. In a play on words, the sign had read: Follow Moly to Leadville. Now the signs were gone, along with the mine.

She watched the familiar scenery fly by the window but saw nothing. Could Callas—*Robocop*—be a killer? He certainly had a hard edge to him, a bitterness. And why *hadn't* he spent Thanksgiving with his family?

Unmarried. No children. Where exactly did he live, how did he spend his off-duty hours? Stalking his next victim? *No, no, no,* Ellie thought, she was leaping to conclusions, grabbing at straws. What she needed was time to get to know him, more time alone with him. She needed him to like her, to trust her, to open up to her. So far she had no idea what he thought. He'd taken her to dinner. Out of politeness? And she knew that gaining his trust was going to test her powers of persuasion. She had her foot in the door. But for how long?

Her mind twisted with thoughts. Everything seemed to be moving so fast now. All these years she'd waited and schemed, bided her time, and finally she'd met one of the players in the drama. But she didn't know what his role was. Yet.

One thing Ellie did know for sure: her father had not attacked Stephanie Morris. Her mother had been out of town, in Nebraska at the farm. But John had been home with Ellie on that New Year's Eve. Ellie's parents had refused to let her testify in court, because they thought it would be too traumatic for a twelve-year-old. And the police had interviewed her, but considered a child's testimony suspect and useless. Even John's attorney had balked at putting Ellie on the stand. The Boulder DA would have accused her of having been asleep at that hour on New Year's Eve, and, more importantly, who would have believed John's daughter?

There had been other similar rapes and two deaths by strangulation on the Front Range that Ellie had learned about. Perhaps there were others. Her father couldn't have done these, because he'd been behind bars. But had the authorities noted the similarities in the cases, had they even looked? *Hell, no.* The cops had taken the path of least resistance and made their arrests based on circumstantial evidence. A belt, a scarf, or another bandana— all found around the necks of victims. Just like her father's bandana. How easy it was. And cops knew the statistics well: 80 percent of all attacks on children were committed by a close male relative.

Goddamn the cops, Ellie thought, as the splendor of the Rockies slid by the bus window. *Goddamn them.*

She put on her happy face for her mother. Janice had enough problems without Ellie unloading on her. And she knew she had upset her mother the other day by telling her about the files she'd been reading. Janice couldn't bear to dredge up the past; she dodged it with ferocious energy despite the fact that Janice herself had first planted the seeds of doubt about the rookie cops in Ellie's young, impressionable head.

The familiar walk from the bus stop to her mother's house on East Fifth Street was quick, past a block of Leadville's downtown, which had been renovated into something approximating its 1879 gold rush glory days. False-front buildings, gilded signs, sidewalks raised two feet from the street, the way they'd been back when mud mired wagon axles. Then the turn onto East Fifth, the ascent into a high-altitude slum, old miners' cottages fixed up with electricity and Depression siding, sagging sheds, everything covered with snow, dirty, gray snow.

The sun was out, but the temperature, even at midday, was bitter at ten thousand feet, and off to the west toward the jagged ranks of the Continental Divide, Ellie could see clouds gathering.

Janice was waiting for her with a lunch of homemade soup and fresh rolls.

"You know," Ellie said, "it's so funny, whenever I'm back here it's so familiar, as if I never left. I fit right in like a pea in a pod. But when I'm in Boulder I feel the same. Weird."

"It's always like that when you've lived somewhere.

When I used to go back to the farm, it was like I never left."

"Strange how the mind can hold two sets of memories equally clearly," Ellie mused.

"I haven't been back to Boulder, not since it happened," Janice said quietly.

"I know."

"I don't know how you can live there."

Ellie shrugged. "I was young. It didn't hit me quite the same way it hit you." She smiled. "But you'll come back when I graduate from law school, won't you?"

"I hope so."

"Mom."

"I will. I'll do it."

Ellie studied her mother. Janice had been so pretty, with Ellie's dark hair and eyes, but with much finer features. Petite, delicate. Now she appeared frail. She was a smart woman, educated, a high school math teacher. She'd kept her husband's books, done his billings. Sharp as a tack.

When she'd moved to Leadville, she gotten a job at the Climax molybdenum mine, the town's largest employer, as an accountant. But the mine had shut down, just like the gold and silver mines of the nineteenth century had, and the town had sunk a little further into poverty. And so had Janice.

"How's your job?" Ellie asked.

"Oh, boring. Routine. Pretty easy. If I took the night shift I'd make more money, but I'm chicken. Besides, they always hire men for that."

Janice worked at the convenience store at the Shamrock station on Harrison Avenue. A job for a high school kid.

"Hang in there. They'll make you manager soon."

"Sure."

After lunch they sat in the living room and talked. It was hard for Ellie to keep up her front in the face of her mother's predicament. This was the house she herself had lived in from the age of thirteen until she'd started college. There were good people in Leadville, and the residents helped one another, gave support to others whom they knew to be having the same kind of financial troubles they had. It was so bad that some of the population commuted all the way to Vail, where there were lots of jobs. But Vail was many miles away, and Janice's old car was not up to the commute.

Janice had moved as much of the furniture from her Boulder house as she'd been able to, but most of it didn't fit into the nine-hundred-square-foot cottage. A kitchen with worn Formica counters, a cracked linoleum floor, an old gas stove, a chipped white porcelain sink. All in shades of faded gold. A living room with unevenly finished walls, the good but aging furniture too large for the scale of the house. Wrong. Big, man-sized couch and armchair in what had once been a lovely stripe, but was now worn and faded.

Two bedrooms: Janice's, with what she could cram in there from her beautiful bedroom set; and Ellie's, left exactly as it had been when she'd attended high school— same posters on the wall, the overly cute canopy bed with a pink spread, and all her stuffed animals. Her books and pictures and mementos, all the same. A museum for a vanished individual.

Once it had been home.

"I hope you're not still looking at those old files, dear. I can't bear the thought of you going back, seeing it all. . . ."

"Don't worry about it, Mom."

"So how's work going?"

"Really well. Ben Torres is letting me help with the Zimmerman trial. Remember, I told you about it, the man who hired a contract killer to shoot his wife?"

"Oh, yes, I remember. That's wonderful, dear. I do wish you'd been able to finish your third year, though."

"I'll do it next year. It'll be a help working at the DA's. School will be a snap after this."

A spurt of anger flashed through Ellie. When she passed the bar and got a good job, she'd buy a nice house for her mother. Here in Leadville, if Janice wanted, or in Boulder, where she'd lived for so many years. She only hoped Janice wasn't too broken, too old to enjoy it.

Damn the man who had ruined their lives. Damn the legal system that ignored the truth and let him go free.

Forcing the anger down, she went back to the subject her mother was really interested in, her job, her career.

"I think Torres has a crush on me," she confided.

"I wouldn't doubt it. You're a gorgeous, intelligent girl."

"And you're not prejudiced, are you, Mom?"

A small curve of Janice's lips altered her appearance and tugged at Ellie's heart. "Of course not. I'm as impartial as a judge."

"Ha!"

"You're not going to get involved with your boss, are you?"

"No, no. My God, the man is married, a pillar of the community."

"But you see a lot of him."

"In the office, sure."

"I trust your judgment, you know that. Now, tell me about this trial you're working on."

Ellie got up and moved around the room. She went to

a window and pushed aside the curtains, gold textured synthetic fabric, water-stained. She'd always hated those curtains. The day outside was bleak, the sky a sullen pewter.

"We have a strong case," she said. "I told you about the deathbed confession."

"Uh-huh. Sounds open and shut to me."

"No trial's ever open and shut, and Zimmerman has a real hot defense team. He can afford it." She hesitated; should she tell her mother? "One of the witnesses who'll be testifying is the detective who was the primary on the case when Danielle Zimmerman was murdered four years ago. Torres has me prepping him for the trial. He'll be cross-examined brutally, no doubt."

"Oh, my goodness, how fascinating. How do you know what to do?"

Ellie smiled. "That's my job. I've had to learn. I study a lot of old trial transcripts. That helps." She paused then, gazing out the window at the lone, bare-branched aspen tree that separated this house from the next. The room was quiet, the only sound the ticking of the baseboards as they expanded from the hot water pumping through them. Then she decided she had to tell her mother. She needed to be truthful with one person. She'd hidden her true self, pretended, acted, for so many years, for so long. . . . She felt as if she were losing track of who she really was—one person to her roommates, another in the DA's office, another to her classmates, and certainly a completely discrete one to Michael Callas.

She turned to her mother. "The detective I've been prepping, his name is Michael Callas."

"What?"

"Michael Callas."

Janice looked puzzled. "But he was the policeman that

found, that was there the night . . . Is he, no, he couldn't be . . ."

"Yes, Mom, it's the same man."

Janice paled. "You're doing it still, aren't you? You're trying to go back. Oh, my God, Ellie, I told you. Don't dig it up. Live for today, not for that, that nightmare."

"I'm working with him on the Zimmerman case."

Janice pushed herself out of her chair, agitated. "You don't fool me. You manipulated the situation so you'd get to meet this, this Callas."

Amazing how her mother knew her, Ellie thought. The only person who did.

"Oh, Ellie, I wish you'd give it up."

"I can't give it up. All right, Mom? And I'm going to try to locate the other policeman, too. His name is Finn Rasmussen, but he's not a policeman anymore, and I don't know where he is. I'll find him, though."

Janice sighed. "You were always stubborn."

"This matters, Mom, a lot." She could have said that her mother had aroused her suspicions in the first place, for God's sake, but instead she said, "I intend to get to know those two men and find out what really happened that night."

"You'll ruin your life."

"Maybe, but I have to do this."

"What . . . what's Michael Callas like now? Does he know who you are?"

"Good Lord, no. He thinks I'm a clerk at the DA's office. Which I am. That's it. As for what he's like . . ." She paused, thinking, trying to put it into words. "He's a tough son of a bitch. Mean, hard. But there's something behind that, I don't know, something vulnerable. A little boy lost. He has a past, I know it, and I'm going to find out what it is."

Janice shook her head. "I wish I could talk you out of this crazy hunt you're on. You'll find nothing but misery."

"I'm looking for the truth, Mom. It's important. It's the most important thing there is."

"No, it isn't, dear. Getting through life is what's really important."

Ellie dropped the subject then. It was a lost cause. Janice would never understand. They went for a walk, a few blocks down, to see a friend of Janice's, Agnes Spanner, who always made a fuss over Ellie.

"The prodigal daughter," she said, a tough old lady, born and raised in Leadville, who'd outlived two husbands. Her five children had all been born in this house. "Got out of this dump. Good for you. Hanging out your shingle yet?"

"One more year."

"Hot damn, whole town's prouder than punch. You go get 'em, Ellie honey."

Janice and Ellie then continued on for coffee at the Motherlode Cafe on Harrison, owned by the father of one of the boys she'd gone to high school with.

"How's Boulder?" he always asked. "They ever get those CU kids to stop drinking beer and busting up the mall?"

"Nope, they never did." Ellie grinned. That's all anyone here knew about Boulder—the wild doings of rich, privileged college students.

They ate an early meal at the Cantina, a Mexican restaurant with such a good reputation people from Aspen drove sixty miles over Independence Pass in the summer just to eat there.

Afterward Janice walked Ellie to the bus stop. They hugged.

"I love you, Mom, and don't worry about me. I can handle it."

"I'll worry. Mothers worry, that's all there is to it."

"I'll call soon."

"Okay. Take care."

"I will. You too, Mom."

Then the bus came and Ellie got on, and she waved through the window at her mother, a small woman in a heavy fleece coat, scarf, hat, and Sorel boots. And she waved again, until the bus pulled away, and she could sit back and close her eyes for a time. She wondered, as the bus sped along the narrow valley where the Arkansas River began its epic journey, would her mother be so beaten down if her husband hadn't gotten sick in prison three years ago? He'd gotten sick with a dumb cold, which had gone into his chest and become pneumonia, and he'd died. Broken by the very system that was supposed to protect and serve its citizens, John Crandall had given up and simply died.

Ellie bit her lower lip and took a breath. Neither she nor her mother had been with him. No one had. God, it still hurt. And someday, someone was going to pay for that.

FIVE

Finn Rasmussen received two presents from his parents on his seventh birthday, a bright red Tonka Toy fire engine from his mother and a black eye from his father. He didn't cry or go to his mother when his father backhanded him, because he knew it would be a waste of time. He slunk away, clutching the fire engine, and retreated into the room he shared with his older brother and sister.

Mostly what Finn recalled of his childhood was his parents fighting, screaming, engaging in drunken battles. A hovering tension even when his father wasn't drunk. Fear.

His sister, Ginny, was frightened and cowed, his brother, Scott, loud and vicious, but Finn was unknowable. His parents, Keith and Becky, were part of the struggling middle class in Milwaukee, Wisconsin. Keith ran a car rental agency at the airport and Becky managed a toy store. They fought over Keith's drinking and money. Constantly.

His mother tried, she really did, but she couldn't han-

dle her job, her children, and her husband, so she chose the easiest to concentrate on—her job.

Even his mother got fed up with her youngest son's bed-wetting, although the entire family conspired to keep it from Keith. No telling what Dad would do if he found that out.

Finn was a darling little boy, a towhead, with Viking blue eyes. His teachers saw him as a quick learner, an intense child, but ultimately too distant. A loner.

The only time he ever felt accepted at school was the day he started a fire on the playground with matches he'd brought from home, and all the other boys had crowded around. His popularity hadn't lasted long—only until a teacher smelled the smoke, came over and stamped the fire out, and took Finn to the principal.

That night he got a bloody nose from his father.

Somewhere deep inside, he determined to live differently when he grew up. He nursed his pain and hated his father, at that age not really knowing that what he felt was hate, and waited stoically.

He was seven. And that was when the racket began in his head, a bizarre concoction of images and voices.

Finn dragged himself back from the noise in his brain and the shifting faces, tossed his head in the bright Mexican sun, and laughed. "That might possibly be the lewdest joke I've ever heard," he said.

Joel Blum, the youngest of the four men who sat at the seedy outdoor bar on the San Lucas dockside, grinned at his boss. "Gosh, sorry I offended you, Finn. I'll buy a round to make amends." He swiveled in the white plastic chair, his T-shirt stuck to the slatted back. *"Cuatro más, por favor, señorita,"* he called to the barmaid.

She shot the *yanquis* a look and gestured with a sun-browned hand. *"Un momento, un momento."*

The fishing trip to Baja California was Finn's treat. Every Thanksgiving he took his most valued—and single—employees to the warm climes of either Mexico or the Caribbean. Some years they golfed and sailed. This year it was sport fishing, though a late Pacific hurricane had nearly ruined the big game fishing this season, and they'd spent most of their time checking out the bars and the women between San Lucas and San Jose del Cabo.

Finn sat beneath the clicking palm fronds at the bar and realized he was having a lousy time. The other men, Joel, Craig Seale, and Matt McLaren were having a ball. They had only been here a few days, and they'd been laid every night—all but Finn. Tonight, though, he was afraid he might have to go the distance. Joel had met four vacationing secretaries from San Diego and fixed everyone up for drinks, dinner, and dancing in San Jose del Cabo. Finn considered claiming an upset stomach and begging off, spending the evening at the fishing camp where they were lodged, but he'd made an excuse every night not to join in the festivities, and he was afraid to do it again. Besides, the date would make a sound alibi.

Male bonding was not one of Finn's pleasures despite the impression he gave. And most women were merely props.

Outwardly, Finn was a man's man. He was big and lean and blond, with intelligent blue eyes, a slightly offset nose, generous features. He was good-looking in a rugged manner, with a deep, compelling voice.

He laughed quickly and easily, and people took to him, calling him charismatic. Men liked and trusted the thirty-eight-year-old Denver security systems entrepreneur, and women sought his attention, which he readily gave, though when the fun and novelty abated, he always backed off. He had a reputation for being fast, a real playboy, and the society columnists loved to follow his escapades. Women never talked about their experiences in Finn's bed, fearing it was they who had not performed to his satisfaction. So his reputation remained unscathed, and he was able to go through women like grains of sand through open fingers.

He usually had a better time than on this particular trip. The poor fishing played a part. But there was more to his discontent. The pictures had come into his head again, the ones he always saw when his need became unbearable. Young girls, faces, swirling in his brain— eyes, noses, mouths, and their mouths were always open, screaming, like the Picasso exhibit he'd once seen: women, their eyes on crooked, huge crystalline tears frozen on cheeks, mouths distended in screams. Square mouths in which the sounds formed in bright cubes that Finn could see but not hear. Cubes that came out of their open mouths and floated, silently, even though roaring filled his head.

The kaleidoscope came to him of its own volition, and he'd known from the first that he could not share its excitement and beauty with anyone. It was his alone.

Outwardly he remained perfectly normal; inwardly he raged and exalted. And planned. The need was all-consuming, a breathless suspense that could only be quelled in one way.

"Damn, it's hot out," Joel said as he tossed a bunch of pesos onto the barmaid's tray. "Well, guys"—he lifted his fresh margarita, the salt on the rim sparkling in the sun—"cheers. Here's to better fishing tomorrow."

Craig clinked his sweating glass to Joel's. "To better fishing. Hell, it can't get much worse."

Finn smiled and looked past Craig's shoulder to where the sport fisherman boat sat rocking at the dock. The crew was still hosing it down from their morning run out onto the blue Pacific Ocean. Alfonso was propping the white vinyl cushions against the bait box to dry, and José was hosing off the last of the bloody bait from the deck.

The owner of the fishing camp and the boat was named Juan Valero, nice man, cheerful and hardworking, whose whole family, his wife and two sons and daughter, all worked at the camp. A real family operation. It was the daughter who'd caught Finn's eye.

Peta was her name. She was sixteen, maybe seventeen, nubile with lovely long dark hair and skin the color of warm honey. She had tiny budding breasts. Finn conjured in his mind's eye the nipples beneath her white T-shirt when her brother had sprayed her with the hose yesterday afternoon. His groin had seized and spasmed and he hadn't been able to take his eyes off her, those tiny, hard nipples and the shy embarrassment. So young. So beautiful. And that was when the faces had swirled behind his eyes. It had been a long time, but this girl was *chosen*.

"Well," Joel said, "I'd rather be sitting here by the dock, lapping up the booze, than freezing my balls off in Denver. Screw the fishing. This is just fine by me."

"Couldn't agree more," Matt said.

"Hell, we'll catch the big one tomorrow," Finn put in.

"Here's to the four-hundred-pounder just waiting out there for me." Joel grinned, and he and Craig clinked glasses again.

Tonight, Finn mused, why not? After dinner and drinks, in the crowded, noisy nightclub, he'd slip off, be gone maybe thirty minutes. He'd be careful no one noticed his absence. If anyone did, he'd laugh and say, "Bathroom. Montezuma's revenge."

He'd heard Peta's father making plans with his men that morning. The mother was away, taking care of *her* sick mother up the coast. Peta was supposed to cover the front desk at the lodge but, as her father had pointed out to her on the dock this morning, no one was due to check in.

Finn was unconcerned. The girl was going to be alone, and no one would suspect him, anyway. Alfonso, one of the crew, was going to take the fall. It was Alfonso's distinctive neck scarf that Finn had swiped yesterday from the galley.

In thirteen years, since he'd first seen Stephanie Morris and his world had spun on its axis, Finn had raped, brutalized, and murdered many more times. He'd been clumsy with Stephanie, his first, leaving her alive but brain damaged. Since then he'd become much more adept, never striking in the same city twice, always changing his MO enough to avoid the cops putting together a serial murder profile. He knew from his cop days that the FBI could probably recognize his signature in the seemingly unrelated attacks, but he'd never given the authorities enough evidence to call in the experts. Besides, he often mused, they always got their man. First it had been that Crandall guy, the remodel carpenter. It had been pure accident that Finn had snatched the man's bandana on the way down to the basement. But after that, after the instant arrest and easy conviction of Crandall, Finn had learned. Always strangle his victim with a weapon that could quickly be traced to either a family member or an acquaintance. The damn stupid police were so eager for an arrest; he found it ironic as hell.

The other mistake Finn had made the first time was not using a condom. Stupid. But even if they had tested his semen, they had nothing to compare it to, no other sample of his. So they could get his blood type, big deal, he was O positive, the most common type. And maybe he was a nonsecretor anyway.

But to be on the safe side he'd always used a condom since Stephanie. Without fail. Even on the one who'd gotten away. That still rankled. He'd been interrupted, and the only good news was that he'd been wearing a mask. He always wore a mask.

"I need a nap." Joel yawned and eyed the barmaid but then shook his head. "Nah, we've got those chicks to-night from San Diego. I'm putting my dibs on that Mar-sha, or was it Marcy? Anyway, the shorter redhead."

Craig sighed. "By the time we bring them home, who'll care?"

Matt smiled and set his glass on the tabletop with a loud clunk. "In that case I'll take Ericka. I like 'em tall and lots of leg. Unless, of course, Finn here . . ."

Finn laughed. "Hey, I'm easy, guys. Besides, my stom-ach's been acting up. Don't know if I'll be able to hang in all night."

"God." Joel frowned. "I hope it doesn't hit *me*. I hate the shits."

Matt said, "Then you should never come to Mexico, my man."

Finn put his arm around Megan's bare shoulder and toyed with the spaghetti straps on her red-and-white-flowered sundress.

She was a striking woman, Finn's age, maybe a couple years younger. And the right coloring for him, dark hair, dark eyes, skin that tanned rather than burned. She had sharp features, almost a hawkish nose, and a wide mouth. He liked a substantial woman, the more substantial the better, as they tended to be more willing and quick to try to please, more accommodating. Control was the key.

"This is a great place, isn't it?" She had to speak loudly in his ear, as the band in the nightclub was in its third set and it was impossible to hear a thing.

He leaned even closer. "Yes, I like it. I just wish I hadn't eaten that last fajita." He put a hand on his stomach.

"I know exactly what you mean." Conspiratorially.

Joel was dancing with Marcy and Matt was at the long curved bar regaling Ericka with stories about the home security business in Denver. Ericka seemed to be hanging on his every word despite the din. Craig and Linda—or was it Lydia? Finn wondered—sat at the round table across from them, Craig with his hand on Linda's bare thigh.

"So you own this business in Denver?" Megan asked over the racket.

Finn nodded. "I was a policeman for a few years and then struck out on my own."

"What's it called?"

"Mountaintech Security."

"So you put alarms and all that into those mega-houses?"

He laughed. "We call them tract mansions."

"Do you own a tract mansion, Finn?"

"Well, it's not a mansion."

"I bet."

"Another Corona?" he asked after a minute.

"Sure. All us girls are going to do is lounge on the beach tomorrow, why not?"

"Be right back."

The band, four young sweat-slicked Latinos in bright orange silk shirts that opened to their belts, and a lead female singer in a short gold skirt, a black spandex top, and knee-high boots, started singing "La Bamba," and the entire, crowded nightclub roared in approval.

Finn made his way through the throng to the bar and checked in with Matt while he ordered the Coronas. "That dinner's sitting heavy," he said in Matt's ear.

"Darn, Finn." Matt turned to him. "You want to go back to the lodge?"

"No, no, I'm okay, but why don't I hang on to the car keys just in case?"

"Good idea." Matt fished the rental car keys out of his shorts pocket. "I could drive you."

"Not necessary. I'm sure I'll be fine in a few minutes. They've got a men's room here, you know."

Matt smiled. "I just meant if it gets bad, like back to the lodge and to bed."

"I'm not there yet." Finn shot him a mock frown. "Well, better see to my lady friend." He picked up the already sweating Coronas and shouldered his way to the table where Megan awaited.

The next half hour went as he planned. He drank a part of his beer and visited the men's room twice, apologizing to his companions, laughing at himself. By eleven the club was maxed, dancers spilling into the enclosed courtyard, where extra tables sat beneath swaying palms.

Shortly after eleven, Finn kissed Megan's neck and rose. "One last trip, I promise," he said into her ear. "This has happened before, and I'm sure I'm fine, just a sudden reaction to dinner. Shall I get you a fresh drink on the way back?"

"I guess one more won't hurt."

He kissed her again, this time on her hot cheek, smiled in apology, and threaded his way toward the bathroom.

He was on fire. The spinning, screaming women hadn't

come to him for almost three years now, and he'd been heating up inside since last summer. There was a curiously exquisite pain whenever he began to see the faces, and he reveled in that pain, much as a person reveled in the sweet agony of prolonging sexual climax. The only escape for Finn was to control, to seize the power over another human being, to inflict pain and terror and take it to the very edge of life and death and only then could he spill himself in release, and the heat would abate until he felt cool, refreshed—until the need began to mount once more.

He never knew when the faces would come. Unlike most serial killers, Finn's heat built sometimes sooner, sometimes later. Which was fortunate. If he ever began to fit into an exact mold someone might catch on.

It was five past eleven when Finn pulled the rental car out of the crowded parking lot across the street from the nightclub. This was the single risky part. He needed to find a spot close to where the car had been when he returned. Otherwise, in spite of all the drinks, one of his buddies might notice.

He drove along the sandy coast road, keeping to the speed limit. It was four miles to the fishing camp and the lodge, and he parked across the road in another hotel's lot—just in case. It was eleven-fourteen when he crossed the road—no cars in sight—and spotted Peta through the plate glass window at the lodge. She was behind the front desk, watching TV. Alone.

He slid around back to where the trash was kept, pulled the stocking mask and the disposable latex gloves out of his pants pocket, and put them on.

He was ready.

He lifted his hand and thumped with a fist on the trash

Dumpster that rested against the thin wood wall of the front office.

A minute passed. He thumped again, as if an animal were trying to get into the Dumpster. He was ready to bang again when he heard the screen door slam shut around front. He slipped to the corner of the two-story building and waited in the blackness.

Five seconds, eight . . .

He sprang on her fast and hard and delivered a numbing blow to the side of her head before she was able to scream.

It was eleven-seventeen.

At eleven-eighteen he slid her semiconscious body onto the sand beneath the pilings of the pier and went to work, stripping her naked, grabbing her and bruising her violently. At eleven-twenty he slid on the condom and thrust himself into her. *Christ, a virgin.* He damn near came, but she started to awaken, to mumble and even struggle, and a firestorm of need burst inside him. This was what he craved, the struggle, the pleading, the terror.

Holding her hands over her head, he pulled out the purple scarf that belonged to crewman Alfonso. He'd knotted it earlier in anticipation, and he easily slipped it around her neck. He could feel her fighting him, her hips rising, legs flailing, but she was impaled by his hardness.

"No, no, no," she whimpered, her tears glistening on her honey-brown cheeks in the half-moon's light. *"Dios, Dios, no!"*

He tightened the scarf and the knot bit into her throat and now the real horror began. He saw it in her eyes, felt it in her desperation.

He pulled out and pounded himself into her, ready now to spill into the condom, his gaze moving from those small brown breasts to her eyes as he twisted the scarf expertly, bringing her to that edge, a little harder, looser now, harder, in rhythm to his thrusting. Don't die yet. Not yet.

Yes yes yes yes.

Finn threw his head back and gritted his teeth. The girl was limp. Wave after wave of beautiful release surged through him. *Yes yes.*

It was eleven-twenty-four.

At eleven-twenty-five her heart stopped.

At eleven-twenty-six, panting, he started the rental car, uncaring that the young girl lay naked and dead on the sand, Alfonso's scarf still twisted around her neck.

At eleven-thirty-three he bumped into one of the cocktail waitresses in the nightclub near the men's room. He picked up her spilled tray, apologized a half dozen times, and tipped her heavily. She was very sweet and very grateful. She'd remember him.

He slid down into the chair next to Megan a minute later. "Goddamn, it's so crowded I couldn't wait any longer to get the beers. Let's just call the waitress over this time."

Megan looked a little puzzled. "We were getting worried. Craig checked the men's room. . . ."

Finn shook his head. "Sorry, I walked outside for a minute. Needed some air."

"Well, that's what we thought. Feel any better?"

"Much, much better," he said, and he put an arm around her shoulders. The car was two slots over from where it had been originally parked. The nylon mask and latex gloves were at the bottom of a reeking trash can across the street from the nightclub. Thirty minutes later he was holding Megan close on the dance floor, hot sweating bodies bumping into them, when out front, practically unnoticed above the noise coming from the club, a police siren whelped by.

SIX

The more Ellie delved into the twelve-year-old court records, the depositions, the Morris trial transcripts and Michael Callas's testimony, the more positive she became that he was the killer. Every word she read, every nuance of his personality, pointed a finger straight at him.

She sat at her desk on Monday morning, where she should have been entering information into Discovery for the Zimmerman trial, and read the pilfered transcripts she'd brought to work. If anyone noticed, she'd say she was studying an old trial to help her on the Zimmerman case.

The words were all there on the twelve-year-old paper, transcribed by the court stenographer, a story resurrected from the past. A story of violence and rape and the Morrises' agony and a whole community's outrage at John Crandall. At her father.

The reading was painful, making her heart pound and her stomach clench, but she had to perservere. She could handle it, she'd told her mother, and she could. She'd have to.

Patrolman Michael Callas had gone on the stand the first day. He'd been questioned by Andrew Harrison, the DA at the time.

Harrison: Patrolman Callas, please tell the court what happened on New Year's Eve last year. In detail.

Callas: My partner and I, Patrolman Finn Rasmussen, went on duty at ten that night. We had the Hill district, and we were not looking forward to it, because the CU students always act up on New Year's Eve. Anyway, we were driving around, my partner was driving, I was riding shotgun when the call came over the radio, missing person at an address on Fifteenth Street. Since we were the closest patrol car to the address, I radioed back that we'd take it and call in if we needed backup.

Harrison: You drove to the address. What time did you arrive?

Callas: Eleven-twenty. It turned out to be the Morris residence. We knocked and the Morrises let us in. They were distraught. They'd returned from a party down the street and their sixteen-year-old daughter, Stephanie, was missing. They were positive she couldn't have gone out because they'd just moved to Boulder and didn't know anyone. Plus Mrs. Morris had spoken to her daughter on the phone about an hour before they got home.

Harrison: What did you and your partner do then?

Callas: I decided to follow procedure, search the

house first. Even though it was unlikely the
girl was in the house, the possibility had to be
eliminated. I told Finn, Patrolman Rasmussen,
to stay with the Morrises in the living room,
to start getting detailed information from
them. I then got written, signed permission
from Mr. Morris to do the search, so we'd be
covered, since there wasn't time to get a warrant.

Harrison: And you did a thorough search?

Callas: It was a very large house, three floors: the
main floor, a cellar—sort of a rabbit warren
of rooms—and an upstairs where the bedrooms were. I went to the cellar first, and I
was going to work my way up. It was just a
lucky break that I found Stephanie immediately in the wine cellar.

Harrison: Had the Morrises searched the cellar?

Callas: No, it had never occurred to them. Why
would Stephanie go down there? There was
nothing but junk and moving boxes, the fur-
nace room, and what I later learned was referred to as the wine cellar.

Harrison: And then, Patrolman Callas, what did
you do at that point?

Ellie stopped reading, took her glasses off, and pinched
her nose where they pressed. She didn't have time to read
any more, but she'd covered the salient part. It was in-
conceivable to her that Michael Callas could enter an
unfamiliar house and go directly to the unconscious girl,
who'd been in the most improbable place anyone could
imagine. *Unless* he already knew where Stephanie Morris

was. Unless he'd left her there a short time before.

Okay, so he'd called it procedure, but the fact that he'd found her so quickly was simply bizarre.

She pushed the transcript under some other papers, but she couldn't rid her mind of the scene. A young, handsome Michael on the stand in his spiffy patrolman's uniform. Her father at the defense table, her mother seated in the courtroom. The Morrises there, too, grieving, hating, wanting revenge for their daughter's assault. Wanting a conviction desperately, even though it was the wrong man on trial.

Michael Callas. She and Ben Torres were meeting him that afternoon for more testimony prep and to look at Hugh Radway's confession.

Could it have been Michael who'd raped and damaged Stephanie beyond repair? He fit the profile. Oh, Ellie had read the literature put out by the FBI's Child Abduction and Serial Killer unit.

Murderers, rapists, and child abusers had invariably suffered abusive childhoods. As children they shared common traits: bed-wetting, starting fires, cruelty to animals. She had a strong feeling that Michael's caustic behavior hid previous abuse. He seemed to hold a lot of anger, especially toward women. He was a loner, she'd gathered. Robocop. He was building a cabin far away from everyone. It appeared he had no close relationships. At thirty-seven he was unmarried, had never been married, didn't even seem to have a girlfriend. She extrapolated from this that he had difficulty with relationships in general. Yes, he fit the profile. So far. But she had to know him better, get inside that thorny barrier he put up to the world.

He could have raped Stephanie—he had opportunity and very possibly motive. And he could have raped the three other girls, one ten years ago from Greeley and seven years ago the girl who died in Longmont. And then there was the victim who'd gotten away in Pueblo. All girls from cities to the north and south of Boulder on the Front Range. And maybe there were more she didn't know about, girls somewhere that were either dead or too ashamed, too afraid to go to the police.

And he'd do it again. When the urge to feed his sickness, to release tension, to dominate and hurt overwhelmed him, he'd drive somewhere and pick a target, stalk her, get her alone, maybe by flashing his badge. Then he'd rape her and beat her and quite possibly murder her. And he'd leave evidence such as a belt or bandana or scarf belonging to someone close to the girl. Calculating. Smart. And very knowledgeable when it came to police procedure.

"Ellie," she heard, and her head snapped up.

"Sorry, I was daydreaming."

"I was going over your notes," Ben Torres said, "and Callas looks like a solid witness. Good job."

"Thanks."

"Did he give you a hard time?"

"Not too bad. He's pretty cynical, kind of mean."

"You said it."

"But apparently a good detective."

"Yes, he is. Has an excellent conviction rate. The Zimmerman case probably drove him crazy all these years."

"He said he knew it was Steve Zimmerman from the beginning, said he had a feeling."

"He has uncanny instincts. I've worked with him before."

"He doesn't seem to have much of a life outside his job," she ventured.

Torres shrugged. "I wouldn't know. Believe me, I keep

my relationship with Callas on a strictly professional basis."

"So, we're on for this afternoon?"

"I called and confirmed. We'll meet him at headquarters at three."

"Great," Ellie said. "Perfect."

She and Ben Torres entered the Public Service Building at three sharp, climbed the now-familiar stairs to the second floor, and located Michael at his desk. He was in his usual shirtsleeves, tie askew, sport coat slung carelessly on the back of his chair. He stood and shook hands with Torres, nodded at Ellie, as if he barely knew her, as if they'd never had dinner together.

They went into one of the rooms that had a VCR and television and Michael had to search for another chair so they could all sit around the table.

Torres started in by buttering Michael up. Ellie could see the detective hated the brand of bullshit the DA was feeding him.

"Miss Kramer has told me what a terrific witness you'll make, and as you know we're very anxious to get a conviction on this one. All of Boulder is rooting for us."

"Yeah, I realize your job's on the line here. Thank God mine isn't."

Torres flushed. "I don't think I'd entirely agree with your assessment, but it sure would be a feather in our collective cap if we put Steve Zimmerman away."

Ellie tried not to smile at the DA's discomfort. Michael didn't give a damn what the man thought of him.

"Well," Ben said, "let's take a look at Radway's videos. I presume you've seen them, Detective."

"About twenty times."

"I've reviewed them, too, of course, but I don't want

any surprises at trial. The defense is trying to get them suppressed, but they won't succeed." Torres loaded the videotape and pressed play.

Ellie hadn't seen any of Hugh Radway's tapes, and she was very interested in this showing. She sat there, her chair squeezed between the two men in the small room, their knees almost touching. Dapper, dark, smooth Ben Torres and slightly rumpled, sarcastic Michael Callas. It made her tense, knowing what she knew about both men. Ben liking her too much, Michael too little. But worse, she kept imagining Michael doing those things to Stephanie Morris. Hurting her, raping, strangling her with John Crandall's bandana. Then answering the frantic call and returning to the scene of the crime. Repugnant.

This man sitting next to her, nearly touching her, the man who'd taken her to dinner and driven her home might be, could very well be, a vicious criminal. She had to stop, she told herself, she also had to compartmentalize. She was good at that, did it instinctively; she had to do it with Michael, too.

The tape was playing, a gaunt-faced man in a hospital bed speaking, the camera on his face.

"Steve Zimmerman called me, it must have been that spring, almost four years ago. I was in California then, and he liked that I was out-of-state. He wanted to get rid of his ex-wife. Said she was sucking him dry. He'd pay me five thousand in cash, half before, half after. Sure, I took the job. It was a day and a half to drive in, a day to case the joint, do her, and get out, drive back home. Easy."

The man's mouth moved, and the words spilled out, but Ellie could not comprehend the reality of what he was saying. Horrible. He talked about the details, the timing, his weapon of choice, all the information Steve Zimmerman gave him so he could get in and out fast. He spoke of his shock when he saw the child. "Hey, okay, so I'm no knight on a white horse, but I don't do babies."

You had to believe him. No jury could disregard these tapes. You knew he was telling the truth. Sure, Zimmerman's defense would try to get the tapes quashed, but the ploy wouldn't work.

They sat through all three tapes, and she was aware of Michael leaning back in his hard plastic chair, hands behind his head, legs stretched out in front of him. She could sense the heat from his body, smell his skin, the scent of him. She was glad Torres was there.

When the tapes were over, the DA got up and gathered them together.

"I hadn't seen them before," Ellie said.

Torres turned, surprised. "Well, what do you think?"

"Effective."

"They're goddamn incriminating," Michael growled.

"We certainly hope so," Torres said.

"Yeah, well, *I* hope you guys have prepared your prosecution real carefully this time. I'd sure as hell hate to see Zimmerman walk."

"We're doing our best."

"It better be good enough."

There was an awkward silence, then the DA said, "We have worked very hard on this case, and I think we've covered all bases, Detective. As you know, the jury selection has been going on since this morning, and my ADA team tells me it looks like a sympathetic group of citizens."

"Terrific."

"Yes, well, thank you for your time, Detective Callas. We'll be seeing you in court on Thursday."

"I'll be there."

Her boss was dying to get out of the police department, away from Michael, Ellie could tell. He was having a hard time dealing with Michael's harshness. Ben liked everyone around him to cooperate—that was a word he used a lot. To cooperate and to relate. Michael did neither.

"Can I give you a lift home?" Torres said, turning to Ellie. "It's cold as the devil out."

She'd love a ride home. It was freezing, growing dark, and she was at least two miles from Marine Street. The bus was inconvenient. It wasn't that she feared the DA's advances, but when she saw an opportunity, she grabbed it.

"Oh, thanks, but Detective Callas was going to give me a lift." She shot Torres an apologetic smile.

Torres looked from her to Michael then back. He tried not to let his surprise show, but the very blankness of his expression was eloquent. "Oh, well, sure. Okay. Uh, I'll be going now. See you tomorrow, Ellie."

She waited, fooling with her coat and her briefcase, surrounded by the featureless walls of the small interrogation room, Michael next to her, very quiet, his face impassive. He'd heard her exchange with her boss and he must have caught on. He must realize she didn't want to get in Torres's car because the DA would try to hit on her. He must know she was angling for a ride home from *him*.

But he didn't say a word, and finally she had to shrug her coat on, heft her briefcase, and walk out of the room.

Michael followed, making her very nervous. What was wrong with him? Why was he deliberately embarrassing her? What a bastard.

"Good night," she said when they reached his desk.

"Yeah," he replied, "bye."

And that was it.

She walked out of the building, the cold stinging like a slap in the face. She was raging inside, disappointed, furious with herself for misjudging him. She didn't understand him. She never would. She'd never get inside his head.

Striding toward Arapahoe Avenue, where she could catch a crosstown bus, she thought hard. Had all her plans, all her manipulations been a waste of time?

She could see the light at the intersection ahead turning red, and the rush-hour traffic on Arapahoe flowed thickly both ways, car headlights on. She wondered how often the bus came, if she'd missed one, how long she'd have to wait in the biting cold.

A vehicle pulled up alongside her, a tall black pickup truck that rolled close to the curb as she walked. The passenger window slid down silently.

"Get in," he said, leaning across the front seat.

Michael. *What?*

"I said get in. It's cold."

She opened the heavy door and stepped up into the cab. Her mind wavered between bewilderment and triumph. And a touch of fear.

"Thanks," she said.

He pulled out, looking straight ahead. "What in hell were you trying to prove back there?"

She, too, stared straight ahead. "He likes me. A lot."

"I could tell."

"Well, then, why did you . . . ?"

"I don't like being played for a fool."

"I wasn't playing you for a fool. I just didn't want to go with him."

"Don't bullshit me."

"Maybe I should take the bus," she said coolly.

"Cut the crap, Ellie."

"God, you're rude."

"Gotta uphold my reputation."

He turned onto Arapahoe. She sat there trying to figure out how to get to this impossible man, how to handle him.

"Okay, I'm sorry, it was a childish trick," she allowed.

He drove without saying anything. She felt her cheeks grow hot and her heart pound. She couldn't figure him out—why had he bothered to pick her up?

Then he pulled off of Arapahoe, turning in to a parking lot, one of the CU student lots, practically empty at this hour. He stopped the truck and let it idle, and Ellie froze inside. Stupid, stupid, she thought, all alone with a predator in the cold darkness of a winter night. She forced herself to stay calm, but a scream was forming, pressing on her rib cage.

"What . . . ?" she began, her voice coming out high and tense.

He slammed the gear lever into park and turned to her, and she inadvertently shrank back. His face was touched by a streetlight in mottled patches, his eyes shadowed hollows.

"What I'd like to know," he said slowly, "is why you're doing this. What in hell is there in it for you?"

"Doing what?" A whisper, a wispy thread of fear.

"Are you one of those women who's hot for guys in uniform? I don't wear a uniform."

"I don't . . ."

"If you're one of those, if cops turn you on, stop playing games. You want a fling, I can oblige."

Everything inside her congealed. The fear fled and anger took its place. He just wanted a fuck. Putting her through all this . . . Talk about playing games!

"Your instincts are dead wrong this time, Detective Callas," she said in an icy voice. She reached for the door handle, flung the door open, and slid out. "Go to hell," she said, and then she slammed the heavy door as hard as she could.

She walked away from the truck, across the parking lot toward the lights of Arapahoe, her heart leaping in her chest. Would he follow? Had she pushed one of his buttons? She reached the sidewalk, striding fast, away from him, from his insults and uncomfortable silences. She wouldn't turn her head to see if he were following, she wouldn't. The cold felt good, the dark hid her mortification. The bastard, the bastard.

She caught a bus a couple of blocks down and sat in it, feeling safe, surrounded by people. Strangers, but not killers, not criminals, not dangerous. Ordinary folk going home.

It wasn't until she entered her house, hearing the familiar voices of her roommates, that she realized she'd had Michael Callas right where she wanted him. She could have accepted his proposal, gone home with him, seen his life outside the police department. That's what she'd wanted all along, what she'd schemed and maneuvered to achieve.

She'd blown it. Had him in the palm of her hand, and she hadn't closed her fingers. How could she have let pride get in the way of her goal?

She'd failed, damn it all. She'd had him and she'd let him go.

On Thursday morning DA Ben Torres, two assistant district attorneys, and Ellie walked down the hall of the Justice Center to Courtroom B. Judge Lorraine Barker was presiding, the jury was sworn in, the defense ready, although Steve Zimmerman's lead defense attorney was still outraged that the judge was allowing the Radway tapes.

Ellie was thrilled that Ben was letting her sit at the prosecution table as if she were a real lawyer. She wore her best suit, a navy blue Ann Taylor she'd bought for fifteen dollars at her favorite thrift shop. She'd had to hem the skirt.

She wasn't to say a word, but Torres had told her to watch and listen, take notes, try to interpret how the jury was reacting to testimony.

It was exciting, sitting up at the front of the courtroom, looking right at the elevated judge's bench, the seal of the state of Colorado, the state flag and the U.S. flag behind it. The jury box on the left, the courtroom done in blond wood and steel blue, almost Scandinavian-modern. Ellie was as nervous as if she were lead attorney herself.

Torres was dressed in an elegant black suit, the two ADAs in close approximations. And to her left, Steve Zimmerman sat with his own team.

She couldn't help a glance in his direction, and she was certain her revulsion showed all over her face. He was one of those Ted Bundy types, collegiate looking, clean-cut, quite handsome. You'd trust him immediately. Would the jurors see past that pretty-boy façade?

She finally tore her gaze away and realized the room was hushed, expectant, the jurors nervous, shifting in their seats. It felt to Ellie as if a contest were about to begin, a life-and-death struggle like the ones that took place in the Roman Coliseum.

The first day consisted of various motions made by the defense, a lot of sidebars, the preliminary jostling for position. Opening statements were made, and only one witness was called late in the day, Danielle Zimmerman's friend who'd phoned the police four years ago to report that she couldn't get through to Danielle.

Routine stuff, but Ellie took notes furiously, studied the jurors, whose names she had on a list in her briefcase. The prosecution had managed to seat seven women on the jury, four of whom had children and could hopefully see past Zimmerman's good looks. Women who'd be excellent for this case involving a dead baby.

She had seen Michael entering the Justice Center that morning, although he probably wouldn't be called. He'd been too far away to talk to, and she was thankful for that. She needed a little distance for now.

She'd thought a lot about it and decided that if he gave her the tiniest opening, she'd try to start over. If he wasn't too angry or too disgusted with her, it could work. And she'd had to admit to herself that she might have come on too strong, too fast, for a suspicious guy like Callas.

Maybe he'd just chalked her behavior up to irrational female urges, hormones or something. Or maybe he had no finesse at all, and he thought his approach was romantic.

God, she'd been an idiot.

She sat in court and listened and felt eyes on the back of her head, as if Michael were in the courtroom. But when she turned around, he wasn't there. Perhaps he'd slipped out, or maybe it was her imagination.

At four Judge Barker called it a day, and everyone filed out of the courtroom. Ellie was afraid she might run into Michael, but he was nowhere to be seen.

"Okay, folks," Torres said, "meeting. Fifteen-minute break then the conference room. With all your notes."

They discussed strategy and the jurors, wrote out specific questions, went over Ellie's report on her sessions with Michael.

"Tomorrow I'm putting Callas on the stand. He's pretty impressive, although he could get nasty if he's cross-examined the way I think they'll do it, go for his throat. But I'll object as much as I can, try to keep the defense from their rhythm," Ben said.

"Judge Barker gets pissed if anyone raises too many objections," one of the ADAs put in.

"I know, I know. I'll keep a close eye on her."

When the meeting was over Ellie left quickly, wary that Torres would once more offer her a ride home. She didn't want to deal with that complication.

At home her roommates barraged her with questions, none of them having sat at the prosecution table in a trial.

"You're learning more than I am," said Bonnie, "and I have to pay tuition."

"It *is* pretty exciting," Ellie conceded.

"Do you think Torres will win?" Celeste asked.

"God, I hate to predict, but the women on the jury sure looked sympathetic when Ben gave his opening statement."

"Was he good?" Jennifer asked.

"Very good, very logical and calm. Very credible, although I think his statement was too long. Too much detail. The jury won't remember it."

"Gosh, I'm jealous." Bonnie sighed. "It's so cool, you sitting up there."

"I don't *do* anything." Ellie shrugged. "I mean, I don't open my mouth."

"But you're there."

There was nothing Ellie could say to that.

• • •

On Friday morning Ellie braced herself to see Michael. He would be the first prosecution witness that day, and she knew she'd run into him.

In truth, Torres took the detective into the conference room the instant Michael got there, and Ellie didn't see him until he entered the courtroom and was immediately sworn in.

He looked perfect. Freshly shaved, a nice dark suit, conservative tie knotted properly. Quite a good-looking man. Tall, muscular, bronzed skin and golden eyes and fine brown hair cut short. He exuded integrity and seriousness of purpose, and she was impressed despite herself.

The man could be a rapist and a murderer, she thought. A contemptible human being, the opposite of what he appeared to be. How could he live with himself?

Ben Torres led him through the whole story, stopping to pounce on crucial facts, bringing the case up to Radway's confession and the subsequent arrest of Steve Zimmerman.

"You were the arresting officer, Detective Callas?"

"Yes, I was. I received the arrest warrant from Judge Kahn, and I took two uniformed officers with me. We served the warrant on the afternoon of March third in Panchito's Restaurant on the Pearl Street Mall. Mr. Zimmerman gave us no trouble."

"Thank you, Detective. That's all I have for now."

Then the lead defense lawyer, a man from Denver named Richard Gardner, stood, shot his cuffs, and approached the witness.

He tried his best to rattle Michael, Ellie had to give him that. He tried threats, which Torres objected to, he tried to trip Michael up in a mistake or misrepresentation, he tried to blacken his reputation, cast doubts on his abilities.

But Michael stayed smooth, competent, unflappable.

"How did you first learn of the existence of this alleged hit man, Hugh Radway?" Gardner rested an elbow on the high rail of the jury box. Casual. The jury's new best friend.

"Radway contacted *us.*"

"Really," Gardner said in disbelief.

Michael said nothing.

"Then we're to understand that this dying man simply called from California and said, Hey, I'm the shooter?"

"That's the way it was."

"Well, then, I imagine you jumped on a plane, and the end result is the videotaped sessions we all watched this morning."

"Is that a question, sir?"

"Ah, no, sorry. I'm merely trying to get a clear picture of the order of events, Detective. I will pose this question, however. Did you suggest to this dying man that he could help serve justice by making a deathbed confession?"

"Absolutely not. *He* contacted us and said he felt remorse and wanted to confess."

"Um. Interesting. I didn't get that impression from the videos. I didn't hear remorse—"

"Objection, Your Honor." Torres rose and shook his head, smiling. "Counsel is not questioning the witness, he's daydreaming aloud."

"Objection sustained. Please put your . . . musings in the form of questions, Mr. Gardner."

"Yes, of course, Your Honor." He turned to Michael again. "Let me be direct here, Detective. Did you locate this dying man, this man who was obviously troubled over the deaths of a mother and child, and suggest to him that he could serve justice by making a false statement that would incriminate my client?"

Ellie saw a muscle begin to work in Michael's jaw. He took a breath and held Gardner's stare. His voice became very soft when he replied. "No, sir, as I previously stated, Hugh Radway contacted us. In fact, we didn't believe him at first, not until—"

"Just answer the question, Detective," Gardner cut in.

But it was the judge who intervened. "You opened this line of questioning, counsel. I'd like to hear what the detective was going to say."

Gardner nodded, found his glass of water, and took a long drink.

Michael's demeanor relaxed. He pivoted toward the jurors, his face open, sincere. "The authorities often keep secret a few details surrounding a crime scene, so we can weed out the nutcases who invariably call in to confess to every crime. Only the real criminal knows those details. In the case of Hugh Radway, we asked him to describe what Danielle Zimmerman was wearing at the time of her death." Michael paused. "Radway described the bathrobe, I believe it's called a kimono, down to the last detail. We knew immediately he was the killer."

Gardner cleared his throat. "Hugh Radway could not have learned this detail in any other fashion? I mean, Detective, four years had passed between the crime and his so-called confession."

"He could not have known it."

"Um. Nevertheless, I still submit that the police, frustrated over this unsolved crime, might have guided Mr. Radway in his confession, whereby my client was incriminated—"

"Objection!" the DA called out, shaking his head, coming to his feet. "Detective Callas has stated under oath that the police in no way coerced Hugh Radway's confession. Your Honor—"

But Judge Barker held up a hand and summoned Torres and Gardner to her bench with a crook of her index finger. When the sidebar was over, Gardner was allowed one more question in the line he'd been pursuing.

"So you are stating categorically, before this court, that the police are innocent of coercing Hugh Radway into making a confession?"

Michael glared at him and then smiled thinly. "That's what I'm telling this court, sir, under oath. I'm sorry if it's not what you want to hear, but it's the truth."

Gardner, seeing that his ploy had backfired, quickly took a new tack. He switched to the day that Michael had entered Danielle Zimmerman's place and found her dead. Gardner tried to imply that the baby had died of SIDS and had already been dead before her mother was killed.

Michael took his time answering that one. He fixed his eyes on Gardner and spoke in a dangerously quiet voice. "Now, you listen, Mr. Gardner. That baby had suffered for three days and died of that. She was in her crib, and she was dressed in shoes, little white shoes, and a pink sunsuit. Now, it's my understanding that SIDS—"

"Thank you, Detective, I believe you've answered the question."

"Not quite," Michael said softly.

"Your Honor," Gardner said to the judge, "this witness—"

"I'll let him continue," the judge said. "You opened the door."

"It's my understanding," Michael went on, "that SIDS occurs when a baby is asleep, and this one, Maryanne was her name, was dressed for the day. The autopsy report shows dehydration as the cause of death. You've seen the report, haven't you, Mr. Gardner?"

"That'll be enough, Detective Callas," the judge admonished. "Mr. Gardner, continue."

"No more questions for now, Your Honor," Gardner said meekly.

Oh, Michael was good, Ellie thought. She'd seen some of the women in the jury box staring at him, unable to take their eyes off him. And when his gaze had moved over the jurors, she'd seen a couple of them shift in their seats. He'd been an extremely effective witness. And he'd put Gardner in his place.

His anger at the crime, his contempt for anyone who'd let a baby die, who'd want their child dead, was evident. Ellie believed him. And yet—she tried to put the disparate pieces of the man together—he was possibly a killer himself, a man who brutally raped and strangled women to death. How could he be so convincing on the witness stand?

Court was adjourned after Michael's testimony that afternoon. Ellie followed him out of the courtroom, determined to speak to him.

"Meeting in fifteen," Torres said to her.

"I'll be right there," she replied. "You did good today, Mr. Torres."

"Callas did good," he answered. "I just asked the right questions."

"See you in a minute," she said, noticing Michael heading for the front door.

She caught him just inside the secured entrance, an overcoat over his suit, fishing around in a pocket for his keys.

"Michael," she called breathlessly. She hadn't had time to grab her coat, and it was cold. She hugged herself.

He turned and looked at her. No expression in the lion-yellow eyes, no change in the artfully carved lips.

"Michael . . ."

"Yeah?"

"Are you angry at me for the other night?"

"Seems to me you were the angry one."

"You . . . you sort of surprised me."

"Uh-huh."

She cocked her head and tried to smile. She was shivering. "A girl likes a little, well, um, lead-in, you know?"

"Is that so?"

"Yes. But you were right. I am interested. A fling would be fun." She couldn't believe she'd said the words. Masking her loathing, flirting with this monster.

He eyed her, as if deciding, as if judging her, and she felt the heat of his perusal, although his gaze didn't warm her at all. The cold bit like a rabid dog. She shivered still, but it wasn't all from the frigid temperature. This was her last chance. What if he wasn't interested?

"Okay," he said, holding her eyes. "Fine. How about I pick you up Saturday morning?"

"Saturday . . . ?"

"For the weekend," he said deliberately. Testing her. "My family has a chalet up near Vail. And bring your skis."

Skis, skis. She didn't own a pair of skis. But that was a minor detail. He'd taken the bait, the hook was in, and she wasn't going to let him go this time. No matter what.

"A chalet? Skiing? That sounds fantastic. Sure, I'd love to go," she said enthusiastically, thrilled, triumphant.

SEVEN

Michael shifted his truck into a lower gear and pulled out around a semi that was crawling up the interstate toward the Eisenhower Tunnel. The road here at almost eleven thousand feet was icy in spite of the sand the state department of highways had laid down.

"God, those big eighteen-wheelers make me nervous on these roads," Ellie said.

Michael signaled and moved back into the right lane. "I take it you don't drive much."

"As little as possible. In the winter, anyway."

She'd grown up in Leadville, he thought, a town that was isolated from anything that was really happening, and she didn't even drive. And yet there was a sophistication and maturity to her that ceaselessly baffled him.

The itch to get inside her head was becoming an obsession, and for the life of him, he couldn't figure why she was interested in him. Hell, more than interested, it appeared; she'd said in so many words an affair was what she was after. Why the abrupt switch?

Well, she was here. And they were on their way to the

family vacation place in Vail. This was not business. They'd ski. They'd wine and dine themselves, and then they'd climb into bed together. That was the long and short of it. An affair. No big deal.

The trouble was, Michael couldn't quite buy it.

She put a cassette in the tape deck and sat back while he steered through the tunnel. She seemed at ease with him, not terribly talkative right now. He liked that. A comfortable silence.

In the background Enya sang a haunting Gaelic tune, and he cast Ellie a sidelong glance. She was wearing black boots, jeans, and a faded green down vest over a heavy Irish knit turtleneck sweater. Her short dark hair curled softly around her face, framing those very lovely features. He'd noticed she had on eye makeup beneath her big round UV-protective sunglasses, and lipstick, a berry color that was mostly worn off now. When she smiled, her teeth were white, and he couldn't help staring at that slightly crooked tooth. That tooth had cast a spell over him.

"Is your family's place right in Vail?" she asked, breaking the quiet.

"Couple miles outside. It's between Vail and Minturn."

"I know where Minturn is. You can take the road from there up over Tennessee Pass and get to Leadville."

"That's right."

"Camp Hale is there. Well, what's left of it. Did you know that's where skiing in the Rockies really got started during World War Two? The Tenth Mountain Division trained there, on skis."

"Very good, Ellie, you're a history buff, too."

"Too?"

"Among your many other attributes."

"Which are?"

"Beats hell out of me, lady, too many to count."

He could feel the weight of her eyes on him as he drove past Dillon and then began the climb up to the summit of Vail Pass. Maybe she was trying to figure him out, just as he was trying to get inside her head. Isn't that what people did when they embarked on a new relationship? Kind of like fencing. You lunge here, parry there, and your counterpart is watching your every move, matching it, sometimes taking the offense, sometimes the defense. When Ellie had slammed his truck door the other evening, she'd been on the defense. Then, yesterday, she'd suddenly gone on the offensive. For the life of him he couldn't figure it. A beautiful woman like Ellie Kramer, smart as a whip, open and friendly, with that rare glow of sunshine . . . Why him?

"God, look how Vail has grown," Ellie said as he sped through on the interstate, the ski mountain to the left, tiers of condos and strip malls on the right.

"Yeah, it has," he said. "When the family bought the lot and built the place, Minturn seemed miles away from the action. Now, whenever it gets used, we're glad it's out of town. Private, you know."

"How often does your family use it?"

"Not much."

"Oh. Why? I mean . . ."

But talking about his mother and his father was the last thing Michael wanted to do.

"It's a long story" was all he said, and then he could feel her gaze riveted on him again, watchful.

The chalet was a sixteen-hundred-square-foot, two-story copy of a real chalet Michael's parents had seen on their honeymoon a million years ago. It was out-of-date and too small for modern tastes. The siding was white plaster cut by dark-brown-trimmed windows with shutters and doors that had Swiss motifs carved in their centers, tulips, even a heart. On the second story was a wood-railed balcony, also stained chocolate brown, extending the length of the structure. The three upstairs bedrooms all had doors leading into the balcony. Close quarters.

Michael pulled into the snow-packed drive that was lined with lodgepole pines and recalled with sudden, painful clarity a snowball fight he and his brother, Paul, had had on that balcony. Michael had lost and run inside to cry on his mother's shoulder. He'd been six years old. Another lifetime.

"It's adorable," Ellie said brightly, hopping out the minute he parked under the sloping carport.

Michael shrugged and climbed out, too. "What it *is,* is antiquated. They haven't built these things in the Rockies for thirty years. It's a scraper."

She took off her sunglasses and blinked. "A what?"

"A scraper. You know, someone buys the place for the property and bulldozes the house."

She spun around and looked at the structure. "You're joking."

He would have asked how in God's name she'd never heard that term, but he let it go. He guessed in Leadville what you bought was what you lived in. "Well," he said, "I guess that's life in Vail."

"It's sick," she declared. "I'd die for a place like this."

He smiled crookedly, a little embarrassed, and then reached their bags out of the truck bed, setting them on the snow. Then the skis and boots. "New skis?" he observed.

"They're borrowed. A roommate's," she said, almost defiantly.

Goddamn, but she intrigued him endlessly. Who the

hell was she? *Which* Ellie Kramer? He carried their stuff to the door, Ellie directly behind him, and found the key on his ring. He unlocked it and showed her in, nodding, his hands busy with their bags.

"Brr," she said, hugging herself, looking around. "Is there a thermostat?"

"Ah, over by the kitchen. It's probably set to fifty-five. Like I said, nobody—"

"I know," she said, turning to look at him, "nobody uses it much anymore."

"Um," he said, setting down the bags, uncertain exactly where to put them. Whenever he came up here, a few times in the winter, he slept upstairs in his old room. Certainly not in his parents'. And never, ever, did he open the door to Paul's room.

He realized, without a bridging thought, that he hadn't brought a woman here before. Of course, there weren't many in his life. A few dates here, a couple there. Never anything with strings attached.

"A fireplace," she exclaimed. "Can I build a fire? Is there wood someplace?"

"Yes and yes," he said, walking across the creaking wooden floorboards to the kitchen, where he began to check the fridge and stove. "Wood's out back. I'll get some in a sec."

"No, no, let me. I've never had a fireplace, Michael, please, let me do it."

"Well . . . sure."

The breaker had gone out on the stove. While he went to flip the circuit switch in the sloping closet beneath the staircase, Ellie fetched wood.

"Kindling? Don't I need kindling? Oh, and newspaper. Oops, there probably isn't any. Matches?"

"Hold on, I'll see what I can scrounge up."

He finally sat on the dusty flowered couch, hands folded behind his head, knees splayed, while he watched Ellie build her fire. She hadn't a clue. Somehow that gave him a shot of childish delight. There was something she couldn't manage to perfection.

He finally said, "You can't stack the wood like that."

She straightened and dusted her hands on her thighs, nicely curved thighs. "Okay, then how do I stack it?"

"Here, I'll—"

"Oh, no. I started this project."

"All right. Well, the fastest way is to make a teepee shape out of them. The oxygen can reach the kindling then. That's right, like that. Now scrunch up the paper and lift the kindling. . . ."

She finally had her fire and the chalet warmed quickly. And then she sat next to him on the couch and smiled triumphantly, curling her legs beneath her, facing him. "I did it. Another first. Did you know there are never-ending firsts in life?"

"Well, I hadn't really thought of it that way."

She laid her head against the back of the couch and gazed at him. A bar of winter sun slanted through the window and fell glowing on her hair, turning her eyes to liquid sable. In a minute he was going to drown in them.

"There's so much out there to do, to learn," she said. "Even little things like building a fire. Gosh, early man knew how to build a fire."

"Only because lightning did it for him first."

She arched a brow. "Ah, a skeptic. Or are you a cynic? Maybe both. Is everyone in your family a cynic, Michael?"

"I really wouldn't know."

"Oh, a man of mystery. Maybe you really didn't have parents at all."

"That's right, I crawled out from under a rock."

"I doubt that," she said airily.

"What about you, Ellie?"

"I already told you. I'm a Leadville girl. My mother still lives there. I got out, though."

"What about your father?"

A shadow scudded across her features. "My father died a few years back," she said, dropping her gaze.

"I'm sorry, Ellie, I didn't know."

"How could you have known?"

"He must have been young."

"Yes. He was."

"An accident. Sickness?"

She seemed to gather herself. "Good Lord, always the detective. Lighten up."

He shrugged, his eyes fixed on her. "Sure," he said. "It's just habit."

What *was* it about her? Okay, she was a woman, and to Michael women were a collection of puzzling contradictions. But Ellie took it further. Oh, yeah. One minute she was soft and feminine and radiant, the next guarded, and then there was that ambition he'd seen, a kind of unfathomable passion burning behind the easy smile. He knew the itch to peel away those layers and get to her core was making him nuts. But worse—and he wouldn't lie to himself—he was afraid he was falling for her.

He frowned. He was as big a sap as the DA. The only difference was, Michael wasn't married. *Goddamn,* he thought, wincing inwardly.

"What?" she said.

"Huh?"

"You looked, well, as if you were thinking about something."

He stood then, too abruptly, and avoided her eyes. "I

was just thinking we better get going to the slopes."

"Oh, yes. Skiing." Ellie also rose. "Ah, where should I change? Your place or mine?"

He didn't hesitate. "My room's upstairs. Last door on the right. You go ahead and I'll check that breaker on the stove. I'll be right back."

"Sure," she said. Then she paused. "I thought you already threw the breaker."

"I did. Didn't hold. Go on."

He watched her climb the stairs and listened to the creak of the floorboards overhead. And then he sat for a moment on the arm of the couch and let out a low whistling breath. No one, no woman, had ever affected him so strongly. She made him crazy, set his blood on fire. He didn't want it. Didn't need it. But then, he thought, when you caught the flu, you didn't want that either. Trouble was, there wasn't a good goddamn thing you could do about it.

Michael stood in line to buy half-day ski tickets, while Ellie waited by the ski rack where he'd stashed their equipment. She looked great in the bright red ski suit, and he wondered if that, too, was borrowed. If so, it fit her as well as if it had been made for her. Interesting, he mused, as he moved up to the ticket window, another revelation about Eleanor Kramer. Another piece to the puzzle, but he wasn't sure where this one belonged— Ellie was poor.

"Two half-day tickets," he said to the girl behind the window, sliding his credit card across.

He could have figured it out, he supposed, because Ellie had told him she was taking a year off of law school to work. He knew she didn't have a car. He should have put those things together and added them up, but he hadn't. She dressed well, had an air about her; she definitely didn't appear to be a poverty-stricken kind of person.

"Thanks," he said, signing the credit card receipt, taking the two tickets.

He handed her one, fastened his own on his parka. "Where do you want to start?" he asked.

"Oh, I don't know the mountain. You decide. Wherever you want to go," she said brightly.

"Okay, let's try Riva Ridge. For a warm-up."

"Sure, whatever."

They walked through the town of Vail; the main village was a pedestrian walkway, no vehicles allowed. It was a thirty-year-old resort, all done in Bavarian kitsch. Stucco, stenciled shutters, very cute. Looming over the town was Vail Mountain, with chairlifts and a gondola crawling up its face and skiers, like ants, dotting the slopes.

"This is pretty," Ellie said.

"You've been here before?"

"No, never."

"You've never been to Vail?"

"Or Crested Butte or Steamboat Springs." She shrugged.

"But you were raised in Leadville. It's so close."

"Well"—she smiled—"my mother and I didn't have a lot of discretionary income. Skiing is a rich man's sport."

They walked through the town, and Michael kept trying to make the pieces fit. A poor childhood, never been to Vail, yet she had looked so good in court yesterday. She'd worn a classy-looking suit; even he could tell when a woman looked good. A bundle of contradictions.

And he badly wanted to find the key to all those contradictions, the one factor that unlocked them, that made logic out of Ellie's inconsistencies.

"Are those bindings set for you?" he asked when they got to the edge of the slope.

She stared at him blankly.

"Jesus, put your boot in and try it."

She stepped in; the binding clicked. It worked. Ellie smiled. "Jennifer told me they'd be okay."

"Jennifer?"

"One of my roommates."

"Is she the same size as you?"

"Close."

"Handy," he said.

He stepped into his skis, a new pair of Salomons he'd bought this fall. You had to keep up with the technical changes in equipment if you took the sport seriously: featherweight poles, shaped skis, boots that were both responsive and comfortable, super-safe bindings.

They shuffled to the Vista Bahn lift, got in place, and were swooped up by the chair.

"I did it," Ellie said breathlessly, her cheeks rosy in the cold.

"Did what?"

"Got on without falling."

"Yeah, that's always a good start."

He traversed the easy road to Riva Ridge, an intermediate run, for a start. Anyone born and raised in Colorado could handle an intermediate slope, he figured.

She did it, following him, trying to follow him, actually, because when he made some turns and stopped, she was still way up the hill, in a mortal struggle with her skis—her roommate's skis—and he had to wait there until she reached him.

"You ski so fast," she panted.

"Not really. But you don't, do you?"

"Well, I'm not a complete beginner. We had some ski trips in school, so I did those, and I learned a little."

"Yeah, a little."

"Oh," she said, her face falling, "you want to go dashing off, tearing up the double black diamond runs."

"No, hey, I don't mean that."

"You'll have to wait for me," she warned, "if you ski with me."

"Well, I invited you on this outing, so I guess you're stuck with me."

"You mean *you're* stuck with me."

He took her to an easier slope, the bunny hill, and he gave her some pointers. She had good skis, a new pair of shaped Volants, and she learned quickly.

"Okay, now weight on the outside ski, the outside, no, the *other* outside," he said, snowplowing along next to her. "Shift your weight over to the other ski, yeah, that's it."

"This is fun," she said, grinning. Her cheeks were red, and she was breathing fast, working so much harder than he was.

"Plant your right pole, shift, look downhill, don't lean into the slope, okay, shift weight and bring it around. Good."

"That's pretty easy," she breathed. "Should we try another run?"

He took her to the Mountaintop Express lift, to some beginner runs, where she did quite well, gaining confidence. Michael couldn't believe how much of a beginner she was. Hell, Colorado kids learned to ski when they learned to walk. But he found he was having fun, actually enjoying himself, watching Ellie improve, watching her have a good time. No games between them, no awkward moments or touchy subjects, just physical exertion, a great sport, cold, clear weather.

And Ellie.

She insisted they attempt a more difficult mogul run, and there she ran into trouble, her skis getting ahead of her, shooting out, deflected by the next mogul, and she fell in a tangle of arms and legs and skis and poles.

He skied over to her quickly. "Ellie, you okay?"

She lay there, spread-eagled, one ski off, her red suit dazzling against the white snow. Hat, sunglasses scattered.

"Ellie?"

"Oh, my God," she panted.

"Are you all right?"

"I thought I was dead."

"Does anything hurt? Your knees okay?"

"I'm fine." She laughed. "I was doing *great,* and then this dumb bump was in my way."

"It's called a mogul."

"I know that."

He reached out a hand and helped her up, helped her get her ski lined up so she could step back in it. He found her sunglasses and her hat.

"I'm trying that again," she said, dusting her bottom off with a glove.

"Persistent."

"No, remember? I'm just plain stubborn."

She wouldn't quit until the lifts closed. She fell a couple more times, but she was learning. She was tough and she was gutsy. And goddamn stubborn.

They walked back to where his truck was parked, put the skis in the back, and drove to the chalet. It was getting dark already, the sun setting behind the mountains, spraying pale fire across the sky.

"My God, I'm exhausted," she said, sprawled on the front seat of the truck, her head back.

"You should have saved some energy for tomorrow."

She groaned.

"You did well," he allowed.

"I kept falling."

"If you don't fall then you're not learning."

"Who said that?"

"Everyone who skis."

"What baloney." She yawned, so unself-conscious, the chameleon, changing her colors to fit into her surroundings. He'd like to know how she could do that.

"I'm starving," she said. "I'm ravenous."

"Can you last until we shower and change? I'll take you to a nice restaurant in Vail."

"Oh, my God, heaven."

"Did you think I'd make you fix dinner?"

"I didn't think. I just came along. But I'm not much of a cook, I have to admit."

She was quiet for a time, then she sat up and turned toward him. "Thank you for a wonderful day," she said softly.

He drove, looking ahead through the windshield, saying nothing. But inside . . . his belly grew warm and liquid.

They ate at a new spot on the western side of Vail, a surf-and-turf restaurant reminiscent of the seventies. "I'm dying for a big slab of meat. And maybe crab. Or maybe salmon instead of meat," she'd declared after a long hot shower. Then, while Michael had showered, shaved, and changed, she'd fallen asleep downstairs on the couch, the fire he'd built up crackling cheerfully in the lichen-rock hearth.

He hadn't wanted to awaken her. He'd stood there in clean blue jeans and a turtleneck and watched her sleep, drinking her in, feeling like a voyeur but unable to stop.

She decided on steak and crab and then peered over the menu at him through her reading glasses. "You'll think I'm awful, though, ordering the most expensive thing. Let me buy dinner, then I won't die of guilt."

He shook his head. "I'm having the same, so don't worry about it."

"But you got the lift tickets."

"Tell you what," he said, "I'll let you buy breakfast."

"Well . . ."

"It's settled. Hey, don't you know men hate to argue over restaurant checks? We'd sooner throw a hundred dollars onto the table to be done with it."

She took off her glasses and cocked her head. "You're right. I get breakfast."

"Done," he said, relieved.

They hadn't had lunch, and they both ate like starving animals. She really did have a good appetite, even ordering dessert, mud pie, which they split. Then she sat back, adjusted the waistband on her black wool slacks, patted her stomach over the emerald-colored sweater she'd worn, and smiled.

"Okay, I'm stuffed."

"You want a brandy?"

"No way. Coffee, though. I need to sit and let the food settle."

"Good thinking." He ordered two decafs, black.

"So," she finally said, "why law enforcement?"

"Huh?"

"Why did you pick law enforcement as a career?"

He wasn't about to tell her that he'd picked it because of the drunk driver who'd killed his brother. So he gave his standard version: "When I was a kid I had a friend who was killed by a drunk driver with four DUIs, no license, the works. I knew right then and there I wanted to be a cop."

"Revenge?"

"You bet. I wanted to put everyone who even spat on a sidewalk behind bars."

"A lot of built-up anger."

"Oh, yeah."

"So you went to college? Studied criminology?"

"Right at CU."

"I didn't know that."

"Why would you?"

She shrugged. "No reason. So, you must have been a Goody Two-shoes."

Michael laughed. "Hardly. I think I lost sight of my goal during the first two years at CU, and I majored in Party 101. I sure wasn't a saint."

"What did your parents think about that?"

He answered before considering his words. "They really didn't give a shit. They'd been divorced for years, and the communication level was nil."

"So you were kind of an emotionally abused child?"

Her expression, the tone of her voice were casual, and yet he knew instinctively there was a real inquisitiveness behind her question. Why? What in hell was he missing here?

He gave her an evasive answer, not lying, not telling the entire truth. "All kids are abused when parents divorce."

"Um," she said, her gaze on him intently. And then she switched gears. "So were you an athlete at CU? You know, football, track, that jock stuff?"

"I did track. Never went too far with it. How about you, Ellie? How did you pick law?"

But all she said was that law picked her, and there it was, another piece of the Ellie Kramer conundrum.

After dinner they walked to the town square, their footfalls crunching on the snowpacked paths. It was a brutally cold night, typical of the shortest days of the year. Their breath came out in great plumes that seemed to freeze and hang in the air. Still, there were plenty of people milling about, coming and going from the hotels and bars and nightclubs. But all Michael could think about was being alone with this woman. He was beginning to burn with need, and he wondered if it was the same with her. She'd come to Vail with him. She'd actually pursued him, said she wanted a fling. Well, it was time.

"Ready to head home?" he asked while they window-shopped.

"Sure. Of course. To be honest," she said, "my legs are really tired."

"Right," he said, unable to take his eyes from her.

He didn't plan the way it went down in the end. It just happened. He unlocked the door at the chalet and stepped aside to usher her in. The warmth seemed to smack him in the face, and suddenly he wanted her there on the spot. He closed the door behind them with a foot and caught her arm.

"Come here," he said, aware of the thickness of his voice as he pulled her toward him.

He kissed her. At first gently, tasting her lips, discovering them. They were deliciously cold from the night, but he warmed them slowly until her mouth grew soft and yielding, and he held her to him tightly, lifting her

to her toes, his tongue probing her mouth then tracing
the line of her lips.

When they finally came up for air, he said, "Go on
upstairs. I'll get the lights."

He wondered if he imagined a moment's hesitation,
but she nodded, turning and shedding her parka and going up the stairs.

In his room, the room that he and Paul had played in
so often, he came up behind her and lifted her arms,
tugging the emerald-green sweater off over her head and
tossing it on a chair. She kept her back to him and he
gently stroked her shoulders then leaned to kiss the nape
of her neck. Her head bent, and he heard her sigh deeply.
The sound inflamed him.

Slowly, tasting each shoulder as he went, the faint
scent of perfume making his head reel, he slid the straps
of her white bra down and then undid it, easing it from
her arms, away from her hands. He couldn't recall making such slow love to a woman, and he knew that somehow he'd always remember these moments.

When he finally brought her around to face him, he
realized that her heart was racing; he could see the quick
rise and fall of her breasts, beautiful breasts, not large,
but perfect.

He looked up into her eyes then and touched a breast
with one hand while drawing her to him with the other.
Smooth, silky skin, but seconds later, as he was about to
kiss her again, he realized there were goose bumps all
over her and she was trembling.

He touched his lips to hers. "You're freezing," he
whispered. "Let's get in bed."

She drew away a little and nodded and then, with no
help, she undid her slacks and slid them off, then her

white panties. She slipped beneath the down comforter so quickly he wondered if she were shy.

A few minutes later, the lights off, he slid into bed naked next to her. He wanted her instantly and had to hold himself in check as he moved against the curve of her body and kissed her, a kiss that began gently, and then the urgency of his desire showed as he crushed his mouth to hers, his hand on her breast, moving to the other and back.

She was still trembling.

He lifted his head, breathless, ready to burst, but something was not right. "Still cold?" he got out.

"I'm . . . fine."

"You want me to use protection?" he whispered.

"It's all right," she said, but barely audibly.

"Ellie, what's wrong?" *Goddamn,* he thought.

"No, no, I'm fine." And then she kissed him, surprising him with the strength of her need. When she moved his head to her breasts and he tasted her, heard her sharp intake of breath, he forgot her trembling, the hesitation, the fleeting moments of awkwardness. He forgot everything but the wild drumming of his heart in his ears.

He made slow and considerate love to her, holding back, giving, holding back until they were both mad for relief. Her hands were in his hair, on his shoulders, her fingers tightening and releasing, tightening again, quicker and quicker. And she whimpered, softly, then more loudly, and she said something, cried something, "Oh, God, oh God," and she held on to him fiercely, and he felt the sudden shudder deep inside her. He was lost, too, awash, drowning, in the sweet agony of fulfillment.

Later—a minute, perhaps an hour—he rolled over and held her, her head on his chest. He might have fallen asleep or dozed, he never knew. But sometime in the long winter's night he became aware of Ellie trembling again, and he thought, bewildered, that she was sobbing.

At dawn he awakened and felt her soft warmth against his hip. He moved a little and kissed the top of her head, a brush of his lips, trying to convince himself that he'd imagined her weeping. He'd dreamed it.

But when the first pale rays of winter sun seeped through the window he saw her eyes. They were swollen and the faint dried trace of tears lay on her cheeks.

EIGHT

Michael got up early Monday morning and dressed for court wondering what Zimmerman's defense team had in store for him today.

He wore his monkey suit, a dark blue wool suit, clean starched white shirt, conservative tie, and then fixed a couple of eggs while the coffee brewed.

His thoughts were on Ellie, the warm kiss she'd given him when he'd dropped her off at home last night, the great day of skiing they'd had—when the phone rang. He strode toward it, checking his watch. Seven-fifteen. Pretty damn early.

But when he picked it up, heard who it was on the other end, he forgot everything, the trial, Ellie, the early-morning hour.

It was the police chief from the Mexican town where Finn Rasmussen had vacationed. Michael had called there a half dozen times, always missing the chief, always leaving a message.

The man's English was passable, certainly better than Michael's Spanish. It didn't matter, though, because the jist of their conversation was all Michael needed. There had indeed been a rape and murder by strangulation over the American Thanksgiving holiday in his town, and an arrest had been made.

"The man's scarf was used to choke the *chica*," the chief told Michael. "Why is it you are curious?"

Michael lied. The last thing he needed was for this man to contact the Boulder PD. He thanked the policeman, said the crime didn't appear to be what he'd thought, and hung up.

He stood in the middle of his living room with murder burning in his heart. Another young girl brutalized, slain; another innocent man imprisoned. How many more victims could he bear to learn about before he took the law into his own hands?

The rest of his breakfast sat untouched on the island counter as he wrote up this latest incident in a notebook. Someday, each entry, each word, was going to be a nail in Rasmussen's coffin.

He arrived at the Justice Center scowling, needing to put aside his frustration, concentrate on the trial and his testimony. So he thought about Ellie, pushing Rasmussen into a dark corner of his mind. Ellie. Yes. He'd see her in a few minutes. God, he hoped she'd flash him one of those smiles. He needed it.

He went in the front door, was subjected to the metal detector and the X-ray belt, even though the guards had known him for years. Ben Torres was waiting for him in his office.

"It's going well," the DA said. "Extremely well. I think Gardner will be through with you today. I want to get on to some of the other witnesses. I'm saving the actual tapes for last, to leave the jury with Radway's confession before the defense presents its case."

"I figured you would."

"So, you're all set? Coffee?"

"No, thanks."

Torres glanced at his watch. "We have a few minutes. I'm going to check on something. Make yourself comfortable, Detective."

Ellie must have been in another room, maybe already in court. He wandered out into the lobby and sat on one of the chairs in the corner.

"Hey hey, Detective Callas," one of the receptionists said.

"Hi, Mary."

"I hear it's going well."

"I guess so." He got up and went to the high counter and leaned an elbow on it. "I think I'm out of here today."

"Short and sweet," Mary said.

Was she flirting? "That's me," he replied, "short and sweet." Amazed at the bit of wit.

Court convened at nine sharp. It wasn't until Michael was reminded that he was still under oath and in the witness chair that he saw Ellie. She was seated between two ADAs, one a black woman, the other an Oriental man. But all he could see was Ellie. Their eyes met briefly across the space; an infinitesimal smile curved her lips and was gone. He felt something inside give way and had to drag his mind back from images of her naked body, her mouth, her hands. Her sobbing.

Today Gardner had chosen one of his colleagues to cross-examine Michael, a handsome young black man in the most expensive-looking double-breasted suit Michael had ever seen. His name was Louis Parks. He sauntered up to the witness chair, full of himself.

"Good morning, Detective Callas," he intoned.

Michael nodded.

"I have a few questions for you this morning. Just to clear up some points."

"Uh-huh." He glanced at the court recorder, then said, "That's fine."

"The court heard your statement last Friday about Hugh Radway's confession. I'd just like to go into a few details concerning your remorseful Mr. Radway."

Michael could see Torres glower. "Yes, sir, go ahead."

"A couple of things. Did you or anyone in the BPD know this Radway or know anything about him?"

"No."

"Did you know he had police records in California, Oregon, and Arizona?"

"We checked up on him as soon as we heard from him. So then we knew, yes."

"This man had been in prison"—Parks moved to the defense table and read from a piece of paper—"four times in twelve years. He'd been arrested seven other times but not convicted. For theft, armed robbery, and fraud. *Fraud.*"

"Yes, sir."

"Hugh Radway was, in your testimony, a self-confessed murderer."

"Yes, sir."

"And yet the DA and the police bought his story, hook, line, and sinker?"

"Yes, sir, absolutely."

"Why, Detective? Radway didn't have an honest bone in his body."

"His confession was the truth."

Parks opened his hands in front of him, lifted his shoulders, frowned. "All you experienced detectives believed his confession?"

"Oh, yes."

"Detective Callas has answered your question. Move on, Mr. Parks," the judge admonished.

"Let's go to the physical evidence." Parks turned to the jury and smiled. "This won't take long, ladies and gentlemen, because there *is* no physical evidence."

"Objection," Torres said.

"Keep your opinions to yourself, counselor. Continue. Let's get this show on the road." Titters rose from the audience.

"All right, at the crime scene we have a woman dead of a wound caused by a twenty-two–caliber bullet that the coroner subsequently removed from the woman's head. Unmatched to any gun you or the FBI files have on record. Correct?"

"Yes."

"No brass? That is," he explained to the jury, "no ejected shell casing?"

"No. Radway said he took it with him."

"Did you ever recover it?"

"No, he threw it away."

"Did you ever find the murder weapon?"

"No, he got rid of it at a pawnshop years ago."

"No brass, no murder weapon. Any other evidence?"

"Not much. Radway wore gloves, used flat-soled shoes."

"No physical evidence." Parks paused dramatically. "To move on. The money Zimmerman *allegedly* paid Radway. Did you ever trace it?"

"It was cash, from the till in Zimmerman's restaurant. It couldn't be traced."

"So there's no proof that Mr. Zimmerman actually paid anybody anything."

"There's Radway's confession."

"Ah, the confession."

"Yes, the confession," Michael said in a quiet voice, and his gaze settled on Steve Zimmerman's impassive face at the defense table.

"Did you ever find proof that Radway received the money? A deposit, something like that. Or even a new car he bought?"

"No, it wasn't the kind of money you deposit in your checking account," Michael said drily.

"Okay, so what we have here—correct me if I'm wrong—is an upstanding member of the community, with a hundred reliable alibis, being arrested and tried for a crime that *somebody else committed,* and for which there is no physical evidence whatsoever?"

"There's the confession," Michael repeated.

"Ah, yes, the whole case is dependent on a criminal's so-called deathbed confession, a criminal who was no doubt coached by the police in the first place, forced to—"

"Objection!" Torres barked, rising.

Parks raised his hand. "Withdrawn, if it please the court."

There wasn't much more after that. Torres remade his points on redirect examination, and Parks tried once more on recross to get Michael to admit Radway had fabricated the confession. But the argument was not convincing, and Michael was finally excused just before the lunch recess.

Torres slapped him on the back. "Good work, Detective. Join us for lunch, why don't you? We've been having sandwiches sent in, so we can talk strategy."

Michael said yes, knowing he was only doing it so that he could see Ellie. Otherwise, he'd never be caught dead eating a meal with the DA.

She sat next to him at the big conference table, while

Torres took sandwiches out of a grocery-sized bag. Gourmet sandwiches, with pesto and olive oil and sun-dried tomatoes and guacamole and crap like that.

"You were very good this morning," Ellie said.

He shrugged, picking some weird pieces of pepper and olives out of his sandwich. "It's part of the job. I've done it before."

"I know, but still. . . ."

Torres was discussing the next witness, the Boulder County coroner, who'd performed the autopsy on Danielle Zimmerman. ADA Gerald Shan was to conduct the questioning, and they were going over a list of points Shan had to make.

Ellie lowered her voice. "I wanted to thank you again for the weekend. I'm so sore I can hardly move." Then she realized what she'd said and flushed. "From the skiing," she added.

"Right." His lip twitched.

"I'd like to do it again. I was just starting to catch on."

"Sure, we can do it again. Like I said, nobody uses the place up there anymore."

She bit into her sandwich, chewed. So pretty, dressed in black today. A black suit with a pale green blouse underneath, framing her neck. Her delicate neck that he'd kissed in the dark. He could see her pulse beating.

"Stop looking at me like that," she whispered.

"Sorry." He took a couple bites of his sandwich, drank some soda, swallowed. "Tonight," he said.

She cocked her head.

"Would you like to come out to the cabin? I'll cook something."

Her eyes lit up. "You'd actually let me into your sanctuary?"

"I asked, didn't I?"

"I'd love to."

"Pick you up . . . ?"

"Five-thirty, okay? We should be done by then."

"Yeah, okay."

He finished his sandwich quickly, thanked Torres, who was deep in conversation with Shan, and left without another word.

He was waiting outside the Justice Center at five-thirty sharp, his truck idling with a low rumble so he could stay warm. He'd already stopped at the Safeway on his way over and bought a couple of steaks and baking potatoes and a bag of salad. He'd bought a bottle of red wine, too, a Merlot that the salesman had said was very good. It had cost enough, but how often did he have a woman over for dinner?

Ellie came out of the building, toting her briefcase. She had on that long black coat and a red scarf around her neck, and she'd changed her pumps for black leather boots.

He got out and opened the passenger door.

"Hi," she said, "am I late?"

"Just got here myself."

He helped her up onto the seat, noting that her hand was cold, as usual.

He got in his side, found Ellie peeking into the grocery bags sitting on the seat between them.

"Wine," she said. "Nice. And some kind of meat, and a salad. Very good."

"I don't cook much."

"Me neither. Okay, so where's your cabin? Where are you spiriting me away to?"

"Up Canyon Boulevard."

"Wow."

"It's a few miles out of town."

"I can't wait. You built it all yourself?"

"Yeah."

"Well, is there hot water, an outside john, or what?"

"The plumbing's all there, one bathroom finished, the other roughed out. I'll get it done someday."

"When do you do all this work?"

"Weekends. Evenings. Vacations. It's taken me three years." He wanted to get the subject off him. "So, how'd the afternoon go?"

"Very well. The coroner was on the stand. They couldn't shake him, especially on the defense's bogus SIDS theory."

"Uh-huh. He's a good man, Dr. Sanders. Knows his stuff."

"Have you ever, I mean, have you attended an autopsy?"

"Oh, yeah. I was at Danielle Zimmerman's, in fact."

"Oh, God, was it . . . is it awful?"

"It's not nice."

"Stop. I'm sorry I asked."

"Not exactly predinner conversation," he said, then switched the subject. "You think Torres will use your reluctant witness, the guy that Zimmerman talked to about hiring a hitman?"

"Um, good question. The guy really does *not* want to testify. He's a businessman, you know. It would look . . . well, seedy at best."

"Yeah, I guess."

"I think Torres is pretty happy the way the case is going. I mean, my God, you should see the faces of the women jurors every time the baby is mentioned. And the coroner's photos today . . ." Her voice trailed off, and he gave her a sidelong glance. It pissed him off that Ellie had seen those photos. That she was even involved in this sordid case at all. Why the hell did she want to be a lawyer? And a criminal defense lawyer at that. On the other hand, if she weren't pursuing this career, he never would have met her.

They drove in silence for a time, out of the city on Canyon Boulevard, up through a narrow notch in the mountains, following the serpentine course of Boulder Creek. The traffic was heavy with commuters going home. Ellie stared out of her side window, but she probably couldn't see much because it was dark out.

"We're here," he said, turning left onto a narrow wooden bridge that crossed the creek. A bridge he'd built. Then up the driveway, pressing the garage door opener, so that a bright square appeared ahead of them.

"Classy," she said, "an automatic door opener. A garage."

They entered the cabin through the garage into a hallway that led to the kitchen. He flipped the light switches and put the groceries down on the center island.

"Oh, my goodness," Ellie said. "It's beautiful. I was thinking of a little cabin in the woods, you know, something sort of primitive."

She took her boots off and walked around in her stocking feet, checking out the cabinets, the range and oven, running her fingers along the smooth granite countertops. Then into the living room. Standing in the middle of it, turning slowly.

"Not much furniture," he said.

"Oh, Michael, it's beautiful. All those big logs. How did you ever . . . ?"

"Had some help with those. Can I take your coat?"

"Oh, sure, yes."

He went to her and stood behind her as she shrugged

off her coat. He wanted to kiss the nape of her neck, breathe in her scent.

She turned, too quickly, and met his eyes. And she knew exactly how he felt.

"Thank you," she said softly, "for having me here. I know it's very special to you."

He only nodded.

He hung her coat in the closet by the front door. Then he hung his next to it and looped his shoulder holster with his gun in it over the doorknob.

"What's that?" She pointed to the loft railing.

"Master bedroom."

"Oh."

"There's another bedroom, right there, but it's nowhere near done. There's only me. I don't need much."

She went to the second room, turned the light on, stood looking from the doorway. He knew what the room contained—a bare lightbulb, a table saw, a pile of boards, sawdust.

"My interior decorator's coming tomorrow," he said.

She turned and grinned.

"Hungry?" he asked.

"Starved."

"I'll get started. I'm just going to microwave the potatoes and grill the steaks."

"Let me help."

"You could put the salad in a bowl. There're dressings in the refrigerator door. Take your pick."

It was strange, very strange, working in the kitchen with Ellie. His mother had never, ever been to his home. Nobody but a few guys, once for a poker game, and a cop friend whose wife had kicked him out had slept on the couch for a few weeks last summer.

Ellie asked him a million questions, didn't seem to

mind his silences. She set two place mats out on the island, along with napkins and mismatched wineglasses.

"I don't have a table yet."

"No prob. I bet you eat standing up half the time. Come on, admit it."

"Sometimes."

She opened the bag and poured the salad into a bowl, searched around in his drawers, clucking, and found the salad fork and spoon. Then she sat on one of the stools, chin resting on her hand, and watched him.

"When did you get on the police force?" she asked out of the blue.

"Straight out of college. Fifteen years ago. After the academy, I was a uniform for two years, then I moved up."

"A uniform."

"A patrolman. In a car. With a partner. We patrolled a beat."

"Did you like that?"

"I did at first, then I realized I wanted more of a challenge."

"You like being a detective?"

"Yeah. I'm good at it."

"It doesn't get you down, all the terrible things people do to one another?"

He checked on the grill's temperature, got the steaks ready. "Sometimes. Like the Zimmerman baby." He shrugged. "Mostly, when a person gets something bad done to him, he deserved it."

"Oh, come on."

"Mostly, it's true. But there are times. A few. . . ."

She played with the fork she'd set by the plate. "Surely there were other cases where the person didn't deserve it."

"Oh, yeah, one or two."

He checked on the potatoes. Five more minutes. "You want to open the wine? It should breathe."

He handed her the corkscrew, then got butter out of the fridge. Salt, pepper, steak sauce. He was aware of her watching him the whole time.

"My father would have loved your cabin," she said. Her voice sounded wistful. "I told you, didn't I, that he was a contractor?"

"Uh-huh."

"But what he really liked was actually doing the work. Building things."

"It must have been hard building in Leadville. Those long winters."

"What? Oh, I guess it was."

"How do you like your steak?"

"Medium rare."

"Okay, just a minute now."

They ate perched on stools at his granite-topped counter. The wine was tasty, sparkling garnet red under the lights. The steak was tender, the potatoes steamed when cut open, though they were a little rubbery, he thought. Microwaved.

"This is good," she said. "Don't tell me you eat like this every night."

"I won't tell you, then."

"You don't."

"You're right."

She drank some wine, cut a piece of steak. "So tell me about when you were a uniform. Did you do those chases you always see in the movies?"

"No, it was mostly drunk drivers, burglaries, and spousal abuse, some assists with campus security."

"Oh, nice." She wrinkled her nose. "Who did you work

with back then? Were you male-bonded, the way you see on TV?"

"My partner?" Boy, she was full of questions. He realized he was being goddamn interrogated. Nicely.

"Oh, I bet it was a female. You had a lady for a partner, and she was tough and beat up the bad guys," Ellie said lightly.

"No, no lady partner."

She cocked her head.

"It was a rookie like me, only he had a couple more years than I did. His name was Rasmussen, Finn Rasmussen."

She didn't reply, just raised her wineglass and drank. But he could have sworn he saw a singular look on her face, a dark, breathless look that gathered then was swiftly hidden behind the wineglass.

"Is he a detective now, too?" she asked.

"No."

"Just no?"

"That's it."

"So you didn't remain close?"

"We were never close."

"I see." Then she was quiet for a time, and when she spoke again it was about inconsequential matters.

He was nervous having her in his place; he didn't quite know how to react. She seemed comfortable enough, but then Ellie always fit in anywhere she was. The only time Michael ever felt comfortable was here or at police headquarters and, he admitted to himself, at a crime scene.

He wondered if she'd stay overnight. He craved her nearness; just the notion of her in his bed made him ache inside. It was hard to keep his mind on anything when she was so close. It was as if he were drugged by an aphrodisiac, making his blood slow and turgid, his heart beat too hard, something tense up under his rib cage. A mind-altering drug.

And yet he knew Ellie was not exactly what she appeared, a pleasant young woman working at the DA's office. No, there was something there, and he wanted to keep her at arm's length and study her, uncover her secret.

"Let me do the dishes," she said when they were done eating.

He sat on his stool and observed. She'd taken off her jacket and wore the long-sleeved green blouse. Such a pretty color against her pale skin and dark hair.

He had to give her the choice of going or staying. It was up to her. No matter how much he wanted her, he had to give her the choice. Especially after Saturday night. Had she really been crying?

He didn't understand her, and he wanted to. He desperately wanted to.

She finished the last dish and turned to him with a smile. "All done."

It was time. "Do you, ah, want a ride home?"

She just looked at him across the central island. "Are you trying to get rid of me?"

"God, no."

"I sort of thought . . ."

His heart gave a leap. "Do you want to stay?"

"I'd like that, as long as you can drop me at home in the morning. To change my clothes."

"Sure."

She leaned across the island and laid her fingers on his hand. "I didn't bring a toothbrush." Her eyes were wide-set and black and bottomless.

"I can probably find one for you."

"Do you have spares for the women you bring here?"

"No, I mean, I don't . . . Ah, I don't bring women here."

"I don't believe you."

He shrugged.

"You mean I'm the first?"

He was silent.

"Why?"

"I don't know. I thought, I guess I thought we got along."

"What a lame answer." She laughed. "Okay, I won't push. I can tell I'm embarrassing you." She stretched. "God, I'm tired. The trial really did me in."

"Trials can do that." He paused. "Would you like to watch TV? I usually try to watch CNN, catch the news."

"I might fall asleep."

"That's okay."

They sat on his couch, the only furniture in his living room besides a battered coffee table full of magazines on building and design.

"I better call my roommates," Ellie said, "so they don't worry."

"What are you going to tell them?"

"The code we have: 'I'm spending the night at a friend's house.' Then no one asks any questions."

"Do you and your roommates spend the night with friends often?"

She taunted him with a smile. "I'm not sure that's any of your business."

"I guess not."

She made the phone call in the kitchen, and he could hear her laugh at something the person on the other end said. A bright, bubbling laugh. He suddenly wanted to make her laugh like that, but he didn't know how.

When she hung up he asked her about her roommates,

what it was like to live with three other people. "Hell," he said, "I can't even remember when I didn't live alone."

Ellie stood between the kitchen island and the living room and raised both brows. "Well," she said, "it's wonderful and awful at the same time." Then she told him about Bonnie, the whiner, and Jennifer, the man-eater, and her best friend, Celeste. She even did a little rendition of Celeste.

"Last year she was into cowboys and the cowgirl look. She lived in jeans and Western-cut shirts and cowboy boots. Her hair was even brassy blond."

Ellie pretended to walk like her roommate, hitching her thumbs into imaginary jean pockets and strutting.

"So what's her look now?"

"Oh, Gothic. This year she's into black. And I mean black. Her hair's dark red and she won't go out in the sun. She's pale as a ghost."

He couldn't help laughing. And even though Ellie was telling tales about her friend, he could see how close they were. Ellie loved this spoiled rich girl. An easy, uncomplicated love. And he wondered: had Ellie ever loved a man like that?

Eventually she came to sit next to him, pulling her feet up under her, leaning her thigh against his. He burned and swallowed. She was so damn casual about everything. He wanted to ask what she felt about him, what she really felt, but the words were locked away inside him in that place where he kept all his hopes and wishes and questions. It was locked, and no one, not even he himself, had the key.

CNN Headline News was on, and he pretended to watch the screen, but his brain didn't comprehend anything except Ellie's body touching his.

She laid a hand on his thigh, so easy, so natural. He felt his skin twitch, like a horse twitching at flies.

"Um, this is nice," she said. "Relaxing. All this beautiful golden wood surrounding us, like a forest. But, you know, you need some area rugs to show off the floor."

"I know."

She drew back. "I'm sorry. I shouldn't tell you what to do in your house."

"No, it's fine. I guess the place could use a woman's touch."

"Some Navajo rugs maybe, or a Kilim. One right here in front of the couch."

"Uh-huh."

She rested her head on the back of the couch and closed her eyes. "You don't have any curtains or blinds in your windows, either."

"No one close enough to see in."

"That's nice."

"Private."

"Um."

He stared at her hand where it rested on his thigh for a long time. Finally he put his hand out and touched her fingers. She didn't move. He wrapped his hand around hers and held it like that. And this time it was warm. Small and soft and warm.

A dark-haired woman was talking on CNN, but he was blind to the color and sound. He let himself feel and breathe, and he closed his eyes, her hand in his, and he shut his eyes for just a moment. Then he lifted his other hand and ran the backs of his fingers over her cheek. She opened her eyes and smiled lazily, hitched a little closer to him.

My God.

He let his hand drape over her shoulder, and he sat

there so long like that Ellie fell asleep—he could hear the rhythm of her breathing change.

She shifted in her sleep, and he brushed the hair back off her temple, the soft dark curls that felt like silk, the way he remembered.

She murmured something in her sleep, and he withdrew his hand.

The lady on TV yattered on, something about Medicare, but he couldn't make sense of the words. He also couldn't figure out how he'd come to be sitting in his cabin with a strange young woman, too young for him, but so lovely, so beautiful and smart. A woman who wanted to be with him. Why? What on earth did he have that Ellie Kramer sought?

He woke her at nine.

"I told you I'd fall asleep," she said in a husky voice.

"You want to go upstairs now?"

She yawned. "Sure, I'm not much use, am I?"

"I go to sleep early, too."

"Wow, we are exciting people, huh?"

He stood, stiff from sitting in the same position for so long, held a hand out, and helped her rise. "Ouch," she said, "sore legs from skiing."

He led her up the open staircase to the loft bedroom. In the room was his bed, an old dresser, and a chair. A down comforter was smoothed neatly over the king-size bed; the clothes hung in the closet and lay folded in the dresser drawers.

"The bathroom's there," he told her with a nod.

"You first or me? And, oh, do you have a T-shirt or something I can sleep in?"

"Sure." He opened a drawer and pulled one out, handed it to her.

"You use the bathroom first," she said. "I'll change."

When he came out, she was wearing his T-shirt, a gray one that had "Vail" printed on the front.

She walked straight up to him, feet bare, legs bare, hair tousled, and kissed him on the lips. "Warm the bed for me," she whispered.

He undressed and got into bed, lay there stiff with want and need and apprehension. He could hear her moving around in the bathroom, the water running, the toilet flushing. Hands behind his head, he waited, body aflame, ready to burst.

The bathroom door opened and she emerged, turned the lights off, and crept into bed next to him. She curled up against his side and laid a hand on his chest. "Oh, God," she said, "I'm really sorry, but I just started my period."

He shut his eyes and felt hollow from disappointment. He took her in his arms, though, because it wasn't her fault, and he wanted to feel her close to him. He wanted her to trust him.

"It's okay," he said. "I don't care. There'll be other nights."

In reply she snuggled closer to him, kissed his chin, his cheek. "Don't be mad," she breathed.

"I'm not." And he pulled her close and buried his face deep in her fragrant neck. It was enough.

NINE

Ellie stood by the fax machine in the DA's office, biting her nails and wondering how long she could play at this dangerous game before she was caught.

Come on, come on, she thought, staring at the machine while she waited for the police report from Pueblo, Colorado.

It was Thursday. The office was relatively quiet—everyone, including Ben, was down the hall in Courtroom B, sitting in on the Zimmerman trial. Ellie had skipped the afternoon session, claiming she had work to catch up on. Which she did. But instead of entering data into the computer, she'd phoned the chief of police in Pueblo and asked for the file on the Holly Lance rape case, telling the chief that DA Ben Torres in Boulder was having her update their database, including all the Front Range first-degree sexual assault cases for the last ten years.

"Yeah, well, the guy who beat and raped the Lance girl is behind bars. Her *stepfather,*" the chief had said. "But if the DA wants the info, fine, I'll fax it up."

"Can you, ah, do it now, Chief?" Ellie had said, in her most persuasive voice.

"Sure, sure. Whatever."

"Thank you, sir." She'd given him the fax number. "Have a nice day."

"Sure, sure, you too."

But she was still waiting. It had been well over a half hour. What if court recessed early? What if Ben caught her at the fax, asked what she was doing?

The fax line rang. Her heart leaped. But it was something coming in from the Boulder cops for one of the ADAs. Ellie put it on the woman's desk.

Then the phone rang again. When the machine began to print, she saw at once that the cover letter was from the Pueblo PD. *Thank God.* She snatched up the ten sheets as soon as they'd all printed out and stuffed them in her briefcase, her cheeks hot, the back of her neck damp. How long could she keep this up?

Celeste was miffed all evening. "Don't tell me you're working again tonight, Kramer. What's with you, woman? Torres must be the slave driver from hell. I'll be good goddamned if I'm ever going to clerk for some asshole like that."

Ellie was fixing a sandwich in the kitchen. "I really don't mind. Honest," she said, slapping mayonnaise on bread.

"Well, you're screwing up our Thursday card game. It isn't just me. Jenn and Bonnie are pissed, too."

"Celeste, there really are more important things than a game of cards."

Celeste arched a pencil-black brow. "No, Kramer, there aren't," she said.

Ellie finally escaped the disapproving glares of her roommates, took her sandwich to the attic, and closed her door.

If only they knew. If only she could confess to them, her best friends on earth. But shame and pride would not allow it. Someday, *someday* she'd be able to hold her head high and tell the world she was Ellie Crandall.

She ate her tuna sandwich with one hand while pulling the fax sheets out of her briefcase with the other, and then she sat on her bed, cross-legged, glasses perched on her nose.

Case file number 21694Z. Lance, Holly Lynn.

The rape had occurred in the Lances' overgrown back-yard in Pueblo four years ago. At the time, Holly had been fifteen, a very mature fifteen. Ellie herself had been just going into her junior year at CU. She'd had the TV on in the apartment that she'd shared with Celeste back then, and the Denver news had run the story. Ellie's ears always perked up whenever there was a sexual assault in the news, and this one had certainly grabbed her attention. Holly had been beaten and raped, but the rapist had been interrupted and had not had time to strangle her to death. Lucky girl.

Holly wasn't able to make a positive ID, although her stepfather's belt had been used as a ligature. Alone at home, she'd been struck from behind, dragged outside, and raped. While her assailant had been strangling her, a neighbor had heard a noise, come out of his back door, and the rapist had fled.

She'd never seen her attacker's face.

Her stepfather, an army sergeant stationed at Fort Carson, had been arrested, tried and convicted within four months. Swift justice.

Ellie put down her sandwich and read the mother's

statement, which had been taped and transcribed word for word by the interviewing officer the day after the rape.

"I had to work at the mall, at the shoe store. I'm an assistant manager. Holly was, oh, God, Holly was baby-sitting for little Carl, he's just five, and his birthday . . . That doesn't matter. Oh, God. My husband and I got separated three months ago. But he's not like this. He's a jerk, okay, but Bob Lance would never . . . hurt a kid. I'm sorry, I need a minute."

Ellie let out a breath she'd been holding, picturing Bob, Sgt. Robert Lance, locked up in prison now, very possibly innocent. It wasn't right. Goddamn it, it wasn't *right.*

She went on reading. "Bob isn't Holly's father, he's her stepfather, adopted her when she was two, raised her, but when my neighbor found Holly . . . out back . . . Oh, God, I'm sorry. Okay, he called nine-one-one and then me right away. It couldn't be Bob who did that to Holly, he loves her so much. . . . Bob's a good father. He is. I'm sorry, I can't stop crying. Anyway, Bob said he got a call from one of the PFCs at the base. Something about a breakdown on the highway, but when Bob got there, to the place the PFC told him, no one was there. I don't understand. I know that belt . . . the belt that was found around Holly's neck . . . I know it's Bob's, but don't you get it? Someone set him up. Sent him on a wild-goose chase so Bob would have no alibi. Used Bob's belt to . . . Bob would never harm anyone."

Ellie then read Bob Lance's sworn statement, which had been taken with a lawyer present. His estranged wife had told exactly the same story as his. Clearly, he had no alibi for the time of the assault on his stepdaughter. And the PFC who supposedly needed help on the highway knew nothing about a breakdown, much less calling his sergeant, Bob Lance.

A perfectly executed setup. Ellie knew it in her heart.

She read the doctor's report on Holly's condition when she'd been admitted to the hospital, and Ellie might as well have been reading the report from the brutalization of Stephanie Morris. The MO was so similar, the signature of the rapist nearly identical, except on Stephanie he'd used John Crandall's bandana to strangle her, and on Holly Lance it had been Bob's very identifiable belt, which he said he hadn't seen in weeks.

Ellie could picture the cops laughing, saying, "Right. Someone broke into your apartment and just stole your *belt*, Bob?"

A slam-dunk arrest, trial, and conviction.

Ellie took off her glasses and stared into the middle distance. Michael Callas. Michael with his ruthless façade. And he'd been emotionally abused—the divorce of his parents.

My God, she mused, he wouldn't even discuss his family. She didn't know if he had brothers or sisters or aunts or uncles, cousins. He was from Colorado Springs. Did both parents still live there?

Oh, Michael fit the profile of a cold-blooded psychopath killer, all right, a calculating son of a bitch. How easily he could have set up Bob Lance. He could have seen Holly anywhere. Pueblo was very near Colorado Springs, lots of malls, movie theaters, fast-food joints. Michael could have seen her on a trip to visit his family. Seen her and lusted after her and followed her home. Then he would have had all the time in the world to stalk her, to learn about the estranged stepfather, the mother who worked weekend nights at the shoe store. He could have broken into Bob Lance's apartment—all cops knew how to pick a lock—and snatched Bob's belt. Finding the name of one of Bob's underlings at Fort Carson would not have been a problem, either.

It had been so easy for Michael, just as easy as the rape and strangulation of Stephanie Morris and God only knew how many others over the last decade.

And you fucked him, Ellie, but, worse, you enjoyed it.

She had to put that thought aside, though. She couldn't afford to think about it now, not in the middle of things. *The end justifies the means.* That had always been her motto. It would have to suffice.

But it was impossible to stop thinking, questioning his every word and gesture, wondering, speculating. She should know if he were evil, shouldn't she? Wouldn't she be able to *feel* it?

And how long could she keep him on a string without sleeping with him again? How many excuses could she come up with? Or did she even want to make excuses? It would be so much easier to give in, to *know* him fully. That was the ugly truth.

He called her that evening just as she was through studying the Holly Lance file.

"It's for you, Kramer," Bonnie's voice boomed up the stairs, and even before Ellie picked up the extension, she knew who it was. Her stomach grew hollow and her head pounded.

"Working late?" he asked when she picked up the receiver.

"Ah, yes. The work of a clerk is never done."

"Torres is an asshole."

"That's exactly what Celeste says. He's not really. Actually, Ben Torres is a pretty swell guy. He's certainly given *me* a break."

"Sure," Michael said, and Ellie heard the skepticism

in his voice. No doubt Michael believed Torres only wanted to get in her pants. Which he did. Okay. But she was also a helluva good clerk and the DA knew it.

"You free tomorrow night?" Michael was asking. "I thought we could take in a movie, if you want. I haven't been to a movie in years."

"Sure, yes, I'd like that." And she knew she would. *Damn, damn.* All she could picture was Michael dragging Holly Lance into a weedy backyard and raping her. But he hadn't been able to finish the job, as he had with the others. No. Holly had escaped the worst fate. And Ellie was sure as hell going to locate her and talk to her. Would she ask the young woman if her rapist had kissed the pulse at the hollow of her neck? If he had smelled like new-sawn wood and soap?

Oh, God.

"Ellie?"

"Yes, I'm here."

"Why don't you meet me at the station? Say around five?"

"I can do that."

"Or, if you want, I'll pick you up at the Justice Center."

"No, no, I'll catch the bus. It's easier."

"Okay, see you tomorrow."

"Yes. Okay, good night, Michael," she said and she hung up quickly.

She dreamed that night about her grandparents' farm, the sweet alfalfa brushing her legs as she and her grandfather walked the fields. The sun was warm on her shoulders, but the fear and insecurity had never left her that long summer so many years ago when her father had been on trial. Her mother had sent her to her grandparents in Nebraska, wanting to keep Ellie away from the ugly publicity, but what Janice hadn't realized was that mere distance couldn't help. The bottom had fallen out of Ellie's world, and she'd had no practice back then of setting aside bad things. All summer her grandparents had tried so hard, but the terror stayed with her. And the distance may have even made it worse.

It had been the summer of hell, but it had been the beginning of Ellie's education in withstanding anguish.

She awoke, used the bathroom at three in the morning, and then she dreamed again about the farm. But only about the good times.

Ellie still felt a little uncomfortable in the detective division, even though she'd been there several times now. She wasn't the only woman; there was another female, a tough-looking young woman detective to whom the other detectives gave wide berth. The woman's name was Rafferty, apparently no first name. But it was a little awkward, all those macho guys swearing, cracking cop jokes, drinking too much coffee. And, of course, they could all tell something was going on between her and Michael—she noticed the knowing grins, the glances.

But she'd met a few of the detectives by now, committed their names to memory, because she might be able to use them to get information on Michael. And yet, today, when she saw that Michael wasn't at his desk, she felt a little lost, not sure what to do.

"He's on an interrogation," came a voice behind her. She turned.

"Oh," she said. It was Rick Augostino, the one with the big belly and the kind eyes. Older.

"He should be back soon. Told me to watch out for you. You want some coffee? A doughnut?"

"No thanks." She smiled at Augostino. He was a nice

man, fatherly. He had powdered sugar from a doughnut on his tie, and she wanted to brush it off but didn't dare.

"You here to do some more prep for the trial?" Augostino asked.

"No, Michael's done with his testimony. I'm, well"—she felt herself blushing—"we're going to a movie."

"A movie." He whistled. "Robocop is going to a movie."

"He's allowed, isn't he?"

"Sure, well, hell, more power to him. You know, he has this rep, I mean, not too many pretty young ladies show up for a date with Callas."

"There's always a first."

"I'm happy for him. About time. Although I don't know what in God's name you see in the bastard."

"If you promise not to tell, I'll confess."

"Cross my heart."

"He's got this vulnerability about him. It's attractive."

"Robocop vulnerable. Well, if that doesn't take the cake. Christ."

"You promised."

"Sure, sure. No one'd believe me anyway."

It came to her then, out of the blue, the perfect opportunity. "Say," she said, "to change the subject. I've been trying to find out about a detective who worked here years ago. My mother wanted to know, because he was her best friend's son, and Mom can't locate him."

"I've been here eighteen years. I probably knew him. What's his name?"

"Finn Rasmussen." She held her breath.

"Oh, Finn, sure. Worked patrol for a few years, broke the Morris case and got bumped up. But he quit shortly after that. Went into the private sector. Home security."

Her heart thumped. Home security. The Morrises' security system intact. "Did he move away somewhere?"

"Denver. Got his own firm, doing well. Puts in security systems for rich people. Lives in Cherry Creek, I think. His company's called Mountaintech. Big-time stuff."

"Wow, that's great to know. I can look him up in the phone book. My mother will be thrilled."

"He should be easy to locate. He's turned into a real playboy."

"Thanks for the info. Mountaintech, I'll remember that."

Michael arrived then, glowering at Augostino. "Sorry I'm late," he said to Ellie.

"That's okay. Rick and I had a nice chat."

They went to a pizza joint to eat and then drove down to Denver to the Mayan, a theater done in art deco, with eucalyptus fronds carved on the walls. She never remembered the movie, something arty and sexy, with subtitles. Michael held her hand halfway through it, and she squeezed his fingers. But her mind was consumed with the knowledge she'd gleaned that day about Finn Rasmussen. In Denver, so close, right under her nose all along. *Rasmussen.*

She didn't spend the night at Michael's, and she wondered how many more lame excuses she could conjure up before he caught on. Tonight it was an early wake-up call for work.

Still, in his truck in front of her house, he leaned over and cupped the back of her head with a hand, drawing her to him. He kissed her gently and then thoroughly and as always that spot deep inside her swelled with longing.

She escaped as quickly as she could, still tasting him, still wanting him, hating herself. She closed her bedroom door and leaned against it. She was worse than a whore. At least a whore went about her business honestly.

• • •

It hadn't been easy to convince Celeste to help her out. Sometimes it was so damn inconvenient not having a car. She'd had to beg and plead, and Celeste had been full of questions Ellie couldn't answer.

"Why do you want to be dropped off there? What's going on? I can't just *leave* you there. You better tell me, Kramer."

But she couldn't tell her best friend. So many secrets, so many ugly, dirty little secrets.

Celeste, all her roommates, knew by now that she was dating a cop. They teased her about it and wanted to know when they could meet him, so when she'd asked Celeste to drive her to Cherry Creek in Denver, her friend had been confused.

"What is this, some trick you're playing on him, a surprise? But he doesn't live in Cherry Creek, for God's sake. What are you doing?"

"Don't ask. Just give me a ride. Early Saturday morning. Trust me, it's important."

"God, woman, you're so full of it. . . . Okay, I'll do it, but you have to tell me why someday."

"I will. Someday. I swear I will."

"Eight o'clock Saturday morning? It's too early. The mall's not even open yet," Celeste had groused.

Ellie dressed for jogging that Saturday morning. Heavy tights, running shoes, a fleece turtleneck, another fleece jacket over it, gloves, a headband. It was cold out. She roused a cranky Celeste, stuck a mug of coffee in her friend's hand, and herded her out to her car. Celeste drove, not saying much, drinking her coffee, shooting looks at Ellie. She got off the Boulder Turnpike at I-25, headed south to Speer Boulevard, then turned onto Cherry Creek Drive.

"What's the address again?" she finally asked.

Ellie had it memorized. "One-thirty-two Gaylord."

"Nice neighborhood. And look at her, dressed like a bum."

"A jogger, I'm dressed like a jogger."

"Right."

She stopped Celeste a block before his house and got out. "Thanks, I mean it. See you later."

"You're crazy, you know that? You're going to freeze to death."

"Bye. Have fun."

And then she was alone on the street, a very private dead-end street of elegant brick older homes, lots of trees, all bare now, and brown, snow-crusted lawns that would be smooth and green in the summer. Watered and cared for by landscapers, in this neighborhood. Patches of frozen ice in the streets and on the sidewalk, unmelted remnants in the shadows.

It was cold. Ellie ran in place for a minute, slapping her hands together. No one would take note of a lone female jogger here. Probably lots of the residents of these houses jogged. Her plan would work. It had to work.

She was a mess of nerves. How long would this take? What if he never came out of his house at all today? She'd try again another time. She had to get his attention.

She jogged slowly along the sidewalk until she was close to his house. It had a security gate around it, a wall, and a locked gate. Well, of course it would. He was in the business. The house itself was brick like the others. There'd been a huge fire in Denver in the early 1900s, which burned the town to the ground, and after that the city council had passed a law that all houses had to be built of brick. The brick factory owner made a fortune.

Solid, substantial, well-kept. Spreading junipers around

the foundation, a flagstone walkway, a three-car garage, doors closed. Patches of dirty snow.

Was he in there? Maybe he was out of town or staying over at a lady friend's place. She should have called his business and asked for him yesterday, given a false name, hung up or something, but she hadn't thought of it.

She stood behind a big tree, watching his house. Cold. She shivered. If she stood there too long a neighbor might notice, might even call the police. It was that kind of neighborhood.

A playboy, Augostino had said. A successful businessman and a playboy. Not married. That meant lots of women. Rich. She bet that one of the cars in that garage was a Beemer. Had to be. She didn't know what he looked like, though.

He was a couple of years older than Michael. That's all she knew about him, really. Michael hadn't said much, only that he and his partner hadn't been close. But, then, Michael didn't say much about anybody.

She stood there, shivering, getting more and more nervous. Maybe this had been a bad idea. Stupid. She could wait here all day while Finn Rasmussen sat inside his warm house and watched college football on his large-screen television set. With a girlfriend.

She ran past his house, to the dead end, then back up the other side, slowly, keeping an eye on his gate. Up to the other corner then back. If a neighbor was looking out his window he'd think she was crazy. Jogging in place, slapping her sides, up the street and down the other side. Her breath freezing, her nose running in the cold, her feet lumps of ice.

Maybe she should just go up to his security gate and ring the bell, say she needed to use his phone. That was lame. He'd wonder why she'd picked his house and not one of the others. She couldn't do that.

How long could she wait? How long until she ran out to First Avenue and called Celeste on her cell phone to pick her up?

She jogged around the block, trying to warm up, deathly afraid he'd slip out while she was out of sight. Behind the tree again, so cold she thought: *Five more minutes, just five more.* And when that was up it was five more.

She was jogging in place behind the tree when she heard a noise. God, his garage door was sliding up. She took a huge gulp of frigid air, ran down the street away from him, just far enough. She could hear a car start up, the low throaty roar of a rich man's vehicle. She turned, judging the distance. His gate was swinging open; he was backing out.

Not a Beemer. A metallic bronze Grand Cherokee. Sure, for the wintry roads. She jogged along the sidewalk, toward him, arms pumping, out for a workout. And then, when he'd turned onto the street and she was in front of him, where he couldn't miss her, she deliberately stepped onto a patch of ice and slipped and went down hard. She lay there, in a heap, the ground like concrete under her. She'd bruised her hip, damn it, and her elbow stung. Would it be worth it?

The Cherokee stopped short, and her heart jumped. *Please, please,* she prayed, and then he was striding around the hood of his car and coming toward her.

"Miss? Hey, miss, you okay?" His voice was deep, pleasing and low-pitched. Worried right now.

She groaned. He knelt down next to her. "You took a nasty fall there. Are you hurt?"

She lifted her head and looked at him. Light blue eyes,

concerned, a large nose with a bump on it, creased forehead, a dark jacket on, sweatpants.

"I fell," she whispered.

"Yes, you sure did. Are you okay?"

"Wow. Give me a minute. I think I got my breath knocked out."

"I bet. Should I call an ambulance? Where do you live? Got a friend nearby or something?"

She shook her head. "No ambulance. I'll be okay."

"Did you hit your head?"

"I . . . I don't think so."

"You want to try to get up?"

"Yes, I . . . it's cold here."

He put an arm around her shoulders and helped her up. A strong arm. He lifted her as if she weighed nothing. She let herself collapse against him, cried out.

"What?" he asked.

"My ankle. I can't . . . ouch. I can't stand on it."

"Oh, hell, you think it's broken?"

"I don't know. No, wait, give me a minute." Gingerly she tried to put weight on it. "Twisted, I think." She clung to his arm.

"Look, maybe I should drive you to the hospital."

"No. I hate hospitals."

"Do you live nearby?"

"No, I . . . a friend dropped me off to jog while she runs some errands. I'm supposed to meet her later."

"Where?"

"The Cherry Creek Mall."

He frowned. "You're kind of stuck, aren't you?"

"Oh, God, I'm so embarrassed. This is awful. It's nice of you to stop."

"You practically fell under my car."

"My name is Ellie, Ellie Kramer," she said, trying to

smile. He was tall, taller than Michael, and his neck had a big Adam's apple, a strong neck.

"Nice to meet you, Ellie. I'm Finn Rasmussen."

"Look, maybe you were on your way somewhere important. I don't want to keep you."

"Only to the gym to work out. Looks like it's safer than jogging." He stood back a little, studied her. "You're freezing. Come on, get in my car."

"Oh, I couldn't. . . ."

"Don't be silly. It's warm. Here, lean on me. Can you put any weight on the ankle?"

"A little."

He helped her into the passenger seat, closed the door carefully, then went around to the driver's side. Ellie slumped back against the beige leather seat, feeling as if she'd run a marathon and won. And it was warm in the car, the heat blasting steadily, the radio on to KVOD, Denver's classical station.

"Better?" he asked. A big man, he filled the front seat. His hands were large-knuckled and powerful looking.

"Oh, God, yes. I guess I didn't realize how cold I was."

"Now look, Ellie. I'm going to drive you to the mall where you're supposed to meet your friend."

"Oh, please, you don't have to do that."

"All right, you tell me how in hell you're going to get there. Run?"

She said nothing.

"I'm going to drive you there and wait with you until she shows up, and I know you're okay."

Tears came to Ellie's eyes. "I'm sorry to mess up your day. This is so nice of you . . . Finn."

"Hey, cut that out. This may turn out to be more interesting than working out at the gym, anyway. Tell me about yourself, Ellie Kramer."

He had a way about him. Easy in his skin. Charming. A playboy, a ladies' man. Handsome in a fair, rugged Northern way. Lines radiating out from his eyes when he smiled, white teeth, that incongrous lumpy nose.

She told him she was a law student from Boulder.

"Boulder," he said, and his tone was odd. He was quiet for a time, as if he'd gone into himself, like dead air on the radio, and she squirmed a bit, feeling awkward. What was there about Boulder that turned him off?

His muteness lasted too long, and she began to babble, desperate to fill the emptiness. She told him about taking a year off, clerking for the DA. Mentioned the Zimmerman trial.

He snapped back to his gregarious mode. "Zimmerman," Finn interrupted. "Sure, I remember that. A few years back, he put a contract out on his wife, right?"

"Uh-huh."

"And you're working on that? Good for you." He paused, gave her a quick sidelong glance as he drove. "I used to live in Boulder myself. Years ago."

"Really?"

"I was on the police force there for a few years."

"No kidding. I've been working with those guys a lot."

He shook a head. "I realized pretty fast I wasn't cut out to be a cop. It was okay, but I'm better at what I do now."

"Which is?"

"I own Mountaintech, a home security company."

"Mountaintech," she mused. "I may have heard of it."

"All I know about cops is that you're either born to be one or you aren't. But, I must say, I learned a lot on that job. A lot."

He was turning into the covered parking lot at the Cherry Creek Mall. He drove right into a handicapped space by the entrance, and Ellie felt a rush of guilt.

"Well, you're handicapped, aren't you?" he said, as if he could read her thoughts.

He came around to help her out of the car, a gentleman. "Here, lean on me," he said, holding her arm.

She hobbled along, her mind whirling. How to attract Finn? What would work? Michael had been easy; all she'd needed to do was be young and fresh and open and show him a little warmth. But Finn was different. He had all the self-confidence in the world. Money, cars, probably all the women he wanted, too. How to hook Finn Rasmussen?

"What time were you supposed to meet your friend?" he asked.

"Eleven-thirty."

"Well, you're early."

"Why don't you just leave me here?" She knew he wouldn't. "I've used up enough of your goodwill."

He pulled on an ear and eyed her. "Are you trying to get rid of me?"

"No, I mean, of course not, but you must be sick of playing nursemaid to a complete stranger."

"You're not a stranger anymore."

"Oh, come on, you barely know me."

"And you barely know me, but you got into my car. I bet your mother told you never to do that."

Ellie raised her brows. "God, was I in some kind of danger? Are you a mad rapist?"

He laughed, throwing his head back.

They stopped in front of a mall restaurant.

"Let me just look for Celeste, in case she got here early," Ellie said.

"We'll both look." And he took her arm and entered the restaurant.

Ellie glanced around. "Nope, no Celeste yet."

They waited at a coffee stand near Foley's. Ellie had a hot chocolate and cupped her hands around it.

"Still cold?" he asked.

"No, not really."

He sat as if he owned the place, one ankle crossed on the other knee, an arm lying along the back of her chair. Not touching her, just lying there, relaxed. He'd ordered an espresso, black.

Celeste hadn't shown up by eleven-thirty. Big surprise. At twelve Ellie began acting nervous. "I don't know what could have happened to her. Honestly."

"Car trouble," Finn suggested.

"I hope not."

"An attack of serious shopping?"

She smiled wanly. "Maybe."

"Some friend."

"She's my best friend."

"With a friend like that you don't need enemies." He tipped his cup up and drank the last of his espresso. His Adam's apple bobbed in his muscular neck. "Now, look," he said, setting the tiny cup down. "I'm driving you home."

"To Boulder?"

"Don't argue. I've made up my mind. It's ridiculous you sitting here waiting when you should be home with ice on that ankle and your foot up."

"Oh, God."

"I'm serious. We're both wasting our time sitting around here."

"Drop me at the bus station."

"No, goddamn it, I'm driving you home. It's no big deal."

"Oh, Finn, I hate for you to . . ."

"Just be quiet. Let's go." He flashed her a roguish smile. "I like you, Ellie, and I'm curious about you. Let's say I'd like to see where you live, get to know you better."

"You're a nice guy, you really are."

"That's what all the ladies say." He grinned and stood up. "Come on, Gimpy, your chariot awaits you."

The roads weren't crowded that cold Saturday afternoon. Before he got on the Boulder Turnpike, Finn went through the drive-up window of a McDonald's and ordered lunch, a huge bag of burgers and chicken nuggets and french fries and drinks, and they ate on the drive to Boulder.

Interesting, Ellie thought. He hadn't asked her what she wanted, just ordered. As if he were used to being in control of every situation in which he found himself.

He drove fast and competently, eating with one hand, steering with the other. Ellie figured she'd gotten off on a pretty good foot with him. He was easy to talk to, funny, smart. He didn't want or need her to keep up the conversation—he handled it himself with perfect aplomb. No awkward moments, no taut gaps in the conversation. A complete antithesis to Michael.

"Then there was the time, when I was starting out, that a woman's lover set off her alarm system trying to get into her house. Oh, she was waiting for him, but he screwed up and set off the alarm, and I rushed out there. That was before I paid guys to sit up all night and do it for me. Jesus, when I got there the husband had come home, and the three of them were going at it." He shook his head, smiling, remembering. "I laughed for a week over that one."

He had more stories, places he'd been, things he'd

seen. He liked to travel, took vacations and went to exotic lands.

"Do you ski?" he asked.

Ellie thought of her weekend at Vail, crossed her fingers surreptitiously. "I'm not great."

"I am," he said, and he meant it. "I'll take you sometime."

"Really?" she said. "You'd go nuts waiting for me, though."

"Get that ankle better, and maybe we'll try it."

She felt good. It was working so far. He liked her. The odd thing was, she liked him, too. He was a lot of fun. A big, handsome man.

She gave him directions, and he pulled up in front of her house.

"Thanks, Finn, I mean it. You helped me out a lot."

"You're welcome, Ellie. I enjoyed it." He reached in his pocket, extracted his wallet, and removed something. "Here's my card. You can always get me on my cell phone." He handed her another card. "Write your number on that." Then he leaned across her to open the glove compartment and fished out a pen. She could feel his elbow pressing against her leg and smell the clean man scent of him. *Very nice.*

She wrote her phone number down on the back of the card.

"Give me a call sometime," he said. "I mean it."

She met his eyes with a frank and straightforward expression. "Well, Finn, I'm afraid I'm enough of an old-fashioned girl that I'm not very comfortable calling men."

"Okay, I respect that. I'll call you, then."

She smiled. "I'd like that."

"You're an interesting lady, Ms. Kramer."

"And you, Mr. Rasmussen, are an interesting man."

He came around to her door and helped her down. "Let's get you inside."

"I'm okay. It's only a few steps. Go on, now, you have to get to your gym, remember?"

"You sure?"

"Yes, I'm sure."

She turned and began to limp up the walk.

"Good-bye, Ellie," she heard behind her, and she pivoted, smiled, waved. Saw him climb into his shiny Cherokee and pull away.

Cool, she thought, and she smiled to herself. She hoped she hadn't played too hard to get, but she knew she couldn't be fast and loose with Finn Rasmussen; he was no doubt surrounded by women drooling over him.

He'd call, he said he would. But what did that mean? Easy for him to say, but it was likely he'd forget her by the time he hit the Denver city limits. What if she'd misjudged him? What if she'd blown her chance?

The smile faded from her lips. God, what if he really did forget her?

And if he called? She closed her eyes for a moment. If Finn took the bait, she'd have to juggle two men and keep each one from learning about the other. It was just like a card game. Bluffing the other players. And only Ellie held all the trumps; the others had gaps in their hands.

Michael. Finn. One of them was a sadistic rapist. A murderer. Maybe. Possibly.

Which one?

She opened the door of the old yellow clapboard house and went in.

"Who was *that?*" Bonnie asked.

"Not the cop," Jenn declared.

"Why on earth are you limping?" Celeste asked.

"Damned if I know," Ellie said, and she walked perfectly normally over to the couch and flopped down.

TEN

When Finn was in fifth grade he began to find himself. He was big for his age, tall and sturdy and good at sports. He never had close friends, but he gained acceptance from his peers through his physical prowess and from adults by his careful politeness and sharp intelligence.

He grew increasingly alienated from his family. His brother, Scott, was fifteen, getting into trouble, flunking in school. His sister, Ginny, was thirteen and colorless.

His father, Keith, still drank heavily. By this time he had lost his job, lost his driver's license. He worked at another car rental agency, but now he washed the vehicles and cleaned out other people's dirt.

His mother had been beaten down by life; the battles were less frequent. Becky gave up.

Finn was ashamed of his family. Teachers at school sympathized with him, became mentors. His fifth grade teacher was a man, the first male teacher he'd ever had, and he learned a lot about how men behaved from Mr. Lundgren. He'd go home and practice gestures in front *of the bathroom mirror, say things he'd heard Mr. Lundgren say. He stayed after school often and took home books lent him by his teacher:* Tom Sawyer, Black Beauty, Tarzan the Apeman. *He read every word, hiding the books under his mattress at home, because his brother would rip them into pieces if he found them.*

Finn started picking up odd jobs that long cold Milwaukee winter. Shoveling sidewalks and driveways, chopping ice buildup from paths. The money he earned gave him fierce satisfaction. He couldn't bear to spend it. His money, too, he had to hide or Scott would snatch it.

He concealed his repugnance for his father, concealed his tears of shame and fear and hopelessness. And rage. A child's deep-seated and inarticulate rage at the unfairness of his existence.

Finn was on his fourth night out in a row and his third woman. The first two evenings had belonged to Suzanne. The third, Donna, and now he was accompanying Julie to the season opening of Tchaikovsky's *Nutcracker,* in the Auditorium Theatre in the Denver Performing Arts Complex—locally referred to as the Plex.

Christmas was around the corner, and Finn's dance card was full.

He folded the playbill in two and slipped it into the pocket of his tuxedo jacket then took Julie's arm, escorting her to their front-row mezzanine seats.

Julie Barrow looked exquisite. She was a twenty-three-year-old model, five foot eleven in her stocking feet, with long, shining, chestnut-colored hair and a reed-thin figure, all legs and slender arms and the neck of a white swan. She wore a simple but elegant calf-length green velvet dress with a deep V that showed off her not-so-natural cleavage. The dress had long sleeves and fit her like a glove. For jewelry she wore a tasteful string of pearls and small matching pearl studs in her earlobes. She wore almost no makeup. Didn't need it.

Finn loved parading his women in front of Denver's finest. He lifted a hand in greeting to the Buckleys and the Romers. The Huntleys and the Butlers and the Greengards all nodded in acknowledgment of Finn's presence. David Chew shot Finn a wide smile at Finn's choice of company for the evening. He and David had once, not so long ago, shared three women in a hotel suite. The experience had been interesting but not Finn's thing. His tastes lay elsewhere.

The lights dimmed and he lifted Julie's long fingers to his lips and kissed them then returned them to her lap, his still covering hers.

"I remember *The Nutcracker* from when I was a little girl," Julie whispered close to his ear, and he felt a tingling in his groin. This excited him. It wasn't often a woman turned him on so easily. Perhaps tonight he'd reach fulfillment.

The ballet was lovely, all those adorable little dancing girls twisting and turning and pointing their tiny toes, their cherub faces made up for the stage, their smiles twanging Finn's heartstrings.

In the second act a new dancer appeared on stage, a girl perhaps in her early twenties. There was something about her, something in the extraordinary grace of her movements, the short, curling dark hair that framed her pretty face, and the way the entire audience instantly responded to her presence, as if she'd carried her own light onto the stage.

It took Finn a moment. Then he had it. The girl reminded him of Ellie.

He'd tried to put Ellie Kramer from his thoughts. There were dozens of reasons Finn did not want to remember her, not the least of which was the fact she was from Boulder, a *law* student, for the love of God, and he shied away from anything connected to that snobbish city where he'd made the amateurish mistake with the Morris girl. He hated that memory, and he hated Boulder because of it.

Forget her, he told himself. Hell, he could have any woman he desired. He didn't need or want the Kramer woman.

After the ballet, Finn took his lady friend to a downtown nightspot on Larimer Square. It was crowded with after-theater-goers who were all high with holiday spirits. Julie was quite a hit in the elegant mass of humanity, and Finn noted many men's eyes fixing on her to the dismay of their women. Julie was a knockout. He felt proud to have her adoring gaze riveted on him and only on him.

But then he saw Ellie again in his mind's eye. He frowned in annoyance. So what if she were pretty, ardent, a warm fire in a cold world? So were plenty of females, especially the very young ones whose bodies had just blossomed. He didn't need some goddamn smart law student cluttering up his well-ordered existence. She spelled trouble. And, besides, he told himself, she hadn't seemed terribly responsive. *Let sleeping dogs lie,* he mused, and he turned the hypnotic weight of his charm onto Julie.

"You know," he said, "every man in this place wants you."

"Don't be silly," she whispered.

But he laughed. "They do. Honest. And for the life of me, I don't know why I should be so lucky."

"You're embarrassing me." She didn't look embarrassed, though; she looked pleased as punch.

He made love to her in the master bedroom suite at his Cherry Creek home. He'd turned out the lights before even undressing her, imagining that he was stripping the clothes from one of his young girls, maybe Peta. Julie's artificially enhanced breasts were a problem, however, so he avoided touching them, concentrating on her slim, almost boyish hips, that did indeed remind him of youth.

He entered her, lost in a whirling maelstrom of disjointed faces: Stephanie Naomi Amy Holly Peta, noses mouths eyes. Spinning. He even whispered thickly in Julie's ear for her to struggle. "It's just a game, darling, it's stupid but it turns me on."

Obviously, it turned Julie on, too. She was quite good at it. Oh, yes, he'd climax for sure. He imaged Peta's face, still so fresh in his mind, and felt Peta twisting beneath him, terrified.

Finn carefully, calculatingly, put his hands on Julie's neck. Oh, how he'd like to tighten his fingers and press his thumbs against her collarbone. He could only pretend, though, and lose himself in fantasy. But it was still good. He thrust, panting. *Good. Yes. Yes.* He was nearly there. . . .

And then he saw Ellie, Ellie beneath him. And it was as if someone had let the air out of him. He withered and shrank and realized he was no longer connected to the woman beneath him.

What in hell?

He rolled away. Furious.

"Finn? What is it?"

He wanted suddenly to strike her, to lash out and bloody that perfect model's face.

He knew he had to say something. Anything. "It's not you, darling," he whispered into the darkness, gentle-voiced, concerned, charmer that he was. "It's ridiculous, and I'm so sorry . . ."

"But . . . ?"

"Just an old football injury. It crops up sometimes. An old groin injury that has a mind of its own. Just give me a few minutes."

He knew a few minutes weren't going to help. He'd deal with Julie somehow. He'd dealt with dozens of Julies before.

Goddamn it, he thought, rising, padding toward the bathroom. "I'll see if a shower won't work it out," he said in an apologetic tone. "You're a saint, Julie."

He took a long hot shower then a cold one. He knew Julie was out there waiting, expectant, disappointed but hopeful. Still, all he could see was the face, that strangely radiant face of law student Eleanor Kramer. He truly hated her.

Ellie looked up from her notepad, took her glasses off, and smiled in genuine sympathy at Holly Lance. "I know how difficult this must be," she offered.

But Holly only sighed. "Have you ever been raped, Miss . . . ?"

"It's Ellie. And, no, I haven't. I'm sorry I said that. It was stupid. I should have said I can't imagine how awful it is to even think about it. If these questions weren't so important, I wouldn't be here dragging you through this again."

"Did my mom give you my address?" Holly asked.

"No, actually, she didn't want me to talk to you at all."

"So how . . . ?"

"I found out you were in Fort Collins from a neighbor of your mother. I called Colorado State University and got your number from Student Services."

"They don't usually give that out." Holly peered suspiciously at Ellie. She wasn't dumb.

"No, they don't. It was a request from the DA's office in Boulder. I told you I clerk there. . . ." *Lies lies lies.*

"I know what you said. I just don't know why the Boulder DA would be interested in me."

"It isn't you, Holly, specifically. We're doing a new database on rape victims. You can understand the value of keeping our records linked up with other cities on the Front Range."

"Sure," the student said. "Let's just get this over with."

"I agree," Ellie said. There was nothing she would like more. She was sick of the lies, the half-truths, the juggling. She sometimes felt as if she'd juggle one of the balls too high, and then they'd all tumble to the ground. It was only a matter of time. Her job, her boss, her roommates, Michael—oh, he was perhaps the most dangerous game she was playing—and now Finn. She'd outsmarted herself with him, hadn't she? Played the game too close to the edge and lost. And she couldn't very well bump into him "accidentally" again. She should have been more interested. She'd let her ego take control. Dumb, dumb.

She let out a breath and focused on Holly again. "Okay, just a few more questions, all right?"

"Go on."

Ellie put her glasses back on. "Did you ever see your assailant, even for just a second, before he struck you?"

"I told you already, I was upstairs checking on my brother. My stepfather hit me from behind. It was lights out. I barely remember any of it. Thank God," she added bitterly.

Ellie nodded. "I need to ask you something that may sound strange now. Will you bear with me?"

Holly made a noncommittal sound.

"Okay. I've read the police report and your statement, of course. But nowhere did I see you actually say it was Bob Lance who attacked you."

"Jesus, what are you getting at? What are you . . . ?"

Ellie put up a hand. "Just bear with me, please. I'm asking if you're sure it was your stepfather."

"Of course it was that bastard! How could you—"

"Please," Ellie said, "just think back. What made you certain it was him?"

"Try his belt around my neck, for chrissakes, lady!"

Ellie nodded. "Yes, I know it was his belt. But was there anything else? His size or shape? His clothes? The scent of an aftershave? Anything . . . ?"

"It was Bob Lance who *raped* me! Are you crazy? What's going on here? I want to know. . . ."

Ellie took her glasses off, put them in their case, and closed the notebook. "I've upset you," she said, rising. "I truly apologize."

Holly Lance said nothing. She only glared at Ellie through unshed tears. Ellie left the student housing a few minutes later. She drove Celeste's car out of the college town of Fort Collins, not even stopping to gas it up, as she'd intended, and she didn't stop till she was exiting the interstate in Boulder. She felt the size of an ant.

Ben Torres sat at his cluttered desk, fingers steepled under his chin, engaged in his favorite pastime—watching Ellie through the open door of his office.

He was feeling down. As low as he had ever felt in his life. It wasn't his job. He loved his work. It wasn't the Zimmerman trial, which was going along quite well, from the prosecution's standpoint. It was his marriage.

It had been three months—no, almost four now—since

he and Marie had had sex. Four months of her headaches, periods, sprained backs from lifting tables at bazaars, exhaustion, telephone calls that simply couldn't wait, appointments, charity events, and even goddamn morning breath.

"Oh, Ben, honey, I should brush my teeth." Had she really said that?

He didn't even want sex anymore. Christ, he just wanted to hold the woman. Five minutes. That was all.

He watched as Ellie rose from her partitioned office and walked to the door leading to the hall. She was toting files. He'd bet she was on her way to Records.

Don't do it. Forget it, he told himself. *Don't fucking do it.*

Ellie's hand flew to her chest and she gasped and dropped the Crandall files onto the cold concrete floor.

"Ben . . . Mr. Torres," she breathed, "you scared me half to death."

"I'm sorry, Ellie, I didn't mean to startle you."

She was trapped in a corner with him, her heart slamming against her ribs. All alone in a dimly lit corner of Records. But worse than that, he'd caught her with files that she shouldn't be looking at, much less taking home.

Ben put a hand on the painted cement block wall next to her and leaned a little closer. "What have you got there, Miss Kramer?" He was smiling, looking down at the file containing the twelve-year-old testimony of Finn Rasmussen during her father's trial. *Shit, shit.*

Smiling herself, Ellie coyly hid the file behind her back. "I wanted to surprise you. It's something I thought might put the nail in Zimmerman's coffin."

"Oh, really? Maybe I could help?"

"No, no," she said too quickly. "I mean, it isn't panning out the way I'd hoped."

"Then let me look at it. I remember those law clerk days, the research, all the files and law books. I used to be pretty good at it, too. Maybe if we got together . . . ?"

"Oh, gosh," she said, "I really want to do this on my own. It isn't that I don't appreciate . . ."

He straightened a bit, and his face grew serious. "Listen," he said, "it's not the work, Ellie. I was really hoping that we could . . . Well, I'm not very good at this." He gave a strained laugh. "Look, would you like to get a drink or something after work?"

Ellie's heart dropped to her feet. "Mr. Torres," she said. Then she had to start again. "*Ben,* I, I don't know what to say."

"Say yes then."

He was so close. And her hands were clasping the file behind her back, making her feel terribly vulnerable. She had to get out of this. Without alienating him. *Talk about work-related sexual harassment,* she thought darkly, and then she realized why so little of it was reported. You didn't dare.

She took a breath. "Listen, I have to be honest, Ben. You're a very attractive man. I'm not just saying that, either. But you *are* married. That's important to me. But if you weren't . . . I mean, if the situation changes someday . . ."

He straightened. "I understand," he said.

"Do you?"

"Yes." Then he gave another tight laugh. "I feel like an ass, you know. I've never done this before. I'd fire someone who did it, in fact. *Jesus.*" He ran a hand through his fine dark hair.

Suddenly she felt sad for him. She shouldn't, but there

it was. "Listen, Ben, I'm not upset or anything. Not at all. I'm flattered." And she was. "You didn't do anything. You asked me out for a drink. No big deal."

"You're . . . sure? I mean, you could go screaming up those steps, yell sexual harassment, you know?"

"Don't be silly."

"We're okay about it, then?"

"We're perfectly fine. Let's go on upstairs, okay?"

"You bet, Ellie, yeah, let's do that," he said.

But that was the last time she attempted to smuggle a file home.

Over the next few days she changed strategy, spending whatever free time she could find at the CU library, looking through microfilm of Denver newspapers and magazines. She searched for anything there was about Finn Rasmussen, eligible bachelor. And there was plenty.

Grainy black-and-white photos of Finn at various social events, charity balls, cultural programs, openings of exhibits at the Museum of Fine Arts.

He was a busy boy. And there was invariably a gorgeous young female on his arm.

She found him in the *Denver Post,* the *Rocky Mountain News, Westword, Colorado Expression.* Handsome, dressed in a tux often enough, smiling. She learned that he gave to many different charities, that he liked to ski in the winter and sail in the summer. Deep-sea fishing and scuba diving were favorites of his, too.

She sat at one of the microfilm machines in the library and read an article about his business, Mountaintech Security. How quickly it had grown, how astute a businessman Rasmussen was, how his company might, in the future, go public. The article even contained a short background of Mountaintech's owner, describing how he'd been a Boulder policeman and received a commendation for solving the Morris case.

"Oh, God," Ellie whispered, and she pushed herself away from the machine, removed her glasses, and sat there for a moment.

She knew he'd been at the Morris house. Of course she knew. He and Michael. But seeing it in the newspaper was hard to take—she hadn't been prepared. She sat in the hushed library and thought back to the morning she'd spent in his company, and it was increasingly hard to imagine the outgoing, vibrant man as a murderer.

Then her thoughts took a 180-degree turn. She was judging a book by its cover, and she should know better. Look at how outgoing and personable Ted Bundy had been. An all-American college type, a regular Joe.

She needed to get to know Finn. But with each passing day that he didn't call, her chances were growing dimmer.

The next morning she woke with a full-blown cold. Runny nose, sore throat, cough. She swallowed a handful of vitamin C tablets and forced herself to go to work, her pocket full of tissues.

Ben was in court all day, but Ellie stayed in the office, coughing, sneezing, blowing her nose, typing up briefs for a burglary case that was on the docket after the Zimmerman trial. She felt lousy.

"Why don't you go home?" Mary, the receptionist, said. "You sound awful."

"I will. I just want to finish this one thing." Her head ached, and she felt as if she could lie down and sleep forever.

"Drink a lot of fluids and get some rest," Mary said.

"I'll try."

The phone on her desk rang at about three, when she

was printing out the last of her briefs. She picked it up, coughed to clear her throat, but even so, her voice sounded nasal and hoarse.

"Ellie? Is that you?"

"Yes, I have a cold. Michael?"

"Yeah, it's me. You sound like hell. Why aren't you home?"

"Well, I have these briefs. . . ."

"Forget it. I'll pick you up and give you a ride. Twenty minutes?"

She hesitated. It had been over a week since she'd seen him. He'd had a couple of night shifts; she'd been busy—the hours in the library researching Finn. Then there'd been the hasty excuses, her fear that she'd weaken and slip again. But she'd never get to the bottom of her father's case if she kept faltering.

"Ellie?"

"Twenty minutes?" she said. "I'll be out front."

She was waiting near the entrance, and she saw him drive up. She climbed into his tall black truck and sighed. "This is great," she said.

"You should take care of yourself, Ellie." He pulled out of the parking lot of the Justice Center.

"That's what my mother says." She took a tissue from her pocket and blew her nose. "Sorry."

"Maybe you should stay home for a few days."

"I'd go nuts." She sighed and settled back against the seat. Miserable.

In the end he didn't just drop her off; he insisted on seeing her inside. She led him into the kitchen, where they made hot tea.

"Look at this mess," she said, eyeing the sink. She slumped down into a chair at the kitchen table and put her head in her hands.

Michael made the tea and liberally laced it with honey. "Your roommates at class?" He set the steaming mug in front of her.

"I guess."

"Well, you ought to drink this and get some rest." He sat across from her.

"I'll try."

"Drink up."

The tea tasted good. *Felt* good, actually, because even her taste buds were messed up. She wanted to talk to him, to let him know she was still interested, but she felt too horrible to deal with the game, the lies.

"How's the trial going?" he asked.

"Good."

"Think they'll finish up before the Christmas holiday?"

Ellie slowly shook her head. "I doubt it."

"That'll piss the jury off."

"How's that?"

"Would you want to take a couple weeks off then have to come back in and sit there again, put up with all that posturing the lawyers go through?"

"No, I guess not."

The front door opened then banged shut. Michael pivoted.

"Celeste. She always bangs the door."

Celeste tossed her coat on the couch then poked her head into the kitchen. "You must be the detective. I'm Celeste, the brains of the outfit."

Michael stood and shook her hand. "Callas—Michael, that is."

Celeste eyed him. "The pleasure is all mine." Flirting.

"Not now, please," Ellie groaned.

"Uh-oh," Celeste said, "still feeling rotten?"

"Miserable."

"Well, then, I'll let you two off the hook. I've got to change, anyway. Hot date."

"Nice to have met you," Michael said.

"We'll have to do this again." Celeste smiled, waved, and disappeared, the staircase creaking.

"Been roommates for long?" Michael asked then.

"Forever."

"Um," he said. "Well, I'll let you get some rest." He stood again. "I . . . Never mind."

Ellie looked up. "What?"

He shrugged. "Nothing."

"No. Go on."

But he wouldn't, and she hadn't the energy to push. All he said was, "I'll call you."

"I'd like that," she replied, still sitting there, and then she could have sworn he muttered something like *Would you?* The next thing she knew he was going. Had she blown that, too? Just as she'd blown it with Finn?

Her head reeled. Michael, Finn. Which one? Which one was guilty? Or, perhaps, neither of them was and she'd wasted all these years, half her life, on a useless quest.

Ellie felt much better by Thursday. She'd gone back to work, even though her nose was still running, and red and chapped, as well. But she was getting over the worst of her cold.

Michael hadn't called, and she wondered about that a lot. She'd thought they'd gotten along. He'd been so solicitous that day, driving her home. He was an endless puzzle to her, leaving her dangling, not knowing, ever, what to expect.

She closed her briefcase, got her coat and boots on, and left the Justice Center to go home that afternoon. Michael still hadn't called, and the weekend was coming up. She didn't know if she was relieved or terribly disappointed.

She walked the familiar route home, along the bike path that followed Boulder Creek. Where did she go from here? She hadn't gotten anywhere at all, really. So much for all her great plans, her good intentions, her lifelong goal. As she walked she tried to think of what to do next, how to attack the problem. Start pilfering files again?

She pushed open the rattly old door with the big brass doorknob, felt the welcome heat of the house surround her. She'd think of something. She'd have to. Her quest couldn't end here.

"Hey," she heard Bonnie call out. "Hey, is that you, Ellie?"

"Yes, it's me."

"Message for you by the phone. He had a great voice."

Message. She stepped over, glanced at the pad of paper. *Call Finn,* it said. Just that: *Call Finn.*

Ellie drew in her breath. He'd finally called, goddamn it, he'd called.

She tossed her briefcase onto the kitchen table, and she did an impromptu jig.

"What the hell?" Bonnie said, coming into the kitchen.

"He called," Ellie said. "Yes. *Yess!*"

ELEVEN

Michael was pouring his first cup of morning coffee at the department when the report came in.

"Callas, Augostino, and Goldman," the dispatcher called out, "we've got shots fired, Thirty-seventh just off Baseline Road." He gave the exact address. "Two units are on their way."

"Shit," Goldman muttered, snatching his coat off the back of his chair.

"Haven't even had breakfast," Rick Augostino groused, scratching his head, looking longingly at his bag of doughnuts.

Michael said nothing. He put down the half-filled coffee mug and got his gun and shoulder holster from where they hung on his chair and slipped them on. *Shots fired,* he thought, *great.*

They signed out two unmarked cars, Michael in one and Augostino and Goldman in the other. Baseline and Thirty-seventh wasn't all that far, and Michael figured the uniforms would be just minutes ahead. They all listened to the radio for updates, but evidently the neighbor who'd phoned in the gunshots was elderly and hiding out in her house.

Hell, Michael thought, the red bubble on the dashboard flashing, it could have been a car backfiring. Happened all the time.

The first thing Michael saw when he got to the address was a patrol car parked at an odd angle to the curb, then he noted the front door of the modest clapboard house standing wide open, and one of the uniforms from the patrol car was leaning over some snow-covered juniper bushes puking his guts out.

So much for a car having backfired.

Michael got out and was informed by the other cop from the patrol car that there was a dead body right inside the front door and that, as far as he could tell, the area was secure.

"We'll just see about that," said Rick Augostino as he strode up to Michael, his service revolver drawn.

As it turned out the assailant had been seen fleeing the area by two neighbors. They even had the make and model of the car and a partial on the plate.

"I'll see if I can get an address," Goldman said. "Hey, Callas, you wanna check the victim?"

"Oh, sure," Michael said. He shrugged at Rick. "Let's do it."

They found the victim right inside the door where the patrol cop had first seen her. She was lying half on her side, still wearing a bathrobe. Her face had been blown off.

"Jesus motherfuckin' Christ," Rick whispered, turning away for a moment.

Michael didn't say a word.

The coroner's tech got there quickly. He took time examining the body in situ, photographing it, searching for wounds, weapons, and identification. He talked a lot, lecturing Michael and the other cops, as if it were a complicated shooting, which it wasn't.

"Now, here we go, one shotgun blast to the face. Cause of death. Does mucho damage, see, fellas? The shooter took the weapon with him, ran like hell, I'm guessing. Anyone know who she is? Norma who? There's her bag over there. Hold on, I'll look. Gotta be official."

And all the while they awaited an address on the partial plate number from the DMV. Michael had spoken to the elderly neighbor who'd made the nine-one-one call and was fairly certain who the perp was—the estranged husband. She'd recognized his blue Blazer.

They'd get him. Even if the bastard fled the state, fled the country, they'd get his ass. No one, no man had a right to do this to a woman. Why was it always the women who were hurt? Had their faces blown off? Beat up, raped, murdered?

While the crime scene technicians moved in to do their grisly work, Michael stood in the cold December morning and thought about Rasmussen—the one who *had* gotten away.

Michael had suspected him for years. When they'd been assigned to the same patrol car, long before the Morris case, Michael had gotten bad vibes from the man. Nothing he'd been able to put a finger on. But something that left a sour taste in his mouth.

Then that night—it had been thirteen years ago—Michael had phoned Finn a dozen times, needing a ride to their ten P.M. shift. There'd been no answer. But later, on the way over to the Morris residence, when he'd asked Finn where he'd been earlier, Rasmussen had lied through his teeth, said he'd been on the phone with some chick. "Man, like an hour and a half," he'd said. Michael never mentioned having called Finn's number over and over and hearing it ring each time.

There had been other aspects of the Morris rape case that had bothered Michael, not the least of which had been John Crandall himself, an educated man, by all accounts a family man, honest, trustworthy, leaving his very identifiable bandana around the girl's neck. Then there'd been Finn. The chilling glow on his face that whole long night. It had taken Michael a few years to see the full picture. A few years and a few more victims and a lot more experience, but then he'd started to put it together. The only thing lacking was motive. What could have turned Rasmussen into a serial rapist and murderer?

A few months. A few phone calls. And Michael had a motive. According to a juvenile caseworker in Finn's hometown of Milwaukee, Finn might very well have been a rape victim himself. His own uncle.

At that point, Michael had gone to his superiors. And had gotten in a shitload of trouble.

He'd needed proof. Hard evidence. He still didn't have it.

Someday, he thought, some goddamn day, Rasmussen was going to slip up and Michael would be on him like a fly on stink.

DMV came through with a license plate match shortly before noon. The old blue two-tone Chevy Blazer seen driving away from the crime belonged to one Lou Diggs. The twenty-three-year-old woman lying inside the house was Norma Diggs, his estranged wife. They figured they had their man. Now all they had to do was find him.

Lou Diggs's address was in a small mobile home park on the other side of town between Yarmouth and Twenty-eighth Streets. Rick called for backup; a single unit was left to make sure the crime scene stayed secure, and the rest of them headed across town. Michael couldn't help his thoughts: Maybe the son of a bitch Diggs had done himself, too, by this time—save them all a lot of trouble, not to mention taxpayer dollars.

Diggs had not done himself. When the fleet of cops pulled up, he took a couple of shots with a ten-gauge out his front window and then holed up behind drawn curtains.

Michael had never fired his weapon except on the target range in all his years on the force. But he knew the drill: He made sure the clip was locked into the handle and slid the first shell into the chamber with a quick, practiced motion. He heard a lot of metal sliding against metal as the cops surrounded the trailer.

Along with the sounds of men readying their weapons, came the rush of testosterone, a high that seized policemen in this kind of standoff. Michael had been in a few of these situations before, and the flood of adrenaline was familiar. Every sense alert, muscles twitching, concentration narrowed to the scratched door of the trailer and the window, its glass broken out, its dirty white curtains flapping in the gusts of cold wind. He welcomed the rush—it could save his life.

SWAT arrived from Denver forty minutes after Diggs had pumped a couple more out his window. The news teams, satellite trucks, the works, were right on the heels of SWAT. And Michael somehow found himself in charge.

He spoke to the head of SWAT. "We wait it out," he said.

"For how long?" the SWAT commander wanted to know. His blood was up, too.

"For as long as it takes," Michael said.

It took three hours and ten minutes. One hundred and

ninety of the longest minutes of Michael's life. Despite
Rick at his side behind their open car doors, the normally
chatty Rick Augostino, hardly a word was spoken. Occasionally the negotiator, who'd come up from Denver,
tried to make contact with Diggs on a bullhorn, but the
man wasn't in a communicating mood. Repeated efforts
to reach him on his phone failed; they could all hear it
ringing and ringing, shrill in the cold silence that surrounded the trailer park.

"Maybe the dude is dead?" Rick said once hopefully.

But Michael thought not. He would have rigged the
ten-gauge in his mouth, and they would have heard it for
sure.

Halfway through the wait the wind began to kick up,
that notorious Front Range wind. At first it was just a
steady, bone-chilling blow, but then the gusts started.
They all knew it would get worse, and it did. Rattling
open car doors, tearing at winter jackets, shaking the
trailer where Lou Diggs was holded up. One gust must
have hit eighty miles an hour, Michael figured.

His thoughts drifted. He saw Norma Diggs—the face-
less Norma—and wondered what she had looked like.
Did she have parents nearby? Were they already over at
the coroner's IDing their child? Then he remembered his
own parents, their trip down to the hospital where Paul
had died. They hadn't let Michael come, and he'd always, reluctantly, had this horrible image of his brother
in death. Even now he shied away from the mental picture.

He thought about Ellie then, telling himself it was just
a way to pass the time, to keep from thinking too much
about Diggs in that trailer or how cold the wind was.
Ellie. Okay. So maybe he *was* obsessed with her. So
maybe she had him as sexually frustrated as a sixteen-

year-old. He couldn't believe she'd do that on purpose. Conversely, he wasn't buying her lame excuses for not sleeping with him again. Hell, *she* started the relationship. Yet she didn't seem to want it to end, either.

He was missing something. He felt as if he were investigating a homicide and hadn't quite put the picture together; a crucial piece of the puzzle was eluding him.

The wind got worse as the standoff continued. The men could barely hear themselves talk when the gusts hit.

"Goddamn," Rick said next to Michael. "Order SWAT to go in."

"Not yet." Michael blew on his fingers. He couldn't wear gloves and fire his weapon effectively.

"This sucks," Rick went on.

"Yeah," Michael concurred, and then the front door of the trailer flew open and every officer jolted to attention.

"What the hell . . . ?" someone nearby said, and they all saw it at once, a white towel held out on a long wooden broom handle.

Lou Diggs gave up.

It was Goldman, on the way back to headquarters, the heater blasting in Michael's car, who said, "Can you believe it? That little coward blew his wife away and didn't even have the guts to do himself. *Jesus.*"

"Yeah," Michael said, "I can believe it. Guys who hurt women are cowards at heart."

And he thought not of Diggs, but of Finn Rassmusen.

He caught Ellie as she was getting ready to leave the Justice Center for the day. When she saw him her eyes widened.

"You were there, weren't you?" she asked breathlessly. "We watched the standoff on TV all day. That man . . ."

"It looked worse than it turned out."

"You didn't know that when it was happening."

He shrugged.

"Oh, stop acting like it was nothing. It was a terrible thing."

"Yeah, it was. A woman is dead for no good reason." He was surprised at the angry edge to his voice.

She put her hand on his arm. "I'm glad you're okay. I was worried."

"I wasn't in danger."

"Sure, right." She grew pensive for a minute. "And now we'll have to prosecute that poor guy."

"Poor guy?"

"He's suffering, he must be."

"And his wife is *dead.*"

She cocked her head and studied him, not saying a word.

"Look, I didn't come over here to talk about that. Let me give you a ride home."

"Sure, that'd be great." She grabbed her coat and briefcase, and they made their way down the corridor, past Courtroom B, where the Zimmerman trial was recessing for the Christmas holidays. They had to squeeze around clots of people exiting the double doors of the courtroom, milling about.

"I'm parked across the street in the big lot," he said. The light was fading, and the same raw wind was still howling down out of the Flatirons.

"Brr," Ellie said, hugging herself.

"I thought you might want to do something this weekend," he said. "Ski maybe?"

"Oh, Michael, I can't." She sounded genuinely regretful, but an alarm went off in his head.

"I . . . I really don't feel all that great yet, and I promised Celeste I'd go Christmas shopping with her, and . . ."

"Okay, I get the idea."

"No, really, I'm sorry. I'd love to, but this weekend isn't good."

"Fine."

"You believe me, don't you?"

"Yeah, sure." He pressed on, knowing he shouldn't, but unable to stop himself from testing her. "Then how about a long weekend over the holidays? At the chalet."

"I'm not sure when I'll be in Leadville." She was looking up at him, a frown pulling at her brows. "I try to spend a lot of time with my mother over the holidays. You know."

They were coming up to his truck. He walked next to her, feeling the swift despair of her rejection. She was playing with him, the way a cat plays with a mouse—let it think it was safe for a second then pounce and tear and hurt. He felt his temper start to erode.

"Michael?" she asked uncertainly.

Something inside him broke, as if a dam suddenly gave way. He spun around, grabbed her shoulders, and pinned her against the door of his truck. Her eyes were wide and scared.

"What the fuck do you think you're doing?" he asked harshly, holding her there.

"What? Michael . . . I . . ."

"What's going on? What game are you playing?"

She stared, her lip quivering, moisture gathering in her eyes. Without thinking, he bent his head and kissed her hard, crushing her mouth, pressing his body to hers. He could feel her squirming beneath him, hear the small sounds of protest in her throat. But he moved his mouth over hers, and for a short time she was his.

He kept her there, pressed against the truck, helpless

and imprisoned, taking the whole rotten day out on her, wanting her, needing her, taking her against her will because he couldn't admit what a shitty day he'd had. He only became cognizant of what he'd done when she managed to get her hands between them and pushed with surprising strength.

He backed off instantly, reason flooding him. And shame. But his anger still roiled close to the surface. He stood over her, leaning on his hands, one on either side of her, breathing hard. "I'm sorry, I shouldn't have done that. But, goddamn it, I'm through with your games, Ellie. You run hot, you run cold. I can't deal with that."

She relaxed then, her back still against his truck. "I'm sorry, too. I didn't mean . . . I'm just . . . God, Michael, I'm confused. You're . . . not easy."

He looked down at her face, her bruised lips. He knew she was right about him, but still, she was making him crazy. Too many paradoxes. Too many secrets.

"Michael," she said softly. "I'm sorry, I really am. I like you. I just don't want to go too fast. We don't know each other very well." Then she reached a hand up and pulled his head down to hers and kissed him on the lips, gently, like a sister.

He knew she was acting. She didn't mean a word of it. Why was she bothering to placate him? She was driving him out of his mind.

"Shit," he muttered. "Get in the truck." He stood back. But Ellie shook her head. "I'll walk."

"Get in the truck," he repeated.

"I think it's better if I don't. I'll walk. It's not far."

"I know how goddamn far it is."

"Michael, go home. Okay? We'll talk later."

"When?"

"Later," she said. She picked up her briefcase from

where she'd dropped it, straightened, and flung one end of her red scarf back. "Good night, Michael." And she started to stride way, the wind tearing at her coat, flapping her scarf like a banner.

He wanted to call her back, he wanted to kiss her again, he didn't know what the hell he wanted, so he just stood there in the parking lot, his expression flat, and watched her until she was out of sight, and even then he stood there.

"Martin Lester? Wow," Bonnie said. "He's a big shot."

"I know," Ellie said. She was looking through her closet, pulling out every dressy piece of clothing she owned.

"No," Bonnie said. "No, nope."

"You don't have a thing that's right." Jenn lifted her shoulders and dropped them.

"Well, how often do I get invited to this kind of event?" Ellie was ridiculously nervous and excited, playing Cinderella, getting dressed to go to the ball with the handsome prince. It wasn't like her at all.

"Let's go look in Celeste's closet. I have a great dress, but it won't fit you."

Bonnie found the dress for her. A high neckline and long sleeves in sheer black, then a knee-length dress, fitted from the bust down.

"I have to ask Celeste," Ellie said.

"She won't care. Try it on."

Jennifer provided her with a pair of strappy, high-heeled sandals to go with it, because they wore the same size shoe.

"Not bad," Jenn said, eyeing her.

Celeste arrived home from class a few minutes later, and climbed the stairs to see Ellie's outfit.

"Perfect," she said.

"You don't mind?"

"Hell, no. It looks great on you."

"Thanks, ladies," Ellie said, and she meant it. Her friends were precious to her, family really. About the only family she had.

"Where're you going?" Celeste asked.

"A Christmas party at Martin Lester's."

"The food'll be good. And you're going with the other one?"

"Finn," Ellie said.

"Finn, right. The one with the voice." Celeste stood, tall and skinny, hands on her hips. "What's the deal, Kramer? You've been avoiding men like the plague for years, and now all of a sudden you're seeing a cop *and* a Denver playboy, too?"

"Funny how it works out" was all Ellie said. God, how she yearned to confide in her friend, talk her wild scheme over with levelheaded Celeste. But she couldn't. Even if Celeste agreed with her plan, she couldn't bear any of her roommates knowing who she really was. She hated the secret that was her daily companion; she hated it yet she held it closely, fiercely, a part of her too familiar to abandon.

Her outfit lying on her bed, she took a shower and washed her hair, shaved her legs. She thought of Michael, unable to pull her thoughts from him. She'd seen a different side to him, and it had alarmed her. If he could do that to her, then he could certainly be violent with other women.

But she had to admit he was right about the games she was playing. She shut her eyes and let the hot water wash over her, as if it might cleanse the guilt she felt. She'd toyed with Michael, and he'd realized it. You can't do that to an insecure man, she thought. It was dangerous.

She tried to put Michael out of her mind. In a few days, she'd call him, or maybe he'd call her. But his temper . . . She shivered under the hot water.

She'd think about Finn, who was picking her up in an hour. She tried to imagine how he'd look, how she'd look, what the party would be like. All those rich people. Not her crowd. Finn's crowd.

Stepping out of the shower she dried her hair with a towel. Slathered lotion all over her body, sprayed perfume on her wrists and neck. She could feel the nervousness bubbling up from deep in her belly.

She was dressed: Bonnie's pearl choker and earrings, Celeste's dress, Jenn's shoes, over her arm one of Celeste's coats, a calf-length, silky tan coat, fully lined in mink.

"Go for it," Jenn said. Proudly.

"We approve," Celeste said, studying Ellie, her head on one side.

"Thank God for all of you," Ellie said fervently.

They heard his car pull up out front. Ellie took a deep breath, suddenly scared. Out of her league. She heard his footsteps approach the front door, and for a split second she wished ardently that it was Michael walking up the front steps. No, no. She couldn't think that. She couldn't falter, not now, when she'd been given a reprieve.

"Wish me luck," she whispered to her three friends. Then she curved her lips into a welcoming smile and went to open the door.

There was no turning back now.

TWELVE

Seductive, exciting, enchanting. Sitting in Finn's car, with its rich scent of leather, feeling beautiful, the fur lining of Celeste's coat tickling her cheek, Ellie's mind conjured up those notions. This was a new experience for her, a first, and she felt as if she'd been touched by a magic wand.

Cinderella.

Finn pulled up to the brightly lit house, which sat on Washington Park, a most prestigious Denver address. He opened her door, handed her out, and a valet whisked the car away. She was swept up the broad stairs, to the columned entranceway, inside to the impact of warmth and voices and music and the aromas of the holiday.

The butler took her coat, and she almost broke into laughter, wild, hysterical laughter. The *butler*. And it was her roommate's coat! She barely had time to collect herself when Finn took her arm and guided her over to the host and hostess, Mr. and Mrs. Martin Lester.

"What a charming dress," Hillary Lester said, taking both of Ellie's hands in hers, and the woman nodded approvingly at Finn. "Have you been keeping Miss Kramer a secret?"

"Yes," Finn said, "I certainly have."

"I can see why," Martin Lester said.

The bantering, the easy witticisms. And Finn fit right in. Ellie glanced sideways at him. He was smiling, relaxed, so handsome in his tuxedo. She took a deep breath. Was this real?

"Go on, enjoy the party," Hillary Lester was saying, "and save me a dance, Finn."

"I will. And I'll try not to step on your toes this time."

Ellie could think of nothing pithy to say. "Thank you so much for having me" was all she got out.

Finn led her past a knot of guests who were talking and drinking champagne punch around the beautiful Christmas tree that was the centerpiece of the huge marble-tiled entranceway. The hall had what must have been a thirty-foot ceiling and a lovely Victorian staircase that swept in a wide curve to a second story and finally curved yet again to a third-story landing. Holly and red velvet bows twined around the entire railing.

"Hillary is a sweetheart," Finn was saying in Ellie's ear, still guiding her into the bowels of the Victorian mansion. "But don't let her fool you. She's got a Ph.D. and an honorary doctorate from Oxford. Anthropology, I think."

"She seems very nice," Ellie said, craning her neck at the tree as they passed. "That's the most beautifully decorated tree I've ever seen."

"Genuine turn-of-the-century. Well," Finn said, "the nineteenth century, that is."

The entire mansion was done up for the holidays in reds and greens and gold and silver ornaments and miniature collectibles, all antique. There was mistletoe and holly framing gilt mirrors, and a red-painted sleigh filled with Christmas presents sat beneath one of the tall windows in the living room. On the other side of the room was the bar, an antique rocking horse to one side of it. A tuxedo-clad bartender filled glasses or ladled champagne punch from an enormous cut-glass bowl. Fresh fruits, artfully cut into little reindeer or snowmen or Santas, floated in the bowl. Ellie would have thought the whole place was overdone, except somehow Hillary's antique decorations were charming and fit the Victorian home perfectly.

"Hungry?" Finn asked, getting them both glasses of punch, and he nodded toward the formal dining room, where there were four enormous tables overflowing with scrumptious foods and delicacies.

"Starved," she said, "but the food looks too pretty to eat. Let's wait?"

"Sure," he said. "Besides, I want to introduce you around."

She had no choice. He insisted she meet everyone, so many new faces that the names immediately went in one ear and out the other. There were more diamonds, rubies, sapphires, and emeralds than in all of Tiffany's, Ellie was sure, and a few of the women definitely eyed her either curiously or with barely veiled hostility.

Finn Rasmussen, the playboy, took it all in stride.

He *was* charming, if a little too used to being in charge. He led her out to a large, cool solarium that must have been filled with potted plants when not being used for a dance. Now it had been cleared out and the tall plates of glass, separated by wrought iron, were decorated with twinkling lights and boughs of holly and evergreens and silk-covered Christmas balls, and there was a tall, wood-carved antique Santa standing whimsically next to the five-piece orchestra in the corner. The Santa had a pipe in his mouth and seemed to be winking at Ellie.

Finn drew her into his arms and led her around the smooth flagstone floor to an old Tommy Dorsey tune. Then, before she could catch her breath, he'd switched partners, and she found herself in the arms of Tyler someone, an excellent dancer, while Finn spun the man's wife gracefully.

It was all overwhelming. At one point she calculated this single party would pay for a full year's tuition at CU law. The extravagancy was mind boggling.

They ate in the formal living room, seated on a green velvet sofa with Victorian roll arms. There was another similar sofa across the kidney-shaped marble-topped coffee table. To her left was the hearth, a fire crackling in it. And hanging from a mantelpiece were handmade Christmas stockings, six of them. They looked well used, too. Above the mantel was a portrait of some terribly distinguished looking gentleman, circa 1930s, and all around the heavy gilded frame were, of course, twists of holly and evergreens. The old gentleman looked quite content.

"Enjoying the party?" Finn asked.

Ellie's mouth was full of shrimp stuffed with crab. She managed to swallow. "It's wonderful."

"Not too pretentious for you?" His blue eyes were dancing, challenging.

"Of course it is." She laughed. "I feel as if I'm committing a sin."

"A sin?"

"Uh-huh. Like buying a Cadbury chocolate, not the little pocket-sized ones, but a big one, and eating the whole thing in one sitting."

"You can do that?" He arched a sandy brow.

"Oh, sure, no problem. If I'm upset, I'm perfectly capable of doing it. Are you shocked?"

"Well . . . I guess not. I knew you were different the moment we met."

"Oh? And how is that?" She was actively flirting now. And enjoying it.

"You seem to fit in somehow," he said thoughtfully. "I mean, even lying in the snow when you fell, you just seem . . . natural in your surroundings. Here, too. I imagine that all this, well, shall we say *money,* is a little much for a college student. But you could have been born to this. Were you, Ellie? Do you come from money?"

She laughed genuinely. "No."

"Really?"

Ellie shrugged. "Really. I promise you, I wouldn't be clerking at the DA's right now if I could afford to finish my last year at law school."

"Interesting," he said, and they went back to their plates.

She was acutely aware of his gaze resting on her. Even when someone spoke to him, and he offered one of his clever replies, she felt his attention on her. Perhaps, she thought, her plans would work out. For all his straightforward, outgoing demeanor, there had to be a hidden side to him. Everyone had their secrets, and so did he. She just needed to dig them out. And she would.

She danced with several different partners after dinner. Engaging, rich men. She *was* having fun. And she knew that no matter the outcome of her relationship with this man—no matter who or *what* he really was—she'd remember this fairy-tale night.

In the powder room sometime after midnight, alone at last for a minute, she leaned against the flowered wallpaper and took a deep breath. So far so good, she decided.

But she knew instinctively not to push. If he found her too interested, if she asked too many questions this early in the contest, she'd lose him. Still, she was dying to know where he came from, who his parents were, brothers, sisters. Had he grown up rich, poor, middle-class? She'd read all those clippings about the security systems entrepreneur, but nothing about his past. No one could be so damn perfect. On the other hand, it was increasingly impossible to imagine him as a mad, calculating killer. It simply couldn't be him.

Then she straightened. Or was she merely seeing what she wanted to see? Had his lifestyle, his rich friends, even his house and the car he drove combined to blind her? Okay, so she was drawn to this glamour. Could she be that shallow?

Or was Finn the good guy?

Michael, she thought abruptly—an antithesis to Finn. He had his dark side, and a brooding quality to him that she knew held secrets. But he kept his past locked safely away, and she was afraid she'd never find the key.

How would Michael Callas fit in with this glittering crowd?

A bubble of laughter rose inside her. He wouldn't fit in. And yet she tried out the concept of Michael, here, her date. Michael in black tie, his arm on her waist, his golden eyes on her, the hint of his beard as his cheek brushed hers. Crazy.

She turned to the sink and dabbed cool water on her cheeks, not enough to spoil her makeup, but enough to bring her to her senses. She was a fool to think about Michael in that way. Sleeping with him, *screwing him,* she thought with a sick lurch of her stomach, had been a necessity. It had worked. And she'd damn well better hope she could keep him on the hook after what had happened in the parking lot that afternoon.

Finn awaited her near the powder room when she emerged, smiling, ready to dance and dance and drink and maybe even eat again. Why not? Finn, tall and so good-looking, possessing a certain grace and athletic quality that was unusual for a big man. There was so much about him that she couldn't help liking, and it was no wonder that women fell over themselves to be with him. He was outgoing and laughed easily. He made her feel beautiful and special, as if she were the only female in the room. She could see how his company could be habit-forming.

He told good stories. Never bragging, just easily carrying her along on his tales of adventure, taking her to places she'd probably never see with her own eyes. He told her about a trip to the Italian Alps, how he'd broken a leg skiing a glacier. He'd visited his family's ancestral home in the Ukraine. He'd taken a cruise on the Nile and been thrown off the back of a cantankerous camel. He'd scuba dived in the Caribbean and on the Great Barrier Reef and big game fished off the Baja Peninsula.

"My buddies and I finally hooked the big one. It was just this last Thanksgiving, in fact, an employee vacation. Our last day. We were hung over, sunburned, and the waves were five feet."

"Is that bad?"

"Pretty rough seas. But we hooked a five-hundred-pound marlin. It took all of us to bring her in. Six hours. I thought my arms were going to come out of their sockets."

"But you landed it?"

"Oh, no." He laughed, his head tossed back so that her gaze fastened on his strong throat above the black tie. "The line snapped. She was two feet from the gaff and it snapped. Gone. She swam away."

"She?"

"Um," he said, "a fishing term, I guess."

"Anyway, you must have been awfully disappointed. All those hours of trying to land her."

"Yes, we were. But every so often you misjudge the spunk in a female. Just when you think she's ready to give in . . ."

But they were momentarily interrupted and he never finished his thought, and Ellie didn't consider his words at the time. It wasn't until much later that she would come to understand exactly what he meant.

She never knew what time he pulled up in front of her Boulder house. She only knew that she'd had a great night, and that he hadn't spoiled it by propositioning her. He was a gentleman till the end. And then some.

"I feel a little like Cinderella," she said in the warm, hushed interior of his car.

He turned toward her and put his arm on the back of her seat. "Can I kiss Cinderella? Is that allowed?"

Ellie felt her heart begin a slow turgid pounding. She said nothing, only smiled and leaned into him. She wanted to kiss him. His lips were soft and warm. She opened her mouth, and he kissed her in passion then broke away, a gloved hand on her chin, holding her eyes for a long heartbeat.

"Don't move," he finally said.

He got out and came around to the passenger door and opened it. The bitter cold air buffeted her. Refreshingly.

"Put your foot up," he said.

Ellie laughed and gave him her foot and he slipped her shoe off then tossed it on the floor.

"There," he said.

"There what?"

"You lost a slipper. Tomorrow your prince will return it."

"Finn."

"On our way to Santa Fe in the morning."

"What?" She shook her head.

"I've got to fly down over the weekend. It's just an hour's worth of business, but it can't be avoided. We'll take my plane."

"You're a . . . pilot?"

"Let's hope so." He grinned. "It's just for the weekend. I've got reservations at La Fonda."

Ellie didn't know what to say.

"Here," he said, and he swooped her up into his arms and carried her to the front door.

"My shoe, Finn," she said; she couldn't lose Jenn's shoe, for Lord's sakes.

"First thing in the morning, Cinderella. Isn't the prince supposed to bring the shoe?"

"Well, yes, but . . ."

"You're coming to Santa Fe with me. This way I know you will. Say yes."

But he didn't give her a chance; he kissed her instead, wrapping his arms around her and lifting her to him.

When she came up for air, a little dizzy, she said, "Yes."

"Good," he whispered. "Seven-thirty okay? I know you won't get much sleep. It's already . . ."

She said yes to everything. Even while a voice in her head cried, *Are you crazy?* she said yes.

• • •

It was still early on Saturday morning when Michael drove down Harrison Avenue in Leadville and turned onto Fifth Street, looking for the address.

He told himself he was doing what he did best—being a detective. He told himself Ellie deserved his snooping into her past. Still, he felt like a heel, had felt this way since last night when he'd telephoned Janice Kramer and said he was going to be in the area and he'd love to stop by and meet Ellie's mother, his *girlfriend's* mother, he'd actually said, the words making him clench his jaw.

"Well, sure, I guess that would be all right, Mr., ah, Callas, did you say?" He'd heard her surprise and hesitation.

"It's Michael," he'd said, "and I look forward to meeting you, Mrs. Kramer."

"Ah, Janice. It's Janice."

"Great, Janice. Would ten be too early?"

"Ah, no, that would be fine."

"See you at ten," he'd said, so nicely, so open. A real good guy.

He didn't exactly know what to expect, what he was going to say. He suspected he'd just plaster a friendly smile on his face and take it from there.

There it was, the address on Fifth Street. He pulled over, parked, and stared at the dilapidated house with its Depression siding, that old fake siding that had been originally earmarked for roofing material.

Jesus, he thought, staring. This was Ellie's home? She'd said she grew up poor, but . . .

It didn't matter. What mattered was solving the Ellie Kramer puzzle. And he sure as hell was not going to leave till he had a few answers.

Determined, he opened the truck door, put on the nice guy smile, and started up the icy walk.

THIRTEEN

The name Michael Callas had been burned into Janice's brain well over a decade ago. When he'd phoned last night, even before he'd said who it was, she had recognized the voice. God only knew, she'd sat in that Boulder courtroom at her husband's trial and listened to a full day's testimony from the rookie. His voice was the same, a shade deeper from age, but she would have recognized it anywhere.

She'd tried calling Ellie immediately but gotten only that confounded answering machine with Celeste's voice. And again before eight this morning. She could have throttled those girls. Didn't they ever pick up the phone?

One thing was for sure: Ellie couldn't possibly know her "boyfriend" was driving up to Leadville. If Ellie had even an inkling of his intentions, she would have warned her mother. Where on earth was that child?

Janice had not slept a wink all night. By eight-fifteen this morning she'd been ready to pin a note to the front door telling Detective Callas she'd had to go out of town—an emergency. But instead here she was, showered and in her best black wool slacks and a royal blue turtleneck sweater, her face made up, awaiting him, convincing herself that the man would never recognize her. They'd never spoken, never met, and she would have sworn he had never once looked in her direction in the courtroom. No doubt he'd been too ashamed. Or too smug. God, how she'd hated him.

Janice could have killed her daughter as she awaited the arrival of the detective, though she knew precisely why he was coming: a fishing expedition. Lord knew, Ellie was an accomplished liar, but this man had nevertheless become suspicious. A detective. Of course he'd seen through Ellie's deception. But he obviously didn't have the whole picture. Not yet.

She wanted to wring her hands as she stood by the front window, the gold-colored drapes pulled aside, staring at the quiet street. There were dead geranium leaves glued to the white vinyl backing of the drapes, and cobwebs in the corners of the windowsill. The paint was chipped. Part of Janice wanted to rush about and tidy the place, hide her shame, but she lacked the energy. Before John had died in the prison hospital, when she'd still clung to the faint hope that the real rapist would be found, she'd had a measure of pride. No longer, though. With John's death three years ago her pride, her will to go on, had drained out of her. Now all she had was Ellie. Her only child, her stubborn, obsessive child, who was playing with fire.

She saw his pickup truck turn onto the street and watched as he searched for the address. When he parked and got out, observing the street with its run-down houses and piles of dirty snow on the curbs, she felt a sob welling up in her chest. Damn her daughter. Damn them both for putting her in this position. And to think—it could have been this man who'd set John up, or even committed the crime himself.

By the time he knocked on the wooden door with its dingy glass panel, Janice was trembling. She knew she had to play this farce out, but no one had given her the rules.

She opened the door. She couldn't even force a smile; her lips were frozen in a timid grimace.

"Mrs. Kramer? Janice Kramer?"

"Why, yes." She cleared her throat. "And you must be Michael. Come in. It's awfully chilly out, isn't it?" There. She'd gotten past square one. She could do this. She *could.*

"Can I take your coat?" She held out a shaky hand for his expensive-looking brown leather jacket—one of those World War II bomber jackets. When he shrugged it off, she carefully hung it on a wooden peg behind the front door. "There," she said, turning back to him, "why not make yourself comfortable?"

Janice could have died a thousand deaths when he sat in the faded overstuffed chair, with its worn arms and the broken springs that creaked beneath his weight.

"So this is where Ellie grew up," he said, knees splayed, his hands clasped in front of him. Smiling. Smiling.

"Oh, yes," she said, no script, no lines, ad-libbing. "We've been in this house a long time." Then she asked, "Does Ellie know you're here?" She was sure of the answer, but she wanted his reaction.

"Well, no, she doesn't. I just made up my mind to come up to check on my family's place at the last minute."

"Your family has a place here?"

"Between Vail and Minturn, actually."

"How nice. Now, Michael, can I get you some coffee? And I made an apple crumb cake."

"I'd love a cup of coffee. Black, please."

"I wasn't sure if you'd want coffee or tea. . . . It'll only take a couple minutes to brew." Babbling, rambling on. Her nerves pricked her skin from the inside.

She went into the kitchen, a separate room directly behind the front room where the cop was sitting, eyeing the shabbiness of her house. But what could she do? She'd lost her job at the mine, and as bad as the hourly wage was at the mini-mart, at least it was a job. There were plenty of folks in Leadville who didn't even have that. Many were on the dole. Others commuted all the way to Copper Mountain ski resort and even farther, to Vail or Breckenridge. By the time they got through paying for gas and tires, they may as well have stayed in Leadville and worked for a minimum wage. As Janice was doing.

"Cold morning, isn't it?" she called as she measured coffee into the filter and shoved it into place, switching on the coffeepot.

"Very," he called back. "I have to be honest, I don't think I could live at this altitude year-round. Have you always lived in Leadville?"

Janice easily evaded the truth, surprising herself with her newfound talent. "Oh, my, no," she said. "I was raised on a Nebraska farm. I married a Coloradan."

"Oh, yes, that's right," he said, having risen and come to the swinging door that was propped open. "Ellie said her father died. I'm sorry."

In prison, you bastard, flew into her mind. "Yes, he did, a while back." God only knew what Ellie had said.

She watched the coffee drip into the clear glass pot and thought how uncomfortable it was to have a man in her little house. A good-sized man. Not chunky or husky, but tall and well built. Reluctantly, she saw the way his green crewneck sweater lay flat against his belly.

"Coffee will just be another minute." A terrible thought struck her, making her grab the counter to support her weight. Had Ellie slept with him? Would her daughter have gone that far?

"Are you feeling all right?" came his smooth, deep-timbred voice.

"I'm fine. A bit of low blood pressure, I guess." She managed to collect herself. "Um, coffee's ready. How about some crumb cake with it?"

"You know," he said, "I'd like that. Sure. Shall I sit here?" He nodded toward the scarred oak table, which was next to a kitchen window hung with lace curtains she'd gotten at a garage sale. On the windowsill a foot below the tabletop sat more of her scraggly geraniums. Why hadn't she cut them back this fall?

Janice put a large piece of crumb cake on a plate, took public prosecutor a paper napkin from a drawer and a fork from the dish rack, and set them in front of him. Then the coffee, which she poured into a plain brown mug, the kind you still found at highway truck stops.

"Black, you said?"

"Yes, this looks great. You know, Mrs. . . . Janice, that is, I really do appreciate you letting me drop by on such short notice."

"Oh, I don't mind a bit. Really."

"It seemed like a good opportunity, and since Ellie is busy this weekend . . ."

Busy? Where, with what? Damn that girl. But she couldn't ask *him*. "So, are you from Boulder, Michael?"

"No, my family's from Colorado Springs."

"How nice. Close but not too close."

"Yeah." Nothing else, just that.

"How did you and Ellie meet?" she asked. A neutral subject.

"Through her clerking job."

"Of course, I should have guessed."

"The DA had her working on my testimony for a trial."

"I see." Janice glanced at him and then her gaze fell to her hands. Oh, how easily she could picture him on the witness stand; even after all these years he hadn't changed very much. There were a few more lines of cynicism around those distinctive amber-colored eyes, but he was still a good-looking man. A little Mediterranean, with naturally golden skin that was curiously close in color to his eyes, hair that was a darker shade, burnished where the light fell on it. A very handsome, striking look. But there was something else behind the friendly façade, a dark vigilance that sent a chill along Janice's spine. *Be careful,* she reminded herself.

"Ellie told me you used to work for the mine?"

"Oh, yes, but that was when there was a market for molybdenum, before the end of the Cold War. You know, it's used to harden steel."

"Actually, I didn't know." He took a large bite of the coffee cake and washed it down. "This is good, thank you." Then he went on. "Ellie has talked about her father a lot."

Liar, Janice thought.

"And she told me he was a builder."

"Yes."

"Here, in Leadville?"

She nodded, smiling broadly.

"I'd think it'd be hard up here with the long winters."

"Oh, well, you know, people need houses, and in the winter there are always remodels." Then, quickly moving on, "And you, Michael. You've always been a policeman?" As if she didn't know. As if the local papers in Boulder hadn't run stories about the terrific job the two handsome young rookies had done on the Morris case.

"Ever since college," he replied, and she thought about how he and his partner had ruined her life. Her happy life. They'd had a modest split-level outside of Boulder, on five acres. Five acres that in today's market would have been worth a million dollars. And her job as a teacher . . . gone, gone. Everything gone. But her child. Yes, she still had Ellie.

It came to her as she rose to get Michael Callas more coffee. Came to her without a spanning thought.

John. He'd been such a nice-looking man. Not terribly tall, but slender, so strong and competent in appearance in his plaid shirts and big work boots. He'd always worn glasses. Round wire-rimmed glasses. With the floppy, light-brown hair that fell across his high brow, Janice had thought he looked awfully intelligent. He had been intelligent.

For years after the move to Leadville, where not a soul had suspected who she and Ellie were, Janice had driven her daughter to the state prison in Canon City twice a month to visit. But then, as the years crawled by, John had lost heart, and their visits—again at his urging—had become less frequent.

"Ellie's a young woman now," he'd said into the phone on the other side of the glass partition. "She needs a life of her own, she needs to put all this in the past. Please don't bring her anymore, Janice, please. I'm begging you. Tell her whatever you have to. But *please.*"

He'd never known how utterly devoted his daughter had been to him. She'd gone to college in Boulder—gone home—and then into law because of him, because of the injustice done to him. And now she was mixed up in this insane quest for the truth, and Janice knew she herself was in part to blame. How many times had Ellie heard her mother sob to the lawyers, the police, and the media, even to the DA, that John had been set up? Ellie had heard her mother accuse the rookie cops, and not just of setting John up, but of one of them being the rapist.

She'd been mad with grief and rage and fear, and she'd sown those seeds in her child.

Janice sat back down. She looked at the detective, and then her gaze slid away. This was *her* fault.

The seeds had rooted and grown. Every move Ellie had made in the last twelve years had led them all to this point in time. Janice had sat in that courtroom and been witness to her husband's crucifixion, and she'd blamed everyone in sight.

Now . . . she braved a glance at Michael Callas. Had she been mistaken? Blinded by rage and hate and wrenching fear? Had she instilled those same emotions in Ellie? Or could this man, or the other one, Rasmussen, truly be guilty?

"So what got Ellie interested in law?" he asked, pushing aside the empty plate.

She forced her glance up to his. "She, ah, just was . . . *is* interested in it. I never knew."

"Maybe her father . . . ?" Michael suggested.

"Oh, well, perhaps, but John worked with his hands, really."

"He died quite young."

"Yes, he, ah, the flu. Went into pneumonia."

"That's a shame. Ellie must miss him. And you, too, of course."

"We do, terribly." That, at least, was the truth.

"Ellie told me about him when she found out what my

hobby was. I guess I'm a little like your late husband, I like to work with my hands, too."

"You build things?"

"I *try* to. I've been working on my cabin for several years. I'm trying to do most of it on my own, but sometimes I screw it up so badly I have to have a real pro come in."

"John was always a terrible plumber," she reflected, and then she looked up fearfully. Why couldn't she leave that subject alone?

But he laughed. "That's funny, I am too. I put the hot and cold water pipes in backward in my bathroom. Never even realized till I turned on the cold water spigot and got burned."

"Oh, my."

"Yeah, it was a mess tearing it out." He looked at her for a long moment, that darkening of his eyes making her nerves twitch. Did Ellie recognize that signal when his mood altered, became watchful? Did her daughter know him that well? *Had* they slept together?

Janice cringed inwardly, willing the thought back into a hidden place in her mind. What was this man doing here, what did he hope to learn? Or had he already learned what he came for?

Suddenly she felt as if the walls were closing in. Had she said something that was going to lead this detective to the truth? She'd put Ellie in grave danger. Oh, dear God. What had she said to him?

But he was pushing himself away from the table, and he was smiling again, the light returning to his eyes. "I've taken up enough of your time," he said.

"Oh, well, that's all right. It's been a pleasure." *Lies, lies.* She wished he'd leave.

She followed him into the living room and got his leather jacket down off the peg.

"Now you have a safe drive over the pass to Minturn. It gets awfully icy this time of year," she said. Wasn't that how mothers were supposed to act?

"I'll take it easy."

"It was nice meeting you, Michael. Maybe next time you and Ellie can come up together."

"Oh, sure. It's been a pleasure meeting you, too. And now I know where Ellie gets her looks." With that, he left.

Janice watched him stride down the short walk and then she closed the door against the bitter cold. She surreptitiously watched him through a crack in the drapes until his truck was out of sight. It was only then that she allowed herself to sag into the same sad chair he'd occupied.

"Oh, God," she whispered.

Michael sat at the stop sign on the corner of East Fifth and Harrison, trying to sort his thoughts out. There was an itch in his brain, but he couldn't reach it.

At the first red light he almost had it. Damn.

It took him another three blocks and then there it was, directly behind his eyeballs, the image of a woman sitting in a courtroom. He drove another half block before the knowledge struck him with a force so hard his breath went right out of his lungs.

Janice Kramer was Janice *Crandall*.

John Crandall's wife.

Then . . . Ellie was . . .

Somehow he drove to the next stoplight.

Ellie Crandall?

"Jesus H. Christ," he breathed.

• • •

The more Michael thought about it the worse it got, a hammer blow that rendered him nearly senseless. He drove away from Leadville, from its rattletrap houses and gentrified downtown, from its cold skies smeared with gray and ten-thousand-foot altitude and shut-down mines, and he never saw the road or remembered the trip until he had to turn off of I-70 to head toward Boulder.

He seethed inside, gripping the steering wheel, rushing past the familiar scenery. He wanted to get home, to go to ground in the only place where he felt secure. He wanted to think this out, this enormous flash of knowledge that had exploded in his face.

The young daughter, Eleanor Crandall . . . *Ellie Kramer.*

Ellie had lied to him from the beginning, sought him out, played with him and made him think, what? That she liked him, wanted to be with him. He'd actually begun to believe he'd found a woman with whom he could have a relationship.

Fool, he raged. *Idiot.*

She'd lied from the first moment, reeling him in, playing, using. All those prying questions.

He turned into his driveway and crossed the wooden bridge over Boulder Creek. He stopped his truck, took a deep breath. Okay, give her the benefit of the doubt. Maybe she hadn't known who he was—she'd only been a kid at the time of her father's trial. He wanted to believe it was coincidence that she'd been assigned to the Zimmerman case. How could she have arranged that? And, hell, he could understand why she and her mother changed their names. Anyone would.

He thought back, dissecting Ellie's questions, his questions. What had she said to him? High school in Leadville. Her father had died a few years ago. Not much more than that.

Michael remembered quite clearly now. Yes, John Crandall had been a builder. He'd been working on the Morrises' kitchen. That much was true.

He went into his cabin, threw his coat angrily over the couch. Oh, how she must have been laughing at him. She didn't give a damn about him, she'd searched him out, chosen him, set out to get him.

It was all a lie. The ultimate betrayal. But why? Why had she done it?

The answer was pushing at the surface of his mind, but he shoved it down deep, unwilling to examine it.

He started to build a fire in his half-finished fireplace. Sitting back on his heels, he watched the flames lick at the kindling and grow, cracking, devouring the wood. If he put his hand in that fire it wouldn't hurt as much as what Ellie had done.

It had begun to snow in the canyon, flakes tapping on his windows, wind swirling around the corners of his cabin. He stood and went to a window, stared unseeing out of it, snowflakes flying dizzily at him, then crushing themselves against the glass.

What did Ellie want from him? Why was she doing this? How had she found him?

Working in the DA's office, of course. She'd positioned herself unerringly. Smart, clever Ellie.

Michael went straight to the kitchen cupboard that held his liquor. Not much there, but he grabbed a bottle of brandy and a tall water glass and poured himself a drink.

"I'm glad you're okay." He could hear her voice inside his head. "I was worried." Her hand on his arm. Had she meant it? Or was it more of her acting?

And the scene in the parking lot. Ugly. Yet she'd still been acting. "You're not easy," she'd said. And she'd kissed him.

He drank the burning brandy, heedless, stalking around his cabin. Ellie Kramer, Ellie *Crandall,* had played him like a finely turned violin. She was a creature of lies and betrayal.

He thought about that weekend at the chalet, his old room, the bed where they'd fucked. That's what it had been. Goddamn the slut. What an idiot he was.

He wondered where she was now. In her funky house, out with another man? A girl like her must have men groveling at her feet. She had a sensuality that came from within. All men had to recognize it. She'd been born with it, and it disturbed and attracted at the same time. He didn't understand the attraction, but he recognized it. And he'd fallen for it.

He drank and watched the snow, stalked around his silent home. Rage consumed him. He finally flung himself down on his couch, the glass resting on his chest.

He could recall with utter clarity every expression on her face, the feel of her under him, her brief smile like sunlight. All lies.

He lay there on his couch, the storm seething outside, and he felt his life pressing on him heavily. So much loss and betrayal. Paul. His parents. And now this. It was no goddamn wonder he'd become a hermit.

Why had she done it?

The truth that he'd been denying smacked him in the face. She'd grown from a girl into womanhood listening to her mother's accusations.

Ellie believed he was the rapist.

The irony of it twisted his lips into a sardonic smile.

Her mother had been right all those years. Ellie was right. The trouble was, they had the wrong cop.

"Christ," he ground out, Ellie was making *him* pay for Rasmussen's crimes. And what was Rasmussen doing? Spending all his wealth on women and toys, free as a bird, happy, free to rape and murder over and over. Clever. Calculating. Leaving no physical evidence. Setting up some other poor sap to take the fall.

He raised his head and gulped a mouthful of liquid fire. His temples pounded and his stomach hurt. Then he thought of Ellie again, the fine-textured skin, the wideset eyes he'd drowned in. Her voice, her scent, her cold hands and silky hair. Her quick wit and easy grace.

Where was she now?

His face set into hard lines. It was a good thing she wasn't here. He'd kill her, choke the life out of her. A man could stand only so much humiliation.

He drank some more and passed out on the couch, the wind screaming around the corners of his cabin and howling through the treetops. He dreamed a lot that night, dreams that in the morning fled like wisps of smoke in the cold air. He never recalled any of them, especially the one about Paul's funeral. He awoke with a single thought only vaguely related to his dreams: Why in hell did his best friend have to die?

The thought was gone by the time his feet hit the floor by the couch, and he realized he had a brutal headache. Shakily, he stood, made his way up the stairs to the wooden rail overlooking the living room, and held on to it to steady himself. And then he saw her as plainly as if she were standing there in his kitchen. Her hair curling, the white sweater, the look of concentration on her face as she'd searched for something in his drawer, something for the salad. Then she'd smiled. A smile just for him.

He held on to the rail, staring down, and he knew if he lived a hundred years, he'd never forget the way she'd looked that night.

FOURTEEN

When their mother got sick and their father lost his job and descended into complete alcoholism, Finn's brother, Scott, was old enough to manage on his own, his sister, Ginny, went to a foster home, and Finn was sent to another.

He thought he was in heaven at his first foster home. Deeny and Brian Hoffman were middle-aged, their own children grown and gone. Unusual in foster parents, they took in children from the goodness of their hearts and not for the state-provided money.

Deeny was a potter, had a studio in their home, and Brian sold insurance. They took Finn in as if he were their own. Deeny hugged him a lot; Brian was not as demonstrative, but he talked to Finn as if they were equals. He told him stories of his boyhood, told him about his two sons and their youthful indiscretions. "Pains in the asses," he called his two boys, but he said it with such love in his voice that Finn wanted more than anything to do something dumb so that Brian would call him a pain in the ass, with that same pride and feeling.

He had three meals a day for the first time in his life, clean sheets, clean clothes. He felt guilty, unworthy of his good fortune, then he realized, he knew, that this was what he'd always been destined for, a life like the Hoffmans offered.

He noted how Deeny ran the house, made shopping lists, thinking hard, chewing on her pencil. "I need onions," she'd say out loud, then she'd write it down.

He loved to watch her turn pots, glaze them. He picked up finished pieces and ran his fingers over their surfaces. He couldn't get over how they transformed in the kiln.

Over Thanksgiving they took him to Chicago; they walked along the lakefront in the cold wind. He had a hotel room of his own, and they ate in restaurants. With enormous menus to order from.

Deeny wanted to visit the Chicago Art Institute. She insisted. Brian joked around about how boring it was, but he went. The museum was a revelation to Finn. Paintings, sculptures, colors, shapes, figures.

He saw his first Picasso there—Deeny told him all about the famous artist. And a Kandinsky that took his breath away. The paintings stayed in front of his eyes for days.

Finn remained with the Hoffmans for six months. He'd practically forgotten his own family, when his mother recovered sufficiently to take her kids back, and his father went into detox.

The Hoffmans drove him home on a spring day. He sat in the back of their car, dry-eyed, suffering. He was only eleven, but he understood that it would be worse at home now that he knew how real people lived.

He ran away that summer, hitching, walking, to return to the Hoffmans. Deeny cried and Brian talked to him

*about responsibility and family loyalty, then they drove
him back to the distraught Becky.*

*The second time Finn ran away, bicycling all the way
to the Hoffmans' on his old junker, there was a new
foster child in their house. A boy close to his own age.*

*He never ran away again, not even later when he was
put in another foster home. No one could call Finn stupid.*

They'd taken off from Denver Centennial Airport before
the storm blew in. Ellie could hear Finn's side of the
conversation with the tower. He had asked about the
weather conditions, but they were well above the clouds
and into the sunlight before she knew it.

He'd fiddled with buttons and switches, and she'd felt
the twin-engine Piper Navajo level off, perfect blue
around them, gray roiling clouds below. She'd felt like a
princess.

Finn pulled aside his microphone. "You've never been
in a small plane before?"

"No. And not often in commercial ones."

"We'll see if we can cure that particular lack for you."

She said nothing, but she was so excited and thrilled
she couldn't stop smiling. She felt almost foolish, inex-
perienced, naïve, but Finn seemed to enjoy her reactions,
so she didn't try to hide the fact that she was having fun.

"We'll be there in two hours, give or take," he said.
"Comfortable?"

"Oh, yes." She gave him a sidelong glance. He looked
so handsome in a pinstriped, double-breasted suit and
pearl-gray shirt with a tie of textured raw silk in the exact
same shade. His cashmere topcoat was thrown carelessly
behind the pilot's seat. He'd apologized for his suit when

he'd picked her up that morning, but he had that pesky business meeting.

"If you want anything to drink there's a cooler right behind you. There should be a thermos of coffee, too. I asked Fixed Base Operations to stock the plane," he said.

"No, I'm fine."

He checked his gauges, and Ellie looked out of her side window, watching the impossibly bright blue sky. She kept telling herself to be on the alert, to be careful. Her common sense, her logic, warned her that Finn Rasmussen could be a wolf in sheep's clothing. But her heart didn't believe it.

She'd been living a fairy tale since last night, and she was reluctant to relinquish it. She'd be all right as long as Finn didn't find out who she really was. Maybe he'd never need to know about the dirty trick she'd played on him.

"So, Ellie, how do you like flying?"

"Better than driving."

He threw back his head and laughed. Her heart sang. This was an *adventure.*

They landed and went straight to the rental car Finn had arranged for. It was overcast in Santa Fe, but warmer than the Denver area, and Ellie couldn't get enough of the scenery.

"Have you been here before?" Finn asked.

"I haven't been anywhere," she replied.

"Santa Fe is a fascinating city. It's got history. Supposedly founded in 1610 by Spanish conquistadors. Taken back by the Pueblo Indians in a revolt in 1680, then the Spanish again. Hell, for a while it belonged to Mexico, then the Confederacy in the Civil War and finally the States."

"You've read up on it." She was impressed despite

herself. Casual tourists didn't usually study the history of their destinations. Neither did businessmen.

"I'm interested in history. Are you, Ellie?"

"It was never my best subject, I'm afraid."

"What was your best subject?"

"Oh, English, and math, believe it or not."

"I believe it."

She looked out the window at the gray winter scenery, the low hills falling back to the cloud-shrouded higher peaks of the Sangre de Cristos. They were in a valley, and there were haciendas and houses scattered about the countryside. Spanish-style houses of adobe with red tile roofs. She really could picture the conquistadors riding up this valley on their horses, holding long lances, followed by dour-faced padres in their brown robes and worn sandals.

"It's wonderful," she breathed. "I feel like I've been plucked out of reality and set down in a movie."

"You haven't seen anything yet. Stick with me, Ellie, and I'll open your eyes." He took his right hand off the steering wheel and patted her thigh, then left his hand there until they turned off the highway into the centuries-old, narrow streets of the city.

I'm a whore, she thought. *Seduced totally by this man and his lifestyle and his money.* She had to be careful, no matter how appealing he was. She had to stay on her toes. But, God, it was hard to keep that in her mind.

They were staying at the La Fonda Hotel, right on the four-hundred-year-old plaza in the center of the city. It was a venerable building, renovated over the years, the walls thick adobe, dark wood beams on low ceilings, and Ellie loved the look of it instantly. Elegant-funky.

Finn had reserved two adjoining rooms. He checked them in effortlessly, and they were swiftly installed, Ellie gaping at her own room. She didn't know what she'd expected, perhaps a modern motel look. What she got was late-nineteenth century. Except for the plumbing in the bathroom, the room would have fit on a Western movie set.

Well, almost, she decided, eyeing the lime-green painted plaster walls and the multicolored, zigzag patterned carpet. Maybe a *Southwestern* movie set.

There wasn't even a phone. A TV—because no one could live without that—but no phone, only a jack in the wall for those either without a cell phone or those who simply had to stay in touch.

"Is it okay?" Finn asked from the doorway.

"Perfect." She turned in the middle of the room, feeling just right in slacks and a sweater and well-worn shoes.

"Now, I'm going to have to leave you for a little while. I have this damn meeting. Call room service if you want anything. Anything at all. A massage, a hair appointment, a manicure. Food, booze, anything. And there's a terrific dress shop in the lobby. Buy anything you want and charge it to me."

"Oh, I couldn't."

"It'd make me happy, Ellie." He stepped into her room, close to her, and for a moment she thought he was going to kiss her, and she wondered what she was going to do if he did. But he only stroked her cheek. "You'll be okay?"

"Of course, I'll be fine. Go to your meeting."

"Don't wander too far. I'll be back in a couple of hours, and I want to show you the town."

"I can't wait."

After he left, Ellie unpacked her few clothes and hung them up in the spacious Spanish-style wardrobe. They'd do fine. Her good navy blue blazer, gray slacks. A red sweater in case they were going very casual. A calf-length skirt, a silk blouse, and her tall leather boots. All well-worn, most of them from her favorite secondhand shop.

She went down to the lobby and wandered around. There was indeed an upscale dress shop, with some beautiful clothes in it, but the price tags made Ellie wince. She most certainly would *not* buy anything and charge it to Finn. What would that make her? She wondered if Finn thought of her as a woman who was for sale, or if the ludicrous discrepancy between their respective financial positions meant nothing to him.

She had a sandwich in the restaurant off the lobby, but, in truth, her appetite had been swept away with her old life. She was too excited to eat much.

Finn knocked on her door precisely two hours after he'd left. A punctual man, organized, perhaps obsessively so. But he had to be that way to be as successful as he was, she decided. Focused, with great powers of deduction and concentration. She was beginning to get the feeling that he was a controller; everything around him had to be under his thumb. Maybe she should talk to some of his employees, see what kind of man he was to work for. But he'd find out, and that could be fatal.

"Hi," he said. "I'm going to my room to change. And then we're going to paint the town red."

"I'll be ready."

She was wearing black slacks and a blue cabled turtleneck. And she'd brought her good black city coat. And the red scarf her mother had given her last Christmas. No gloves, as usual. She always lost them.

Michael. Had he tried to call her? Maybe. But her roommates had been instructed to inform him that she was away for the weekend. It would be okay. And she'd think of something to tell him if he asked. If he even bothered to get in touch again. After that scene in the parking lot . . .

God. Forget it, Kramer. She'd deal with Michael later.

Finn took her out onto the plaza, the cobblestone square surrounded by dun-colored adobe buildings that housed tourist shops, and began pointing things out to her. One side of the plaza was taken up by the Governor's Palace, the Palacio Real, which was an original building, headquarters of the colonial Spanish governors of New Spain. Across its one-story, flat front was a portico, almost as ancient, a carved and roofed walkway the length of the block. The plaza and the side streets were lined with tall cottonwood trees, bare-branched now, but in the summer, she thought, they would provide shade on the old narrow roads.

"It's very different," Ellie said. "As if it hasn't changed in centuries."

"It hasn't. They work very hard at historical preservation here, keeps the tourists coming. You know, in the summer, Indians are lined up under the portico, their wares on blankets. Silver, turquoise, jewelry, belts, rugs, pottery."

"Oh, I'd love to see that."

"Okay, we'll come back next summer."

She flashed him a quick smile. Next summer? She couldn't think beyond the next hour.

He took her to a bronze plaque off to one side of the plaza.

"This," he said, holding her arm, "is the end of the Santa Fe Trail. Read it."

She read. It was on this very spot, right on the corner where La Fonda Hotel stood, that the wagon trains had reached the end of their long and perilous journey from St. Louis, Missouri.

"Wow," she said.

"This town is full of stuff like that. It makes cities in Colorado seem like babies."

They walked around the plaza, window-shopping. Native American and Hispanic painters, sculptors, potters. Beautiful things. Clothes embroidered in vivid Mexican style. Ellie loved to look at it all.

Finn took her hand as they strolled. "Your hand is freezing," he said.

"They're always cold."

"You're not wearing gloves." He covered her fingers and chafed them.

"I lose gloves. I probably have a dozen single ones in my room."

"We'll buy you a pair," he said, stopping, stroking her palm, raising it to his lips and kissing it.

"Oh, really, I'll just lose them. I'm used to not wearing gloves."

His eyes bored into hers, very blue, the outside edges turned downward, the big bumpy nose, the wide sensitive mouth. "You're also not used to flying away for weekends, but it sure is nice when you can have the pleasure. Isn't it, Ellie?"

"Well, yes, but . . ."

"Come along." He tugged at her hand, striding swiftly by the storefronts. She had to walk fast to keep up. He went into the first shop he came to that looked as if it sold gloves and asked the saleslady to show them to Ellie.

"Hm, about a size seven?" he asked, holding her hand up.

"Sure." She was a little embarrassed, a little swept off her feet. No one, much less a man, had ever taken her shopping like this, not since she'd been a young kid when her father . . . But no. Now was a lousy time for *that* recollection.

The saleslady brought out a clear plastic drawer of gloves, size seven. Ellie could tell the woman was impressed with Finn, with his size and his looks and the elegantly casual clothes he'd changed into: cords, a cashmere polo shirt, and a soft brown suede jacket. And gloves. Fine, soft leather gloves lined with fur.

"Try these," he said, holding a pair out to Ellie.

She tried them on; they fit, lovely black lined gloves. "They're fine."

"No, no, let's try that pair." He flashed his smile at the saleslady, and the woman almost fell in.

"Finn, those were fine."

He turned his gaze on her, but he wasn't smiling. "I want the best, only the best. Put these on."

Avoiding the saleslady's eyes, she tried on three more pairs before Finn was satisfied. He had the woman tear the price tag off before he pulled them on Ellie's hands.

"Now," he said, "*now* we can walk around Santa Fe."

Back to window-shopping, feeling the soft lining of the gloves on her fingers, Ellie was confused. Happy but confused. She wasn't used to take-charge guys. Mostly *she* took charge of situations. But Finn didn't allow it. Things went his way, or . . . She wasn't sure what would happen if she crossed him. On the other hand, the things he did were generous, and he enjoyed doing them.

Should she just give in and accept his largesse? Moot point, she thought. She was already doing just that.

They walked around the plaza then went down a few side streets, narrow winding streets lined with Spanish colonial buildings. People were out Christmas shopping. The galleries were full. Finn took her into one.

"I like the artists this woman commissions. I've bought some pieces from her over the years," he explained. "I like to take a look at her new collection when I'm in town."

A quiet word to a salesman and the gallery owner appeared as if by magic, a heavyset woman swathed in bright colors, loads of turquoise and silver jewelry, and too much makeup.

"Finn, darling," she cried, and she held her arms out. Finn grinned and embraced her, air-kissing both of her rouged cheeks.

"Marisol," he finally said, "I'd like you to meet my new friend, Ellie Kramer."

They shook hands, Marisol sizing her up, and then she took Finn aside to show him some new paintings.

"I'll just be a minute," he said. "Look around. If you like something I'll get it for you."

She looked, strolling around the gallery, enjoying the paintings. Some were very good, but what would she do with them? And why did Finn press so much on her? Was it pride or was he trying to impress her or was he simply, astonishingly, generous?

He was by her side again shortly, his hand at the small of her back.

"Did you see anything you liked?" she asked.

"Not this trip. And you?"

She shook her head.

"You certainly are hard to please, Ellie," he said, mock-scolding her.

"Finn, honestly, I didn't agree to this weekend to go home loaded with presents. I wanted . . . I want your company."

"Nicely said, very nicely said. I'll take it on advisement."

But he led her into a jewelry shop next and, despite her protests, he bought her a sterling silver chain necklace with a silver lariat knot at the end.

"It's you," he said. "I can't pass it up. Think of it as an early Christmas present."

It was either accept it or cause a scene. She could send it back to the shop later if need be. And it was lovely. He clasped it on over her blue sweater, centering the lariat knot at the front, then kissed the nape of her neck, whispering, "Beautiful things for beautiful people."

When they returned to the plaza, snowflakes were drifting down; the storm had followed them from Colorado. It was dusk, and the store windows had lights in them. The *luminarias* had been lit, small perforated tins with candles inside, lining walkways. They were a Mexican Christmas custom, twinkling paths in the darkness.

It was a Christmas card, Ellie thought. It couldn't be real.

Finn pulled her arm through his as they walked, holding her close. "Are your hands warm?" he asked.

"Every part of me is warm," she replied. "It's so beautiful here."

They went down to dinner at the La Fonda Hotel's restaurant. It seemed the easiest thing to do, and Ellie mentioned how much she loved the atmosphere.

An elegant-looking Spanish guitarist played, his fingers picking and strumming, fast flamenco, soft romantic tunes. The food was excellent, and Ellie wore her good silk white blouse with her black skirt. And the new necklace.

They had drinks first, a glass of wine for Ellie and a back shelf vodka martini for Finn. He was easy to talk to, more and more charming as the evening wore on. She felt comfortable with him, more comfortable than she'd ever felt with Michael. He was so much easier to get along with. She didn't have to try so hard, to work so hard at creating a relationship. He helped it along, too.

He was a good listener, and she found herself opening up to him much more than she usually did. She tried not to dwell on her money problems, but the subject was impossible to avoid, as it formed the perimeters of her life.

"So I decided it was better to work for the whole year, save up some money, and finish school next year. And, really, I enjoy working at the DA's office. I'm learning so much, I think it'll give me a leg up with my classes when I go back."

"Can't your parents help you at all?"

She fixed him with a look. "My father died years ago, and my mother has money problems of her own."

Finn swallowed a forkful of free-range beef, not replying.

"I'm doing all right," she said, fending off pity. "I'll be all set for next fall. Then I take the bar exam and go to work."

"Where do you think you'll want to practice law?"

"I might stay in Boulder."

"Um." He thought for a minute. "What kind of law do you want to practice?"

"Criminal defense," she said promptly.

"You have *that* all figured out."

"Yes, I do."

"May I ask why?"

"I believe that people need to be protected from the huge machine of the law. Little people. They can get bulldozed in our system. They do all the time."

"Interesting. Then why not go to the public defender's office?"

Ellie swallowed the garlic mashed potatoes, practically swooning with pleasure. Then she leaned forward, elbows on the table. "I may be idealistic, but I'm not crazy. Public defenders make peanuts."

Finn nodded, lifted his wineglass, and she could see his throat work as he drank.

In the background the guitarist was playing "Malaguena." What a wonderful place this was, and she never would have experienced it but for the man sitting across from her.

"Enough about me," she said. "I want to know about you, Finn. Are you originally from Denver? Family?"

"Born in Milwaukee. I have an older brother and sister, still there. My family was middle-class, very ordinary, except for one thing. My father, bless his soul, was a falling-down drunk." He said it lightly, spearing a piece of steak and lifting it to his mouth.

"Oh, I'm sorry," Ellie said.

He waved his left hand. "No, no, I didn't mean for you to feel that way. I'm far beyond him and my whole family. Left Milwaukee as soon as I graduated from high school. And I've never been back."

"Never?"

"Nope. Not interested. I send some money and a Christmas card to my mother, and that's it. My father died a few years ago, but she still lives in the same house, my brother and sister within blocks." He frowned. "I don't know how they do it."

Ellie thought of Janice. *Because they have no choice.*

"So you're the family success story," she offered.

"I am that. But I worked hard to get where I am. It wasn't handed to me."

"I know how that feels."

He put his fork down and leaned across the table. "My

poor mother. I'll never understand why she put up with him. She was weak. A foolish, weak woman."

"You shouldn't . . ."

His broad shoulders rose and fell. "I see the truth. And"—he put a hand on her cheek—"I see the truth about you, Ellie."

Her heart halted.

"I know that you, for instance, would never be weak like my mother. It's one of the things I find so attractive about you. You have strength and passion and a vision of your future." He let his fingers trail to her chin then pulled her face close and kissed her gently on the lips. "I'm glad you came. Are you glad, Ellie?"

She smiled, her heart beating again. "Oh, yes, it's been wonderful."

"And it will be more wonderful."

What did he mean? Was he going to sleep with her? What would she do if he tried? She kept the smile on her face, but inside she felt trapped. He was a Prince Charming, but she wasn't sure she was ready.

Trapped. The food was gourmet, the bar entwined with holly and evergreen and twinkling white lights, her room charming, but there really was no way out. Not if Finn didn't want to let her go.

She needed time, a little more time. She'd tricked him into this sudden relationship, just as she'd tricked Michael, but Finn, the playboy, was used to moving much faster. What woman would turn him down?

She tried desperately hard to be lighthearted the rest of the evening, not quite sure she succeeded. They had dessert then coffee, then they strolled around the lobby, looking in shop windows. He put his arm around her shoulders, and often he bent his head and kissed her cheek or her ear. Goose bumps raised on her skin, but she didn't know if they were from cold or nerves.

"Early to bed," Finn said, as they sat at the lobby bar, drinking cognac from huge snifters. "I've got a big day planned for you."

"What are we doing?"

"I'm driving you to Chimayo, an old village north of here. It's famous. And there's a terrific place to have lunch up there."

"Sounds great."

Eventually they took the elevator up to their floor. She steeled herself, excuses ricocheting around in her head. But Finn only pulled her close, kissed her thoroughly, and let her go. "Tomorrow," he said.

"Tomorrow," she replied, holding his hand as he backed away, until the distance between them broke the grasp.

"Sweet dreams, Ellie."

"You too, Finn."

In her room she sank onto the bed, shaking in reaction. She'd had too much to eat and drink, but he'd insisted, and now she felt slightly nauseous. She got into her nightgown, brushed her teeth. In the bathroom mirror her face looked unfamiliar. Who was she? Was she the con- niving female Michael thought her? Was she the strong passionate woman Finn saw?

No, yes. Both at the same time. Neither. She wondered for a moment why she didn't fly apart into all the dif- ferent women who lived inside her. Maybe she would one day—just explode—and there'd be dozens of mini- ature Ellies running around, each one a foreigner to the rest. She splashed water on her face. How long could she keep this up?

Finn. Michael. She lay down on the soft springy bed, her head spinning from wine and cognac and the thrill of what she'd accomplished. Lying there, it occurred to her that Finn might knock. Maybe he'd given her the privacy to get ready for bed, and he was just waiting to knock at her door. She didn't know the rules for high-society affairs, and she wasn't sure what she'd do.

She lay there in the dark, awaiting the knock, certain it would come. When it didn't she wasn't sure if she was relieved or disappointed.

It was snowing lightly the next morning, the ground covered with an inch already. The windshield wipers were going, and Ellie was feeling extraordinarily content, croissants and cappuccino for breakfast, another adventure ahead of her.

"Everyone thinks New Mexico is a warm state, but Santa Fe is at six thousand feet. It's the highest state capital in the country," Finn said.

"I thought Denver was, but it's only the Mile-High City."

"Uh-huh. We're on what's called the High Road to Taos, the original, winding road. Most people use the new highway, but this is so much more scenic."

"How far is Chimayo?"

"Oh, about thirty miles. And every one of them packed with history."

"Is this snow going to be a problem when we fly out?" she asked.

"I checked the weather this morning. The front should be through here by this afternoon."

"That's good. What if I had to call in to the office tomorrow to tell them I was hung up in Santa Fe?" She laughed; it was too ridiculous.

"It happens when you fly. But then I'd have another

night in your company, and that wouldn't be half bad."
He winked at her.

Mountains rimmed the world. Snow drifted down, not
sticking on the road but powdering the dead buck brush
and trees. The High Road snaked between hills, passing
road signs for exotic-sounding places: Tesuque Pueblo,
San Ildefonso Pueblo, Pojoaque, Nambe.

"They're Pueblo Indian names. They still live in their
pueblos. Some of the most beautiful pottery comes from
these places." Finn gave her a heart-melting smile.

"This is the best guided tour ever," Ellie said. She felt
languid, as if she'd given everything up for the day—her
plans, her manipulations, her judging of the two men. It
was all on hold. She sat in a warm luxury car with a
handsome man who seemed to really like her. She
wanted to take the day at face value; she wanted to rest
for a while. If only she could.

"Here we are," Finn said, pulling off the road. "The
Santuario de Chimayo."

She saw a small, squarish adobe building. There were
some cars parked in a lot nearby, people walking around
the grounds. Tall cottonwoods with bare branches surrounded the small, homely sanctuary.

"I know it doesn't look like much, but it's called the
Lourdes of America. A place of many miracles."

"Miracles," Ellie mused.

"Healing miracles. Cures."

They walked across the snow-dusted grass, arm in arm,
and went inside the door. Cramped and dark, full of a
kind of reverence. There was a side room where for years
people had left their crutches and braces along with written prayers and drawings.

"I could almost believe in this," Ellie said thoughtfully.

"It's nice to think it's true, that people come and get cured of their ailments, isn't it?"

"Yes."

They stood there for a while, shoulders touching, hands clasped, studying the relics people had left there.

When they were back out in the fresh air, Ellie shook her head. "It's not my world. I respect it, but I can't . . . belong."

"Yes, this place is out of a simpler time. You have to have faith for it to work," he said.

"Never mind. It's good to know it exists and that it's there for the people who need it."

They had a leisurely lunch at a nearby restaurant. The waitress told them it was usually quieter in the winter, that their business really began at Easter, with the pilgrimages to the *santuario*. "But Christmas is coming up. You know."

"What have you got planned for me next?" Ellie turned her attention to Finn.

"Oh, I'm not sure. When we get back to Santa Fe, I'll check on weather conditions again. That might determine our schedule." He played with the tips of her fingers on the tabletop.

"It's been so much fun. So different for me," Ellie said. "Tell me the truth, Finn, are you trying to impress me?"

His blue eyes met hers, crinkling at the corners as he smiled a little self-consciously. "Don't men always try to impress women? Isn't that the name of the game?"

"I'm usually impervious to being impressed. I like to judge people by what they are, not what they have."

"Usually?" His blond brows raised. "Then I made it through that armor-plate of yours?"

"I guess so."

"Well, what am I like, then?"

"You're a gentleman, very generous. Smart, thoughtful."

"Really?"

"Yes."

"To hear people talk you'd think I was a playboy, different girl every night."

"Is it true?"

"Yes, it is. Until now."

"Oh, Finn, we hardly know each other."

"I know what I feel, Ellie." His eyes were serious, locking onto hers.

"Finn . . ."

Things were moving too quickly. It was scary. What if she'd tracked down a perfectly innocent man, tricked him, and he'd fallen hard for her? She'd be guilty of being unethical, irresponsible. Playing games. Only Michael had looked at her suspiciously from the first; Finn had no idea what was going on. No idea at all.

She *liked* him, though. Liked him a lot. And if they got to know each other over time, there could be something between them. It could grow.

"Do you believe in love at first sight?" she asked.

He thought for a minute. "Yes, I think I do." He enclosed her hand in his. "And you?"

"I don't know. I don't think so."

"That doesn't discourage me a bit," he said.

The weather cleared that afternoon, and he called Fixed Base Operations to ready his plane.

"I don't want to leave," Ellie said wistfully as the bellboy loaded their bags in the trunk of the rental car—Finn's crushed leather one next to her cheap nylon one.

"I know."

"But we both have to go back to work," she said. "The real world calls."

"We'll do it again soon. Over Christmas. We'll fly somewhere south, where it's warm. How's that?"

"Perfect." She sighed. She took one last look at the plaza, at the La Fonda Hotel, and wished suddenly, fiercely, that she could forget about everything except wonderful long weekends with Finn, fine meals, quaint hotels, travel. It was seductive, and Ellie was weaker than she'd imagined.

The flight to Denver was uneventful, the clouds thinning out as they headed north. Finn pointed out landmarks to her: the Rio Grande Gorge, Sand Dunes National Park, Pikes Peak. Then they were landing, a squeak, a bump, and they were on the ground.

It was a tremendous letdown. The minute she got into Finn's Cherokee, her life came rushing back, filling her head with unwelcome questions.

There was Michael to deal with, and her mother and, of course, Finn. Juggling and lying again. Work and cold and her obsessive search.

"Happy?" Finn asked, and he gave her a quick sideways glance.

"Sad," she said. "It's over."

"No, Ellie, it's only beginning."

He drove through Denver and up to Boulder, past rolling dry fields covered with snow, so familiar. Home. He didn't need directions to her address, even though it was growing dark.

The lights in the Marine Street house were on. Good, at least she wouldn't be alone. Maybe they could play cards. Jenn could tell some of her dirty jokes, and they'd laugh.

He pulled up in front of the house and came around to open her door and get her bag out.

"Home sweet home," he said.

"Thank you. Thank you more than I can say. It was a very special weekend."

He put his arms around her, and she tilted her face up. He kissed her, squeezed her tight, and kissed her again.

"I'll call you," he said.

"Yes."

"Don't work too hard."

"Okay. Whatever you say."

"That's my girl. Good-bye, Ellie."

"Good-bye, Finn."

He kissed her one last time, and she walked up the porch steps, carrying her cheap nylon bag with its broken zipper and the secondhand clothes folded carefully inside. She opened the door, warm and glowing inside, missing Finn already.

She closed the door behind her, and she never saw the black pickup truck parked in the shadows across the street, never saw the murderous look in the golden eyes that had watched her every move.

FIFTEEN

Rick Augostino got the call Monday morning. "Come on, Callas," he said, "a body on the CU campus." There was something in the older man's voice that made Michael look up.

"It's a coed. Campus cops just secured the crime scene. They think it's a rape-murder." Augostino sounded sick.

"Shit." Michael's voice was barely audible. "I'll get my coat. You want me to take this alone, Rick? I'd be glad to. . . ."

"No, no."

Michael knew why Rick looked ill. His daughter was a coed—not at CU—but this sort of heinous crime did them all in, especially Augostino.

They got to the campus, parked, and were led on foot to the scene by a campus cop shortly before ten A.M.

"It's an isolated area in winter," the cop told them en route, "off a footpath behind the Student Recreation Center. We figure she died sometime on Sunday."

"How's that? Has the coroner . . . ?"

"No, he's on his way to do the preliminaries."

Michael jammed his hands in his parka pockets and ducked his head to the cold. "So what makes you think she died on Sunday?" Campus cops, he thought, about on a par with security guards, rent-a-cops. Although this guy seemed okay. At least he'd done the right thing, called the BPD and the coroner immediately. Still . . .

The cop shook his head. "She's pretty . . . frozen, you know?"

"Uh-huh," Michael said.

"ID?" Rick asked.

"Yup. He left her backpack. Student card, the works. It's in my patrol car."

Michael swore. "You shouldn't have touched it."

"Well, I, I was careful. I even used gloves."

Michael grunted.

At first the body just looked like a dark hump in the snow between two small fir trees a hundred yards along the path behind the Student Recreation Center. Then they went in closer, trying real hard not to disturb the scene any more than it already had been. The snow was recent—from that storm on Saturday. Michael remembered it well. The bottle of brandy. The excruciating hangover Sunday morning.

"Oh, man, I hate this," Rick breathed at his side.

Then Michael stopped short, a sudden pain in his chest.

The victim was sprawled facedown in the snow. She had short dark curly hair, which was frozen at the tips now, and she was wearing a long black wool coat.

All he could see was Ellie. Her beautiful face pressed into the hard-packed snow. His stomach clenched like a fist.

But then Rick leaned down, snapping on latex gloves, and moved her head slightly.

Michael took a hard look. Not Ellie.

After the coroner arrived and did the preliminary examination, a few photos and body temperature check, Michael and Rick spent hours at the crime scene with the crime techs, the police photographer, instructing him to take shots of everything, samples of everything, right down to collecting some of the pine needles on the trees. You never knew where you'd find fibers. There were plenty of footprints, too, and after photographing them, Michael wanted the loose snow bagged in plastic and checked for dirt and fiber when it melted. They might get lucky.

It definitely looked like rape. Beneath her coat her clothes were torn away. She hadn't been strangled, though. On the coroner's initial examination, it appeared as if her assailant had struck her with a blunt object on the back of her head. It was up to the coroner, of course, to determine the exact cause and time of death and whether death had occurred before or after the rape.

Although Michael knew the MO of this crime was totally wrong, he nevertheless thought about Rasmussen. Always did.

And Ellie—goddamn her cheating heart—had spent the weekend with the man. What if Rasmussen had . . . ?

But he couldn't let himself go there; this poor girl was lying on the snow dead, and a murderer was on the loose. Then there was her family. Who would be assigned to tell them? Did they live in Colorado? Maybe right in Boulder. *Jesus.*

"I guess we'll start with the known sex offenders and then widen the investigation to some of the townies," Rick said.

"Yeah." Michael frowned. "And I'll get her roommates and boyfriends, if there are any. God, I'm going to hate telling her friends."

"It's hard. But I appreciate the help here, you know?" Michael nodded. He knew.

It took most of the day to locate and take statements from the girl's roommates, who were all sophomores. So damn young. And all the while Michael kept having to shove aside thoughts of Ellie. Ellie, the accomplished liar. Ellie, Rasmussen's latest lady friend. Michael's brain pounded with images and questions and more images.

Had she seduced Rasmussen, too? Had she *fucked* him?

He searched out the rape victim's boyfriend, who had a part-time job at a fast-food joint on Arapahoe. Taking the kid to an isolated booth in the back of the restaurant, Michael taped the boy's statement. Or tried to. The kid could barely stop blubbering long enough to answer Michael's questions. If gut reactions meant anything, Michael would have sworn this boy knew nothing about the murder and rape of his girlfriend. It was a tough interview, the toughest kind there was, next to talking to the parents. Michael figured the Chinese had gotten it right when they'd said there was no worse fate in life than outliving your children. Like his own parents. And Paul.

He left the restaurant a few minutes before two P.M. and met up with Rick back at headquarters, where he learned forensics might already have a lead. Apparently, and this was very preliminary, something had turned up in the plastic bags of melted snow, a loose car key, of all things. If the key was an original and the serial number could be traced, they might just be looking at a fast arrest.

The worst part of policing was writing up the formal reports. Some of Michael's notes were easier than others to transcribe, usually his crime scene notes, ones he'd had the time to scribble down properly. But the notes or

tapes taken during interviews were more difficult. Those
you had to get exactly right. Michael preferred taping
everything. It was too bad he was still and always would
be a hunt-and-peck typist, and thank God for Spellcheck.

He began typing up the reports from the interviews
he'd conducted that day but found his mind wandering,
his fingers hovering, unmoving, over the keyboard.

Ellie Kramer. *Crandall,* rather. Her game was obvious.
She suspected either he or Rasmussen had something to
do with her father's conviction, perhaps planting evidence. Such as John Crandall's bandana. Of course Janice Crandall had carried on for months, until the trial was
over, about evidence tampering and police setups.

Janice Crandall. It was a wonder he hadn't recognized
her sooner.

What did Ellie expect to find? Trying to prove, after
so long a passage of time, that her father was innocent,
that either Michael or Rasmussen had set the man up?

Michael typed for a minute and then went inside himself again.

Or were Ellie's suspicions deeper? Did she think one
of them was the rapist? And if she thought that, even
suspected it, she was out of her mind to be pursuing
either one of them.

Had Ellie believed *he* could be a rapist when she'd
slept with him?

He sat staring into the middle distance. If that were
true, then wouldn't he have to admire her tenacity, the
fact that she'd overcome a hundred obstacles to get as
far as she had? Shouldn't he respect her courage? She
was deliberately putting herself in intimate situations
with a rapist. For her father.

How had she located Finn? He thought back and realized she'd been trying to get the information from him,

asking him about his rookie days on the force. "I'll bet your partner was a woman, a tough lady." She'd said something like that, leading him.

He had trouble concentrating all afternoon. He had to let her know about Finn. What if she were going out with him again, say tonight? He had to tell her. My God, what an insane, foolhardy, fearless lady she was.

At four P.M. he filed his reports and then accompanied Rick to the coroner's over at the Boulder Community Hospital. This was the fun part, he thought darkly, having to look at the young girl's naked body, all her decency and humanity stripped from her on a cold stainless steel autopsy table, the scales suspended above her, the microphone, the sink, and her lifeblood dripping into the drain. He hoped to hell when his time came it would be in a ball of fire, nothing left for the coroner.

Rick entered the room but hung by the door, eyes averted. Fortunately, the doctor performing the examination was a real pro who had enormous respect for the dead. That had not always been the case in Boulder. Years ago, there'd been a young hotshot who'd cracked every clichéd sick joke there was, the old eat-at-Luigi's jokes, when he'd been examining brains or contents of intestines. Michael never knew if the guy had done it for his own amusement or for that of the cops, but Michael hadn't seen an ounce of humor in it.

The truth was he despised this part of the job. Some guys got over it after a time. Not him. There was something about the stench of human blood and organs and waste, something that stirred a primal fear deep inside.

The coroner nodded at him and said hello to Rick, who was still avoiding the corpse. "Just finishing up," the man said.

"Uh-huh," Michael said, hands in his pockets, gaze

averted from the table. "So what have we got here?"

Michael had never liked to look at a cadaver. No one did. He hadn't seen Paul right after the accident. But at the funeral, for a few minutes, he'd been allowed into the viewing room with immediate family to pay his last respects. It had been a shock. At first he'd thought his brother was just asleep. Someone had made a terrible mistake. But then after a minute, staring wide-eyed at the lifeless form, Michael recognized the horrible finality, the empty husk just lying there. Then, for a moment his brain had done a reversal and he'd thought, no, no, Paul *was* asleep—look at all the color in his face, the slight, peaceful smile. *Wake up. Wake up. For the love of God, Paul, wake up.*

"I'm going to stick my neck out and fix the time of death between nine and ten P.M. last night—Sunday," the coroner was saying.

Michael took a breath. "Okay." He made a note in his black book. "Rape?"

"Definite rape. And there's semen, too."

"Good. Good." More notes. "Doesn't look like a serial rape, either," Michael said.

"No, wouldn't think so. Nowadays repeat rapists usually don't leave evidence like this behind."

"Okay. What else?"

"Death by hypothermia, after losing consciousness from a blunt instrument blow to the back of the head. All the technical stuff will be in the report, but between you and me and the walls, Callas, I'd say a rock, a smooth rock not much larger than my hand. Clumsy job, too, though there were no fibers, such as wood, in the wound, so unless you find the exact weapon and some blood I won't be able to help much in court."

"Was she hit before or after the rape?"

"Definitely before. My guess? I'd say your guy got scared. Maybe he only wanted to shut her up long enough to do his thing. He may not have intended to kill her. Probably didn't or there would be a deeper wound or several wounds, and certainly in a more select area on the cranium."

Michael thought about the girl's boyfriend but again aced him out. He'd said he and the victim had an active, normal sex life. Her roommates had confirmed, albeit with many tears and much embarrassment.

"Listen," the coroner said, "I'd like to get her cleaned up here. The parents"—he glanced at the institutional wall clock—"should be arriving in under an hour."

"Of course," Michael said, "anything else we need, we'll get from your report."

"Any suspects?"

Michael shook his head, but it was Rick who answered. "We'll get the little fuck. And he better hope I'm not alone with him when we do."

Michael exchanged a look with the doctor and then ushered Rick out.

He never got a chance to phone Ellie until he dropped Rick back at police headquarters and they switched to their own vehicles. Of course, he acknowledged he'd been putting the call off since seeing her with Rasmussen, the goddamned way Rasmussen had touched her, kissed her, held her so close. As if he owned her.

Forget it, Michael told himself, sitting in his truck, looking at his watch. She'd be leaving the Justice Center soon. Maybe Rasmussen was picking her up. Maybe he'd take her home with him, home to that big expensive house of his. And there, maybe he'd screw her brains out.

It doesn't matter. It was painfully obvious to Michael

that Finn must seem like the good guy to her. Why not? Finn, the big handsome ladies' man, Mr. Charisma. And Michael, the inarticulate loner, Robocop. Of course Ellie believed he was the mad rapist.

Well, she had to be warned. If he let it go, if he stayed away from her to keep his sanity, then she was wholly at Rasmussen's mercy. Michael had found out the truth about her, and sure as hell Finn would too. Rasmussen was a sick puppy, but he wasn't stupid.

Michael dialed the number on his cell phone, half wishing she'd gone home, half panicked that he'd missed her. It was nearly five.

He got through to her almost immediately. Her voice, picturing her, then seeing behind his eyes that pretty coed in the snow, her dark curling hair frozen, was more than he could handle.

"I have to see you tonight," he got out and then, shocking him, he realized he was choked up. About ready to goddamn cry. He hadn't cried, even come close, since they'd shoveled dirt on his brother's coffin.

"Michael?"

Jesus. "I need to see you, Ellie. It's important."

She hesitated. Of course she did. She thought he was guilty. "Well, I was going to—" she began.

"Look," he cut in sharply, "this can't wait. I'm serious." Just her name on his tongue was torment. *Don't lose it now, man.*

"Well, okay, sure, if it's important."

"It is. I'm off work. I can be there in, say, ten minutes."

"I'll meet you out front. Where are we, ah, going?"

Worried. Her voice was saturated with concern.

"We'll get some dinner" was all he'd tell her, and then

he severed the connection. Wouldn't it be great if he could cut her out of his life as easily?

He backed out of the parking slot then twisted the steering wheel till it squealed. Ellie with that sick bastard. How could she be so blind? How could all Rasmussen's women be so blind?

He didn't stop at the sign when he exited the police lot, and a patrolman looked askance at him. Turning onto Arapahoe, he barely saw the heavy rush-hour traffic. He merged into it and cut into the left lane, receiving a horn blast from some irate driver. Road rage. By the time he was crossing Twenty-eighth and heading along Boulder Creek his temper was barely in check.

Ellie in bed with Rasmussen, screwing him.

He wondered, stopping at a light, if she'd cried afterward.

Ellie stood in the parking lot and watched for his truck. She was on pins and needles. Despite her mother's assurance when they'd finally talked on the phone that Michael had gotten nothing pertinent out of her, Ellie couldn't be sure. She knew only that he'd driven up to Leadville on his fishing expedition because he had been suspicious of her. He was closing in on the truth, and when he reached his goal . . .

What *would* he do? It wasn't as if she'd proved he was the rapist. Still, God only knew what murky waters ran beneath his surface. Would he try to shut her up?

A cold wind tore through her coat and she hugged her briefcase and hunched her shoulders, desperate for him to arrive in his warm truck, dreading the moment she'd see him again. She'd never counted on her strong feelings for both these men. Surely the fates were laughing at her. Michael, Finn, Michael—one of them a monster.

She looked up, focused on the road, and saw him, and her heart gave a sudden buck.

He pulled up to the curb, leaned across the passenger seat, pushed the door open for her. Even in the waning light of the winter evening, she instantly recognized a tightness to his expression, a fire burning behind the golden flecks of his eyes.

"Hi," she said, closing the door. "Cold out, isn't it?"

"Very. Want more heat?"

"No, no, feels fine." There was something. . . . "Bad day?"

"Um," he said.

And then she remembered, the office had buzzed with it: the rape and murder at CU. "Were you involved with that . . ." She couldn't choke the word *rape* out. "With the thing over on campus?"

"I'm afraid so."

"Awful," she whispered, her gaze fixed on the road. Was she, *could* she be having this conversation with a rapist, a murderer? Oh, not the man who killed that poor coed, the MO was too far off. But was it possible for Michael to rape, strangle, to rip a woman's soul to shreds before taking her life?

Her mind cried no. Yet who was he?

He drove for a couple of blocks in silence, the stillness of him, the quiet, warning her that something was terribly wrong. It must have been the events of the day. *Sure.*

She ventured a glance at his profile. "Well, where are we going? And what was so important?"

"My place."

"Oh."

"Worried, Ellie?" he asked, and he shot her a look.

"Of course not. Don't be silly. Should we stop at a

store on the way? I'm famished." Babbling, babbling, trying to think.

Worried, he'd said, and the word was like a pebble thrown into the dark waters of her consciousness, where endless ripples of meaning spread out in an ever-widening circle. *Worried.* Why would he ask such a thing? Unless, of course, she had good reason to be concerned. Could Janice have been so wrong? Had he realized who she was?

"You know," she said after a moment, "I should let Celeste and the girls know where I'm going. I mean, this is one of our card nights. Could I use your cell phone?"

"Battery's dead."

"Oh," she said.

It was pitch-black out by the time the pickup truck crossed the loose boards of his driveway across Boulder Creek. When Ellie got out she was aware of the darkness around his cabin, the utter silence. She felt as if the canyon walls and the sky were closing in on her, and she had to take a calming breath and let it slowly out of her lungs. She was okay. She'd be okay. The mantra played over and over in her head.

He opened the door from the garage, held it for her, followed her in, and switched on the lights. The sense that something was terribly wrong persisted and grew, a bubble of apprehension swelling in her chest.

He took their coats and hung them up and she gave him a pathetic smile. "Well."

"There's a bottle of wine in the cupboard." He nodded toward it. "You want to get it out? I've got to change, I stink like the autopsy room."

"Sure, go ahead."

Then he disappeared up to the loft.

Change his clothes? He was only prolonging the tension, making her wait. And squirm.

Ellie looked furtively around the cabin, wildly, searching for his phone. It was the only edge she had. She found it on a base next to the couch, snatched it up, and pressed talk, then stabbed in her home number. If no one answered—and they rarely did till they knew who was on the line—she'd leave a message or fake a conversation.

No one was at the Marine Street house. She took a breath and left her message just as Michael reappeared, his sport coat gone, pulling a heavy beige sweater over his head while he came down the stairs.

"Okay, well, bye, see you shortly," Ellie said into the receiver and then she broke the connection. "I'll, ah, get the wine, all right?"

"That's fine. I'll build a fire."

"Oh, great, it is a little chilly."

She was freezing, goose bumps raised on her flesh beneath the black knit tunic and the black tights she was wearing. "This bottle, Michael?" She held up a bottle of cabernet sauvignon, an everyday brand.

"Yeah, sure."

She opened it with a corkscrew she found in the drawer next to the sink, all the while studying his back as he stooped over and shoved kindling and logs into the hearth. He was so quiet. Far too quiet. And she remembered that stillness from his days on the witness stand at the Zimmerman trial. The angrier he was, the more contained he became, but the anger leaked out around the edges.

"Wine's ready," she called.

"Be there in a sec."

When the fire caught he straightened and brushed his

hands on his slacks. Under most circumstances she would have found that amusing, his using his good trousers as a rag. But not tonight.

What if he'd learned who she was? What if he'd found out where she'd spent the weekend? And with whom?

He finally approached her and picked up the glass of wine, took a long drink, his gaze fixed on her. He was standing across the granite island from her, the overhead lights burning in his eyes. Eyes as golden as a cat's, as watchful. Her heart was beating a furious tattoo against her ribs. He knew everything. How stupid could she have been?

He put his glass on the counter with a clink. "All right," he said calmly, his gaze pinning her like an insect, "you've got two minutes to come clean, Ellie."

SIXTEEN

Ellie stupidly repeated the words. "Come clean?" Her head spun, and her lungs ached as if all the air had gone out of the room. "What are you talking about?"

"Spare me the innocent act." His voice was very contained, very quiet. She wished he'd yell.

"I'm sorry, I have no idea . . ."

"Ellie, I know who you are."

"Of course you know who I am."

He gave a disgusted shake of his head. "Your name is Crandall, not Kramer, and your father was John Crandall."

"John *Kramer,*" she said, stubborn, terrified.

"Jesus Christ, the game's over. Don't you get it? You lost."

"Michael, you're confusing me. I . . ."

He moved closer to her, and she could see the harsh set of his face. "John Crandall, Ellie, and he died in prison."

"No," she cried. "You're talking about someone else."

But he stood there over her, unrelenting. "I recognized

your mother. I know who she is. I saw her in that courtroom."

She felt the blood leaving her face. And then the words
spilled out of her mouth. "I was going to ask you about
that," she said angrily, pacing around the room, her arms
folded defensively across her chest. "I thought that was
pretty sneaky, Michael, going up to Leadville behind my
back and *investigating* my mother."

He gave a short laugh.

She paced, and her mind tried a thousand possibilities
on for size, discarded them, tried on new ones. Not a
word came to her.

"I know everything. I even know what you did over
the weekend." Steel shavings curled off his voice.

Her eyes flew to him.

"Finn Rasmussen," he said.

"Are you *spying* on me?"

He shrugged.

"Finn and I . . . we're friends."

"Friends."

"I just met him. He seems very nice. How *dare* you
spy on me?"

"Because I knew you were lying about something."
Quiet, measured words. Only the truth.

There was no out in that direction. She switched
abruptly, holding her hand up, warding off what he might
say. "Okay, I admit I was interested in the Morris case.
But only after I met you, only after we worked together.
I didn't know before—"

"Cut the crap."

"It's true. I met you and . . . and I read up on your past
and . . ."

"Me and Finn both, huh?"

"Well . . . sure."

"Coincidental, right?"

"Yes, I . . ."

"Ellie, you've been planning this for years. Revenging your father."

"He was not . . . that man in jail was not . . ." Her voice clicked off.

"He was your *father,* Ellie, and he worked in the Morris house, and I"—he took a step closer—"*I* found his bandana around Stephanie Morris's neck, and my partner, Finn, and I put him away."

"Oh, God," she whispered.

"You had to meet both of us, judge us, pick our brains. Get *close* to us. Oh, yeah, it worked, didn't it? You got to fuck both of us."

"No," she said, "no, it wasn't like that. No. I got to know you, and I *liked* you, Michael. I really did."

"The same way you *liked* Finn?"

"No, no, we're just friends."

"Platonic friends." Scathing.

"I . . . I didn't sleep with Finn, I swear, Michael, I didn't. But you . . . it was different. It *is* different. I care about you . . . deeply."

His hand sliced the air, making her jerk back. "Stop lying, Ellie." Then he looked at her closely. "You're scared to death, aren't you? You're standing there, shaking like a leaf, because you think you're my next victim. You think I'm going to rape you. Murder you. Or maybe I'll kill you just because you know too much."

She shook her head mutely, tears gathering in her eyes, her nose starting to run. Shaking.

He smiled, a grim, ironic twist of his lips. "You've got the wrong man. Finn's the one you want. He's the one who raped Stephanie Morris."

She felt her gorge rise. Saliva gathered in her mouth. *Finn.* "No," she breathed.

"Yeah. Sorry."

She sank onto the couch, afraid she was going to be sick. "I can't . . . I don't . . ."

"Proof. You want proof? I don't have anything but circumstantial evidence, but it was him. And you know what, Ellie? Stephanie Morris wasn't the only one. There were others. . . ."

"Holly Lance?" she got out, her thoughts running wildly, beating at her brain. He was accusing Finn. Lying to save himself?

"You *have* done your homework. Holly in Pueblo, and a decade ago he murdered Naomi Freeman in Greeley and Amy Blanchard in Longmont seven years ago, and just this past Thanksgiving, he killed a sixteen-year-old girl in Mexico. Her name is Peta, and one of her father's employees was arrested because—hey, listen up, Ellie— his scarf was tied around her neck."

She couldn't find her voice.

"I have proof Finn was in Baja over Thanksgiving. I've got a big fat file on my good old partner, Finn."

Somehow she found the courage to meet his eyes. He was lying, wasn't he? Covering his own tracks?

"Every time your friend has raped and murdered I can place him in the town. Use your head, for chrissakes. Or are you as snowed as all the rest?"

"No, I . . ." But she knew he was right. Finn had snowed her. "You, you really can place him in Pueblo and Greeley?"

"*And* Mexico, just a few weeks ago. You want to talk to the police there? *Do you?* And you know it wasn't me. Shit, Ellie, you're my alibi. Wake the hell up."

She closed her eyes and took several breaths. Why

would he be lying when it was so easy to check?

Finn. The ladies' man. What a fool she'd been. She bit her lip and opened her eyes. "Why . . . if you knew all this, why didn't you tell your captain or somebody? Why did you just let him go on doing it?" she cried.

"I tried, believe me. After your father's trial, after the murder in Greeley with the same MO, I started suspecting Finn. But he'd quit the force by then, and I had no proof, nothing to go on. Eventually, I brought it to my commander's attention, and I got my ass reamed out."

"No one believed you?"

"Hell, no. Not when there was a convenient, made-to-order suspect in each case. Cops don't look very hard for things that disprove their theories. Some cops, that is. Plus everyone knew I hated Rasmussen."

"My father—"

"And plenty of other men, too," he cut her off bitterly. "There's Naomi Freeman's neighbor, that was ten years ago, and Amy Blanchard. Her older stepbrother is still in prison for her murder. She died, raped and strangled in Longmont. That was seven years ago now. And let's see. Oh, yeah, Holly Lance. Finn screwed up with her."

"Yes," Ellie said, biting her lip.

"And of course Peta, in Mexico. Let's not forget her. Some poor sap who worked for her father is taking the rap."

"I . . . I wonder . . ."

"How many more there are? Girls we don't know about? Beats me, *Ellie*. Now, where did Rasmussen take you?"

"Santa Fe," she whispered.

"How cozy. In that plane he's got?"

She nodded slowly.

"Jesus, Ellie, are you out of your mind?"

She looked up at him, sniffing. "I went with you."

"Don't goddamn put me in the same classification as that piece of filth."

"I didn't know. How could I know?"

"Does your mother have any idea what you're doing?"

"Some."

"Huh, no wonder she was so nervous. She must hate my guts."

She bit her lower lip again.

"Well, tell her I'm sorry. She had the wrong guy, too."

Ellie found her briefcase on the bar stool and searched for a tissue, blew her nose. She was not afraid anymore, but she was sick, empty and bare to the world. Naked. And so ashamed.

"You wish it was me. Go on, say it."

"No, no, Michael. I didn't lie . . . about that."

"You wouldn't know the truth if it slapped you in the face. You and Finn make a good pair."

"Stop," she breathed.

"He's a great guy, lots of fun. Rich, good looking. But he's really screwed up. I've done my research, too, and I got hold of one of Rasmussen's social workers in Milwaukee."

"Social worker?"

"He was in foster care for a while. His father was in jail, and his mother couldn't take care of the kids. They went to foster homes. Finn was the youngest."

"He told me about his father."

"Did he tell you about his uncle?"

"No."

"For a while he and his sister stayed with their uncle, and the social worker I talked to was convinced that the uncle did something to Finn. Her educated guess was sexual abuse."

"Oh, no."

"She had no proof, but she knew the kid had problems."

Finn? Handsome, thoughtful, charming Finn? Her mind couldn't cope with the idea.

"Well, Ellie, what do you think?"

"I . . . don't know. I have to sort it all out. . . ." She looked up at him, at the hard, chiseled face, anger held tight behind his golden eyes. "What are you going to do, Michael?"

"About Finn?"

She shook her head silently.

"About you? Nothing. I'm not going to do a goddamn thing. If you have a date with Rasmussen, break it."

She looked at her hands. "I want to catch him."

"What?"

"We have to catch him."

"We? Jesus, Ellie, give it up."

"You want him, don't you?"

"Yeah, I want him. But not until I have hard evidence."

"Don't close me out, Michael. He killed my father. He put my father in prison and it killed him."

"Close you out? You were never in."

"Michael, please. . . ."

"You lied to me about everything."

"I didn't . . . not about everything. Not about how I feel about you. I swear."

"Ellie, I wouldn't believe you if you had your hand on a Bible and a noose around your neck. You don't know how to tell the truth." He moved close to stand over her, and she shrank back.

"I don't hurt women," he said in a ruthless voice. "Now, get your coat. I'm taking you home."

"Wait, Michael, can't we . . ."

"What?"

"Can't we talk . . . just a little while?"

"About what?"

"I . . . I don't know. I'll try to explain. . . ." Tears ran from her eyes silently, and she wiped at them. "I care so much about you. Michael . . ."

"No."

She was afraid then, of his implacability. Not only had she lost him, but her search was at an end. She knew who the guilty man was, but she couldn't do anything about it. Michael would stop her.

"I don't want to give up," she said in a stronger voice.

"Here's your coat." Roughly, he shoved it at her. "Don't forget your briefcase."

He was opening the door to the garage already. She tried to think of a way to get through to him, but he was too angry, his surface slick as marble, no cracks, no way to gain a hold.

Woodenly, she shrugged her coat on, picked up her briefcase, and followed him. There was nothing else to do.

He didn't say a thing the whole way back down Canyon Boulevard into Boulder. She sat huddled in the truck against the door, shaking. She couldn't stop shaking. She thought once, *Is this what the truth does to you? Then I don't want it. Leave me the comfort of my lies.*

He drove fast, jerking the wheel savagely, and she was relieved when they shot out of the narrow canyon into city traffic.

It was over, she kept thinking. Everything was over. She'd lost the game. Michael had said that, and he was right.

A red light stopped him at the intersection of Canyon and Sixteenth Street, and he waited impatiently, drumming his fingers on the steering wheel, looking straight ahead. His profile was as sharp against the streetlight glare as one of the warriors on a Greek temple frieze.

She couldn't bear it another moment, the silent shrieking furies flailing in the truck. She opened the door, slid down to the street. "Wait," she heard him say, surprised, but she slammed the door and darted away to the sidewalk. She walked fast, then, breathing in the cold air, angrily wiping away the tears that still came. For a few blocks she was aware of him tailing her, but she wouldn't look. She kept her eyes on the sidewalk, concentrated on her breathing. What had she done? All these years of scheming and it was over, in the blink of an eye.

She walked a long ways, farther than she had to; her house was only a few blocks away. She did it to calm herself down, to start working on the barriers she would have to construct in her mind to protect herself from the God Almighty truth. And she walked, also, because she was afraid Michael might have driven to the house to wait for her.

She thought of Finn and shuddered, and she recalled the small things about him she'd wondered at—the need for control, his too-easy way with women. His father, his mother. The small things. The way he always had to have his hands on her, as if he owned her—or was he afraid she'd slip away?

It was cold out. She shoved her hands in her coat pockets to try to keep them warm, and she felt the gloves. The soft black gloves Finn had bought her in Santa Fe. Crumpled, stuck in her pockets that morning when she got to work.

She tugged them out, warm, cashmere-lined gloves that had cost a fortune. They'd feel wonderful on her hands—they'd been so warm that morning going to

work. She held them for a moment, and she could feel
Finn's hands on her, smell his male scent, taste the food
they'd eaten, hear the guitar. Then she flung them away,
onto somebody's lawn, and walked past swiftly, shoulders hunched to the cold, hands in her pockets.

She was ashamed. She should have known, should
have *felt* it. She'd been seduced by his money, his house
and car and airplane, his friends. The things she'd wanted
all her life, her nose pressed against the glass looking in.

From the very first Michael had been different. She'd
felt something real but denied it, because it wasn't convenient, and she'd thought, God help her, she'd thought
he could be the rapist, the murderer. She'd slept with
him, and he'd opened his life to her, and she'd betrayed
him. She couldn't blame him for being angry—she deserved it.

It was late by the time she walked home. Cold, her
feet icy, shivering, she opened the door to the familiar
warm place that was more home to her than anywhere
else.

"Here she is," yelled Celeste.

"Where in hell have you been?" Bonnie asked. "Your
mother's been calling."

"Look, she's half frozen. What happened, Ellie?" Jennifer asked.

Ellie sank down on the old couch. "I'm okay," she
said. "I was walking."

"Walking? In this weather? At night?" Celeste cried.

"You've been crying," Bonnie noted.

"I thought you were with Michael," Celeste said.
"When you didn't come home . . ."

"I was."

"You had a fight." Jenn shook her head.

Ellie almost smiled. *A fight.*

Celeste ran upstairs and got the duvet from Ellie's bed. "Take your coat off and put this around you. What happened?"

Ellie looked up at her good friends, their faces worried, hovering over her. She pulled the duvet around her shoulders. "Sit down," she said. "I have something to tell you."

"What?"

"Come on, Ellie. . . ."

"No, wait," Celeste said, "let her talk." She sat, sinking down onto the floor in a lotus position. The others sat, too, waiting, expectant.

Ellie swallowed. Could she do this? Confess? All these years. So many lies. She felt a terrible sob well in her chest.

"Ellie?" they chorused.

She closed her eyes for a moment. When she opened them, she said, "I'm . . . I'm not who you think I am."

"Ellie . . ." Bonnie protested.

"Shush," Jennifer said.

"I've lied to you all this time, to Celeste the longest." She met her friend's puzzled gaze. "My real name is Crandall, Eleanor Crandall, and I'm originally from Boulder."

"Crandall?" Celeste said.

"My mother had our names changed legally because . . . because my father was arrested for a terrible crime and convicted, and we couldn't live here anymore," now the words tumbled out, "and we moved to Leadville." She stopped for breath. "I was twelve years old, and my father was arrested for raping a girl."

"Oh, my God." Bonnie's fist went to her mouth.

"But he was innocent. He didn't do it. I know he didn't do it because he was with me that whole night. And all these years, all this time, I've been looking for the man who did it." She stopped and searched her friends' faces. Shock, sorrow, Celeste in tears. But none of the disgust or rejection she expected.

"I believe you," Bonnie said, nodding now. "I mean, you were with your dad."

Celeste rose from her lotus position, tall and skinny, her black jeans worn through at one knee, and she put her arms around Ellie. No words, just her embrace.

"I'm sorry," Ellie mumbled. "I apologize to you all."

"Shush. Don't be silly," Jennifer said, and she and Bonnie followed Celeste's lead, embracing Ellie in a tangle of arms and hair and hands patting with fevered comfort.

Ellie sat there, the center of the outpouring of love, and she felt shamed again, shamed to the core of who she was. She thought of her friends and of Michael and held on to the girls tightly. She didn't deserve their love or their forgiveness. How could they forgive her when she couldn't forgive herself?

"It's all right, it's all right," Celeste whispered. "Shh."

But Ellie knew. It was not all right. *He* was still out there. Free to rape and murder and destroy.

SEVENTEEN

Michael wondered if he should have told Ellie he was sorry about what he'd done to her father. He'd been thinking about it for two days now: Would it have done any good? He kept trying to convince himself that it was water under the bridge—*Ellie* was water under the bridge—but his mind insisted on circling back with irritating regularity to that scene in his house, to her slipping out of his truck, dodging cars, running away from him. Maybe from herself, too.

Ah, forget it. Forget her, he thought about a hundred times.

Then he got the call from his informant Pete Stone. "Rasmussen's seeing this lady on a regular basis," Stone began.

As if I don't know, Michael thought.

"Haven't got a name yet, but he drives to Boulder to pick her up. He flew her somewhere over the weekend. . . ."

"Uh-huh."

"They sure looked lovey-dovey. About made me puke."

"Is that so?"

"I never saw your man act that way before. He couldn't keep his hands off her. She's a fox, though. And young."

"I know who she is," Michael said.

"Well, shit, you still want me to keep tabs on him?"

"Absolutely," Michael said. "And you'll be compensated as usual."

"Okay, talk to you."

"Yeah, sure," he said, and he hung up scowling. Lovey-dovey. Christ, he couldn't get away from her. Ever.

He and Augostino had been working on the coed homicide. Her name was Valerie Girard, she had been a CU student, twenty-one years old, from Omaha, Nebraska. All the patrolmen and detectives were working overtime, canvassing the area where she'd been found, talking to her friends and classmates and professors. Over and over.

She'd been last seen working out at the Student Recreation Center. She'd left around ten, which matched the coroner's time of death in the autopsy report: between ten and midnight.

Someone had stalked her when she left the Recreation Center, grabbed her, raped her, hit her on the head, or maybe she'd been hit first, to keep her quiet. She had not actually died of the blow to the head; that had only rendered her unconscious. She had died from hypothermia. And the killer hadn't even taken her wallet or her money.

"It has to be some crazy," Augostino kept saying, his brow furrowed. He'd been the one to coordinate with the campus cops, making sure all CU students were on high alert, no coeds walking alone at night. Publicizing the campus service, Night Ride–Night Walk, on television, radio, and in print.

"He got scared when he saw what he'd done," Michael agreed, "and just ran. There was no planning to this one. A crime of opportunity."

They were both walking around the crime scene, in the tracked-up snow, one last time, trying to figure out exactly where the killer had come from, where he'd hidden, where he'd waited, which way he'd run when it was over. But the snow had melted, and nothing looked like it had that dark night.

Experience told Michael they weren't going to run the killer down by walking the same old turf; much more likely they'd track him through the car key they'd found. Jim Chambliss was working that angle.

"Any news from Chambliss yet?" Rick Augostino asked, idly nudging aside a frozen lump of snow with the toe of his shoe.

"Not yet. Apparently the key is an original, and Jim's got the VIN from the manufacturer, but DMV's still searching the back records for the present owner."

"Christ, they're slow. Anyone tell those bureaucrats this is murder?"

"Jim's on their asses."

Augostino grumbled something unintelligible.

There were CU students walking along Boulder Creek, coming out of the Rec Center. They all stared at the two cops, and they saw the yellow crime scene tape, knew what had happened there. Maybe some of them had known the Girard girl, the poor kid, dead long before her time.

Michael recalled his reaction when he'd seen the girl's body lying there that cold morning. *Ellie,* he'd thought. *Ellie's dead.* It had grabbed him with shocking force for a moment, just a moment, until he'd seen that it wasn't her. And now Ellie was as dead to him as Valerie Girard.

He was obsessing over Ellie, and he knew it. Ready to forgive her everything one instant, damning her soul to hell for her betrayal the next. All these years, all these long years, since Paul's death and his parents' rejection, he'd kept his emotions in that vault inside himself. Carefully, safely locked away. And then Ellie had come along, and he'd thought that maybe he was capable of caring, even of love. *Goddamn her.*

"Well, I can't find a thing," Augostino said. "We need the car, damn it. Chambliss has to get it."

"So meanwhile we keep digging. The usual. Maybe someone will get lucky and find a witness. It could happen," Michael replied.

Uniforms were already checking neighboring buildings and the faculty-staff housing across Boulder Creek. Ten o'clock on a Sunday night wasn't late, and there had to have been people out. People who saw someone who didn't quite fit in, someone running or looking frightened. Out of synch with the rest of the campus crowd. Based on local demographics, most likely a young, white male.

He and Rick walked to where their car was parked. While Michael drove, his mind returned stubbornly to Ellie. Almost worse than his anger was his fear for her safety. Because he knew she wasn't about to stop pursuing Rasmussen. She'd gotten him interested in her, and she wasn't going to give up just because Michael had told her to. She didn't give a damn what he said or what he thought or how he felt.

Persistent Ellie. She'd waited and schemed for years; now, thanks to him, she finally knew the truth. Maybe he shouldn't have told her about Rasmussen, but he'd had to. He'd had to, or she would have gone on thinking it was *him.*

All afternoon Michael went through reports that had come in regarding possible sightings of the Coed Killer, as the TV and newspapers had dubbed him. He sifted the good reports, the ones that had a modicum of value, from the bad, took notes. Thought about Ellie.

She wouldn't stop. She'd go out with Rasmussen and try to find a chink in his armor, try to push his buttons. She'd try to get some kind of proof that he was a criminal, and that her father had been unjustly arrested, tried, convicted, imprisoned.

He should have apologized. He should never have told her about Rasmussen. He should never have believed in her in the first place.

At home that night his mother called: "You'll come for Christmas, Michael, won't you? You missed Thanksgiving, and I do want to see you. You work too hard. For goodness' sake, you can take a few days off."

"Okay, yeah, I know. I'll be there, sure I will."

"Well, it's not like you're that far away. I'd drive up, but you know I get nervous on those icy roads. And we all want to see you."

He'd heard it before, and he knew he'd have to go, but he shriveled inside at the thought of sitting down to Christmas dinner without Paul.

There was a Christmas card from his father in the mail, too. A scribbled note and a query as to why Michael hadn't called lately.

He thought back to the last time he'd seen his father. A year and a half ago? His father lived in the mountain hamlet of Manitou Springs, to the west of Colorado Springs. He'd been on his way to Cheyenne, Wyoming, and he'd stopped in Boulder for lunch. Their get-together had been typical.

"How's the car dealership going?" Michael.

"Oh, fine, fine, a good living. And you?" Paul Senior.

"Oh, fine here, too."

They'd never had much to say to each other. Not before Paul Junior's death, and certainly not afterward.

Ah, hell, he thought. So he'd call the old man someday soon. It was Christmas. He'd be magnanimous.

He sprawled on his couch and watched the news on television. And all the while he was imagining Ellie sitting right there. Her smile, her gestures, that warmth of hers that lit up the whole room. Her body next to his in bed. Her back as she washed dishes there, at his sink.

And then, superimposed on those images, he saw her crying, terrified, white and sick as he'd bludgeoned her with her lies. Threw them in her face.

If she weren't putting herself in such deadly danger, he'd admire what she was doing. They were on the same side, the side of justice, but he'd let himself get emotionally involved, and now they were enemies.

He knew he had to protect her from her own foolhardy courage. He'd have to keep an eye on her, follow her when he could, stop her from putting herself at risk.

He turned the TV off, went upstairs. In bed, he thought again, his old familiar refrain, that if Rasmussen did it again, only one more time, Michael might be able to put together enough evidence to reopen the Morris case—or one of the others. Sooner or later Rasmussen would slip, either through overconfidence or carelessness. Sooner or later.

He had a dream that night. Ellie was with Rasmussen. She was wearing a wire, and Michael was listening, but he was also somehow right there with them, seeing everything. Rasmussen started to get rough with her. She cried, "No, no," but he didn't care. He was pulling at her clothes, and she was crying. Michael listened, but he also saw; he was with them, in the manner of dreams. Rasmussen overpowered her and raped her, then he started to choke her; Michael was still there, listening and watching. He had the evidence this time, absolute proof. He had it on tape and he was an eyewitness. He'd put the man away this time. He had him.

But why wasn't he happy in his dream? Fractionally awake, still asleep, he manipulated the scene until he understood: It was too late for Ellie to celebrate. Rasmussen had choked the life out of her.

Ellie was done crying. She was done feeling sorry for herself. Michael was finished with her. She'd stupidly blown her chance for a real relationship, but she couldn't, wouldn't think about that now. She didn't have the leisure or the energy to dissect the awful mistake she'd made.

No, she wouldn't think about that, because she had to focus on Finn. She wasn't about to let him go, not when she knew he was the man she'd searched for all these years. To hell with Michael's warning. The cops hadn't caught him thirteen years ago, they hadn't caught him when he'd raped and murdered those other women, and they weren't looking for him now.

She had to do it.

Schemes chased themselves around in her mind every waking moment. *How to get proof?*

By God, she'd let him rape *her,* if it would nail him. But, strangely, Finn seemed uninterested in sleeping with her. Much less raping her.

Finn called her a week before Christmas, on a Thursday.

"How have you been?" he asked, and Ellie was surprised that he had the same smooth baritone as usual. So nice and polite and concerned. The perfect gentleman.

"Fine, good," she said. Could he tell she knew about him?

"Listen, I have a couple of tickets for *A Christmas Carol* on Saturday night. At the Buell Theater. Great seats. Can you make it?"

"Dickens's play?" She didn't want to seem too anxious.

"That's the one. It's a charity affair, you know, money goes for abused kids."

"I'd love to," she said.

"Dinner first?"

"Sure, wonderful."

"I'll pick you up early, so we'll have plenty of time. Six o'clock."

"Perfect," she said.

"See you then."

"Can't wait," she purred.

"That's my girl."

When she hung up she noticed that her hand was shaking.

She borrowed another dress from Celeste, a red one this time. She'd never worn a red outfit in her life, but it looked good on her, a slim knee-length dress with a bolero jacket to match. And the mink-lined coat.

It was a lie, all a lie, but wasn't that the point?

"You look great," Celeste said.

"I promise I'll get it dry-cleaned if I spill food on it."

Celeste laughed. Her generosity stabbed Ellie. For all the truth she'd supposedly confessed to her roommates, she hadn't said a word about Finn being a rapist, a killer. She couldn't. They would try to stop her. But the absence of truth and her store of ugly secrets made her sick and ashamed. Someday it would be over, she swore, her life an open book. No more dirty secrets.

"Have fun," Celeste said.

Fun. "I will."

He took her to dinner at a small cozy Thai restaurant near the Plex, so they could walk to the play.

He ordered for her, didn't even ask if she liked this or that. "Pad Thai," he said, "and that whole fish cooked in ginger, what's it called? Oh, and the shrimp curry. Not too hot, now."

The food was marvelous, but Ellie had to bite her tongue to keep from asking him if it wasn't impolite to order for his date.

"So," she said, twirling pad Thai noodles around her fork, "tell me more about these charities of yours."

He used chopsticks—deftly, easily—and he scooped up some rice before answering.

"I've been very fortunate," he finally said. "I've been successful, and I believe in sharing my good fortune."

He meant it, she realized. This brutal murderer believed that charity began at home.

"I can't give to everyone, you know, there are just too many, but I have priorities. Some of the arts. Well," he said, flashing his roguish grin, "in a small way. But my real interest lies in children. Abused children. The young ones."

"I think that's terrific."

"I feel for those kids. You know, I told you about my folks, so you can see I don't come from a rich family. I do what I can to help." He reached across the table and stroked her fingers. The hair on the nape of her neck rose.

He went on. "Once a year I do a real special thing. There's an organization called Mountain Dreams, have you heard of it? Volunteers take groups of abused kids up to the mountains. We have a permanent setup near Aspen. And we camp out and hike and climb. We push those kids, but it's good for them."

"And you go on these trips?"

"I'm a team leader."

"That's very generous."

"I enjoy it. Hell, I think I get more out of it than they do."

She smiled at him and turned her hand over so that her fingers rested in his. "You're a good man," she heard herself say.

"I do what I can," he repeated.

She could almost believe that Finn was a nice guy she was dating, a sincere guy who helped kids and took her to Santa Fe in his plane. If she closed off one small part of her mind she could believe it.

But if she didn't close off that part of her brain, she had to sit across the table from him, smiling, making conversation, knowing that he could turn into a vicious killer. A completely different person, afflicted with schizophrenic rage. It was impossible to comprehend.

After dinner they walked to the Plex, part of a stream of well-dressed Denverites in a holiday mood. He held her hand, and then he drew it up in front of him.

"Where are your gloves?" he asked. "My God, your hands are freezing."

Her heart stopped for a moment. *The gloves.* "Oh, God, I left them home. I told you I wasn't used to gloves, Finn. I bet they're in the pocket of my black coat."

He chafed her hands, first one then the other. "You silly girl."

"I know, I know."

Their seats were center front, two rows from the stage. An impeccably dressed older woman sat next to Ellie, and next to Finn was a man he obviously knew.

"George," Finn said, "meet my friend Ellie Kramer. George Midkiff and his wife, Marion."

Ellie leaned across Finn, smiled, said hello. Lovely people, she thought, coming to this play, which they'd probably seen a dozen times, to benefit a charity.

The familiar scenes unfolded: Bob Cratchit, Ebenezer Scrooge, Tiny Tim. Ellie sat there, her arm touching Finn's, his hand on hers. She could hardly breathe. She prayed he couldn't feel her trembling. Surreptitiously she tried to take deep breaths to slow her heart. He couldn't do anything to her here, not with all these people around them.

A lot of the play went past her. The scenes she saw were in her head; she couldn't stop them: Finn's big hands on a girl, on Stephanie Morris or Holly Lance or the Mexican girl. Ripping at her, jamming himself into her. Then the choking—with a scarf or a bandana or something that belonged to an innocent man. His face hidden by a ski mask, gloves on his hands, clothes that he threw away after the attack. This man next to her, hurting, forcing, strangling, killing.

Suddenly she wanted to run out of the theater, race away into the cold night. She wanted to see her mother, to hug her, to stay in the little house in Leadville.

And she longed, desperately, to call Michael, to see him, to beg his forgiveness. To say something as simple as "Merry Christmas, Michael."

"Isn't Scrooge great?" Finn whispered in her ear.

She nodded, shuddering inside, but she forced herself to pay attention, to stay away from those frantic thoughts.

The Ghost of Christmas Past was speaking, showing
Scrooge what he'd been. A morality play, but so true, so
true. What had Ellie's past been but a life put aside in
waiting and waiting for this moment? Losses suffered—
her father, her mother, she herself. Pain and sadness. She
felt tears fill her eyes, for Scrooge, for herself.

And the Ghost of the Future. The tombstone. Tiny Tim
dead. The waste, the misery. She saw into her own future,
and it was only desolation.

After the play Finn drove her to his house. She'd seen
it before from the outside, but when he led her in, she
was taken unawares. While the exterior was standard-
issue brick, the interior was stark contemporary, glass and
chrome and pale wood floors and track lighting. A large
beige leather sectional curled around a chrome-and-glass
coffee table. There was a long table in the dining room,
heavy smoked glass, with upholstered chairs in gray. The
kitchen was all stainless steel, commercial gas stove, Sub
Zero refrigerator, sinks. A central island of marble.

"My goodness" was all she could find to say for a
moment.

"It's different, I'll admit. My decorator wanted to make
a statement."

"Well, she certainly did."

"He," Finn said.

She walked around, trailing her fingers over the butter-
soft leather. There wasn't a speck of dust, a crumb, a
magazine out of place. The house looked as if no one
lived in it.

"Beautiful," she finally said.

"I'm glad you like it."

Would he show her his bedroom? Would he . . . ?

"Let's have a glass of wine," Finn suggested.

"That sounds nice." The paintings on the walls were

all modernistic, slashes of black and white and red, to go with the decor. Hideous, Ellie thought, but maybe they were valuable pieces of art. She thought of Michael's cabin, the comparison so shocking it was almost comical. She wished she were there, not here, but that didn't count. It didn't matter.

Finn handed her a crystal wineglass filled with white wine. "This is a vintage Chardonnay," he said. "I hope you like it."

He was proud of his house and his wine. He was showing it off to her, she realized. He wanted, needed her approval.

He raised his glass to hers. "A toast," he said, "to many more evenings like this."

"To many more," she said, clicking her glass against his.

"Let's sit over here," he said, as always directing the show.

She sat on the soft couch, reaching out to set her glass down on the table, when a napkin appeared as if by magic. She looked up at Finn. He was smiling, content. Compulsive. A neat freak.

"Do you entertain much?" she asked.

"Well, I do from time to time. I have to. I do a benefit for Mountain Dreams once a year and business dinners."

"You cook yourself?"

"Good God, no. I get a caterer in. It's so much easier. That's why my decorator planned the kitchen the way he did."

"You have a fantastic setup here."

"It's comfortable."

The bedroom. His bedroom. Was it on this floor? Would he . . . ?

"Uh, do you mind, I'd like to use the powder room."

He ushered her down a hallway off the living room. Two other open doors led off it; in one she could see a blinking computer screen—his home office. The bathroom was shining, spotless, the toilet and vanity in black ceramic. Black. Starched hand towels hung in precise lines. She used the toilet then washed her hands, staring at herself in the mirror above the sink. She was astonished at how normal she looked. He couldn't have noticed the pinpoints of fright reflected in her pupils. He'd never notice that.

But Michael would have.

"My, my, a black bathroom," Ellie said lightly when she sat down on the couch again.

"I know." He shrugged, his big shoulders rising and falling. "My own bathroom is much more traditional."

Her heart squeezed. His bathroom. Oh, God.

She sipped her wine; it was very good, a touch of fizz to it. They made small talk. Finn sat beside her, their thighs touching, and he often stroked her hair or her cheek or ran his fingers along her neck above the high collar of the red bolero jacket.

"It's late," he finally said. "I've got to get you home."

"Yes," she said, barely audible. "It's late." And she studied her hands, afraid he would see the immensity of her relief if she looked at him.

He drove her to Boulder. There wasn't much traffic this time of night, so the trip went fast.

"I'm sorry you have to keep driving me back and forth," she said.

"Oh, no problem. I'm on the road a lot with my business. I have security systems everywhere from Colorado Springs to Fort Collins, a hundred-mile radius."

"How many employees do you have, Finn?"

"Eighty-two."

"My God . . . I had no idea. That's huge. Where are your offices?"

"Right in Cherry Creek. But there are district branches up and down the entire Front Range."

No wonder he was so wealthy, she thought. And how easy it was for him to select and stalk a victim, find out all about her, her family, friends, neighbors. Ellie knew in her heart there would be a Mountaintech Security sign posted on the lawns of the victim's home or a neighbor's home. He would cruise neighborhoods at will in his official car. Who would ever suspect him?

He pulled up to her house. *Home free,* Ellie thought. *A few yards and I'm safe.* She shouldn't think that way, though. She should try to be with him as much as possible, figure out how to get to him. What buttons to push to anger him, make him lose his steely control.

And why didn't he want to sleep with her? What was the matter? Maybe he could only get it on with his victims, and Ellie was in a different category. *Disgusting.*

She was so torn, wanting him gone, wanting him close. She had to fight her strongest feelings every second she was with him, then she had to fend off regret when he wasn't there. Every time he left her, she thought: *This is it. I've lost him. He won't call.*

He opened her door, helped her out of the car, walked her up onto the porch.

"Thank you for a wonderful evening," Ellie said.

"My pleasure. I'll call soon."

"Yes, please do."

"It may have to be after Christmas, though."

"I'm busy, too. I want to visit my mother."

"Of course." He was staring at her upturned face, staring as if he wanted to understand her expression, memorize her features.

"Ellie," he said, and he put his arms around her and kissed her hungrily, a long, passionate kiss. His hands pressed against her back through the thick fur of Celeste's coat. She moaned, deep in her throat, hoping he didn't recognize it for what it was.

"Good night, Ellie," he finally said, his embrace softening.

"Good night, Finn."

And then she was inside, her back against the door, trembling, gagging, hot tears spurting behind her eyelids.

A sound, a knock at the door, the vibration reaching into her, touching her backbone.

It was *him*. What did he want?

She took a deep quavering breath and wiped away the tears.

She opened the door, her lips curling into a smile.

"That was quick," she started to say, and then her blood froze. It was Michael. Standing on the porch. Michael, his face, in the light, set hard as a rock.

EIGHTEEN

Finn steered along the Boulder Turnpike with the taste of Ellie fresh on his lips. He waited, almost longingly, for the familiar kaleidoscope to start wheeling in front of his eyes: the faces, and with them this time would be Ellie's face, brightly hued, her mouth open in supplication.

Images catapulted around his brain, but they were not the ones he was used to. They were all Ellie. Sitting next to him in the dimness of the theater, the pearly white of her cheek, the slight flare of her nostrils, her delicate nose, the way her slim fingers lay on top of her beaded purse. Her smile, her glow, her heady scent. Ellie. Ellie. Ellie.

He'd never burned for a woman like this. It was not the same desire he felt when he stalked his victims. This was astoundingly unique. He was scared, right down to the nuclei of his cells, that he was falling in love.

He dared to imagine life with her. Ellie in his home. Ellie, her stomach swollen with a child. *His* child. It was unthinkable.

He was out of control. It was like a disease. The cure was simple—abstinence. He could do it. Just stop seeing her. Then he'd recover.

How could he have let this happen?

He signaled and merged into the southbound traffic on I-25 and suddenly he hated her with a ferocity he'd never known.

Out of control again.

But he was strong. He'd been the strong one his whole life. In strength there was survival.

His brain pounded against his skull; the noise filled his head. She'd done this to him. With that bright smile and inner warmth, she'd brought him to his knees.

Good cop or bad cop? Tonight, Michael decided it had to be good cop. There was no other way to lull Ellie into submission.

He stood on the threshold of her house and masked his anger, letting the fire in his gaze burn down, willing his taut muscles to relax.

"Mind if I come in?" he asked, trying not to take in her attire, not to notice the slight swell of her lips where Rasmussen had just kissed her.

What else had Rasmussen done?

"Michael, I didn't expect you," she was saying, her words tripping out.

He hiked his shoulders.

"Were you, ah, waiting outside? I mean . . ."

"Yes."

He watched her duck her head as she kicked off her shoes, two frantic spots of red appearing on her cheeks.

"*Can* I come in?"

"Look, it's late and . . ."

"I just want to talk."

Then she laughed. "Oh, Michael, *please,* don't you think I know a lie when I hear one?"

"I didn't come here to argue. Let's just sit down and talk a minute. Your roommates home?" He looked up the staircase then back to her.

"I don't know. Maybe. They might be asleep. Or out doing the town."

"Okay, well, can we sit?"

"I . . ."

"Please?" Oh, what *that* cost him.

"I . . . all right, sure, but I really am tired."

"I bet" came out before he swallowed it.

She shot him a sharp glance, and then she seemed to acquiesce.

He sat in an old comfortable chair opposite the couch; Ellie settled on the edge of the couch, her hands on her knees.

"You're playing with fire," he began.

"Michael, you don't want to talk. You're about to read me some sort of a riot act here, and it's a waste of your breath."

"What if I told you *I'll* handle Rasmussen?"

"How?"

"I'm working on it."

"No, you're not. You have no idea how to catch him."

"Not true."

"Another lie?"

He shook his head. Damn, but she could be one tough cookie. "I'll get the bastard, Ellie, you can take that to the bank."

"Maybe you will. But when? How many more girls have to die first?"

"Soon."

"Oh, bullshit."

He wondered how she could do that, curse and make the word come out sounding like a blandishment.

It was torture sitting there so close to her, unable to touch her, to feel one more time the silken texture of her shoulders, her hips and thighs moving against him. Even from four feet away he could smell her, perfume and woman. And Rasmussen had just, minutes ago . . .

Christ, he thought.

"Look." She leaned toward him. "I've spent the best years of my life working to see that justice was served, and—"

"Let's call it what it is, Ellie: revenge."

She sat back as if pushed. "Okay. Let's call it revenge then. Fine. It's just a word. The end result will be the same."

He smiled thinly. "You're going to get hurt. You aren't trained for this. And how do you think your mother will feel?"

"Now you're hitting below the belt."

"Let the professionals handle Finn. I'll talk to my superiors again, see if—"

"No, Michael, I'm already on the inside track. You can't stop me."

"I could arrest you," he said abruptly.

"Oh?"

"Sure."

"On some sort of trumped-up charge? How about drugs? Or robbery?"

"You think I wouldn't?"

She shook her head slowly, her eyes holding his, *knowing* him too well.

He took in a long breath then let it out slowly. "There's another option. We send in a female undercover officer. There's a detective I know from Lakewood. She's a real good sport and a helluva looker. She can handle—"

"Finn can have any woman he wants. And it's me"—
Ellie glanced down—"It's me he likes. He's asked me
out more than any other—"

"All right, all right," he said curtly.

"I know I can get him to lose it, to lose control, Michael. I can do it. And if we work together on this, we
can get him cold."

He was shaking his head. "I can't believe you're even
considering this. You screw with his power trip and he'll
kill you. For chrissakes, I found out who you were, and
so can Rasmussen. I want you out."

"No."

He was starting to lose it. So much for the good cop.
"Don't see that asshole again. Do you understand me?"

"I hear you, Michael," she said, her voice so soft he
could hardly make out the words. "But you know you
can't stop me. You know I'm the only one who can get
close to Finn. We're both after the same goal, and we're
nearly there. Please, I need your support. I need your
help. Help me."

Was she trying to tear his heart out?

He stood and jammed his hands into the pockets of his
leather jacket and started to pace.

"Michael." Her voice was seductive now. "You know
I'm right. You're being the stubborn one now. You're
smarter than this."

"Don't fucking patronize me."

"You're mad."

"I am not mad."

"You are. Your voice gets this certain way."

"What the hell are you talking about?"

"See? Just like that. Quiet."

He stopped and glared at her. "You're out of your mind."

"Am not."

"I'm not amused, Ellie."

"I only want you to calm down and be reasonable."

"And let you put yourself in harm's way?"

"Did it ever occur to you that I can take care of myself?"

He laughed mirthlessly.

"This is all pointless. The fact is, *I'm* the one he wants to be with. I'm the only shot we have right now. It doesn't matter what I'm feeling . . . what *you're* feeling. . . ."

"I'm not feeling a thing, Ellie."

"I'm asking for your help."

That was the last straw. He hissed, "No goddamn chance," and then he stormed out. Was this what caring for a person did to you? Well if it was—he yanked open his truck door so hard it nearly came off the hinges— then he didn't want it. *Ever.* Screw her and screw Rasmussen.

He fumbled for the key in his jacket pocket then got in, slammed the door, and jammed the key in the ignition. The veins were sticking out on his neck and his jaw was locked so tight it hurt.

Then came the *tap tap tap* at his window.

He twisted his head. *Ah, shit.*

He pressed the window button and it rolled down. "Get back inside, Ellie," he ground out, "it's below zero out here. Look at your feet. Stockings? Are you crazy?"

But she was shaking her head and even in the dim glow from a neighbor's outdoor Christmas lights, he saw the tears, rainbow streaks on her cheeks.

"Come on, Ellie, let's not do this," he tried.

"Michael, I'm asking, no, I'm *begging* you to help me. I don't have anywhere else to turn. I can't bear the weight of one more innocent girl, one more innocent man behind bars. . . . I *would* rather die. . . ."

"Don't say that."

"I mean it. Say you'll help me. I know I . . . hurt you, but . . ."

He swore and pounded his fist against the steering wheel.

"Michael?"

But he couldn't speak. He couldn't even think, for chrissakes. "Don't," he finally said. "Go away, go inside, Ellie."

"Michael, *talk* to me."

"Go the hell inside. I'll . . . I'll call you."

"When?"

"In the morning."

"You promise?"

"Yeah, sure."

"And we'll work this all out. We will. I know we will."

"Please, go inside. That's all I need," he said thickly, "you freezing to death out here."

She finally backed off. "Okay, okay. And you'll call? You promised."

"Right," he said, and he turned the key, put the truck in gear, and sped away from the curb. The worst part, the very worst, was that he knew everything she'd said was true.

He was going to help her. Help the stupid woman because he couldn't stop her. It was going to kill him.

He didn't phone her in the morning. And he didn't phone her at lunch. He sat at his desk, still working the Valerie Girard homicide, typing notes, sitting on hold on the telephone, stewing. How in hell had he let himself get into this fix with John Crandall's daughter?

He was still on hold, needing to clarify something in a witness's statement, when he got a high sign from the desk sergeant, who mouthed, "Lady on line six for you, Callas."

Michael shook his head, cupped his hand over the receiver, and said, "Tell her I'm out."

Rick Augostino, three desks over, gave him a look.

Screw it, he thought.

At one the commander walked into headquarters and Michael frowned. He was out of options with Ellie. He couldn't let her keep seeing Rasmussen without backup, and short of hog-tying her, he couldn't stop her. The trouble was, he wasn't sure the commander would go for it. He sure as hell hadn't before. And if the man didn't, what was plan B? *Good goddamn question,* Michael thought, his frown deepening.

The commander's name was Sam Koffey. A big guy, but not doughnut-eating big, mostly bald, who'd come up from the ranks, fifty-five-year-old Sam was built like a two-hundred-pound drill sergeant. Funny thing was, the man's disposition was gentle as a lamb. He was no pushover, though, and Michael knew convincing him to authorize surveillance on Rasmussen was going to be touchy. Maybe impossible. Koffey distrusted cops' hunches. Hard evidence, okay. But those gut feelings didn't cut it with him and, if Michael cared to look at it through Koffey's eyes, that was about all Michael had.

At one-thirty he rapped on Koffey's glass-paneled door.

At two o'clock Michael was on the phone with Ellie at the Justice Center. His news wasn't good.

"Look," he said, "I laid it all out to the commander. I

gave him my notes, the computer printouts. Times, places, names. I showed him every poor slob who was convicted for a crime he didn't commit."

"And?"

"Went about the same as before, until I laid the Baja murder notes under his nose. *That* got his attention." He could feel the expectation in her silence. "I asked him for permission to get a warrant from the judge to set up a wire surveillance on Rasmussen. I told him about you, Ellie. Had to. And that's where it fell apart. He says he'll think about a wire, think about going to the judge for a warrant, he even said he'd think about who we could use for the wire, but, and I quote, *no civilians.*"

Michael could not have been more shocked by her response. "You tell him," she said in a sharp tone, "that I'll be there in fifteen minutes."

When he found his voice, he began, "That's a bad idea," but she'd hung up on him.

Later, when he thought about it, Michael realized he should have seen it coming; he never should have underestimated Ellie Kramer for a moment. But he did. And so did Sam Koffey.

She entered Koffey's office, Michael right on her heels, took her coat off, folded her arms—refusing a seat—and within ten minutes she convinced Koffey to let her in on the operation.

Michael stood with a shoulder to the wall, his arms folded across his chest also, and wondered if his jaw was as slack as it felt.

She was *good.* As good as any trial lawyer pacing in front of a jury who believed passionately in her client, the case, and in her abilities. *Goddamn, but she is amazing,* and he knew all over again why he'd fallen for her in the first place.

"I've spent my entire life trying to prove my father's innocence," she launched in. "He's dead now, Commander, but there are other men rotting in prison at this very moment who still have a chance. I'm sure Detective Callas had laid out the evidence for you, and I realize it isn't hard evidence. But as for circumstantial, it doesn't get much better. Not after the Mexican trip. And two things I do know. . . ." Her dark eyes held Koffey's unflinchingly. "First, my father and I rang in New Year's together. I know, because we were having pizza and watching videos and wearing stupid hats that my mother got for us before she left for her parents' farm, when Rasmussen turned Stephanie Morris into a vegetable."

Ellie took a breath and began pacing again. "And second, I'm the first woman Rasmussen has asked out more than twice in his entire life. There isn't anyone else you *can* use to get inside.

"Commander, if you say no, you can go to your grave with the knowledge that we could have stopped him here and now. We can save God only knows how many innocent victims to come. A little risk to my safety pales in comparison, doesn't it?"

Koffey sat back, steepled his fingers, and studied her.

"One last thing," she put in, her tone softening, "and I've told Michael this, too. With or without your help, I'm going to continue to see Finn until I find a way to trip him up."

"Or he figures your game out and kills you," Koffey said quickly.

Just as rapidly, Ellie fired a return salvo. "Well, Commander, when you find my body, at least you'll know where to start your investigation."

Five minutes later, Koffey sighed and said he'd talk to the judge about a warrant for surveillance.

All Ellie said was "Thank you. You won't regret it."

But Michael wondered. Maybe Koffey wouldn't regret it. And Ellie sure wouldn't. But all *he* could see was that picture in his head of Rasmussen choking the life out of her.

He and Koffey talked for a couple minutes about contacting the CBI to request their surveillance van and wire equipment.

Michael explained to Ellie. "It's kind of like getting preapproval for a loan. You don't know if you'll need it, but it'll be there if you do."

"Maybe Ben Torres could talk to the judge," she began, but he saw her expression cloud over. Of course, Torres had no idea who she really was. If he had known, he'd have realized she'd used his office and used him, too, on this wild quest of hers. Torres wouldn't like it any better than Michael had.

"We'll handle it," Koffey said, and Ellie nodded. If she was relieved, she hid it really well.

They were leaving Koffey's office, half out the door, when the commander crooked a finger at Michael. "Can I see you alone for a sec?"

Ellie waited by Michael's desk. The door to Koffey's office closed again, and the commander said, "Okay, are you doing her, Callas?"

Michael donned an innocent mask. "Huh?"

"Don't act stupid."

Michael shook his head. "How dumb do you think I am, Sam?"

The commander glared at him. "And whoever said cops weren't good liars."

Wisely, Michael got the hell out of there.

"What did he want?" Ellie asked, her eyes bright with her victory.

"Ah, nothing," he said.

"So tell me how this wire thing works. I—"

"Hey," he cut in, "we're not there yet. And I can guarantee nothing will happen till after Christmas."

She didn't look in the least disappointed. "But we still need to go over stuff, have a plan, right?"

"Look," he began, his tone curt. "Sorry, but can't this wait?"

She frowned.

"All right, all right," he said. "Listen, I have to go to the Springs tomorrow for Christmas Eve. Family. But as soon as I—" Then, without thinking it through, he said, "What are you doing over Christmas?"

"Well, the roomies are all gone and I promised Mom I'd spend Christmas Day with her. Otherwise . . ."

"Okay. Then drive down to the Springs with me tomorrow—you can use the guest room—and I'll put you on the train or bus up to Leadville first thing Christmas morning."

Her face lit up as if someone had turned a spotlight on it. "Really? You mean dinner and everything, with your family?"

He didn't hesitate. "Ellie, it's business. Of course we'll have dinner, I only meant we could work on the plan on the drive down."

The spotlight switched off as fast as it had come on. He hadn't meant to sound so bitter, but it was for the best.

"Okay," she said, "as long as I make an early bus on Christmas morning." She shrugged eloquently.

"Fine. No problem. We'll talk on the way."

"Great," she said. "I guess I'd better get back to the Justice Center now."

He opened his mouth to say he'd drive her but closed

it. The less time he spent with her, the better. He never asked himself why he'd invited her to his family dinner. He didn't have to. He'd already convinced himself the drive down would give them time to work on the plan.

Still, he found himself watching her—as were all the guys—thread her way through the maze of desks toward the stairs, and a heaviness settled in his stomach. He dared, for a fraction of time, to recall that radiance in her face when he'd first asked her to ride to the Springs with him. The moment passed. Ellie disappeared down the stairwell and he went back to the Girard case.

I am a fool, Ellie told herself as she sat in Michael's truck. *I am a damned fool and he's going to hurt me again.*

They were heading south on I-25 out of Denver toward Colorado Springs. It was a sunny afternoon but cold, the Rockies to their immediate west rising from the high plains in ramparts of brilliant white peaks wreathed in clouds.

Christmas Eve.

She had her overnight bag and a present for her mother. She had a big box of chocolates for Michael's mother. She sat on the broad truck seat stiffly. How to behave with Michael? Businesslike? Friendly? Neutral? What would his mother think? Had he told her who he was bringing?

She wished she felt comfortable enough to ask him all those questions, but she didn't. She couldn't even think of anything to break the taut silence in the truck's cab.

Fortunately, Michael broke it. "That was quite a stunt you pulled yesterday." There was no inflection to his voice, so she wasn't sure how he intended the statement.

"You mean . . . with Commander Koffey?"

"Yeah."

"Well, I didn't have much choice, did I? I had to convince him."

"You convinced him, all right."

"Are you sure he'll let us go ahead with it?"

"Pretty damn sure."

"Oh, God, I hope so."

He fell silent, and the road unrolled monotonously ahead of the truck. South of Denver, they passed acres and acres of prosperous new subdivisions, the stomping grounds of Yuppies who were reaping the rewards of the city's burgeoning economy. Clouds sat on the mountaintops, billowing gray, but out here on the plains the winter sun shone. The rolling land, the rooftops of the distant houses, the farmland and barns were all winter gray, the snow melted, the trees bare, the grass flattened and colorless.

Ellie had rarely felt so ill at ease. Michael had asked her to accompany him on this trip, a visit to his family on Christmas Eve, ostensibly to discuss their plans. But so far he hadn't said much about the operation, or about anything else for that matter, and she couldn't figure out why he wanted her along.

She'd known since yesterday it would be awkward, but wild horses couldn't have stopped her from going with him. And, surely, when he got to his mother's home he'd have to be pleasant with his family there. He'd have to be.

She kept going over in her mind what she could have done, what she should have done, to be on better footing with Michael. Her thoughts chased themselves around in her head over and over, like a tape looping without end.

Scenes came to her, Michael furious and betrayed. Maybe she should have leveled with him earlier. But, no, she'd thought he might be the killer. Or in the parking lot that night—she should have been more receptive, kissed him back with feeling. Or the night at his cabin—it could have gone so differently.

She relived the scenes, trying out new dialogues, new actions. Over and over.

As they passed Castle Rock, he finally broke the silence. "Do you have any definite plans with, uh, with Rasmussen?"

"Not really," she replied. "He said he'd call soon, but probably not till after Christmas."

"Huh."

"Is there any kind of place you particularly want me to avoid? Or places where it's easier to—what is it called? record me?"

"The best situation is for you to be in a small building, say, a house. Big buildings, like a mall or office building, create too much interference with the recorder."

"Okay."

"You're going to have to do this by feel," he said. "Have you come up with any ideas on how to, um . . ."

"Get to him," she finished for him.

"Right."

"Well, first of all, he's a control freak. He orders the food in restaurants, never even asks what I'd like. He doesn't ask my opinion, he tells me what he thinks. His house . . . well, it's strange. Ultramodern, perfect, not a speck of dust. Control again."

"Uh-huh, that's consistent with what we know about serial killers." .

"Really," she said, as if she hadn't read everything put out by the FBI for the past decade.

"They're a mess psychologically, but you couldn't call them clinically insane. They're rigid and they crave structure. They're arrogant; they have what we call an incomplete conscience. They know right from wrong, but they ignore it when it suits them."

"Yes," Ellie said emphatically. "That's what he's like. You've done research. . . ."

"I've been reading about it for years. I can spout all sorts of psychobabble. A typical serial killer is a white man between twenty and forty, average to above average intelligence, compulsive, a perfectionist. Rasmussen has the advantage of having law enforcement training, so he knows how to avoid leaving evidence. He's clever enough to steer clear of patterns to outsmart us. He moves around, picks different types of victims. What we call surface variables. But the core of the crime is consistent. He can't help it."

"That's impressive," she said quietly. "You've got him perfectly."

"I don't have him at all. That's the trouble."

"But we'll get him. This time we'll get him."

He didn't answer, and she could see his jaw tighten. She knew he hated the idea of her being involved. She'd forced him; she'd forced Koffey. But, damn it, somebody had to do it.

He said nothing for a long time, and she looked out her window, not wanting to push him. She had to be careful, so very careful. He'd take offense at the smallest thing. He was so hard yet so vulnerable, and she was crazy to be here with him.

"I wanted to apologize," he began, out of the blue.

"Apologize . . . ?"

"The other night . . . I should have . . . Look, I'm sorry I was the one who arrested your father and testified against him. I've been sorry about it for a long time."

Ellie looked down at her hands. Her eyes suddenly stung. "Thank you," she whispered.

"And I'm sorry he died in prison before we could nail Rasmussen."

"Me too."

"And you were with your father that New Year's Eve."

"Until long after they found Stephanie Morris."

"They should have let you testify in court."

She blew out her breath. "My parents were adamant about keeping me out of it. And who would have believed me, anyway?"

"Mm," he said.

He drove, looking straight ahead. They were passing the Air Force Academy, nearing Colorado Springs. Closing in on Michael's home and his family.

"Well," Ellie said lightly, "that conversation wasn't exactly full of holiday cheer."

"Guess not."

"I'm glad you told me, though. It . . . it means a lot, Michael. What you think . . . it's really important to me. I . . ."

"If . . . when we do this," he said as if he hadn't heard, "you're going to have to break his control. You're going to have to get inside his head and figure out how to push him over the edge."

"I know."

He shot her a sidelong glance. "It'll be a fine line. You piss him off too much and he could get violent."

"I know," she said again.

"The closer . . . the closer you get to him, the more . . . intimate, the better the opportunity."

"Yes." She cringed inside. Michael hadn't said the word, but she knew what he meant: sex. "Um, you know, he hasn't, I mean, he doesn't come on that way, almost as if, well, he's afraid of . . ."

"He'd be uncomfortable in a situation where he's on equal terms with a woman. On a date. It doesn't fulfill his control fantasy." His voice was flat.

He was right. Of course. No wonder Finn hadn't tried to have sex with her.

"He might even be," Michael continued, "dysfunctional."

"Oh," Ellie breathed.

She let a little time go by, then she asked a question she'd been wondering about for a long time. "Do you think Finn gets into people's houses because he knows so much about security systems? That's what caught my attention at first. You know, the Morris case."

"It's possible, although we'll never know. Maybe Stephanie let him in, maybe not. It's a dead end, I'm afraid."

"And I thought I was so clever."

There were several cars already pulled up in front of the Tudor-style house. A large wreath hung on the door, and there were decorations in the windows.

"Jesus," Michael growled, "Joy is here."

"Joy?"

"One of my cousins. With a mouth on her."

"How many cousins do you have?"

"Oh, about ten. My mother had three sisters and a brother."

"How wonderful. A big family. You're very lucky, Michael."

"Yeah, lucky."

He opened the front door and ushered her in. The house was full of cooking aromas: ham and fragrant baking and rum punch. There was a Christmas tree in the corner of the living room with gifts under it, and an amazing array of people sat on couches and chairs or stood around the fireplace. Several small children played on the floor.

"Oh, my goodness," Ellie said.

"Uncle Mike, Uncle Mike!" cried a small boy, and he ran, short legs pumping, and grabbed Michael around the knees.

"Michael's here!" several voices cried out. "Martha, Michael's here!"

Martha, Michael's mother, bustled in from the kitchen, an apron over her sweater and skirt.

"Michael, at last," she said, and she hugged him.

"This is Ellie," he said, disengaging himself subtly. "Ellie Kramer. This is my mother."

"Hello, Mrs. Callas," Ellie said. "Here's a little something for having me." She handed Martha the gaily wrapped box.

"Oh, you didn't need to," his mother said. "Thank you so much."

"It's good of you to have me, Mrs. Callas."

"Martha, please." She smiled, a nice-looking woman with something of Michael in her eyes and her jawline. "I'm so glad Michael brought you. Merry Christmas."

Then there was a bewildering flurry of introductions. So many people. Aunts and uncles and cousins. And the small children, Michael's nieces and nephews. *How fantastic,* Ellie kept thinking. *All this family, all these relatives.* She smiled and shook hands and tried to remember names: Al and Janey and Frank and Linda and the big-mouthed one, Cousin Joy. And Beryl and Robert and Richard. My God.

In the dining room a long table was set with linen and silver and crystal and candles. Richard, not a cousin but married to Beryl, got Michael and Ellie glasses of punch.

"My special punch," Richard warned.

"Lethal," Michael agreed. "Richard, did you meet Ellie?"

"Not exactly, but I saw her across a crowded room. How come you've managed to put up with this surly son of a—"

"All right, all right," Michael said. "This is a business trip."

"Where'd you meet the lovely Ellie?" Richard asked.

"We're doing some work together. A case."

"Work, a case. Right." Richard went back to his punch bowl.

"Shit," Michael muttered.

Ellie felt her cheeks grow hot.

Martha didn't pry; she moved around her son carefully, as if she, like Ellie, were afraid of setting him off. There was a tension there, something Ellie recognized but could not understand. She noticed Martha watching Michael surreptitiously, even though she was busy, and there was a kind of sadness in the woman's eyes.

Ellie knew Michael's folks were divorced, and the family was mostly from his mother's side. They seemed so normal, Michael and his mother the aberrations.

Before they began the meal, Martha approached Ellie.

"It was good of you to come with Michael. I worry sometimes, oh, you know mothers. I worry that he's lonely and works too hard."

"He's one of the best detectives in the department," Ellie said. "He was terrific on the stand in the Zimmerman case."

"The Zimmerman case?"

"He didn't tell you."

"No, he doesn't confide in me much."

"Michael doesn't confide in anybody much."

"No," Martha said thoughtfully, "I suppose not."

Ellie had to tell her about the Zimmerman case and Michael's role in it. Martha seemed impressed, and she sent more sidelong glances her son's way. He must have noticed, because he left the cousin he was talking to and came over to Ellie and Martha.

"Ellie's been telling me about the Zimmerman trial, Michael. I had no idea . . ."

"It's my job, that's all. No big deal."

"Michael, of course it's a big deal."

"Please, spare me, Mother."

"Michael . . ."

His expression cut off whatever she was going to say, and Ellie saw the sadness cloud her face again.

"I've made the turkey the way you like it, Michael, and the stuffing. Everything you loved as a boy," Martha went on, trying hard.

"That's nice."

"I'm sure it'll be delicious," Ellie put in, attempting to lessen the awkwardness.

Martha said nothing more, only put a hand on her son's arm, touching it lightly as if to make a connection. Michael withdrew his arm, and Martha gave up. She forced a smile and said, "Well, I better get back to the kitchen."

They all sat at the table, actually two pushed together, and mismatched chairs were pulled up from all over the house to seat everyone. It was a noisy, friendly meal. Ham and sweet potatoes, rolls, vegetables, an abundance of food.

Ellie found herself between Michael and Cousin Joy, a plump lady who was married to Frank. Two of the children belonged to her.

"So, where did you and Michael meet?" she asked while passing the potatoes.

"We were working on a case. A trial."

"Are you a lawyer?"

"Not yet," Ellie said, "I'm clerking at the Boulder DA's office."

"Ah, I see. What case?"

"The Zimmerman trial. Are you familiar with it? The man who's accused of having his wife killed?"

"Oh, sure, that bum. Frank, hey, Frank, this girl's working on that Zimmerman case!"

"That's nice, honey," Frank called from down the table.

"Do you know, you're the first girl Michael's ever brought home?" Joy said, spearing a piece of ham.

"I am?"

"I swear, I don't think he's ever had a serious girl-friend. At his age. God." She rolled her eyes. "You kids! Get out from under the table. Now, Ellie, where were we? Oh, yes, you're the first girl I can remember—"

"I'm not his girlfriend," Ellie pointed out. "We're do-ing a job together."

"You *look* like his girlfriend."

"I'm not, honestly."

"Ellie, I'll tell you, we all think Michael *needs* a girl-friend."

"But I'm not . . ."

"Leave it alone, Joy," Michael said, obviously over-hearing the conversation.

"Okay, sure. Don't get in an uproar."

Ellie wondered if anyone at the table noticed that Mi-chael rarely spoke to her. He talked to his cousins, even laughed with the little ones, but there was that curious strain between him and his mother.

There were three pumpkin pies for dessert, each helping piled high with homemade whipped cream. One of the ladies—Michael's aunt?—got up to make coffee.

"Oh, God, I ate too much," Joy said. "And I was on a diet."

"She's always on a diet," the man across from her said.

"Shut up, Bobby."

"Ever since she was twelve," Bobby said.

Joy waved a dismissive hand at him. Oh, what Ellie wouldn't give for a clan like this, squabbling and all. To belong, without lies or questions. And Michael didn't appreciate it—that was evident.

Joy was eating her pie. "I can't resist," she kept saying.

"It's Christmas, don't worry about it," Ellie offered.

Joy leaned close to Ellie and said quietly, "How well do you know Michael?"

"Oh, not that well."

"Do you know about Paul?"

"Paul?"

"His older brother."

"I didn't know Michael had a brother."

"He doesn't anymore."

Ellie was speechless.

Joy leaned closer. "You don't know? Paul was killed when he was nineteen."

Ellie drew in her breath sharply.

"It was pretty bad, you can imagine. The family fell apart. That's why Aunt Martha and Uncle Paul, Michael's dad, got divorced."

"How . . . ?"

"Drunk driver," she whispered.

"Oh, my God . . ."

"Michael was fifteen. It hit him hard. His parents just

couldn't deal with him after that. He barely hears from his father."

Ellie turned toward Michael; he was talking to his uncle, his face averted. Yes, of course, it all fit. Tears filled her eyes.

"Well, you can imagine," Joy went on relentlessly, "we were all horrified by the way Michael's mom and dad treated him. I mean, everyone knew Paul Junior was the apple of their eye. Okay, so he was smart and athletic and all that, but so is Michael. It was just one of those things. And nobody dared say anything to Paul Senior or Martha. We were crushed, you know?"

Yes, Ellie thought, *and so was Michael.*

Joy prattled on, but Ellie was looking away from her round face to Michael. If only, she thought, if only she could tell him that he never had to be alone again.

NINETEEN

Christmas morning, when all was said and done, Ellie missed the bus that ran through South Park into Buena Vista and on up to Leadville. She and Michael stood next to his truck at the bus station and stared at the empty bus lane.

"Oh, Lord," Ellie said, gripping her suitcase, "I'll call Mom right away, tell her I'll catch the one o'clock. Damn."

"I'll drive you."

She pivoted and cocked her head. "Don't be ridiculous. Your family is waiting to open presents and all that."

"They'll still be there when I get back."

"It'll be hours and hours, Michael. No. You go on back and I'll just wait. . . ."

"Ellie, shut up, will you, and get in the truck?"

She argued for a few more minutes but in the end he had his way. She would have liked it to be her company he sought but now, after talking to Cousin Joy, she knew better. He'd do anything to avoid the discomfort of his memories.

She sat next to him again in the warm cab, while he used his cell phone to call his mother, and realized she felt protective of him, so protective she wished she could erase his pain. How sad, she thought, casting him a furtive glance, both their families ripped apart. There was one huge difference, though; whereas she and her parents had never stopped believing in one another, loving one another, tragedy had torn Michael's family asunder.

What had Joy said over coffee as they'd sat around the living room? Something like, "Oh, yeah, Paul was always the favorite, the perfect son. It seemed to the whole family that if Martha and Paul Senior had to choose, they'd have sacrificed Michael. And believe you me, he knew it, too."

Ellie had thought her heart would break.

They drove across the sixty-mile-wide expanse of South Park, a perfectly flat high-altitude plain where only grass and sage survived the harsh elements. They were on Highway 24, which met the Arkansas River Valley south of Buena Vista and then snaked its way toward Leadville. To their left rose the Collegiate Peaks, a part of the Sawatch Range: Mt. Harvard, Mt. Princeton, and Mt. Yale, all towering over the valley at fourteen thousand feet. Salida and Buena Vista sat at the base of the mountains and enjoyed a banana-belt climate, the bad weather blocked by the ranks of the tall mountains. Leadville, at ten thousand feet, seemed to suffer the opposite effect. It began to snow, in fact, several miles past Buena Vista.

"Oh, Michael," Ellie said, "now you've got to drive through this mess."

"Doesn't bother me."

"Well, it does me."

He shot her a look. "That's right, you hate to drive."

She sighed. No reason to lie anymore. "The truth is, after we sold the Boulder house and moved to Leadville, Mom let the insurance lapse on our car and some guy, uninsured, too, broadsided her, and for years we didn't even have a car. I was eighteen before I learned to drive."

"Jesus," he said.

"I'm not ashamed. Mom spent what little we had on lawyers."

"Appeals?"

She nodded. "For all the good it did."

There was nothing for him to say. He'd already apologized. And, really, she was glad he knew about her, glad he now knew why she could hardly ski and why she didn't have a car and why she spent half her life in thrift shops. She wondered if he suspected how much she'd been attracted to Finn's lifestyle, the house, the cars, the plane and trips and lavish parties.

Then she thought, well, of course Michael had figured that out. Any idiot could have. She wouldn't apologize, though. Her reaction to Finn had been predictable. She was poor. He was wealthy. No. She'd never feel guilty for enjoying the finer things in life. Her guilt lay elsewhere, in her failure to have seen the truth about Michael. She knew now. And she knew exactly why he came off as such a prick sometimes. Maybe she could have helped him, once, before she'd blown his trust.

He pulled up in front of her mother's house shortly before eleven. They'd beaten the bus by forty-five minutes. Ellie saw the curtains part, and she realized, suddenly, how awkward this was. She couldn't invite him in, and yet she knew that sometime, someday, he was going to owe the same apology to her mother.

But Michael solved the problem. "I'd say hello to your

mother," he said, "but it's probably better if I let it lie for a while."

"I understand," she said. "Well, thanks for the ride. And thank everyone again for the dinner and everything. I really did have a good time, Michael."

"Um, I'm glad." Words with no meaning.

He got out then and lifted her suitcase from the truck bed, handing it to her on the sidewalk, the snow settling noiselessly on their shoulders and bare heads.

"Now listen," he said, "put Rasmussen off till Sam Koffey can get to a judge for the okay to go ahead with the surveillance."

"Okay."

"I mean it. No games, Ellie."

"I heard you the first time."

"Yeah, well, I don't know if I trust you to use your head when it comes to Rasmussen."

And before she could sort out exactly how he meant by that statement, he walked around the front of the truck, lifting a hand in a dismissive farewell. "I'll be in touch," he said, and then he was in the truck, turning on the ignition.

She stood on the sidewalk, suitcase in hand, snow blinding her, and watched him turn around and drive back the way he'd come.

"That was Michael Callas," Janice said when she pulled the door open for Ellie. Accusation dripped from her voice.

Ellie hauled her suitcase into her old room. "Yes, it was," she said, Janice directly behind her. "I'll explain everything, but first, Merry Christmas."

They hugged and Ellie pulled out her present for her mother and then Janice got Ellie's from under the small tree that sat in a corner of the living room.

Christmas had been an unhappy time since her father's arrest and conviction. Ellie recalled the better times with warmth, and she'd learned to cling to those memories: leaving milk and cookies for Santa, shaking her parents awake excitedly at dawn, the presents under the tree, the stockings hung from the mantel and filled to overflowing, her father building a cozy fire while her mother made hot chocolate and cinnamon buns.

For a few years, after John's imprisonment and at his insistence, Ellie and Janice had spent the holidays in Nebraska at the farm. But then Ellie's grandparents had passed away and the farm had been sold, its debts paid—what was left had gone to the appeals lawyers—and she and her mother celebrated Christmas in Leadville.

They had friends there. Close friends from school and work, but it was never the same. Then John had died three years ago, the week before the holiday. Now Christmas would always be a time of reflection and little joy.

Janice made hot chocolate, and they opened their gifts. Ellie had brought along presents from her roommates and Janice had several gifts from friends and neighbors, and soon the living room floor was littered with red and green and silver paper and ribbons.

"Oh, Ellie," Janice exclaimed when she opened her gift and held up the sage-colored sweater and matching shell, "they're beautiful. Perfect."

Ellie smiled. She knew her mother's taste as well as her own.

Then Ellie's gift. A new leather briefcase with her initials on it in gold. It had to have cost Janice several hundred dollars. Ellie held it to her chest and cried.

"Well," Janice said, "my lawyer daughter can't go around carrying that dreadful old one and make a good impression."

"It's the best gift ever, Mom." She meant it.

Michael's name never came up again until they were stuffing the torn wrapping paper into a trash bag; in a few minutes they'd be going over to a neighbor's for eggnog cocktails.

"About Michael," Ellie began, cramming the paper in the trash bag, and she went on to tell Janice how wrong she'd been—how wrong they'd both been about him.

"It's the other one," Ellie finally said, sitting on the edge of the couch, "it's Rasmussen." Then she told her mother everything she'd learned and everything Michael had put together over the years. She said nothing about her seeing Finn, though. She only told Janice that Michael had a plan.

"And just how involved are *you* in this so-called plan?" Janice asked.

"Only peripherally, Mom."

"Really?"

"Really."

"Hm," Janice said.

Ellie quickly changed the subject. "Michael really feels awful about coming up here like he did and trying to deceive you."

"I bet."

"No, Mom, he really does."

"Then he should have come inside this morning and told me so."

"He . . . Well, he isn't that open, if you know what I mean. He's not very in touch with himself in that respect."

"So he never said he felt badly."

"He apologized to me, Mom."

"You seem to know him quite well," Janice began, but Ellie wasn't about to tell her mother the whole sordid story, certainly not that she'd duped him and slept with him and doomed whatever relationship they might have had together.

She stared for a moment into the middle distance and thought about Michael, now back at his family's house, the sad things his cousin Joy had told her, and she wished, so very desperately, that she could turn the clock back.

"So, he took you to his family's for Christmas Eve," Janice was saying.

"Just to tell me how he plans to bring Rasmussen down."

"And he couldn't have done that in Boulder? *Humph,*" her mother said.

They ate too many goodies and drank too much rum-laced eggnog at the neighbor's, but it was a fun time. As much fun as Ellie could remember having for a long time. Except for Santa Fe, she thought once, but then she knew that didn't count. She never should have let it count.

It snowed that whole afternoon and night, and the following morning they put on every warm thing in the house and went for a long walk through town. For all the hard times Leadville had suffered in the last century, the historical society had still done an amazing restoration of the town core, and it was like strolling arm and arm through a Victorian wonderland, the quaint street-lamps decorated, the store windows all lit up, a foot of fresh snow glistening on the sidewalks and rooftops, hanging from eaves and pressing the boughs on the evergreen trees nearly to the ground.

A part of Ellie felt hopeful about the future. Would she change her name back to Crandall? Would her mother? Would Janice come to live with her in Boulder?

She was on the brink of something wonderful, and as

she and Janice walked, she dared to voice her excitement. "It's going to work, Mom. Michael is going to get that bastard."

"Ellie."

"Well, that's what he is. Oh, Mom, think of it." She squeezed her mother's arm. "Just think about how great it's going to be. I know Dad's not here to share all this, but wherever he is it's okay. He'll know, Mom."

"Yes, I think he will." Then Janice stopped on the sidewalk. "But you better be telling me the truth, young lady. You better not be doing something stupid with that Finn Rasmussen. Something dangerous."

Ellie sighed and shook her head. "Oh, Mom, the cops aren't going to let me put myself in harm's way. Don't be such a worrywart."

"It's just that I know you. You can be awfully . . . pushy."

Ellie punched her mother in the arm lightly. "Pushy, maybe, Mom, but not stupid. Okay?"

"Well, okay," Janice said doubtfully, and they walked on into the cold winter's morning, Ellie promising herself that she really wasn't lying this time—she wouldn't do anything stupid.

Her good intentions lasted less than twenty-four hours.

When she arrived home to the still-empty Marine Street house, she found a zillion messages on the recorder. But only one interested her.

"This is for Ellie. Finn here. If you're free this coming Thursday, I've got some hockey tickets. Give me a call."

She stood over the recorder and thought about phoning Michael. Maybe, even though it was still the long holiday week, Sam Koffey had gotten hold of a judge and gotten the warrant issued. Maybe . . .

But she knew that wasn't the case. If the cops had a warrant, Michael would have contacted her. And out of the zillion messages, there were none from him. Not even one wondering if she'd gotten home okay.

And just how long could she keep Finn dangling before he gave up on her?

She thought it over, biting her lower lip. She knew what she'd told Michael. Even told her mother. But how long *would* Finn hang in there?

Slowly, thinking, her hand went to the phone. She was actually trembling, she realized. It didn't stop her from picking it up, though.

She took a breath and dialed.

Finn was kicking himself for calling Ellie. He'd managed to stay away from her since that last time, but then he'd grown weak. He wanted to see her so badly. He *needed* to see her. It was as strong an impulse as the other need, but different. With Ellie he felt out of control, on shaky ground. She wasn't one of his . . . one of the others. She was a strong and vibrant woman who could say no to him, who could turn him down. He couldn't imagine doing to her . . . No, that didn't feel right. She was too rare.

He drove to Boulder from Denver on a windy night to pick her up. They were going to a Colorado Avalanche hockey game in the new Pepsi Center, where Finn had treated himself to a luxury box. Tax deductible, of course. Business expense.

His heart hammered in an unfamiliar way. Ellie, Ellie. He felt an erection starting, but he couldn't do that to her. He wanted to, but he couldn't imagine it—the scene would not coalesce in his mind. Yet.

He knocked on the rickety wooden door of her house, and she opened it instantly. Beautiful Ellie, in a green

sweater and gray slacks that clung to her hips with exquisite grace.

"Hi," she said, smiling.

He kissed her on the lips. "Merry Christmas," he said,
"a little late."

"Same to you." She cocked her head in that charming
way that was achingly familiar to him. "Let me get my
coat, just a sec."

In his car, he put his hand on hers. "I missed you."

"Me too."

"Do you like hockey?"

"Never been."

"Good God, I have a lot of experiences to introduce
you to."

"Okay," she said lightly.

She told him what she'd been doing since he'd seen
her last as he drove back to Denver.

"My mom was so glad to see me. I think she's lonely.
Well, she has friends, but, you know. It was good to see
a lot of old friends from high school. And, oh boy, I ate
way too much."

" 'Tis the season for that."

"So I keep telling myself."

He didn't talk about what he'd done in the last week.
He'd been alone, except for when he'd driven out to Limon, where he'd studied the small town on the prairie,
studied the stores on Main Street and the movie theater,
where the teenagers on Christmas break hung out. One
girl . . . But he had time to plan that later.

The Pepsi Center was impressive, his private box even
more so. It was right on the red centerline. "Rock and
Roll Part Two" played, that earthy, bump-and-grind piece
that always introduced games in Denver. The crowd
roared as the starting line skated on the ice, big men

made bigger by their helmets and pads and gloves. Gladiators.

"I love this," Ellie said, clapping with the music.

He had to point out to her the rules of the game: icing, off sides, and high sticking and checking. He told her about strategy, about the forwards and the defensemen.

"It's kind of like soccer," she said. "I played soccer in high school."

"Yeah, it is. But faster. And you don't check in soccer." He held her hand and watched her more than he watched the game. He loved the way her face grew animated, and she jiggled in her seat when the team was close to the goal.

"Want something to drink?" he asked. "I can order whatever you like."

"That'd be nice."

He ordered two imported beers; beer always seemed right for hockey games.

"Oh!" she cried. "Get him!" A defenseman headed off the other team's center.

She sipped her beer, which he'd poured into a glass with the perfect inch-high head.

"Good?" he asked.

She made a little face. "Well, actually, I'm sorry, Finn, but I don't like beer very much. It's bitter."

"You don't like beer," he said obtusely.

"Could you order me something else? Do you mind? I'm so sorry."

He ordered her a glass of wine. He knew she liked wine.

The crowd roared—an Avalanche goal. The music blared again; the huge men were in a scrum, their arms around the scorer. "A goal by *Le Toreau* at ten minutes, fifteen seconds into the first period," chanted the announcer. "Assisted by *Hendersen.*"

The wine arrived. She smiled and took a drink. "Much better," she said.

He put his arm around her. She was warm and pliant, and he could feel her move when there was some action in the game. He desired her. He could sleep with her, plunge into her. Into Ellie, no fantasies, no whirling screaming faces, a real woman. He could almost imagine climaxing inside her without any of the planning, without the crying and struggling and pleading. He'd be able to do it. Soon. He was sure of it.

"I'm starving," she said. "Can you get food here?"

"I can get anything I want," he said, "but I thought we'd go out afterward and grab a bite. Someplace nice."

"Oh, Finn, I'm so hungry. I can't wait. I didn't have time for dinner. Please." Her dark eyes pleaded.

"Okay, sure, what do you want?"

"A hamburger. I'd adore a hamburger."

He didn't have anything himself, so he watched her eat. He was a little upset, his plans spoiled. She'd never want to eat after the game now, and he'd planned to take her to one of his favorite sports bars, where they had great barbecued ribs.

She was halfway through the hamburger when she set it down, hesitated, and said, "It's too rare for me. I can't finish it."

"Too rare?"

"Could you send it back, Finn? All they have to do is grill it a little longer."

"Do you want another one? Or something else?" He was aware his tone was a touch peevish.

"No, no, this is fine. Just cooked a little more."

He sent it back. He was sharp with the service person.

All Ellie's fault. Had she been this picky before? He didn't think so. Maybe she was in a mood. Women had moods. She'd be sweet, pliable Ellie again soon.

The Zamboni machine came on the ice to clean it after the second period. Ellie stood up and stretched. "Where are the rest rooms?" she asked.

"Just outside the box and down the hall."

"Okay. See you in a minute."

But she wasn't back in a minute. She hadn't returned in fifteen minutes. Or twenty. The third period started, and she still wasn't back. Finn went out into the corridor, pacing back and forth in front of the ladies' room. No Ellie. He wanted to ask some of the women exiting if Ellie was in there, but he felt it would be really dumb. *Can't keep track of your girlfriend,* they'd think.

Eventually he returned to his box. He was angry; he almost felt like crying. Where in hell *was* she? Had she left him there, *ditched* him?

She breezed in five minutes later. Smiling, full of good cheer. "Sorry I took so long" was all she said, and she gave him a quick kiss on the cheek. Her cheerfulness did not dissipate his irritation. He knew he was sulking, that it was immature and ugly, but he couldn't help it.

Ellie didn't seem to notice his bad humor, though. She watched the game, yelled with the crowd, jumped to her feet.

"I love hockey," she said. "I never knew how great it was."

He should have been mollified that she was happy, enjoying herself. He tried to be, but a small bud of doubt had found fertile ground in his imagination. And it only made him want her more. He craved her undying admiration and uncritical adoration. He wanted to possess her in all ways, to shape her and coddle her, to protect her and own her.

"Great game!" she cried when it was over and the Avs had won. "Can we come again?"

"Of course we can."

"Thanks, Finn. Thanks for all this." She gestured at the luxurious box. "I'm having so much *fun.*"

He wanted to drive her to his house and make love to her, all night long. Slow, sensual love. But he'd been thrown off by her behavior that evening, and he wasn't ready. The time wasn't right. He required everything to be just right. Ellie needed to be the nice, easygoing girl he'd thought she was. And he had to be on top of his game, not tainted with residual irritation.

No, he wasn't ready yet.

"Listen," he said in his car, "you don't mind if I drop you off early? I've got a breakfast meeting tomorrow. Clinching a big deal."

"Oh, but I thought you wanted to go out to eat."

"You already ate."

"But you didn't. I don't mind. I'll sit with you."

"Never mind. Not tonight. The meeting . . ."

"Sure, it's fine. Whatever you want, Finn." The soft, sincere voice, her hand on his thigh. That was better.

He raced back to Denver after dropping her off. He was sweating, his stomach in a knot, his heart drumming. He shouldn't see her again. She was an addiction, a dangerous narcotic drug. She was gaining a control over him that was frightening. He should give her up.

He'd go out to Limon again on the weekend. Hang around, look for that high school girl. Find out who she was, where she lived, who her male friends were. Or maybe she had a stepfather. Stepfathers were good. Neighbors, too. He recognized the need in him, but it wasn't growing the way it usually did. The thought of doing the girl in Limon was almost too much trouble to bother with. He wondered at that. It hadn't happened before, and he knew it was Ellie. She was standing between him and fulfillment.

He knew it was because he had to possess her first, before he could turn to anyone else.

Ellie, Ellie.

He tried to sleep in his comfortable, familiar bedroom, with its king-size bed and expensive linens picked out by his decorator and the silver-gray duvet cover on his bed, the cool, shiny silver that usually delighted him so.

But he couldn't sleep. No matter how he tried to conjure up his conquests, the soothing memories, he failed. Because Ellie's face kept superimposing itself over the others, stopping the kaleidoscope, narrowing his field of vision to her alone, ruining his fantasies, destroying his peace of mind.

TWENTY

Sam Koffey gave Michael the news a couple days before
New Year's Eve.

"It's a go," the commander said. "Judge Worrell issued
the warrant. He wasn't thrilled about it, Callas, but he
did it. I've got the equipment and a van lined up with
the CBI."

"Okay."

"This better not turn into a media party. The Boulder
police have had enough bad press."

"Goes without saying," Michael replied.

He should have been happy as hell. *His* operation, *his*
warrant, the whole thing based on *his* evidence. If he got
Rasmussen he'd be owed a whole shitload of favors, a
commendation maybe, not that he cared about that, but
he'd like one for catching the right guy this time.

He should have been happy, but he wasn't, and it was
easy to figure out why: Ellie. She was putting herself on
the line, and he was afraid for her. Rasmussen was big
and strong and smart and crazy as a loon. A lethal com-
bination.

He phoned the CBI and spoke to the tech guy who was going to bring the equipment from Denver. They'd do it tomorrow. He hung up and his mind clicked into gear, making plans. He was going to have to let Augostino and Chambliss work on the Girard case while he concentrated on Rasmussen. And he needed Koffey's help to free men from their regular schedules to man the van. Ellie couldn't be left uncovered one second.

Then came the hard part—he had to call Ellie. He'd avoided her like the plague since Christmas Day, since he'd dropped her at her mother's house.

He reached her at work after lunch. "It's a go," he said.

"Oh, my God, it is? Really? Michael . . ."

"Got the warrant. The CBI will be here tomorrow morning with the equipment. Can you get off for a couple hours?"

"Yes, sure."

"Look, does Torres know anything about this?"

"No, nothing. Nobody knows."

"Okay, leave it that way for now. We may need him later."

"Okay."

"I'll pick you up at nine at the Justice Center tomorrow."

"Fine, okay. I'm so thrilled, Michael. I know this is going to work, I know it."

"Thrilled, huh? You should be scared to death."

"That, too," she said lightly. "Michael, um, I've got to talk to you about—"

"Tomorrow," he said brusquely and placed the receiver down hard.

He picked her up the next morning. It was cold and sunny, and her cheeks were pink from waiting outside, and when her hand brushed his it was cold as ice.

They met with the CBI technician in one of the larger interrogation rooms. His name was Ron Tuttle, and he was a tall, skinny black man. He looked like a basketball player.

"Miss Kramer," he said, shaking her hand. "Detective Callas. Nice to meet you. Well, I've brought you a whole bunch of Christmas presents."

He handed Michael a set of keys. "The van's in your parking lot. Unmarked, because you said you'd mostly be doing this one at night. No way can we park a Public Service Company van on some suburban street, right? It's all fitted out. No video on this one, you said only audio."

"How far can we receive?" Michael asked.

"Several blocks unless she's in a big building, the usual. You said probably a private home, so it'll be fine. This device works on line of sight, so if the receiver has a clear line of sight to the person wearing the transmitter, you should be okay.

"This is the transmitter." He held up a tiny radio transmitter. "It will be inside the lining of this purse. Your new purse, Miss Kramer." He held up a black leather shoulder bag in his other hand. "Keep this bag as close to you as possible, so the receiver can pick up your conversations. It's battery-powered, self-contained. You turn it on like this, and then just leave it."

Ellie was staring at the microphone as if it would bite her. She was nodding her head, listening intently.

"It's pretty foolproof. The receiver is also self-contained. It's in the van, all set up. It will record as well as transmit the conversations.

"Now, if you find that the van has to be more than a few blocks from the radio transmitter, we'll need to fix you up with a repeater to broadcast the signal farther, but we'll worry about that if and when."

"I think we can get close enough," Michael said. "Shouldn't be a problem."

"Let's take a look at the van," Special Agent Tuttle said.

"Can I come?" Ellie asked.

"Sure. You should know what it looks like anyway," Tuttle said.

The van had tinted windows. It wasn't old and it wasn't new. A nondescript tan color, not too battered, not too shiny. Ordinary Colorado license plates, the green mountains on a white background. Tuttle slid the side door open and climbed in.

There were two swivel seats, a counter containing the receiver and a tape recorder, carpeting on the floor and walls for soundproofing. A television screen was attached to one wall. Very high tech.

Michael looked around, checked out the interior; he'd probably be spending a lot of time in there.

"Okay, so here's the switch for the receiver; here's the one for the tape recorder. It has very slow speeds for long recording. There's a supply of new tapes, right there."

"Can we check it out?" Michael asked. "A test run?"

"Sure thing. Miss Kramer, here, take the transmitter, put it in the purse, yes, there in that slit in the lining. Okay? Turn it on. Like that. Walk on over to, oh, say the entranceway. Then just talk."

Ellie held the purse with exaggerated care. She looked a little intimidated. *Good,* Michael thought. He watched her walk to the door of the building.

Tuttle clicked everything on. They waited.

"Okay, I'm talking," came Ellie's voice, surprisingly loud, electronically amplified. The tape recorder spool turned on by itself.

"Voice activated," Tuttle explained.

"Can you hear me? One, two, three, testing. Michael, am I talking loud enough?"

Tuttle stepped outside the van and waved her over.

"Could you hear me?" she asked breathlessly, striding up to them.

"Clear as day," Tuttle said.

"Was I loud enough?"

"Plenty loud. That transmitter will pick up much quieter conversations. Want to hear yourself?" He rewound the tape, then pressed play.

"Okay, I'm talking," came Ellie's voice. "Can you hear me? One, two, three, testing. Michael, am I talking loud enough?"

"Oh," Ellie said.

"See, nothing to it."

Tuttle left shortly, picked up by another CBI agent.

"Whew," Ellie said. "This makes me nervous."

"Good."

"But there's no danger. He'll never find the transmitter. Why would he suspect anything?"

"Rasmussen's smart. Don't underestimate him."

"I don't underestimate him, believe me," she said sharply.

"Don't overestimate yourself, either."

"I don't need any lessons from you, Michael. I already—"

"You need every goddamn bit of help you can get, Ellie. Don't kid yourself. Every edge. This is no walk in the goddamn park."

She stood there in the cold winter sun and glared at him.

It was impossibly hard to be with her, to accept the fact that he was sending her into this volatile situation.

Into the arms of Finn Rasmussen. Suddenly he felt his stomach clench. It made him sick, to send Ellie in alone, unprotected. But she was right, someone had to stop that son of a bitch.

"Okay, I'm sorry," Ellie said. "I know you don't want me to do this. But you also know I'm the only one who can get him. Let's not fight, let's not. . . ."

"I'm not fighting."

"All right, Michael." She studied his face for a moment, then she said, "Did I thank you for Christmas Eve? I wrote your mother a note."

"That's nice."

"I enjoyed it. All that family."

"Yeah."

"Your cousin Joy . . . I liked her."

"I saw you two talking. That's Joy, blabbermouth."

"She told me . . . she told me about Paul, your brother Paul, and I wanted you to know how sorry I am. . . ."

He froze as if liquid nitrogen had been injected into his veins.

"Michael?"

"Don't go there, Ellie," he said harshly.

"Okay, sure, sorry. But Michael . . ." She was searching his face with those big dark eyes, trying to make him *feel,* and he didn't want to.

"Come on," he muttered, "I'll drive you back to work."

Neither one of them said a word the entire way.

He pulled up at the main entrance to the Justice Center. Ellie didn't make a move to get out of the unmarked car.

"Michael," she said, "I have to tell you something."

"Go ahead." He kept his hands on the wheel, eyes forward.

"I saw Finn the other night."

He swiveled his head. "You *what?*"

"He called. I was afraid to put him off. I knew you wouldn't have anything ready yet. I wasn't even certain the operation was on for sure."

"Goddamn it all."

"He took me to a hockey game. Michael, I got to him, I really did. I irritated him. It worked, I'm telling you. He's easy to push."

"You little idiot."

"Don't, Michael. I had to keep him on the hook. You see that, don't you?"

"I don't see anything. You went with him, alone, no backup."

"Nothing happened to me. I'm fine. He—"

"Did you sleep with him?" he blurted out, the words forming in his brain and vomiting from his mouth.

He saw the hurt and the shock in her eyes. It made him feel good in some indefinable way.

"Oh, Michael," she said, and she shook her head, infinitely sad.

"Well, did you?"

She didn't answer, only opened the car door and got out, slammed it behind her. He watched her walk to the Justice Center entrance, her back straight in the black coat, her red scarf like a slash of blood against the dark wool. She carried the new purse with the radio transmitter in it over her shoulder, its gold catch glinting in the bright sun.

Then she was inside the door, and it closed behind her, swallowed her up, and Michael shifted the car into drive and left.

"Tomorrow night," Ellie said quietly into the phone at her desk.

"You mean New Year's Eve?"

She knew Michael was pissed the moment she heard his tone. "Well, it figures Finn would ask me out then."

"Does it." Flatly.

She let it go. "I know you and the other men probably had plans. . . ."

"That's not important."

"He said he'd pick me up at eight sharp."

"Okay. Just in case, did you get an address?"

"Michael." Her voice grew louder. "How could I ask him for an address? All I know is he said a friend's party in Castle Rock. He told me it was dressy, so I figured I'd—"

But he cut her off. "I'm sure you'll handle that end," he said, all business, brusque. "We'll just have to be on your street at seven-thirty and hope to hell we don't lose you in traffic. And for God's sake, Ellie, don't look for the van. Not on the street and not on the interstate. You understand?"

"Of course. But what if you *do* lose us? I mean . . ."

"We'll pick you up later at Finn's house."

"But what if we don't go back to his place?"

One of the ADAs was standing behind Ellie now, talking to a clerk. She pivoted in her chair and lowered her voice. "I mean, Michael, what if he takes me someplace?"

"Listen, the odds of that happening are next to nothing. He'll take you home or he'll take you to his house."

"If you say so."

"And we won't lose you in traffic. Okay?"

"But you said . . ."

"I know what I said. I was thinking out loud and I was wrong."

"Maybe you were trying to rattle me," she couldn't help pointing out.

"Don't be ridiculous."

She took a breath. "Listen, Michael, you have to understand, it's important to me that you know I never did anything—"

"Drop it," he said sharply.

"All right, all right." God, she was going to scream. "But you need to know that I'll do everything in my power to keep him from touching me. Michael?"

"Whatever," he said. "We'll be there tomorrow night. Your street. Seven-thirty. If anything changes, call."

"Sure, I'll—" But he'd hung up.

She wore a black blazer and a midcalf black skirt, a functional raspberry-colored rayon shell under the blazer.

It had taken her hours to dress. Hours of agonizing with no one to advise her—the girls weren't due back for two more days.

She knew she was going to push a few of Finn's buttons with her choice of attire. He'd said dressy. But if she dressed down too much, he'd get suspicious. So no jeans or slacks. Still, she wondered if her work clothes weren't too nice for what she had in mind. On the other hand, she couldn't afford to have him get furious and dump her on the spot. She needed to annoy him, to disobey him, not set him into a rage. *Right.* She was sure he still liked her—even desired her in some sick way. She couldn't blow that.

Five minutes before eight she flew up the stairs and used Celeste's most expensive perfume. Just a hint. *Don't overdo.*

The purse, the little transmitter in its lining, was waiting on the table by the door. She didn't want to be holding it when Finn arrived. *Pick it up casually,* she thought.

Still, it seemed to be pulsing out a beacon: *The transmitter's in here.* Over and over.

At two minutes till eight she panicked—she couldn't let Finn see her clothes yet.

Her coat.

She grabbed it and threw it on and stood near the front door, trying very hard not to peek out the living room window.

Was Michael out there? Waiting, watching? Should she turn on the transmitter now or later . . . ?

She heard a car pull up out front. *Finn.* She grabbed the purse, fumbling in the lining, switching it on. The damn battery had better last. Should she test it, say something?

His knock on the door.

Her heart leaped and a hot prickly sensation crawled up her neck. When she opened the door, she was clutching the black purse so tightly her fingers were cramping.

"Hi." She beamed. "I'm all ready."

"You're cheerful tonight."

"Oh, yes, well, New Year's Eve. One of my favorite nights." Perhaps the biggest lie she'd ever told. She hated New Year's. Champagne. A god-awful headache in the morning. Cotton mouth. The night Stephanie Morris had been raped.

He'd driven his BMW because the roads were dry, and she slid into the hushed warm interior gratefully, having walked all the way to the car and not once glanced up or down the street. Had Michael noticed her restraint?

Don't think about him, she admonished herself. *Pretend he's not there, listening, hearing every word. . . . Stop it.*

Finn, as always, was the perfect conversationalist on the drive south to Castle Rock. He talked about another show he'd gone to over the holiday and asked how she'd liked her first hockey game the other night.

"I loved it."

"Then we'll go again. Would you like that?"

"Oh, yes, I really would."

The party ended up being at a fabulous home in the gated community surrounding the Castle Pines golf complex. The gate and guardhouse troubled Ellie, but Michael would figure out how to get in without alerting the security man as to why he was really there. *If* Michael hadn't gotten lost in traffic.

The house was a modern white structure reminiscent of Frank Lloyd Wright: big, sweeping, all white and gleaming chrome and glass, no corners, only curving panels that gently climbed a rocky hillside overlooking two golf course fairways.

On the walk up the curving, heated drive, Ellie craned her neck. "My God, it's magnificent," she breathed.

"You like it?" His hand was at the small of her back.

"Oh, yes."

"Too modern for me."

"But your home is modern, Finn."

"The interior is. But I purposely chose brick and wood for the exterior. It fits. This is too California."

"Well, I hate to disagree," she said, her words well planned, "but I adore it and I haven't even seen the inside."

"It's the same as the outside. *White.* Frankly, Ellie, I'm surprised by your taste," he said, and she heard the disapproval in his voice. *Good.* Wait till he saw how she'd dressed.

At the impressive chrome double-doored entrance, she turned for a second and couldn't help scanning the street below from her position. She thought she saw a van down the road, parked on a curve. *Line of sight.* Yes. If that was Michael, he'd have a clear line of sight.

The minute Finn helped her out of her coat for an awaiting maid, and he saw how she was dressed, his shock was evident. "Jesus Christ, Ellie, what were you thinking? I specifically told you this was a formal affair." He glared at her, obviously caught between anger and humiliation.

"Did you?" she replied mildly. "Oh, gosh, Finn, I don't remember you telling me. Do I look awful?"

"Never mind," he said, cutting the air with a hand, "I'll think of something to tell people. But, Jesus, woman, you should try listening once in a while."

She didn't apologize. She only smiled her prettiest smile and saw a flurry of emotions sweep across his face until his expression returned to neutral.

There wasn't a thing he could do or say as their host appeared and introductions were made, and Ellie and Finn were carried along with a group of guests toward the largest living area she'd ever seen. Finn had been right. Except for the modern artwork on the walls, everything in the enormous, curving room was white to off-white, even the metal dividers on the huge plate glass windows that curved on and on around the room.

At one end was the food and liquor. In the center a quartet played. There was more than enough room to sit or dance or merely stand at the plate glass windows and admire the night views. Ellie wished her mother could see this. Hell, she thought, she wished she could buy it for Janice.

True to form, Finn was the consummate companion, attentive, charming, his hand always at her back possessively. When he introduced her around, he had a ready-made excuse for her dress.

"My poor Ellie," he must have said twenty times, "I snatched her right from work. She's a soon-to-be lawyer, you know, clerking for the DA up in Boulder."

Oh, yes, Ellie thought each time he made excuses for her, he was still miffed.

She kept her purse tucked under her right arm. She wondered, a thousand times, if the transmitter was working, or were the men in the van just picking up cluttered voices and background noise? Could Michael tell how angry Finn was? And she was just beginning.

They danced two dances, and she managed to hold the purse in her hand behind his back. Nonetheless, she was positive the signal was blocked. On the other hand, there was nothing being said worth recording. There would be, though. She was determined to get under this monster's skin and dig away until he did or said something so incriminating they'd have him.

Over a light supper, during which they stood with their plates near the windows, Ellie tried to pry into his childhood. On the surface he'd always been open about his dysfunctional parents. But if she could scratch that fragile surface . . .

"So, Milwaukee, you said," she began. "Tell me more about where you grew up."

"I got out of there the minute I could. It's a terrible place. Cold. Long, cold winters and the wind off the lake. I hate Milwaukee."

"When did you leave?"

"The day I graduated from high school. And I never looked back."

"But you went to college," she urged.

"Yes, I did. I went to CU." He grinned at her. "That was the only advantage of being dirt poor. I qualified for a full scholarship."

"Boy, do I know that story," Ellie said. "I did the same thing."

"Kindred spirits," Finn said, taking her hand and squeezing it, his blue eyes kind.

She lulled him into a false sense of security then went in with a jab. "And you mentioned your uncle. Didn't you tell me you stayed with him for a while?"

His gaze clouded over, his features froze, sudden harsh lines appeared around his mouth; he seemed to go inside himself. Ellie stood there, still holding her dinner plate, and ignored the lengthy silence.

Finally, he replied, "You must be thinking of someone else." His voice was thick, and his mouth twisted in a rictus.

"Oh, sure, I got confused there for a minute. But you did tell me that you have an uncle. I'm sure you did. Is he in Milwaukee, too?"

"I don't have an uncle in Milwaukee or anywhere else," Finn said.

Could Michael hear the edge to his voice?

She backed off when they finished the meal, and then she threw another punch. "It must have been awful, growing up with a father who drank. Didn't you tell me you were in foster homes?"

He snatched her unfinished plate from her hands. "You're done, aren't you?"

"Um, sure."

"We're going to dance now. I love to dance." He was breathing a little too fast.

"I'm sorry," she said sweetly, "I've upset you."

He relaxed as the New Year approached, spinning her around the dance floor, his old charming self. She was beginning to wonder what else she dared to pull when an opportunity fell in her lap and she seized it.

"Finn," came a male voice, "mind if I cut in? You're hogging the prettiest lady here, buddy."

Finn allowed his friend to sweep her away.

"Leo Shoemaker," the man said in her ear. "And you're . . . ?"

"Ellie. Ellie Kramer."

"Well, Ellie Kramer, I'm trying not to feed you a line here, but where have you been all my life?"

Ellie fell happily into the game and played it without a hitch, right up to exchanging phone numbers after the dance, when Finn was within earshot. She knew, too, that Michael was hearing every word and a small spurt of satisfaction coursed through her.

Leo left her, winking at her so that Finn saw. It couldn't have been more perfect if she'd planned it.

Finn was seething. "What the hell was that all about?" he demanded to know, and he dragged her aside—to a few raised eyebrows.

"What?" she said innocently.

"Are you telling me you didn't give Leo your phone number just now?"

Ellie blinked. "Well, yes, of course I did. I mean, after all, Finn, it isn't as if we're married." Then, the icing on the cake, she gave him one of her glowing smiles.

She could see a vein swelling in his temple and the hard set of his jaw. *Go for it,* she thought. "Finn? Is there a problem?"

"Is there a *problem?*" he hissed. "You accept a date with a stranger at my friend's house? At a party that I brought you to? You're acting like some cheap whore."

"Finn. I—"

"We're leaving."

"Leaving? It isn't even midnight. What about—"

"Fuck that," he ground out.

She had no choice but to let him usher her across the big room. He concealed his temper well, nodding and smiling at people. But she felt a flush of satisfaction—she'd gotten to him, made him lose control. She couldn't back off. Michael was out there. She'd be okay. Maybe this was the night. Maybe she'd brought him to the edge, and he was ready to step off into darkness.

Somehow he said his good-byes to the host and made their excuse for leaving sound believable. She went along docilely, smiling too, her lips brittle. Miss Innocent. But what now?

They marched back down the curving drive, and she could see the van clearly now. Finn still had her by the arm, his big hand over the sleeve of her coat. He was deathly silent.

"Where are we going?" she tried.

"I'm taking you home," he snapped, but then he stopped in his tracks and brought her up against him so hard her breath was knocked out of her lungs. "No, we're not going to your house. I think we'll go to mine. We've got a few things to work out, don't you think?"

Before she could catch her breath he kissed her, a cruel grinding of his lips to hers, and then he let her go abruptly.

She staggered. Began to say something as her hand came to her lips, but she held her counsel. What had she expected?

"Get in the car," he said, fishing his keys out.

She fought fear. God, how she hated him. *Michael, Michael, I should have listened, I can't handle him.*

Finn drove in silence and there was nothing she could find to say. She spent the time collecting herself, convincing herself that she'd taken Finn's power from him tonight, and she had to make the best use of it she could.

This was what she'd dreamed about. For an eternity.

Don't stumble now. Don't be afraid.

He threw open the door to his house and glared at her. "Go on in," he said, nodding.

She did, but not before imagining she could hear the sound of the van's tires as they rolled to a stop just down the road. Now was the time to go for the jugular.

"Why are we here?" She turned to him in the hall and cocked her head. "I mean, Finn, you're so mad at me, why bother?"

He only walked past her into the living room, switched on the lights over his wet bar, and poured himself a stiff brandy, chugging it in a single gulp. Only then did he offer her one.

"No, thank you," she said, standing in the half light near the sectional, clutching the purse. "I think you owe me an explanation."

"I owe *you?*" He laughed humorlessly.

"Yes, you do," she dared. "I have every right to see whoever I want, whenever I want. Did you really believe you were the only man I dated?" *Oh, God.* Her heart was fluttering like a bird's wings against her ribs. "Well? Did you really believe that?"

"You bitch," he got out. "I'm telling you right now . . . I forbid you to see anyone else. Do you understand? *Do you?*"

Here goes. She laughed lightly, incredulously. "Oh, please, Finn, we're not living in the Dark Ages, for Pete's sake."

He reached her so quickly she had no time to react. He was just there, his hand raised. He slapped her. She collapsed against the arm of the couch and slid to the floor, the hot copper taste of blood against her teeth.

She stared up at him, her fist pressed to her mouth,

hate and terror in her eyes. Somewhere a voice called from the recesses of her mind: *You have him now.*

Then a thought slammed into her consciousness: Michael. If he came busting in here too soon ... "I'm all right," she said against her fist. "I'm all right."

And Finn sobered. He came back into himself as if a bucket of cold water had been thrown in his face and he reached for her, apologizing. "Oh, God, Ellie, I'm so, so sorry. I don't know ... I've never ... It's just that you're so different. I've never wanted a woman ... not like this ... Ellie, forgive me. Here, let me help you up. I'll get some ice. Oh, shit, I'm so sorry."

She wanted to cry. So close. She'd been so close to breaking him.

He made an ice compress for her, and then she said she just wanted to go home.

The ice pack still on her lip, she sat next to him in his car, unable to collect her thoughts. If only she hadn't said she was all right. If only she'd said something as she'd planned, an insinuation, one of the murdered girl's names. Or she should have fought back physically. She should have grabbed her chance. Had she chickened out? Or had she been trying to keep a lid on Michael's reaction?

Finn said he was sorry a dozen times, but she barely heard. She clung to the notion that he still cared about her—all was not lost. He'd come back for more. She just had to keep him dangling. But how long could *she* keep this up? No one, not even her mother, had struck her before. It was a sobering experience, humiliating. Curiously, she almost felt guilty. Was this why battered women were incapable of leaving their tormentors?

She let Finn touch her beneath the porch light at her house. He put one hand on her coat sleeve, the other on her chin, trying to tip her head gently toward him. With that same hand that had choked the life out of how many young girls? Bile rose in her throat. She couldn't imagine Finn on top of her, pressing himself into her, his hands on her throat. No.

"Ellie," he said, "I'm sorry. I hate what I did. But it's because I care so much about you, you know that, don't you?"

She said nothing.

"Forgive me."

"I . . . I'll try."

"I'd never hurt you, Ellie."

"Good night, Finn." She opened her door and went inside. She heard his footfalls crunching in the hard snow on the walk. His car door opening. Closing with that rich man's *snick*. He drove away, and she sagged against the door and held back tears, hating him, hating herself.

And someone knocked on the door.

Finn? Or Michael? It didn't matter. She couldn't take any more. *No more, please, no more tonight.*

Another knock. Insistent.

"All right," she said weakly, "all right." She wiped away her tears and opened the door, reluctantly.

It was Michael. *Oh, God.*

He came in before she could stop him. "Listen," she began, "I'm really tired. Can't this wait?"

But he didn't hear. Or maybe he didn't care. He put his hands on her shoulders and forced her around into the hall light. "Let me see your face," he said.

"I'm fine. Really." But her voice was quivering. She cleared her throat and tried to pull away. "I said I'm fine."

"Sit down. In there."

She said again that she was okay, but he was still ignoring her, turning on the lamps in the living room, making her sit, easing her face toward the light.

He never said a word. He only examined her lip, murder in his eyes.

"It doesn't hurt much," she lied.

He snorted.

"Honest, Michael. This was what we wanted. I expected something like this. Finn almost—"

"I'm calling it off."

"No."

"Too dangerous."

"No, Michael, God, don't even think that."

He straightened then and jammed his hands in his parka pockets and began to pace. "It's too goddamn dangerous."

"We almost broke him tonight," she said in a quiet voice. "Don't you see, we nearly had him. I only said I was all right because I was afraid you'd come storming in or something and . . ."

He stopped and pivoted. "I nearly did. Parker had to stop me."

"See?" She tried to smile. The cut in her mouth hurt. "You see? And next time we will have him. It's not over."

He glared at her, his amber eyes seeing past her prevarications to her fear. He looked dangerous, a big cat ready to pounce.

"You know I won't stop seeing Finn, no matter what you do. I'm going to break him," she finally said.

"Even if it kills you?" he asked, his voice so soft, so quiet, so menacing.

"It won't kill me. You're there in the van."

"You push him too hard, he breaks, and you're dead before I can get to you."

She shook her head. "That will never happen."

He stared at her for a long time. She felt like squirming.

"Stubborn," he said, shaking his head.

"It isn't your decision to make. It's mine."

"It's my case. I'm responsible for you."

"The hell you are."

He moved away from her and started toward the door. "Michael?"

He halted, turned to face her. "Okay, Ellie, you win. It's on your head." Then he continued walking away from her.

"Michael, don't, don't just leave like this. You're always . . . running away. There's so much I have to say, things I need to tell you. Stay a minute," she said, astounded by her boldness. But this couldn't go on. The wanting, the guilt, the need to know he forgave her. If he'd just let her inside. Just a little . . .

"I'll call" was all she got, and then he was gone. She sat on the couch, the living room lit up like a Christmas tree, alone. Her world narrowed to the beating of her heart.

TWENTY-ONE

It was a Monday morning when Rick Augostino put a hand on Michael's shoulder. "Chambliss finally got a registration out of DMV to go with the key."

"The key?" Michael said blankly.

"Jesus, Callas, the key we found in the Girard case."

"Oh, right. Sorry. Hey, that's great news." He was having a hard time switching his mind off Ellie and Rasmussen these days. He'd been up late all weekend, in the van, following them, and a couple of nights last week, and the weekend before. He wondered how in hell Ellie kept up the pace between work and dating, how she kept her cool with that madman, needling him, then cooing, then needling again.

She was good.

So far Rasmussen had neither said nor done anything they could use against him. Either he was extraordinarily careful, or his persona was so submerged in denial that he really believed he was a normal functioning guy when he and Ellie were together.

How long would it take? How long before the man

broke and said something incriminating or trapped himself by physically going after Ellie?

Maybe he never would.

There was one certainty in this whole goddamn mess: Finn was in love with her. You could tell. The other cops on duty in the van joked about it with savage cop humor, but Michael didn't find it the least amusing. He knew precisely how Rasmussen was feeling; Ellie was easy to love.

He'd sat in that van for over two weeks now, listening to the two of them together, listening, listening. Hearing the rustle of her clothes when she sat or crossed her legs or walked alongside Rasmussen. He could tell what she was wearing just by the sound of the fabric, jeans or wool slacks or hose. Hearing every word, hearing Rasmussen's sweet nothings, Ellie's replies, hearing, feeling, living the kisses, the murmurs, the flares of the man's rage that made Michael's body tense with readiness and made his hand seek his weapon.

But so far Rasmussen had managed to keep himself under control.

The cracks were there, though. There and growing. Ellie was prying them open wider every day and Finn was showing the stress. It almost seemed that the harder Ellie pushed, the more obsessed he became. Hell, he even drove to Boulder now just to take her out to eat on her lunch hour.

Ellie had the routine down pat.

"Michael," she'd say on the phone, "tonight at seven. He's taking me to the movie at Arvada's downtown art center."

"Okay."

"You won't be able to hear when I'm in the theater."

"No, but he won't do anything in there."

"No, I suppose not." A pause, then. "I'm trying. If I can get him mad enough, I'll throw in a name, one of his victims. I'll say I know about him. I'll—"

"Take it easy."

"I know, but it's hard. I want this to be over."

"Do you?" he'd ask.

His relationship with Ellie was completely professional these days, exchanges of information about locations, times, addresses.

Michael had never apologized for asking her if she'd slept with Rasmussen, but he knew now, listening to every word, every sound between them, that she hadn't. The sicko couldn't get it up. He fit the serial murderer profile so well it was amazing to Michael no one had seen it before now.

He couldn't have intercourse with a woman he loved, because the situation was alien to him—he was utterly out of control, his emotions running amok, and sex was impossible. It was that dysfunction Michael had warned Ellie about.

But he suspected the man was working up to it.

His phone rang that afternoon: "Michael?"

"Jesus, not again."

"Not tonight. He's taking me out tomorrow night. To a dinner he gives every year for his supervisors. It's going to be at The Fort, you know, the one in Morrison?"

"Yeah, I know it."

"I think it's small enough for you to hear everything."

Michael and Leland Kirkner sat in the van the next night; Cam Parker drove. There was a lot of background noise, but he could make out Ellie and Rasmussen; she must have the purse right in her lap.

"Honey, get the buffalo tenderloin," Rasmussen said.

"No, Finn, honestly, it's too much for me. I'd prefer the chicken."

"The buffalo is the house specialty, Ellie."

"I don't care. I want the chicken."

Then Rasmussen's voice took on that dark edge Michael had come to know.

Later on there were a lot of toasts and a speech by Rasmussen, the usual rah-rah crap. The tape turned slowly, monotonously. Michael was bored, but at the same time he was aware of Ellie, a hundred yards away, next to a maniac, egging him on, hoping he'd go over the edge and incriminate himself.

They followed Rasmussen's car home. Tonight he'd taken the silver-blue BMW, not the Grand Cherokee, because the roads were dry, and the route up to the restaurant in Morrison outside of Denver was a two-lane winding highway, where he could set the Beemer to rocking and rolling. Showing off for Ellie.

Rasmussen didn't take Ellie back to Boulder that night; he went to his house in Cherry Creek. Cam Parker pulled up where the street crossed First Avenue; Rasmussen's house was near the dead end, two blocks away. They could hear perfectly.

"Why didn't you wear that red dress?" Rasmussen was asking.

"I told you, it's my roommate's dress. I can't keep borrowing it like that."

"I'll buy you a dress, Ellie. I'd have bought you one for tonight. I'll buy you a dozen dresses."

"No, Finn. You like me, you like my clothes, too. I won't pretend or change how I dress, and I won't let you buy me anything."

"Christ, Ellie, you're so stubborn."

"Maybe."

"I want to be proud of you."

"You're looking at superficial things, Finn. Now, come on, lay off me."

"Did you like dinner tonight?"

"The place is overrated. Just because President Clinton was there once . . ."

Silence. "You ungrateful little bitch."

Michael froze.

"Whoo, he's pissed," Kirkner said.

"Sorry, Finn, but the restaurant took you for everything you're worth."

A noise. Something falling. A vase? A lamp? Michael half stood in the van.

"Finn" came Ellie's voice, "my God, you scared me." She began to cry. "I don't like it when you get like that. I don't like it! Will you take me home now? I want to go home, Finn."

Would this be the time? Had she pushed him too hard? Was he going to do something to her, rape? Choke? Kill the woman he loved but couldn't possess?

They followed the BMW all the way up to Boulder. Rasmussen drove too fast, flashing along the Boulder Turnpike. There was nothing said between him and Ellie on the drive; the tape remained unmoving until he pulled up in front of her house.

"Good night, Finn. I . . . I'm sorry I made you angry. Are you still angry?"

"Yes."

"Give me a kiss, Finn. We'll kiss and make up, okay? I'll be in a better mood next time."

Michael and Kirkman heard the kiss as clearly as if it had taken place in the van itself.

"Good night, Finn."

"Good night, Ellie."

Michael couldn't see her house from where the van was parked, around a corner a block away. He was tempted to ask Parker to drive there so he could go in and see how she was, but just then her voice came over the receiver: "It's okay, guys. He's gone and the house is locked up tight. Thanks. Good night."

So he couldn't see her. It'd look ridiculous to the two cops with him. But at least he knew she was all right. This time.

"Jesus, that guy's a wimp," Parker called back to them from the driver's seat. "Lets her get away with so much shit. I'd dump the chick so fast."

"He can't help it," Michael said. "He's in love." ·

He wondered endlessly what she would do if Rasmussen got up his nerve to sleep with her. He was terribly afraid she'd do it, just to get inside his skin, to gain his trust, to alleviate his suspicions. She'd go that far, yes, she probably would, because she was so determined. She'd do anything to trap the man.

And what would *he* do if that happened? If he was in the van listening, and they made love, and he had to sit there and hear every sound, every moan, the whisper of flesh against flesh, and remember how she felt beneath him?

He became adept at turning those thoughts off.

The next day in the office he sat in on a meeting with Augostino, Chambliss, Commander Koffey, and one of the assistant district attorneys, Gerald Shan. They'd asked him to join them only because he'd started out on the Girard case, a matter of professional courtesy. He hadn't been involved for a while now.

"Okay," Shan said, "what have you got?"

"Yesterday Detective Chambliss and I went to see the

kid who the car was registered to. A CU student named Roger Landis," Augostino said.

"Let me get this straight," Shan said, "you got the car's VIN number from the key you found at the crime scene?"

"Yup." Augostino held the key up. It was in a plastic bag. A ring was attached to it. "Found in the snow near her body."

"Go on."

"We talked to the kid. He'd just bought the car and had to wait awhile to save up the money to register it, which is why we couldn't find him for a bit."

"So, is he good for this?"

Chambliss shook his head. "No way. He was home in Glenwood Springs that weekend, until his first class Monday morning. Went with his sister."

"Well?" Shan asked, raising a brow.

"*Well,*" Augostino replied, "he let a friend borrow his car."

"Ah."

"Friend named Alan Sorelli."

"So, where's this Sorelli guy?"

"He's in Boulder, flunked out, kind of a bum. We've got him under surveillance. What we want to know is, will your office issue a warrant? Think we got enough?"

Shan pondered for a minute.

He'll say no, Michael thought.

"No," Shan said. "Not yet. Bring him in and question him. Routine. I'll watch. Let's see what he does."

"We have no prints. We do have a preliminary report on the semen. He was a secretor, but the type's O positive," Koffey put in.

"Too common to mean much," Shan reflected.

"We'll get the markers in a week or so. Should narrow

it down. Otherwise, there's not much hard evidence," Koffey said.

"Break the kid," Shan said. "Call me when you've got him in here. I'd like this tied up fast."

The men stood, shook hands. "We'll pick him up to-day," Augostino said. "Callas, you want to go with us?"

"No, this is your thing. I've got my hands full. Good work, guys."

"You sure?"

"Yeah."

He went home early that day, and he laid stone on his fireplace, climbing up the ladder with each piece, fitting it carefully on top of the layer below, taking it out, trow-eling in the grout, then tap, tap, tap, fixing the rock in place with great care. He laid a whole layer of stone that afternoon, accompanied by loud music from a jazz radio station. It was therapy for him. Thank God he had it.

Ellie called him at work on Thursday.

"Saturday night," she said. "Dinner at Morton's. Then back to his house. He bought a new painting he wants me to see."

"A painting."

"He's into that modernistic stuff. I think it's ugly, but he collects it."

"Huh."

"He's picking me up at six-thirty. Drinks first. He's got it all planned out."

"We'll be there," Michael said. He paused. "You still okay with this?"

"You don't really think I'd stop now, do you?"

"Guess not."

"He's close, Michael. I can tell. He's irritable, and I know he's not sleeping well. He's going to break."

"Nailing him isn't worth you getting hurt."

"The hell it isn't," she said.

Brave Ellie. And foolish. But more to the point, would Saturday be the night Finn took her to bed? It was coming. Michael knew. And he dreaded it.

Ellie could feel the panic bubbling up inside her during dinner at Morton's. She had to force the food past the lump in her throat. Finn was different tonight. More confident, a smug smile on his face, a big hand on her always. Two bottles of wine. Expensive wine. She sipped, tiny sips, but he kept her glass full.

He was different. It was as if he'd made up his mind about something. She knew what it was, what it had to be.

Michael, she cried silently, *don't leave me alone with him.*

And she knew Michael wouldn't. He'd be listening. He was parked somewhere nearby in the van, and he'd follow them to Finn's house after dinner, and he'd hear everything.

Could she really go through with it? Sleep with Finn? A rapist, a sick, brutal killer?

She'd always believed she could do whatever it took. Sleep with him. Worm her way further into his confidence. Or at the opportune moment, push him away, drive him to the brink of sexual insanity. She'd believed she could control the situation. She'd convinced Michael she'd handle it.

Oh, they'd never talked it all out. But both she and Michael knew the score. So why was she so panicked?

The black purse sat at her feet. Close enough. She knew they could hear.

"I've decided," Finn said, "I've decided something."

He was eating a filet of sole in a sauce of sun-dried to-matoes and mushrooms.

"What have you decided?"

He put his fork down and leaned close, setting aside the candle in the center of the table. "I've decided that you're feeling insecure and that's why you've been so . . . moody with me lately."

"Insecure," she said.

"Yes, you don't know where you stand with me. I haven't let you know what my feelings are."

"Ah," she said, "I see."

"Am I right?"

She thought a minute. Where was this leading? "You could be."

"I knew it." He smiled. "So I'm going to let you know exactly how I feel, and the problem will be solved."

Ellie had been eating shrimp etouffé. She put her fork down, too, and cocked her head. "How *do* you feel about me, Finn?"

He lowered his eyes, almost as if he were embarrassed. "I'm crazy about you."

"You are."

"I think I love you."

"You *think.*"

"Ellie, please, I'm new at this. I've never loved a woman in my life."

Michael is hearing this.

"Oh, Finn," she said.

"That's it, 'Oh, Finn'?"

"I . . . I don't know what to say."

"Say you love me, too."

A heartbeat of hesitation. "I think I do, Finn. I really think I do."

He smiled and put his hand on hers and raised his

wineglass. "To us," he said. "To happiness."

She raised her own glass. The words made her choke.
"To us," she said.

*My God, he's, he's working his way to a climax. To-
night.* She couldn't put it off. What to do? Could she let
Finn do that to her?

The painting was hideous. Very large, on the wall behind
the smoked glass dining room table.

"Look," Finn said proudly.

She looked. Harsh colors, brutal, slashing strokes. A
clown. His false grin in one corner with sharp teeth, his
bulbous red nose in another. His hands clutching at his
ruff, which was painted delicately, in detail and color,
right in the center of the canvas.

"Oh," Ellie said. It was frightening. Sullen, despite its
subject. Swollen forms, a darkness that unfolded when
you stared at it for long. It was a brilliant painting if you
liked nightmares.

"It's a Lassiter."

"A . . . Lassiter."

"Yes. And it cost me a pretty penny."

"I bet. Wow, it's really something, Finn."

"You like it."

"Oh, yes, it's . . . powerful."

He brought out his fine crystal glasses and filled them
with wine. Ellie sat on the leather couch, crossed her legs,
and set her purse on the seat next to her. She sipped her
wine.

"I love it when you're in my house," Finn said. "You
make it come alive." He stood watching her.

"What a nice thing to say."

"I'd like to see you here more."

"But, Finn, you know how busy I am. My job, and law school next year."

"I'll buy you a car. You can commute."

"I wouldn't let you buy me a car."

"Ellie, Ellie, what am I going to do with you?"

He was different tonight. He refused to become irritated with her. She couldn't get to him.

He loosened his tie, then reached a hand out to pull her up.

"Yes?" she said, breathlessly, and he mistook her breathlessness for passion.

"Come here," he said. He enfolded her. He kissed her, ran his hands up and down her arms. She felt his erection press into her stomach.

Michael is listening.

Letting her go, he brushed her hair off her forehead. "My bedroom," he said.

Oh, God.

She just had time to scoop the purse off the couch and carry it along. In his bedroom—ebony furniture, a huge canopied bed with a silver spread, white carpet—he shed his coat and tie and opened his collar button.

"I want you in my bed," he said softly. "With me. I want to see you. Without your clothes, Ellie."

She was trembling; maybe he'd think that too was passion. "Oh, Finn," she mouthed.

He unbuttoned her blouse, slowly, carefully. Unzipped her skirt, her plain black thrift-store skirt. He nuzzled her breast above her bra. She closed her eyes and pretended it was Michael undressing her, Michael whose hands were on her bare skin. Michael.

Her shoes, her panty hose. Goose bumps rose on her. Finn was nude, his body big and hard and pale in the dim light.

Could she do it? She tried desperately to go out of herself, to let her mind break free of her body. It was impossible. His hands . . . She couldn't bear it. *Oh, Michael.*

On his bed, smooth sheets like satin, the comforter rolled back.

"Ellie, Ellie," he said. "I've wanted you so much. You have no idea. I waited. For you, I waited."

He undid her bra, kissed her breasts, one at a time, reverently, pulled down her panties.

Her breath was coming in terrified hiccoughs; she was stiff as a board. He must think that, too, was passion.

His hands stroked her hips and thighs. His mouth moved from one breast to the other. Her flesh recoiled and a scream formed in her throat. She couldn't breathe. She couldn't go through with it. *Yes, you can, you have to.*

Michael!

But it was Finn who parted her thighs with his big hand; Finn whose teeth were on her breast; Finn who moved and poised his long body above hers, holding himself now, seeking her, ready to . . .

She knew in that flash of time that she couldn't do it, that denying him was going to have to work.

"No," she choked out.

"Ellie," he moaned.

"No, Finn." She pushed him away, getting her hands against his chest, shoving hard.

"What?" he cried.

"I said no." Frantically.

"What do you mean, no?"

"I can't sleep with you." She lay under him, panting. He was so heavy.

"What?" He held himself above her on his arms.

"Let me go."

"Oh, Ellie, darling, honey, come on. This is no time . . ."

She pushed again. "Get off me!"

"What's the matter? Are you . . . ?"

"I want to go."

He moved off her. "What in the hell's the matter with you?"

"I want to go home."

"What are you, Ellie, a cock-tease? Do you know what you just did?" he yelled. He grabbed her and shook her. "What's the matter with you?"

"Stop!"

"I will not. You bitch. You're crazy!" He held her arms in his hands.

"Let me go!"

"Let you go? Let you go?"

She tried to scoot backward, away from him, but he held her, and his hands moved quickly, like a snake striking, to her neck. "You're mine. I won't let you go, you crazy bitch." He squeezed, and she flailed about, hooking her nails in his hands, trying to drag them away from her throat.

Michael! her mind screamed.

"What are you doing," she managed to croak, "raping me?"

He cursed, but that was all. No self-incriminating confessions, nothing.

Finn was eleven years old the summer his mother, Becky, fell sick again. His father, Keith, was in jail for sixty days on a drunk and disorderly charge. But this time Becky had a plan—her brother would take Finn and his sister, Ginny, so they wouldn't go to foster homes.

Finn's uncle was a big man, a bachelor, and he welcomed his niece and nephew to his house. Within a week he was coming into Finn's bedroom in the middle of the night, at first only stroking and talking to the pretty blond boy.

Then he forced himself on Finn. The memories were so clear, so explicit, that they rolled in front of Finn's eyes like a movie, over and over and over.

First his uncle's face, then his hands, his mouth opening, saying words. But Finn never heard the words, because a noise filled his head, blotting everything out.

At first he thought his mother would come and save him. But she didn't. Couldn't. She was too weak, used up, a coward, he realized eventually.

Didn't she know?

Finn fought with everything in him, but it was no good. His uncle easily forced him over the side of the bed and . . .

Dread and searing pain and shame, shame that never left, pain and more pain. He tried to scream, someone would hear, Ginny would hear, save him, but his face was pressed into the sheets and his mouth felt as if it was tearing away from his bones, his nose was squashed crookedly. Couldn't breathe. Eyes were forced so hard into the sockets his brain ached. So much pain.

He never told anybody about his uncle, knowing instinctively it was too evil to mention, but whenever he saw a big blond man even vaguely reminiscent of his uncle, the noise started in his head.

And then, years later, Finn discovered girls.

Ellie couldn't get her breath, his hands squeezing, her chest heaving with effort. He kneeled above her, straddled her, her struggles of no account against his strength.

This was how he'd done it to Stephanie Morris. But he'd raped Stephanie first. He wasn't going to rape Ellie, he was going to strangle her to death.

Michael!

Abruptly the hands were gone, and air came rushing back into her lungs. She lay there, faint, gasping, naked. Finn had rolled away. He was cursing, sobbing and cursing, raging.

"I'm all right," Ellie said, "I'm all right." Praying Michael heard, praying she could stop him. Would he smash the door open, burst in, gun in hand, and ruin everything? "I'm fine, I'm okay."

Finn flung the comforter off the bed, and Ellie curled up in a protective ball. A lamp crashed to the floor.

"Goddamn you! Goddamn women! Filthy, lying slut!"

No, Michael, her mind shrilled. *Not yet.* Finn was ready to break. He was over the edge now.

She cringed back against the headboard. "Do you have to choke all your women, Finn?" she cried.

"Get out," he screamed. "Bitch, slut."

Ellie slid off the bed, keeping it between them. She gathered her clothes, the purse, torn between escaping this horror and staying, trying one last time to get at him. She was shaking in terror.

"Get out! I won't drive you home," Finn raged. "Get a cab! I never want to see you again. Cock-tease!"

She dressed quickly in the living room, half her buttons undone, panty hose balled up in her coat pocket. Scared, still trembling but knowing now with a sick finality: *It didn't work. I failed.*

Finn appeared in the doorway, a tall nude figure, his face twisted. "Here, take this, get a cab." He threw bills at her; they fluttered to the floor, then he disappeared, and she heard a door slam, shaking the house.

Then he was there again, a pair of pants on. "I said get out!" He took her arm and propelled her to his front door, opened it, and pushed her out into the night. Pushed her hard, so she stumbled. Then he slammed the door behind her.

Ellie stood in the cold dark and cried. She cried from fear and relief and disappointment.

She'd failed. It was over.

TWENTY-TWO

The Zimmerman trial was over. It had gone to the jury yesterday, and everyone in the district attorney's office was on pins and needles. Nobody could concentrate; the staff stood around in knots, debating, guessing, second-guessing, dissecting every word of Torres's closing statement and every word of Richard Gardner's closing statement for Steve Zimmerman.

The consensus was that the prosecution had done its job for the people of Colorado, but one could never count on a jury. Never.

Ellie sat at her desk, trying to get some work accomplished. She'd been given the police reports on the interview with Alan Sorelli, the prime suspect in the Girard case, and all the transcriptions of their taped sessions. The kid had folded and confessed, but Torres wanted no out for him, and Ellie was to go through every word again, taking notes on possible glitches. She was also charged with writing up a pretrial motion for DNA testing of Sorelli, so he could be tied to the semen the coroner had recovered from Valerie Girard.

Routine work. Stuff she would have done diligently in the past, proud of her meticulousness and insight. But she couldn't concentrate, although it wasn't the Zimmerman verdict that had her attention wandering. It was Finn and her failure. The end of her life's work.

She read two pages of the thick Girard file, but she didn't comprehend a word. It was useless.

And Michael—she hadn't heard from him in over a week, not since that night. The guys in the van had driven her home; Michael had called off the operation and that was that. Not a word or a phone call.

She felt like crying all the time. She'd lost her appetite, couldn't sleep, couldn't think. Her roommates kept at her, asking what was wrong, but she was unable to tell them. Secrets again. Ugly secrets.

The worst was the paranoia. She tried to convince herself she was merely exhausted, suffering from sleeplessness and depression. But she kept thinking she saw Finn's Grand Cherokee at a distance. She was imagining it, of course. Imagining that he was stalking her the way he'd stalked his other victims, that he was following her, watching, planning.

She was desperate to tell Michael. She longed for his company, his protection. His forgiveness. But she couldn't phone him with paranoid delusions. He had to make contact. And she knew he wouldn't.

She put the file aside and started to compose the motion for DNA testing of Alan Sorelli, twenty-six years old, address . . . She clicked "save" on the computer and sat there, head in her hand, just sat there.

"What's up?" a voice said behind her.

Startled, she straightened and twisted on her chair. Ben Torres.

"Nothing much," she said.

"You looked like the world was on your shoulders."

"Oh."

"Hey, Ellie, I don't want to pry, but you've been . . . well, preoccupied lately. Is something wrong?"

She was going to force a smile and say, "No, I'm fine, just a little headache," but she couldn't get the words out.

"Ellie?"

Tears filled her eyes, and she gazed up at him. "I . . . I'm sorry . . . I . . ."

He leaned down and lowered his voice. "I was thinking maybe it was me, you know, because of . . . that day I asked you to go out. And I wanted you to know that I'm still sorry about it. It was stupid."

"Oh, Mr. Torres, really . . ."

He held up a hand. "I've reassessed a lot of things, Ellie. My wife and I, well, I'm not sure it'll work out between us, I don't know, but we've been talking lately."

"That's good."

"Yes, it's good. Clear the air, you know. So you don't have to worry about me."

"It's not . . . it wasn't you. I . . ."

"What is it then?"

"Oh, God, I . . ."

His expression went from mild concern to lawyerly blankness. "In my office," he said.

She followed him. He shut the door and gestured for her to sit, and all the while Ellie knew this was it, this was the end, her day of reckoning. She didn't have the energy to lie anymore.

The DA sat, his fine-featured, patrician face impassive except for a furrow on his brow. He steepled his hands on his desk. "Okay, let's hear it."

The words spilled out of her, the first time she'd willingly confessed to anyone but her roommates, and even with them she'd kept secrets.

"I'm not who you think I am. My name isn't Kramer. It's Crandall, Eleanor Crandall. My father was John Crandall."

"John Crandall . . . ?"

"The convicted rapist. Thirteen years ago. You weren't the DA yet, but you must remember. . . ."

"John Crandall? The— Christ, the Morris case?"

She nodded. Her head bowed.

"Your *father?*"

She looked straight at him. "He was innocent. I knew it, and I had to prove it. All my life since then, I've been trying to find out who really raped Stephanie Morris, and I went to law school so I'd know how to proceed, and I applied for this clerking job so I could study the files. The files right here in Records. The trial, the police reports, everything."

"You've been taking files out of Records?"

"Yes."

"Ellie, that's—"

"I know."

Emotion finally played across Torres's face. "I don't believe this, I can't believe you'd do it. You know the rules."

"But I had to, for my father. And it worked. I started with the two cops who were on the case, the ones who 'solved' it. The ones who came to our house and arrested my father and testified against him."

"Jesus, Ellie."

"I lied and I stole and I used you. But I found out who set up my father. I know who it is, but I can't prove it."

"Whoa, slow down."

She told him about Michael and Finn. She told him

everything: Michael's notebooks, the surveillance, the van, the other women Finn had raped and murdered, her failure to get anything incriminating from him.

"Callas? Detective Callas? And you've been going out with this man, this Rasmussen? Under surveillance? I had no idea. Not even a hint. And a judge okayed it? Good God."

"Rasmussen is guilty, and there was no other way. There's evidence, it's all circumstantial, and we needed hard proof. God, we tried, I did everything I could to get something on him, but it didn't work. Nothing worked, and now it's over, and I . . ."

"Finn Rasmussen. Sure, I remember the name from when he was with the department. He was a good cop, was the impression I got."

"A good cop."

"Who knew?" Torres raised his shoulders. "A murderer? Jesus."

"Four, no five, that we know of. And he'll do it again, and I can't stop him."

"If this is all true . . ."

"It's true. Oh, God, it's true."

"I'll talk to Sam Koffey, we'll start an investigation, we'll work on it, Ellie. There's got to be something. . . ."

She shook her head. "There's nothing more I can do. I'm done. I've lied and cheated, and I don't deserve to work here, and I don't deserve a law degree. I'm done. I'm quitting. I can't do this anymore."

"Don't make any big decisions right now. You're upset."

"Yes, I'm upset."

"I have to admit, I want some time to consider what you did here in the office."

"I know."

"Let's take a few days. I'll think about it."

"*You* think about it. I can't. I can't."

"Ellie . . ."

"Everything's a lie. My life is a lie. I wanted to find the truth, but I lived a lie. I thought I could help other people, but I can't even help myself."

"Give yourself some time. You're a smart lady. You'd make a great lawyer."

She shook her head again.

"Look, let's talk later. I've got to be ready for the Zimmerman verdict."

"There's nothing more to talk about."

"There's always something more for a lawyer to talk about."

"I'm not a lawyer," she said dully.

The Zimmerman verdict came in at four o'clock that afternoon. Torres got the call; the office seethed with curiosity, apprehension, anticipation. Torres came out and spoke a few words to his staff. "Whatever the outcome, we did our job, folks. I'm proud of you."

He buttoned his suit coat carefully and walked down the corridor to the courtroom. Everyone followed, clustering outside the closed double doors, but only Torres and the two ADAs on the case could enter. The press crowded the hallway, too; outside in the parking lot were news vans and cameramen and TV anchormen.

Ellie stayed in the office. She couldn't face people today. She'd barely spoken to a soul. She had packed all her belongings into a box, and she was ready to leave the Justice Center for the last time.

Only an infinitesimal professional curiosity remained inside her; she'd stay to hear the verdict. Then she'd go home and figure out what she was going to do with the rest of her life.

She heard the cheer echoing from down the hall, and she knew what it meant—a guilty verdict. Zimmerman was finally going to pay the price for his crime. But Ellie couldn't summon up the proper amount of satisfaction; it all seemed futile and insignificant.

The staff poured back into the office, everyone grinning, talking, yelling, embracing. Torres walked in. Smiling, happy, a success.

He'll keep his job, Ellie thought. *He'll get reelected for sure now.* But it didn't matter to her, not really.

She took a last look around the office. She wouldn't say good-bye; she'd just slip out.

But Torres had other ideas. He came to her desk and stood over her. "You helped, Ellie, you helped a lot. You got Zimmerman convicted as much as anybody did."

"Um," she said, keeping her eyes lowered.

"Don't rush into anything. Take a few days off. Then we'll talk about Rasmussen. Okay, Ellie?"

"You talk about it. I'm finished."

"Hey, Ellie, wait . . ."

But she picked up her box and her coat and new briefcase and walked out of the office.

Finn was stalking a girl.

He was driving around Limon. He'd taken the afternoon off work and, without thinking, he'd found himself heading out I-70 to the small town on the prairie.

The pictures had come into his head on the drive; he had no control over them. He'd been seeing them a lot lately, wildly gyrating faces, mouths open but soundless. Bright colors, frozen tears.

He pulled himself back from them in time to make the Limon exit. A close call.

One of the faces in his head was the girl in Limon,

the high school kid. It twirled behind his eyes. He needed her, needed her under him, needed to control her so that his mind would rest.

She was there, hanging around with her friends after school. But she didn't match the picture he had in his head. Her hair was stringy and her clothes hung on her, and she wasn't very attractive after all. As he watched her, it seemed to Finn as if her face melted and rearranged itself, and there was Ellie's face superimposed on the high school girl.

Ellie, Ellie.

She got in the way of everything. He couldn't stop thinking about her. He hated her, he loved her, he could never forgive her for what she'd done to him. But he couldn't live without her.

A plan had been forming in his brain. Slowly. Amorphous, yet taking shape in small increments. If he couldn't have her, if he couldn't satisfy his needs with her, he had to rid himself of his obsession. His life would not return to normal until she was erased from his thoughts, his soul, his memory.

He'd never suffered like this, not when his father was drunk, not when his mother gave her kids away, not when his uncle . . . But he wasn't a child any longer. He had control over his life now. He could accomplish what was needed.

He parked his car and watched the girl for a while longer before deciding she wouldn't do. Nobody would do but Ellie.

He thought about his next step for a long time, calculating, going over every possible detail. It had to be right. Everything needed to go according to plan. It all hinged on whether she'd say yes. She always had before. She would this time, too. Sure she would. She was crazy about him. She'd *told* him she loved him, hadn't she?

He phoned her that night. He had the perfect opening gambit: the Zimmerman verdict. A roommate answered, yelling for Ellie. Then she was picking up the phone, and her face flew into his mind as if she were in front of him.

"Hello?"

"Ellie, it's Finn."

Silence.

"Please, listen. I'm sorry about that . . . that night." Kind, charming, apologetic.

"You hurt me."

"I know, I know. But it's because you drove me crazy. You know that, don't you?"

Silence.

"Oh, God, I wish . . . Listen, that's not why I called. I wanted to congratulate you on the Zimmerman verdict. I know how hard you worked on that trial."

"Thanks."

"You should be proud. Justice was served, and you helped."

"I hope so."

"Of course you helped. You have a brilliant legal mind."

"Oh, please, Finn."

"Ellie, I miss you. I tried not to call, but I had to. Can I see you again?"

"I don't know. You scared me."

He gave a short laugh. "I scared myself." He paused for a moment. "I'm going to Aspen this weekend. Have you ever been there?"

"Once. A long time ago."

"I'm staying at the Hotel Jerome, a great place, renovated so beautifully. We could have a nice weekend. Skiing, the best restaurants, whatever you want."

"I don't know."

"Please say yes." Then he remembered to add, "Two rooms. I swear I won't touch you if you don't want me to."

"Aspen," she said thoughtfully.

"It's a beautiful place. The town, the skiing. They really know how to do things right."

"I'd like to, but . . ."

"Please. You're breaking my heart."

"Okay," she said after a moment.

His spirits soared. "Good. Wonderful. It'll be a great weekend. Better than Santa Fe. A perfect weekend."

"I hope so."

"It will be. You'll see. I'll pick you up. Can you get off work early? Say one o'clock?"

"Ah, oh, I guess so, sure."

"See you then."

"See you then, Finn."

He hung up, suffused with a ferocious joy. Every cell of his body craved the fulfillment only she could provide. And then the pictures came back, the kaleidoscope of faces. The eyes, the tears, the colors and hair and skin and chins. The open screaming mouths.

But this time all the faces were the same, and they were all Ellie.

Michael was on the phone with Valerie Girard's father. Since the Rasmussen surveillance had ended, he was back on the case, although it was nearly tied up now.

"Yes, Mr. Girard," he was saying, "the boy confessed. It's in the bag."

"I want the filthy murderer to get the death penalty for what he did to my daughter. Will you ask for the death penalty?"

"It's not up to *me* to ask for anything. The Boulder County DA will decide that. But, I have to tell you, Mr. Girard, the DA probably won't go for the death penalty, because it wasn't murder one."

"He deserves to die."

"He deserves to be punished, absolutely."

"I want him to suffer," Mr. Girard ground out.

"I understand. But he may even plea-bargain, and then his lawyer will be negotiating with our DA."

"I feel like, I feel like it's all slipping away, and Valerie, my little girl, will get nothing, no revenge, and that kid, that disgusting *kid,* will get away with murder."

"That won't happen, Mr. Girard, I promise. Alan Sorelli will be prosecuted to the full extent of the law."

"I hope you're right. I hope to hell you're right."

Michael hung up. The poor guy. His daughter was killed senselessly. He wondered if the Girards had other children and if they did, how those kids were doing. He hoped the Girards treated their other children better than his parents had treated him.

Paul. It always came down to Paul.

He sat back and stretched his legs out, hands behind his head. Rick caught his eye, frowned, and Michael shrugged just as Commander Sam Koffey appeared in the doorway, back from a week's ski vacation with his family.

Shit, Michael thought.

Koffey made his way straight to Michael's desk. "In my office, Callas, now."

An already lousy day was about to get worse.

Office door open, Michael's boss read him the riot act. You could have heard a pin drop in the department.

"Goddamn, Callas, I'm on vacation in Breckenridge and the CBI calls me at the hotel to bitch about tying up their equipment for weeks and we come up with squat."

Michael's face remained impassive.

"And to top *that* off, I gotta explain to the judge what went wrong. He didn't want to issue the surveillance warrant in the first place. Do you know how embarrassing this is? I look like a fool."

"Um," Michael said. How did Koffey think *he* felt?

"After all this, what did you come up with? Reels of useless tape is what."

"That's about it," Michael conceded.

"Well, I want your notebooks. Everything you've compiled."

"It's all circumstantial, sir."

"I don't give a damn. I want it all on file. *Everything.*"

"Yes, sir."

"And I want it yesterday, is that understood?"

"Yes, sir."

"You're telling me there's a murderer on the loose, and we can't do a damn thing about it. And you put a civilian in danger. If this gets out, Callas, we're all dead ducks."

"Yes, sir."

"Go on, get out of here. I need to think about this."

Michael left the commander's office. Every detective in the department raised his head to stare, their eyes like the feet of a thousand small animals walking on him.

He got a call from his informant Pete Stone later that afternoon.

"Rasmussen's on the prowl," Stone said. "He's been driving around a lot. Out to Limon a couple of times. Not on business, either."

"Limon."

"Strange, huh? I think the man's losing it. The word

at Mountaintech is that he's not around much, and he's weird when he is there."

"Interesting."

"The foxy chick, the one you said you knew who she was, hasn't been out with him in a while."

"Okay, Pete, thanks. Listen, my other line's lit up. Gotta go."

"Want me to stay on him?"

"Sure."

He and Chambliss took a couple of calls that afternoon, one at a liquor store and a domestic disturbing the peace. Routine. Chambliss, thank God, said nothing about Michael getting chewed out in front of the whole department. Not that Michael could have felt any worse.

On the ride to the liquor store, Chambliss did have one thing to say, though. "I don't know if you've heard . . ." He hesitated.

"Heard what?" Michael stared out the passenger window.

"Your friend Ellie, she quit the DA's office."

"Huh."

"Didn't know if you'd heard."

Michael hiked his shoulders.

"So, Zimmerman came in guilty," Chambliss said, changing the subject. "Wonder what they'll give him?"

"Beats me," Michael said. He couldn't muster the energy to think about it.

They were turning the unmarked car back into the motor pool, when Chambliss said, "Listen, I know it's none of my business, but Augostino and I were talking, and . . ."

"And what?"

"Well, we're friends, right? And, well, we think you ought to give Ellie a call, you know?"

Michael swung open the car door. "You're right, Chambliss," he said, "it's none of your business."

He spent an hour transcribing his notes on the liquor store robbery then just sat staring at the screen saver on the computer and felt his stomach twist. What a mess he'd made of everything. He'd like to blame Ellie—she'd convinced him they could get Rasmussen. But he couldn't lay it on her. Hell, he couldn't even stand to think about her, much less analyze what had gone wrong.

He'd finally managed to forget her and put Rasmussen aside for a full minute, when someone called, "Line three, Callas," and he picked up the phone, punched the blinking button, and there she was.

"Michael, it's Ellie."

Her voice struck him like a soft blow. He straightened.

"Michael, are you there?"

"Yeah. I'm here."

"I have to talk to you."

He said nothing.

"Can you come over to my house?"

"I heard you quit your job."

"I don't want to get into that," she said. "Just tell me if you can come over."

"Now?"

"Yes. It's important."

"Rasmussen?"

"Just come, Michael, please."

"Give me a few minutes." And he heard the click as she broke the connection.

He drove to her house, his brain buzzing. What did she want? Not for a minute did he think it was to see him again. *Shit.* This was going to hurt like hell.

He parked in front of the shabby yellow house, walked

up the familiar walk. It took more courage than appre-
hending an armed suspect.

She'd opened the front door and was waiting for him.
"Michael."

She looked drawn, dressed in old jeans and a heavy
black sweater, white wool socks on her feet, no shoes.
Her hair mussed carelessly. No makeup. His heart
squeezed.

"Come in," she said.

"Anyone home?"

"No, they're all at class."

They were standing in the middle of the living room
facing each other. The moment stretched out like a string
drawn too tightly, vibrating, ready to snap.

"Let's sit down," she finally said.

"Just tell me what you want." He remained standing.

"God, Michael, sit down and give me a minute, will
you?"

He sat on one of the tattered armchairs, and she
perched on the edge of the couch, her hands clasped in
her lap.

"Okay," he said, "let's hear it." She looked exhausted,
strung out. He noticed a couple of bags sitting at the base
of the stairs. Was she leaving Boulder? *Jesus.*

"Finn called me last night."

Michael's eyes cut to her face.

"He asked me to go to Aspen with him this weekend."

"You're . . ."

"I'm going, Michael. I told him I'd go."

"*This* is what you called to tell me?"

"I thought you should know. It's one last chance, one
more shot at him. Maybe this time . . ."

"Are you out of your fucking mind?" He stood
abruptly.

"I'm going, Michael."

"Is that what those bags are for? A trip to Aspen?"

"No. Actually, my mother was going to take me home to Leadville. But now . . . I *am* going with Finn."

He stared at her in disbelief for so long that her knuckles turned white.

"Say something," she finally whispered.

"Say something?" His voice was barely audible. "How about over my dead body."

TWENTY-THREE

Ellie hadn't been to Aspen since she was seventeen, on a school trip, and then it had been in late April, what was known by the locals as mud season. She remembered the mountain playground with new buds on the bare-branched aspens and cottonwoods, melting piles of dirty snow against north-facing structures, and a patchwork of mud and snow on the slopes of Ajax, the ski mountain that hovered over the town like a tidal wave ready to break.

But now it was the dead of winter, everything covered in clean white snow, Christmas lights twinkling merrily in the street mall, in windows, and on trees, and coiling up the quaint Victorian lampposts.

It was a fairyland, a rich man's mecca. Whereas Boulder was home to upper-class working men and women, students and intellectuals, Aspen appeared to be the home of the jet set. Finn had even pointed out the dozens of corporate jets lining the airport directly outside of town.

"And that's only half of them," he'd told Ellie. "The rest of them landed here, dropped their passengers, then had to fly into Grand Junction just to park."

"It's so beyond my comprehension," she'd said, "all this money."

"I hate to tell you," he had said, "but it won't be long before I go in on a jet with a couple of other men from Denver. I'm working on it."

"Like a co-op? For jet-setters?"

"Exactly. A new kind of time-share. I'll have my license to pilot a small Lear in less than a year now."

No, you won't, Ellie had mused. If it killed her, she was going to see him behind bars before that year was out.

He got them checked into the Hotel Jerome, two adjoining rooms, as promised. He had reverted to being the complete gentleman. He was either afraid of losing control again, or he was terrified of having sex with her. She'd never be able to comprehend how he fancied himself in love and yet was incapable of performing normally in a sexual relationship. What doors in his mind did he keep closed to function as he did?

But none of that mattered. She was here for one reason. This was her last chance, and she couldn't afford to squander it with thoughts about Finn's dysfunction. The last-ditch effort. And she was going to stick to the plan no matter what. But God, how alone she felt right now—all on her own. No backup. No nothing. Michael might as well have been a million miles away.

Their rooms were exquisitely appointed Victorian boudoirs. Ornate and elegant. Lace curtains, gold, green, and burgundy flowered carpeting, antique oak dressers and chairs, brass beds covered in ivory duvets and big lace-edged pillows, real claw-foot tubs in the white-tiled bathrooms that were scented with English soap. Ellie stood in her room, thinking she was in heaven. Except for the devil himself just on the other side of the wall.

He hadn't been the devil on the drive to Aspen. He' d spent the entire four hours apologizing for that horrible, horrible night at his house.

Ellie had sat in the car and listened to him, nodding demurely, accepting his apology. But she'd known he was trying to justify his actions to himself.

"I can't imagine behaving so badly," he'd said. "That's not like me. Even though, Ellie, I still don't know what happened or why you . . . changed your mind. Obviously it got to me. If only I had understood at the time."

She still hadn't offered an explanation. What could she say? That she hadn't realized until the very last that she could never, ever sleep with him? And with Michael listening? *My God.*

He rapped on the adjoining door to their rooms at five. "I thought we'd take a walk before dinner," he said, and as always it struck her that he never asked. He instructed. He commanded.

"That would be nice. I'll get my coat."

The dress in Aspen ran the whole gamut. There were women in long furs and soft leather and big Stetsons and cowboy boots. There were brightly colored down parkas and mittens and jeans and tall boots. There were sequined jackets and sequined cowboy hats and glittering high heels. No problem on the heated sidewalks. Ellie herself was a parka-and-jeans tourist in black boots. Finn wore brown leather and was also in jeans. She couldn't help eyeing him as they crossed the postcard-perfect Victorian lobby. He looked good in leather, but not half as good as Michael. Then she shut the notion down cold. This was her mission, the end of her long quest. It was going to be all or nothing and to hell with her career, Michael, to hell with everything but the task at hand.

God, she was scared.

Still, it was smile smile as they darted through Main Street traffic and walked into the heart of the old silver-mining town, Finn protectively tucking her arm into his.

He took great delight in window-shopping, especially at the myriad art galleries. One new artist in particular struck his fancy, and after chatting up the gallery owner he whipped out a platinum credit card, bought the modernistic oil titled *Dying Flowers in Vase,* and arranged to have it shipped to Denver.

Ellie smiled smiled. "Oh, yes, it's great, Finn."

In reality, the cut-up rendition of wilting flowers gave her the creeps. If she had her way, if her plan worked, Finn was never going to see the painting hung. Too bad for Finn; too bad for the artist.

She was sweetness and light, clinging to his arm, smiling smiling, bolstering his schizophrenic ego as they continued on, occasionally ducking into a shop out of the cold, but mostly strolling the brick-paved malls of downtown.

In front of Amen Wardy, where you could buy a ready-to-display Christmas tree for your second home for a mere eight thousand dollars, Finn rubbed her hands in his. "You forgot your gloves again."

"I am hopeless, aren't I?" she said sweetly.

"I assume you remembered ski gloves for tomorrow?"

"Of course." But tomorrow might as well be a thousand years off. She couldn't help thinking about her ski weekend with Michael, that night in his cozy chalet, the gentleness of his touch, his breath in her hair, his weight pressing down into the soft mattress. Had he and his brother, Paul, roughhoused on that old bed?

And she'd cried on that bed.

"You're awfully quiet," Finn said.

She smiled.

Aspen was packed with tourists despite it being low season, that lull from New Year's to mid-February.

Finn explained the crowds. "It's a local festival week they call Winterskol. Lots of ski events and a parade and fireworks on the mountain tomorrow night. I come up every year. Usually alone. But I wanted you to see it."

"Can't wait," Ellie said.

They ate dinner at the base of Aspen Mountain—Ajax to the locals—at the Ajax Tavern, an intimate, very *in* restaurant that offered a large menu, small portions, and substantial prices.

Finn ordered for them both and selected a reserve bottle of an Italian chianti, which was much too hearty for her.

"Excellent, don't you think?" he asked, clinking his glass to hers over the candle, sipping.

"It's delicious," she lied.

"Not too robust?"

"Oh, no really. It's perfect."

They had all four courses, à la carte. Creamy cucumber soup, salad of baby field greens in a raspberry vinaigrette, sliced tenderloin of free-range beef with a dollop of creamed horseradish sauce, shallot potatoes garnished with flowering chives, baby brown-sugared carrots, and then, when Ellie was sure she was going to burst, sapphire pudding topped with fresh blackberries.

She sat back, smiled at Finn, and thought what a hell of a last supper this was.

After dinner she continued to stroke Finn's ego, biding her time. She wanted him relaxed, comfortable with the power he believed he was exerting over her. Finn in absolute control of his realm. She was so pliable, so sickly sweet, she wondered if he noticed, if a tiny part of him didn't see straight through to the core of her repugnance.

After-dinner drinks at Bentley's were Finn's idea. She liked that. A crowded bar. Finn hated above all else to be defied in public. *Perfect,* she thought, her nerves beginning to prick at her skin as they entered the bar in the historical Wheeler Opera House.

Again he ordered for them, two snifters of Grand Marnier. The cocktail waitress said, "Two agent oranges it is."

Ellie was careful to sip hers slowly. Finn drank his in two swallows and then grew impatient with her dallying.

He glanced at his watch. "I'd like to get an early start on the slopes tomorrow," he said.

"Oh, I'll be ready soon." But she only took a wee little sip.

"It's best to drink those things in a swallow."

Ellie screwed up her nose.

"At the rate you're going, we'll be here all night."

"And this is just my first one," she said.

"Excuse me?"

"Well, we aren't really going back to the hotel yet, are we? I want another one of these. They're delicious."

"And you're a little drunk."

The cocktail waitress could not have timed her appearance more perfectly. "Two more?"

"Oh, yes, please." Ellie beamed.

Finn put up a hand. "Just the check, miss."

Ellie frowned and looked at the waitress. "Well, *I'm* having another."

"No," Finn said, "you aren't. The check, please."

Ellie shook her head. She was aware of the sudden hush from the surrounding tables. "Miss," she said, "I *will* have another. You can give me a separate check. I have my own money if he won't pay."

Finn was speechless for a terrible moment. When he found his voice it was low and quivering. "We are leaving, Ellie, right now. I've never been so embarrassed in my life."

She struck with the swiftness of a snake. Loudly, she said, "It's a good thing we're in public, isn't it? You wouldn't dare hit me here."

He was stunned. Everything he held of importance, his desires, his entire belief system had just tumbled around his ears. "Goddamn you," he snarled.

Ellie came to her feet. "I'm going to the ladies' room. If you're here when I get back, fine. If not, I'll see you at the hotel when I get there."

He just glared at her, his jaw trembling, his neck a furious red. By now, everyone in the bar was watching them.

Ellie pushed her chair aside, shrugged at him, and began to shoulder her way through the throng.

Her only focus, the single image that kept her putting one foot in front of the other, was the look of pure malevolence in Finn's cold blue eyes. This time she had him.

It began snowing in the Rocky Mountain states on Saturday and continued through Sunday. In the heart of the mountains, near the Continental Divide, some of the ski areas reported up to thirty-three inches of fresh powder. CNN covered the storm nationwide, and reservations skyrocketed. Nothing like free advertising.

The Front Range was another story. Pueblo and Colorado Springs were spared the bulk of the storm. Denver got twenty-four inches and Boulder just over a foot. Nevertheless, the roads were a mess right through rush hour on Monday morning, when the snowplows finally got on top of the storm.

It was a slow drive into Denver on the Boulder Turnpike.

"Man, this traffic is bad," Augostino said, from the passenger side of the motor pool SUV.

Michael only nodded, then pulled out into the passing lane, going around a semi, the windows of the SUV getting coated with gray slush from the snow-melting goop they put on the roads now.

"Goddamn," Rick breathed.

Michael was oblivious. He was thinking of only one thing, getting to Rasmussen's house.

Augostino and the uniformed patrolman who sat in the back wisely shut up. No one talked to Callas when he got this quiet. Rick let his gaze shift to the morning edition of the *Denver Post,* which lay open on the console between the seats.

The headline screamed up at him.

University of Colorado Law Student
Murdered in Aspen

Rick didn't have to read the text to remember it. He'd already seen it twice. Practically knew it by heart.

Slain student Eleanor Kramer was found late Sunday in a room at the historic Hotel Jerome. Death appears to have been by strangulation, and there is suspicion of sexual assault. The Boulder Police, in conjunction with the Boulder County District Attorney and the Aspen Police, are confident of an imminent arrest, which may also tie in to several other attacks on women on the Front Range.

Rick whistled between his teeth. *Jesus H. Christ,* he thought. *Little Ellie.*

They arrived at Rasmussen's shortly before nine A.M. "You want me to handle this?" Rick said, starting to open his door.

Michael shook his head. "I need to do it," he said in a tight voice. He swiveled around to address the uniform. "You back me up."

"Sure, Detective."

They had to ring the buzzer on the gate. If Rasmussen wasn't home, they'd look for him at his office. Michael didn't give a shit where they located Finn, so long as he was the one to haul the son of a bitch in.

But it was still early and Rasmussen was home. The gate unlocked electronically, and Michael saw the front door open. Lying in the unplowed drive when they went through the gate was a rolled-up *Denver Post.* Michael made eye contact with Rasmussen then stooped, picked up the orange-plastic-wrapped paper, banged it against his leg to shake off the fresh snow, and strode toward his nemesis.

"What the hell?" Rasmussen said when Michael stood eye to eye with him. "Callas? I can't believe it. What's it been, ten, twelve years?"

But Michael wasn't in a chatty mood. He shoved the paper at Rasmussen's gut as if passing the man a football, and said, "You can read it on the way to headquarters."

"Headquarters?"

"You're wanted for questioning in connection with the murder of Eleanor Kramer."

"*Murder?* What the . . . ?"

"Let's go, Rasmussen," Michael said. He nodded to the uniform. "Take this man to the car."

"Wait a minute. This is goddamn ridiculous! *Murder?*"

"Shut up," Michael said, and his tone brooked no argument.

Rasmussen fell silent and the patrolman took his arm and led him away through the deep snow. Michael let out a ragged breath, locked his jaw, and followed.

Ben Torres paced in front of the interrogation room, one hand on his hip under his sport coat, the other rubbing the back of his neck.

Finally he pivoted to Michael and Commander Koffey. "Look, I want this done by the book. Rasmussen's no dummy. He's lawyered up. We wait till his attorney gets here. This is for Ellie, goddamn it. We do it right."

"Fuck it," Michael said in that soft voice, and then he saw Janice Kramer sitting in a corner by the window, Rick Augostino handing her a coffee. She was the color of ash. They owed her. They had to do it right. They owed *Ellie,* for chrissakes.

"Okay," he said, his eyes moving to Ben Torres. "We wait. But not for long."

"Take it easy," Koffey said, his brow furrowed.

Rasmussen's lawyer arrived shortly after noon. He popped out of the stairwell, his gray cashmere overcoat askew on his shoulders, briefcase in hand. He was big and out of breath.

He introduced himself, shaking hands with Torres and Koffey. Michael kept his own hands in his pockets. "Ralph Sempler," the attorney said, still a little breathless, red in the face. "What's this all about, anyway? Koffey, what are you charging my client—"

But Michael cut him off. "You can stay out here and

talk all you like. I'm going to start the interview. I'm sick of waiting."

Sempler looked perplexed.

Michael opened the door to the interrogation room— the same room where he and Ellie had talked the first time. He felt as if there was a steel vise on his heart, tightening. *Ellie,* he thought, *this is for you.*

On the outside, Michael appeared calm and under control as he checked the tape recorder that sat in the center of the table and pulled out a chair. On the inside, he was seething, the vise unrelenting around his heart, his stomach a pit of writhing vipers.

"Mind if I tape our session?" he asked, sitting, his gaze lifting to Rasmussen.

"Where the hell is my lawyer," Rasmussen began, but then Sempler walked in.

The only thing Michael had to say was, "You keep a lid on it, Sempler, or you're out of here."

"Now listen," Sempler began, but something in those gold eyes silenced him. He cleared his throat, looked away, and muttered, "We'll just see how this goes."

Michael turned to Rasmussen. And it began. "We can do this the easy way," Michael said, "or the hard way. Either way, we're not leaving this room until we have your signed confession for the murder of Eleanor Kramer. I believe you knew her as Ellie."

"Yes, of course I know Ellie," he started in, leaning forward, his expression sincere and open, concerned.

Michael punched the record button and so it went for the next hour. Michael asking questions, Rasmussen answering candidly for the most part. Then Michael would back up a step and make the ex-cop repeat himself. Over and over. And they'd only scratched the surface. To get his confession, to break him, was going to take great patience and a lot of exhausting hours. Rasmussen was no one's fool. Then again, Michael knew where and when to place his punches. Sempler, though thorough and attentive, was not able to say much. For the most part, the lawyer seemed stumped as he madly scribbled on his yellow pad.

Michael felt a grim but fierce satisfaction in his work. Paring away the bullshit to get to the truth. It had to be done with a sure hand and firm knowledge of the goal—breaking the bastard. There were moments, though, when he wanted to just pull his service revolver and put one between Rasmussen's blue eyes. Then he thought of Janice out there waiting. All the years of suffering.

Time went by. Rasmussen was restless, the hard plastic chair uncomfortable. He squirmed, he stood, he sat. He rolled his shoulders to rid them of tension. So did Sempler. Michael was as still as a statue.

"I've got to get to the office," Rasmussen said. "I have a contract to negotiate. Goddamnit, this is crap. Sempler, do something."

The attorney shrugged. "Just let them ask their questions, Finn. Get it over with. And then we'll sue the lot of them."

"Mind if I take a piss?" Rasmussen asked.

"Not at all," Michael said.

While Rasmussen was gone, Sempler leaned forward. "Look, have you got anything on my client? Anything solid? Or is this just a fishing expedition?"

Michael smiled.

"Christ, you cops. Goddamn Nazis," Sempler muttered.

Finn returned and sat down in the uncomfortable chair. He'd loosened his tie; his suit jacket hung from the back of the chair. His shirtsleeves were rolled up. A handmade shirt in pale blue with a monogram on the pocket. Perfectly starched. Michael guessed it must have cost two hundred bucks.

"Okay," Michael said, "let's go over this again. You admit to dating Ellie."

"I've said that ten times."

Michael put up a hand. "Okay. Let's go to last Friday."

"Yeah, let's," Rasmussen said, obviously tiring of the whole thing.

"You picked the deceased up at her house on Marine Street at one P.M. Does that sound right?"

"Yes, yes, I told you that. One sharp. I even saw one of her roommates. Okay. I'm not goddamn denying I took Ellie to Aspen."

"Careful," Sempler put in.

Rasmussen shot him a look. "I don't have anything to hide, for chrissakes. I drove her to Aspen. We got rooms. *Two* rooms."

Michael cut in. "Why two rooms, Rasmussen?"

"Hey, I don't care what fucking century this is, I respect women. My God, I was going to . . ."

"Going to what?"

Rasmussen squirmed, recrossed a leg. "I was thinking about buying her a ring."

"An engagement ring?"

"Yes."

"Okay. So you checked into your hotel—two rooms— and then?"

Rasmussen recounted the evening. Dinner then Bentley's and the two Grand Marniers. "And I'm telling you, Ellie said she was going to the bathroom and she never came back. Ask the cocktail waitress, for chrissakes, I had everyone in that place looking for her."

Michael folded his arms, rocked back in the chair.

"The Aspen cops *have* talked to the waitress, Rasmussen, and it seems you and Ellie had a pretty good row. Lots of witnesses, in fact."

"It wasn't a fight." Rasmussen drew his sandy brows together. "Ellie wanted to stay. I wanted to get some sleep so we could get an early start on the slopes."

"Uh-huh. So then why didn't you contact the police when she didn't show up?"

Rasmussen snorted. "You don't know her. She's stubborn. I finally went back to the hotel, thinking she'd be there. But she wasn't."

"And that didn't concern you?"

"I don't know. Maybe a little. But Aspen's a party town, and I guess I figured she'd found another bar."

"Go on."

"Well, then two o'clock rolled around, and she still wasn't in her room."

"And you didn't call the cops then?"

"You know I didn't, Callas."

"Then tell me what you did do."

"I went to bed."

"I see. And you weren't worried. All her clothes were in her room, but you still didn't worry?"

"To be honest," Rasmussen said, his blue eyes sliding up and to the right, "I thought she'd either been so pissed that she found someone driving back to Denver and figured I'd bring her stuff with me, or she picked someone up in a bar and . . . Shit, I don't know. But this isn't the first time Ellie ran off."

They stopped for lunch then; the idea was to let Rasmussen stew. The longer the better. Staying power was the key now. And Michael figured time was on his side.

The worst hamburgers in town were delivered to the interrogation room. Michael had deliberately put the order in to Drive-Thru Burgers early that morning, with explicit instructions to cook them up then and bring them to police headquarters at two.

"But, geez, man, they'll be like rubber," the kid on the phone had said.

"Just do it," Michael had replied.

"What is this shit?" Rasmussen asked angrily, as the grease-splotched paper bag was set on the table before him.

"Hey, the taxpayers of Boulder can't pay for gourmet food." Michael shrugged.

"Let me order out then. I'll pay for something decent myself."

"Sorry, no can do."

"God," Rasmussen said, and he didn't touch the burger.

Michael ate his, every bite. Then he took his time straightening the cluttered table, stuffing the foil burger wrappers and torn ketchup packets into the paper bag, leaving the room. Through the one-way mirror he stood with Torres and Koffey and observed Rasmussen as the man conferred heatedly with his lawyer.

"He'll break," Michael said, as much to himself as to the others.

"I hope you're right," Koffey said, staring through the glass.

Michael checked with Janice then, striding over to where she sat waiting with Augostino, still wringing her hands. She cried silently when Michael told her Rasmussen was ready to crumble.

By the time he got back into the interrogation room Rasmussen was furious. "You can't just leave me in here to rot, Callas. What the hell . . . ?"

"Shall we continue?" Michael said, sitting, his face a study in neutrality.

Then he started in again, the line of questioning clear in his mind. "Are you aware that Ellie didn't run off that night?"

"What do you mean?"

"She returned to the hotel, and sometime early Saturday morning, and I admit the time isn't fixed yet, but sometime before noon on Saturday, Miss Kramer was raped and strangled, resulting in her death by asphyxiation." *God Almighty,* Michael thought, his fists clenching. He wanted to break everything in the room. He wanted to smash that face across from him, and keep on smashing it.

Michael took a breath. "Did you hang the Do Not Disturb sign on Miss Kramer's door and leave it there all weekend? Till you checked out?"

"No, goddamn it, why would I do that?"

"So that the maid wouldn't find Miss Kramer—*Ellie*—till long after you'd gone. The way I see it, Rasmussen, you got mad, you tried to make love to your girlfriend. Maybe she rejected you, and then it got out of hand. You panicked. You knew you couldn't dispose of her body, so you put out the Do Not Disturb sign and left."

Rasmussen shook his head adamantly. "No. That's not true."

And Michael came in with one huge blow to the gut. "Oh? But it's happened before, hasn't it? First time, I believe, was right here in Boulder. Remember Stephanie Morris?"

"What the . . . ?" Sempler came half out of his seat.

But it was Rasmussen whom Michael was watching.

Michael followed with a second blow. "But you learned. Learned to choke them just right. There was

Holly Lance and Naomi Freeman and Amy Blanchard and Peta Valero."

"You're . . . you're fucking out of your mind!" Rasmussen screamed, pounding the wooden table. "What is this? What the . . . ?"

"Yes," Sempler said, staring at Michael and then his client and back again. "Do you realize what you're saying? This interview is over. Finn . . . ?"

But Rasmussen wasn't moving. "You're insane," he hissed at Michael. "You always resented me. And now you're trying to pin some kind of bullshit on me."

"Okay," Michael said, putting up a hand as if backing off. And he suggested they take another break. A uniform escorted Rasmussen to the bathroom, then Michael saw him and Sempler talking by the pop machine, drinking from cans.

It was between rounds. Time for a gulp of water, time to catch your breath and get a pep talk from your trainer. Only Michael didn't have a trainer and he didn't need a pep talk.

He saw Janice Kramer standing down the hall with Augostino. She was staring at Rasmussen as if he were the devil. It wasn't policy to allow civilians to watch an interrogation, but Koffey had made an exception in Janice's case. There wasn't a patrolman or detective in the building whose heart didn't go out to the woman.

After the break, Sempler and Rasmussen were escorted back into the claustrophobic interrogation room. Finn looked smug, confident. The pep talk. Right.

But Michael had it all planned out. A solid blow to the solar plexus. He sat back and watched Rasmussen wordlessly for a long time, then he said in a mild voice, "I guess you know that Ellie Kramer was really Ellie Crandall?" He let that sink in a second. "*John* Crandall's daughter? The man that went to prison for the rape of the Morris girl?"

Rasmussen fell back in his seat.

Sempler stared, uncertain which, if any, of his client's rights had been violated.

Michael was on a roll. "Ellie *Crandall*. The way we see it, Rasmussen, you, or maybe it was Ellie, had some ugly unfinished business from thirteen years ago."

"No," Rasmussen whispered, as if someone had knocked the breath from his lungs. "I . . . She was the Crandall kid?" He was stunned. Almost down for the count.

"It gets worse," Michael said, leaning forward now, his gaze pinioning the man. "We have a witness who saw you and Ellie, Ellie *Crandall,* at breakfast in Aspen early Saturday morning. Witness said you were arguing with Ellie, and then the two of you went to the elevators. Is that when you did her, Rasmussen, right after breakfast?"

"No no no. Impossible." Rasmussen shook his head vehemently, still totally done in by the knowledge of who Ellie really was. "No no. I swear I never saw her after Bentley's."

"Then the witness is lying?"

"Yes. Yes, of course he is."

"I didn't say he."

"Whoever, for chrissakes."

Sempler came to his feet. "I'm advising my client—"

"Sit the fuck down," Michael said in a voice so still it barely registered on the tape. Then, before Sempler ruined it, Michael said, "Did you kill Ellie, and rape and murder all those other women, because your uncle raped you, Rasmussen? Is this what it's about?"

Rasmussen flew to his feet and began yelling, swearing, even shoving Sempler back when the lawyer tried to control him. "Fuck you, Callas!" There was spittle at the corner of his mouth.

And Michael delivered the knockout punch. "I don't suppose any of this matters, really." He reached in his coat pocket and pulled out an evidence bag, letting it drop quietly in front of them.

Rasmussen, still standing, ranting, shut up and put his fists on the table, leaning over. "What the hell is . . . ?"

"It's a necktie. Looks like a custom-made necktie. And you'll never guess where we found it."

The blood drained from Rasmussen's face.

"Around the neck of the murder victim. Around Eleanor Kramer's neck."

Absolute, pulsing silence in the room. Rasmussen looked as if he'd been poleaxed. He tried to say something but nothing emerged.

Sempler stared at the evidence bag and then his gaze rose to Rasmussen. "Take it easy now, Finn. Not another word." He glanced at Michael. "There's no proof this belongs to my client. You can't . . ."

"No . . ." A groan came from Rasmussen's throat; an oily slick of sweat formed on his face. "No. I . . ."

Michael smiled wickedly. "*Your* monogram. *Your* tie. Not real good planning on your part, pal."

There was a sudden panting hush. Only the faint whirring of the tape recorder could be heard. Rasmussen began to breathe hard, his chest rising and falling as if he couldn't get enough air. He stood and stared at the plastic bag, his big hands forming fists at his sides, his neck veins bulging.

Then he exploded.

He fell back against the wall and it came gushing out. "How stupid do you think I am! Using my own tie!"

Sempler rose quickly and tried to shut his client up. "I want to see that tie, Callas," he demanded. "I don't see a monogram. How do we know this belongs to—"

Rasmussen was still bellowing, bouncing off the walls. He shoved his lawyer and pounded the table so hard his knuckles began to bleed. "Why the hell would I blow it this time! When everyone knew where Ellie was! Whoever killed her has to be a copycat! Knows how I work! Do you think I'd be so stupid after all these years, all those stupid little women! Me? Finn Rasmussen? I've built an empire, for chrissakes, I . . ." He began to blubber. Then rage. Then blubber again, tears rolling out of his eyes. "I . . . I loved Ellie. The others, they were just *things*. But Ellie . . . You should have seen the ring I was going to buy her."

Michael spoke in a deadly quiet voice. "But we know you *killed* Ellie Kramer."

"No, no," Finn brayed. "I didn't!"

"And I suppose you'll deny you attacked Stephanie Morris, too. Hey, Finn, what about Stephanie?"

"Yes, Stephanie, yes, but not Ellie!"

"And Naomi Freeman?"

"Yes, fuck you, yes!"

"Amy Blanchard, Holly Lance, the one that got away, and Peta Valero."

"Yes," he yelled, his face twisted, and he lunged across the table at Michael, then flung himself against the wall where he sagged, spent, and slid down until he was curled in a fetal position, rocking back and forth, his arms hugging his knees to his chest, mumbling.

"Dear God in heaven," Sempler moaned, and the door opened. It was Torres. He looked at Michael then switched off the recorder.

"Enough for you?" Michael asked.

"Oh, yeah, I think this will do."

Then every head in the room swiveled as the door opened again, and Eleanor Kramer walked in.

TWENTY-FOUR

She couldn't think. She felt as if she were stranded in a dream, a voyeur, standing motionless, watching Michael yank Finn up by an arm.

Finn stared at her, even as Michael pushed him, the man's wild gaze fixed on her.

She wanted to say so much, to gloat, to hear his shock verbalized, but neither of them uttered a word.

Where was the overpowering sense of victory she'd anticipated for so very long?

There was only a hollowness inside.

Voices drifted in and out of her head. Michael instructing a uniformed officer to book Finn. Sempler telling his client not to panic. "You'll be out by tomorrow morning, Finn. This is a travesty."

And Torres's voice from behind her. "We'll just see if a judge goes for bail." Torres chuckling, triumphant. "Not a chance."

Where was *her* triumph?

Her thoughts reeled. No more young girls raped and murdered; no more families devastated; no more innocent men imprisoned. And Torres would see to it that those falsely convicted men already behind bars were freed.

Another uniformed cop appeared and, shouldering his way past Ellie, clamped a beefy hand on Finn's other arm. He was muttering now, mucus on his upper lip, spittle at the corners of his mouth—broken, crushed. Suddenly so small.

For an instant his eyes met hers again as he was led out of the room. Sanity touched his gaze. "You bitch, whore . . ." he breathed, and Michael, behind him, gave him a hard hand between the shoulder blades.

"That's for hitting Ellie," he said between gritted teeth.

Sempler protested, ticked off all the charges he was going to file against the department, swore if Michael touched Rasmussen again he'd have his badge.

Michael only grinned.

And still Ellie couldn't find her voice.

Where was the victory? She'd done it, gotten him. But at what cost?

Michael never looked at her as the room emptied into the corridor. She made eye contact with her mother, who was standing between Commander Koffey and Rick Augostino. Janice smiled and nodded at her daughter—perhaps the only one in the crowd who truly understood the emptiness of revenge.

As Finn was led away, shoulders sagging, his arrogant demeanor gone, the crowd thickened in the hallway. She spotted all the familiar faces, even the guys, Parker and Kirkner, who'd manned the surveillance van. The atmosphere was the same as the scene at the Justice Center when the Zimmerman verdict had been announced. Smiles, high-fives, laughter, congratulations. Manly slaps on the back. Cop talk: "You fucked him over good, Callas." "Never see the light of day again." "See him go nuts in there?" "Thought I'd crap my pants when the girl walked in."

Janice finally came over to hug her. Neither said a thing for a long moment; they both fought tears, and Ellie clung to her mother. Then, Janice's voice in her ear, "Your father would be so proud, Ellie. So very proud."

There was no opportunity to talk, though, as Rick appeared. "Come on, ladies, if ever there was a time to celebrate . . . We're all headed out for a few brewskies and you're both coming. The guests of honor."

Surprising Ellie, Janice was all for it. "Hell," she said, "why not? Ellie and I will follow you in my car."

But Ellie begged off.

"You sure, Ellie?" Rick said.

And Chambliss. "Just for a couple?"

"No, really," she said, finding a smile. "I've got to pack, all that stuff. Really."

Then Michael. Whom she hadn't spoken a word to since he'd picked her up in Aspen last Friday night outside Bentley's and driven her back to Denver.

"Let her do her own things, guys," he said. That was all. Cutting her loose. He disappeared.

Augostino helped Janice into her coat.

"I'll see you at the house in a little bit," her mother said.

"Fine, Mom, have fun." She meant it, too.

Most everyone was gone when she felt a tap on her shoulder. Michael? But it was Torres.

"Well, we got him. God, what a coup." He smiled and took her hand. "I was telling your mother that I'll ask the governor to issue a full pardon to your father. Even if it is posthumously."

"Thank you."

"It's the least I can do." He hesitated, then said, "Ellie,

come back to work for me. Get your law degree. Don't waste your talent. I can use you on this case. There's so much to do. You know Rasmussen's lawyers will pull every legal stunt in the book."

"Their tricks won't work," she said.

"No, they won't, but we need to be prepared. That's what we do. We prosecute criminals. Come on, Ellie."

"I'll think about it." She wouldn't; she'd made up her mind.

"You do that. The job's yours. Take all the time you need to decide."

"Okay," she said, and then Torres left, giving her a thumbs-up as he disappeared.

She was alone in the corridor, the hollowness spreading in her belly. There was nothing to do, though; it was over. Thirteen years since her father's arrest, thirteen years of plotting and scheming. Why couldn't she rejoice?

She found her coat on a bench near the stairs, longing to search the detective division for a sight of Michael. Shouldn't she say something to him? Congratulations? Thanks? Sorry I *screwed* you?

She picked up her coat. *Oh, God.*

Then his voice. "Wait, Ellie," and her heart squeezed. She turned.

"That was good work," he said, and he offered his hand.

She stared at it dumbly for a moment then reached out her own. "Thanks, Michael. The credit's all yours."

"No. No, it isn't. You know that."

"Well, anyway, good-bye, I better be going now." She only wanted to withdraw her hand from his as quickly as possible, because his touch was torture. His skin warm, his grasp firm. She'd thought, crazily, that she could love this man, but she'd ruined it all. The cost, she thought again, was too high.

"Good-bye, Ellie."

She walked down the stairs, shrugging on her coat. It was snowing out. It had been snowing fitfully all day long, while Michael had battered away at Finn. She pulled up the collar and wrapped her red scarf around her neck. She needed to walk. She needed to cry her heart out. It was over. It was all over.

She walked across the black marble floor of the lobby, past the curved, faux-marble reception counter and the two stainless steel columns and the black leather benches. She pushed open the door and stepped out into the whirling storm.

Wind lashed at her, and she hunched her shoulders, set off down the walkway toward the street. She heard a sound, which she thought at first was the wind howling, but it was too insistent, and then she realized someone was calling her name.

She stopped, lifted her head, turned.

Michael. He was striding after her, no coat, no hat, no gloves, the wind slashing at him, his hair blowing about.

"Wait, goddamn it, Ellie, wait a minute," he said, and then he stood before her.

"We said our good-byes, Michael. Don't . . ."

"Damn it, Ellie, I'm not going to let you just walk away. Everyone in my life has just walked away, and I'm goddamn sick and tired of it. This time I'm doing something about it. I'm a coward. Whining all these years about Paul and my parents. Never asking or trying to find out why or . . . *pushing* anyone.

"Look, I don't know what the rules are when it comes to love. I'm a loser. No practice at all. But, Ellie, I swear, I can't spend the rest of my life wondering every goddamn minute where you are, if you're okay. What son of a bitch married you, what your goddamn kids look like. I . . . I want you, Ellie. I want those kids to be mine."

She stood there, shocked to the core, snow plastering her coat, hitting her face, making her blink. Her mind stuttered.

"*Shit.* Well, *say* something."

"I don't know what to say."

"Jesus, maybe I . . . Maybe I got it all wrong. I thought, hell, I thought you and I . . ."

"Felt something for each other?" she ventured.

"Yeah. At least I . . . hell, I care about you. Ellie, I want to try. I want us both to learn how to trust."

"And you . . . love me?"

"I said I did."

"No, you said . . ."

"Stop being a lawyer."

"So we love each other, right?"

"Yes, we got that straight. Ellie, you're killing me."

"Michael . . ."

"Come on. I'm making an ass out of myself here and I'm freezing. Yes or no."

"It's not that simple, is it?" she said, dazed.

He shook his head. "How the hell should I know? It's worth a try, I figure."

"You mean it, Michael?"

"You think I'm standing out here in this cold playing games?"

"No," she breathed.

"Look, you go back to the DA. Get your degree. Forget the stuff about Leadville. We get married, and you're close to school and to work." He reached out a hand and touched her cheek. "Then when we start a family"—he grimaced—"I'll have to add on to the cabin."

"A family."

"That's it," he said. "It took me thirty-seven years to pour my guts out, and it'll be thirty-seven more before I do it again. Just tell me, Ellie; yes or no."

She only blinked once. "Yes," she whispered against the storm. Then, more clearly, "Yes, yes, yes."